THE REBEL PIRATE

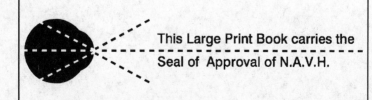

This Large Print Book carries the
Seal of Approval of N.A.V.H.

RENEGADES OF THE REVOLUTION

THE REBEL PIRATE

DONNA THORLAND

THORNDIKE PRESS
A part of Gale, Cengage Learning

GALE
CENGAGE Learning·

Farmington Hills, Mich • San Francisco • New York • Waterville, Maine
Meriden, Conn • Mason, Ohio • Chicago

GALE
CENGAGE Learning®

LIBRARY OF CONGRESS CATALOGING-IN-PUBLICATION DATA

Thorland, Donna.
    The rebel pirate : renegades of the revolution / Donna Thorland. — Large
print edition.
       pages cm — (Thorndike Press large print romance)
    ISBN 978-1-4104-7066-9 (hardcover) — ISBN 1-4104-7066-0 (hardcover)
    1. Massachusetts—History—1775-1865—Fiction. 2. Great Britain. Royal
Navy—Fiction. 3. Smuggling—Fiction. 4. Large type books. I. Title.
PS3620.H766R4 2014b
813'.6—dc23   2014012593

Published in 2014 by arrangement with NAL Signet, a member of
Penguin Group LLC, a Penguin Random House Company

Printed in the United States of America
1 2 3 4 5 6 7 18 17 16 15 14

For my husband, Charles,
who gave me time
and a room of my own

ONE

April 20, 1775

The gold was Spanish, the chest was French, the ship was American, and the captain was dead. James Sparhawk, master and commander in the British Navy, on blockade duty patrolling the waters north of Boston, took one look at the glittering fortune in doubloons and swore.

He was supposed to be thwarting smugglers. Petty criminals. Sharp traders who had weighed the risk of prosecution against the reward of profit and decided to defy Parliament with a cargo of outlawed goods bound for Rebel Boston. He was supposed to be confiscating Dutch tea and French molasses, punishing the disobedient colonists by stopping their luxuries and cutting off their trade.

Instead, he was standing on an American schooner, the *Charming Sally,* which he had chased halfway to Marblehead and been obliged, finally, to dismast. And she was carrying one hundred fifty tons of musket flint for ballast and a fortune in foreign gold into a country on a knife's edge of war.

He closed the chest and turned to his lieutenant, one of Admiral Graves' innumerable nephews, and said, "Not a word about the gold. To anyone." Even English sailors might be tempted to mutiny for such a large sum, and half the crew of Sparhawk's twenty-gun brig were Yankees pressed off American merchant vessels and the docks of Boston. "Have the chest moved to my quarters. Tell the marine guard on duty that no one is to enter."

Lieutenant Francis Graves pursed his lips. It had been clear from his first day aboard the *Wasp* that he did not like serving under James, a man only a few years short of thirty who had made captain with little of the navy's vital currency, *interest*. Not when Graves' well-connected cousins had commands of their own. It proclaimed him to be the only scion of that seafaring family whose talents did not make up for his temperament.

"What am I to say is in the chest?"

A better officer would say nothing at all, but discretion did not come naturally to a Graves. "Paper, *Lieutenant,*" James replied.

"Rebel documents."

"It is far too heavy for paper."

"Make the Rebels carry it," James said. *They* would already know — or suspect — what was in the chest. He could not press the whole crew, even though his ship was shorthanded and could use the men. The *Wasp* already had too many disgruntled Yankees on board.

That was the problem with service in the North American squadron. *Nothing* was simple. If he did not press sailors, he put his vessel and the lives of his crew at risk. If he carried out the press, he risked touching off a bloody confrontation with the locals, and Lord knew no one needed another Boston "massacre." The navy expected its serving officers to strike a near-impossible balance between following standing orders and acting with autonomy when confronted with unusual situations. Unfortunately, there were no *usual* situations in New England these days.

"Order the Americans to throw the flint overboard." Upon that point, at least, King George and his standing orders were clear: *take the most effectual Measures for arresting, detailing, and securing any Gunpowder, or any sort of Arms or Ammunition, which may be attempted to be imported into the colonies.*

The rest, Sparhawk would have to improvise.

"Then press their ship's boys. The youngest and the smallest. They should be able to reef and hand as well as an adult, and they're much less likely to cause trouble. Or to be believed if they talk about the gold. Lock the rest of the Yankee sailors in the *Charming Sally*'s hold."

Graves departed with ill grace to dispose of the flint. James did not like having to trust him with a prize crew. He was too inclined to flogging. A good officer rarely needed to resort to the cat, but young Graves was not a good officer.

Sparhawk remained behind to search the dead skipper's cabin for real Rebel documents. He quickly grew discouraged. There were papers everywhere: charts and bills of lading and letters. It was a mess, and he had no time to sort it. He would leave it for the prize court in Boston. He took only the *Sally*'s log. Its presence was another sign of the late captain's incompetence. Her log *should* have gone over the side at the first sign of pursuit.

And James should never have been able to catch her. She was built for speed, sharp-hulled and square-rigged. Properly loaded, with her cargo and ballast stowed correctly, she should have outrun him. She had been handled badly, and the dead captain had only himself to blame for his fate. James had suspected from afar, and discovered for certain up close, that the bungling skipper had set too much sail, driving her weighted hull down into the water instead of skimming it along the surface as her maker had intended.

The man's cabin was of a piece with his sailing. Merchant crews were allowed to dabble in private ventures, of course, as long as they did not consume space meant for the owner's cargo. Normally that meant some small objects of high value, such as might fit in a sea chest. A conscientious captain did not cram his living quarters — which were his work quarters as well — with bolts of cloth and boxes of pepper. James had to resist the urge to sneeze after examining the chests.

If the prize court ruled the *Charming Sally* a legal capture, he would see a share of the pepper, the cloth, and the French molasses weighing down her hold. And when she was sold, or more likely bought into the service — Admiral Graves was desperate for seaworthy ships — James would see a share of that as well. Some captains had made fortunes patrolling the Massachusetts coast

11

for smugglers.

But the gold was another matter entirely. It smacked of foreign intrigue, the kind the Admiralty wanted to keep quiet, the kind every officer in the undermanned, cash-strapped North American squadron feared, because the Rebels had a thousand miles of tricky coastline and enough ships, if they found the money to arm them, to spit in the eye of the British Navy. And that was something the French, the Dutch, and the Spanish — in that order — would enjoy seeing.

James returned to the deck. He counted sixteen American sailors, only two of them boys, formed up in a human chain from the hatch to starboard, heaving casks of flint over the side under the watchful eye of a five-man marine detail.

"The chest is stowed in your cabin," Graves reported.

"Very good, Mr. Graves. Take the boys on board the *Wasp* and return with a prize crew."

Graves took a step toward the American boys, and every Yankee sailor on the crowded deck paused and tensed, all eyes fixed on those two small forms. The Americans were suddenly ready — as they had not been when boarded — to do violence.

James looked at the boys again. The smaller one was no more than eleven years old, the same age James had been when he'd unwillingly gone to sea. He was towheaded and slender; his fair hair was sun bleached, his skin deeply tanned, and his gray eyes wide with fear.

The older boy was taller, slimmer, perhaps as old as fifteen, but James could see nothing of his face beneath the broad-brimmed hat. The boy pivoted, sensing James' scrutiny, and in one fluid movement pulled the younger child behind him. It was a protective gesture, and spoke of courage in the face of the enemy, but it had nothing of masculine bravado about it.

Because the older boy was no boy at all.

"Belay that, Mr. Graves." James crossed the deck to confront the boy who was not a boy. Her face was still obscured beneath the hat. Her form, now that he was aware of her gender, was plainly feminine: wide hips, narrow waist, and fine bones in her slender wrists. She was not an ordinary sailor's trull either, to judge by the pale skin of her hands. And no one would bother with the precaution of disguising a trollop during an enemy boarding. Only a lady merited such treatment.

She looked up.

He was right. She had fine skin, luminous brown eyes, and a dusting of freckles to complement honey blond hair much like the boy's. Her disguise had been hasty. Pearl bobs still hung from her ears, and a fine gold chain circled her neck. She took a step back, out of his reach, barring his access to the child with her slim body.

"Your son?" he asked, but he knew as soon as he spoke that this could not be the case. She was too young — twenty-five or six at the most.

"My brother," she said. "He is a passenger."

"The calluses on his hands say otherwise. I am very sorry, but the king's ships must have men."

"He is a child," she said.

"Can you reef and hand?" he addressed the boy, who looked up nervously at his pretty sister.

"Every child on the North Shore can do as much," she said. "I can reef, hand, and steer the *Sally,* but you're not going to press me."

She did not intend a flirtation. He knew that. She had none of the jaded sophistication of the Boston ladies he entertained himself with, but he could not resist a smile. "The thought is tempting."

The girl paled, and he regretted the statement immediately. This was not a London drawing room, or even a Boston parlor. She was alone on a smuggler's ship, with only a small boy to defend her, and his suggestion, in this context, must sound far from playful.

"Your brother," he assured her, "will do well on the *Wasp*. She is a good ship, with," he lied immoderately, "an excellent crew. We hardly ever resort to the cat." That much was true. "You may come aboard to see for yourself, and we'll get you safe to Boston, or wherever home might be."

The girl narrowed her eyes and scrunched her nose. It was wildly unbecoming and charming all at once. So charming, he realized too late, that it was a signal. He heard a scuffle behind him. He did not turn to look, because she raised one slender arm and captured his full attention.

"I have a better idea," she said, leveling her pistol at his head. "Order your marines off our ship."

Two

Sarah Ward's heart hammered. She'd heard of James Sparhawk. Coastal gossip accounted him a good seaman and a conscientious enforcer of British policy. Normally, these were qualities she admired. She was no Rebel, and the Wards were no more smugglers than most of Salem's merchant families, which was to say they dealt in contraband only when it was more profitable than legitimate cargo.

He could not have Ned.

"Put the pistol down," he said, living up to his reputation for being coolheaded, "and we will discuss the boy."

"Without the pistol," she said, "I suspect our conversation would be one-sided." And it would end with Ned pressed aboard a British ship, never to be seen again, all because they'd agreed to Micah Wild's scheme. "I won't let you take my brother. Order your marines back to your ship, and

I promise we'll put you and your lieutenant ashore — unharmed — at the first opportunity."

Mr. Cheap, her father's formidable sailing master, had felled the lieutenant in question with a sack of flint. The Graves boy was curled up on the deck, gasping for breath. She supposed a few bruises — and perhaps a broken rib or two — were to be expected. Lucas Cheap had endured six weeks of sloppy sailing under the command of Micah Wild's hired captain without a word of complaint, but the prospect of going to jail for the man's intrigues evidently palled.

Sparhawk's marines had fared little better. The *Sally*'s crew now possessed their muskets. The lobsters looked worried, with reason. A sailor might do anything — even murder — to avoid being pressed. No one, particularly not the British officers of the North American squadron, had forgotten that business on the *Rose* in '69, when a group of Yankee sailors had barricaded themselves in the forepeak and harpooned the British lieutenant who hadn't had the good sense to let them be.

Sparhawk was at least exhibiting more tact than the unfortunate captain of the *Rose*. He made no sudden moves, no threatening gestures. Nor did he take his eyes off Sarah Ward.

"Smuggling is one thing," he said. "You'll pay a fine and lose your ship and cargo. Kidnapping officers of the king is quite another. It will get you hanged."

"So, I suspect, will the chest of French gold in your cabin," she said. "No matter that it has nothing to do with me or these men. They'll still suffer for it. And so will the wives and children who depend on them."

"They should have thought of that," Sparhawk said, "before they signed aboard a smuggler."

He could afford to be smug, this tall, glittering captain with his gold braid and gilt buttons. "Your king's taxes," she replied, "have made it impossible for them to earn a living any other way." Her father had tried trading in legal British goods. It had brought him to penury and her to something worse. "These are desperate men, Captain Sparhawk. Even if your crew swarmed over the side and retook the *Sally,* you and your lieutenant would die."

"If I return to Boston without the gold, I'll like as not face a firing squad. *'Dans ce pays-ci, il est bon de tuer de temps en temps un amiral pour encourager les autres.' "*

Candide. Surprising reading for a sailor, but then by all accounts James Sparhawk was no ordinary sailor. *In this country it is a good thing to kill an admiral from time to time to encourage the others.*

"Then you will understand that I am just tending to my own garden," she said, answering him in kind.

His blue eyes widened fractionally. She had surprised him. Of course she had. Sailors' women did not read Voltaire.

"My choice," he said, "would seem to be a bullet now or a bullet later, unless we can reach some agreement about the gold."

He was right, of course. Micah Wild's French gold wasn't just a fortune — it was enough money to arm most of the smugglers on the coast. And after seven years of crippling tariffs, there was hardly a sloop in New England that didn't carry illicit goods — or wouldn't mount a pair of four-pounders and add a dozen rough men to her crew if she could afford it. A British captain who let such a dangerous fortune slip through his fingers would pay a high price.

The treasure was a bargaining chip, and she would use it to save Ned and the *Sally*'s crew. What Micah Wild would do to her later, she didn't care to contemplate.

19

"The gold," she said, taking a deep breath, "may remain aboard the *Wasp.*"

"The *Wasp* is more likely to end up in one of the Dutch free ports than Boston with that chest full of gold — unless she is officered," Sparhawk countered. "Release Mr. Graves to captain her home."

"Mr. Graves," she said, "makes an excellent hostage. The admiral is reputed to be inordinately fond of him." He was also reputed to be the boy's real father, the only plausible explanation for why the admiral still worked so hard to advance the lieutenant's career. Cruelty was often forgiven at sea. Ineptitude was not.

"I suspect my prospects will be little improved," James Sparhawk said dryly, "by allowing the admiral's nephew to be kidnapped. He might think me careless. Let the gold go to Boston with Mr. Graves. Take me as your hostage, and I give you my word that the *Wasp* will not pursue you."

He didn't say, *No ship will pursue you,* nor could he make such a promise. If the *Wasp* met another navy vessel on her way home to Boston, another captain would not be bound to honor James Sparhawk's word.

Their only chance was to run for home, and fast. The *Sally* should just make it — if the weather held.

"Agreed," she said at last.

Sparhawk nodded, but Lucas Cheap cast her one of his looks — dark as the threatening sky. He had some inkling of what had passed between her and the man who had jilted her, and he could guess the price she would pay for crossing Micah Wild.

The *Sally,* being a merchant vessel, didn't have a lockup, so her ruffian of a sailing master confined Sparhawk in the captain's cabin. This suited Sparhawk, as he wanted another look at the *Sally*'s papers. Capturing one chest of foreign gold was not enough. There would always be another. If the money wasn't French or Spanish next time, it would be Dutch. And it would be used to buy powder and shot and the blood of British sailors.

Sparhawk had not entered the navy willingly, but the service had been mother and father, school and church, to him; the King's Rules and Admiralty Instructions his Bible, the Articles of War his Book of Common Prayer. He would not see the service become prey to the machinations of foreign powers.

The French king Louis and his ministers would deny any involvement, of course, leaving the British Navy to round up and hang the American traitors if it wished to put a stop to the flow.

If he could not bring the *Sally* home to question her crew, then he needed names — the dead captain's for a start, the owner's and investors' if possible.

The girl's.

He did not like the idea of a noose around her slender neck. The fine gold chain was a far better ornament, and her misguided defense of the boy had reminded him of another woman and another boy a very long time ago.

He might have been able to disarm her, but the situation in New England was delicate. The blockade, in place for nearly a year, had failed to chastise disobedient Boston, and tensions between Britain and her colonies were running higher than ever. If a pretty young American girl were hurt during a customs search, the rabble-rousers like Adams and Hancock and their counterparts elsewhere would brew a tempest in a teapot — with open war the result.

But these were no ordinary smugglers. He'd been on deck as the Americans began their repairs, and while he could not put his finger on any one thing, the Sallys sported an altogether more raffish appearance now that the British were gone. They had rolled up their sleeves to clear the wreckage off the deck and heave the dead captain's body overboard, and Sparhawk had seen that every man jack of them bore a tattoo — many more than one.

This was unusual in the merchant marine, where crews were often filled out with one-timers. Only a career sailor opted to go under the needle, to be marked for life as a man who had stood before the mast. There was also a preponderance of that antique fashion, earrings, and Sparhawk was surprised to see more than one diamond bob glinting on the sun.

Raffish or no, these were the men the Admiralty — and every post captain worth his salt — was worried about. The navy needed these hands to man its warships, and the trouble in America was playing merry hell with the recruiting. If these sailors evaded the press in numbers, if the smugglers of New England began to arm schooners like this one, fast, strong, innovative, the already overtaxed British Navy would be unable to stop them.

The shallow anchorages of New England were no place for British ships of the line, and the North American station was perilously short on seaworthy small craft, while Yankee schooners were numerous and widely held to be the best in the world. The *Sally* had been such a sleek and lovely thing, even badly handled, that it had pained him to fire on her. James had coveted a fast vessel like this his whole career — damn her dead captain for a fool.

Sparhawk had crippled her twice over when he'd splintered the mast and killed her commander. Merchant crews were tiny. The skipper had not been a credit to his calling, but there was no one to replace him. The sailing master's business, contrary to his title, was not sailing. It was navigation: charts and angles and stars, and this close to home, dead reckoning. He was a capable man with a compass and a sextant, no doubt, but no captain.

Sparhawk caught the fellow's name as the crew responded to his orders: Mr. Cheap. A good hand in a fight — Cheap had proved as much leading the *Sally* against Graves and Sparhawk's marines. James watched the man dash back and forth across the deck, hauling on lines and splicing cables when he should have been standing still and issuing orders. And every few minutes he stopped what he was doing to lay eyes on the girl.

He did not look at her with lust, but with concern. Mr. Cheap was desperate to get her and the boy clear of the *Wasp*. That was why he was crowding on too much sail. The girl they deferentially referred to as *Miss Sarah* and the boy was *Young Master Ned*. There was as much tugging of forelocks as on a royal vessel, but to a slip of a girl and a wide-eyed boy.

This display of deference and loyalty shocked him. He had not attempted to press any of the regular sailors, just the girl — until he discovered her sex — and the boy. Smuggler's crews usually got off easy with a few weeks in jail and a loss of wages. It was an accepted risk.

Rebels were another story. The navy had decided to treat Rebel sailors as pirates. They could be tried and hanged for resisting a boarding. The crew of the *Sally* risked a great deal for these two.

And while Mr. Cheap might not be fascinated by the girl's — *Sarah's* — body, Sparhawk was. He did not know how he had ever mistaken her for a boy. She was not tall, but she had distinct curves and a slender, defined waist. Like one of those headless Venuses that were all over the Med, she was sculpted along classical lines.

She was decidedly feminine, yet there was nothing fussy or delicate about her. Sparhawk had entertained ladies aboard his ships — if the men were allowed trollops in port, he saw no reason to deny himself — but the bored wives and merry widows he consorted with, even those married to other captains, didn't have legs like this girl. She stood as lithe and easy on deck as any of the Sallys, graceful hips and round bottom outlined in canvas trousers, adjusting instinctively to the pitch and roll of the ship.

Mr. Cheap caught him watching the girl, or more accurately, one specific part of the girl, and that was when the sailing master smiled wide — revealing three carved gold teeth and no goodwill whatsoever — and directed him below.

"Who are they?" Sparhawk asked as Lucas Cheap thrust him not at all gently down the hatch.

"Passengers."

James felt his way aft through the shadowy main deck, where only scattered light filtered through the hatches, the redoubtable Mr. Cheap a palpable menace behind him. "That girl is no passenger," James said. Her pistol had never wavered. "She has the sea legs of a Jack Tar." Neither the wind nor the roll of the ship, nor "feminine" qualms, had disturbed her aim when she drew a bead on him. Nor had she blinked at the gore on deck or the rivulet of the dead captain's blood that had snaked past the toe of her shoe.

"This is Naumkeag," the sailing master said. James knew the Indian name for Salem and her shores. *The fishing place.* "Our women are bred to the sea."

"And to the *Manual of Arms,* it would seem," Sparhawk said under his breath.

He regretted it at once, reminding Cheap of circumstances and testimony that hung over the girl's head like the Sword of Damocles. Sparhawk had grown too used to his own quarterdeck, but he was not master and commander here.

Lucas Cheap moved like a snake. He seized James by the collar, swung him around, and slammed him back against the bulkhead. Sparhawk found himself staring into Cheap's gimlet eyes. Slatted light glimmered off the sailing master's gruesome gold teeth, and James could feel the man's heated breath against his face — and the cold sting of a short blade pressed to his ribs.

"She promised you'd get to shore in one piece," Cheap said, "and I won't make a liar out of her. But if you know what's good for you, you'll forget all about that girl. Ask anyone on the coast. Or the Lord God himself. They'll tell you. Lucas Cheap sailed with the Brethren. He makes good ever on his threats."

Sparhawk didn't doubt it. He had spent his childhood — brief though it was — in the West Indies. The buccaneers were greatly reduced since Morgan's day, but they made up in viciousness for what they lacked in numbers. Lucas Cheap had the cut of such a rogue. "You are devoted to her," James said.

"I've followed her father to sea, man and boy, these forty years. And his daughter might not have been born with a silver spoon in her mouth, but she *is* a lady, and on the *Sally,* she is treated as such."

"I did not mean to imply otherwise," Sparhawk said. "Only to observe that she is remarkably brave."

Lucas Cheap released Sparhawk, stepped back, and looked him over. Finally he grunted and said, "A pretty sentiment, Captain. You might even mean it. But she's not fair game for your sport."

Sparhawk's reputation must have preceded him. The Massachusetts coast, as he was often reminded, was shaped like an ear. It heard everything.

"Understood. I have no designs on her." His own personal code would not allow it, no matter how intriguing she might be.

"And I meant the boy no harm, Mr. Cheap. I went to sea myself at that age."

Lucas Cheap snorted. "With a midshipman's berth, a sea chest full of warm clothes, and no fear of the cat. As a young gentleman is privileged to do, eh?"

"As a common sailor," Sparhawk replied, "with nothing but the clothes on my back." He risked a great deal saying so. There were only two men in the world who knew how he had been pressed into the navy. One had saved his life. The other had tried to take it from him.

"Then I've no need to tell you what might befall a boy under a bad captain."

He knew all too well. When he thought about it, he could still feel Captain Slough's hand on the back of his neck. "That does not happen on my ship." He made certain of it.

Cheap shrugged his powerful shoulders. "It happens enough. *That's* why the girl was on board, to look out for the young master on his first voyage and after the family interests. The gold was the hired captain's private cargo. It had nothing to do with her. When you report to your admiral, you'll leave the girl out of it."

"I shall do as duty and honor demand," he said.

Lucas Cheap surveyed him with a jaundiced eye. "I've served in your navy. There was plenty of duty and precious little honor in it." He removed an imaginary piece of lint from Sparhawk's epaulet, fingered one of the silver gilt buttons atop his snowy lapels, then sliced it neatly off. "Something to remember you by, Captain," Cheap said, and dropped it in his pocket.

Then he let James into the skipper's cabin and locked him within.

If Sparhawk were lucky, they wouldn't take the ship's log off him when they put him ashore, but he couldn't count on that. He must read it and find the names he needed now. He had scarcely cracked the book open — had learned nothing more than her tonnage and registry — when the key turned in the lock and the door opened.

The girl — *Sarah* — stood shivering on the threshold. She had changed her clothes, but she was as fascinating in a swallow-tailed calico jacket and rustling silk petticoats as she had been in sailor's togs. Her eyes fell immediately on the log. "I believe that belongs to the *Sally,*" she said, holding out her shaking hand.

"It should have gone over the side before we caught you," Sparhawk said, hoping to distract her.

"Captain Molineaux was nothing if not consistent," she said, her attention still focused on the slim volume in his hand. "He proved unprepared for *every* eventuality."

There had been no opportunity on deck for her to make any expression of outrage or grief over the death of the captain. It had not occurred to Sparhawk until now that the man might have been someone important to her — a lover perhaps.

An unwelcome thought. Her words now argued otherwise, but he found he needed to know. "Who was he to you?" Sparhawk asked.

"The captain was hired by one of the *Sally*'s investors," she said. "For his politics, and not, more's the pity, for his skill as a sailor."

The ship chose that moment to lurch alarmingly to starboard. She'd walked with an effortless sailor's gait earlier, but her sea legs deserted her now, and she tumbled into the room, a mess of honey blond hair and pale, cold skin.

He caught her. "You're trembling," he said, tucking the log discreetly into his pocket.

"It's cold," she said, disentangling herself from his arms.

It wasn't. Not in the cabin, and not in the

stuffy main deck she had just crossed to reach him. "No," he said. "It is the aftermath of the tension on deck." He snatched the coverlet off the bed and approached her with it. She backed from him warily.

"You have nothing to fear from me," he assured her. "If I had the stomach for hurting a woman, I would have disarmed you on deck earlier."

Her pale complexion turned ashen. "Why didn't you, then?" she asked.

"Because if I had touched you, I believe your crew might very well have begun a war over it." He dropped the blanket loosely over her shoulders and stepped back.

Duty said he should push her out the door of the cabin and lock it from inside until he'd memorized everything he needed from the log.

Honor said she was a lovely young woman — with an unfortunate fondness for firearms — in distress.

"I take it you don't make a habit of kidnapping naval officers," he said.

It was difficult now to imagine this fashionable young girl leveling a pistol at him. Her jacket was Indian cotton, brightly printed, and smartly laced in front with a green silk ribbon. The glimmering lattice tempted his eye down to a neat, defined waist. Her clothes were stylish and spoke of money and leisure, but her skirts were hemmed country-high, as though she were a farmwife or a shopkeeper. Not that he minded the extra inches of stockinged calf on display.

"No," she said. "Do *you* make a habit of abducting children?"

The ship rolled once more, and he reached for her automatically. Earlier he had held no doubt that she would have shot him to protect the boy and that the standoff on the deck would have dissolved into a bloody slaughter if he had tried to disarm her. The events of the last hour had taken a toll on her. She was shaking so hard she could barely stand upright.

"Children, no." He led her to the bunk. "Able-bodied men of seafaring habits, yes. Your brother counts as such if he has been working a merchantman. And manning the *Wasp* is one of my responsibilities as an officer."

She wrinkled her nose. "You would not have caught the *Sally* had my father been at the helm. Your *Wasp* is a lubberly brig. Sluggish and in need of careening. I grant that you handled her well for all her faults, but she does not, from what I saw of her, have an excellent crew."

He was most definitely not on his own quarterdeck with this girl. "I might have exaggerated on that point," Sparhawk said. "But your brother would not have been mistreated on my ship. And it is in my power to press whom I see fit."

She sat and pulled the blanket tight around herself. He'd had his first glimpses of a tempting female form in three months, and he found he sorely resented the embroidered coverlet. Nevertheless, when she shivered once more, he took his coat off and draped that too around her slender shoulders.

"My brother is hardly a hired hand. This is our father's ship. And considering that I have kidnapped you," she said, acknowledging the loan of his coat with a nod of her head, "you needn't be so gallant."

Earlier, he'd thought her pretty, but nothing truly out of the ordinary. Now she smiled, and he revised his opinion. It was more than the pleasing curve of her full lips, the light in her wide brown eyes, the hint of strawberry in her honey gold hair. She had a daring and directness that made her an original. He felt strongly the unwanted tug of desire.

He retreated to the other side of the tiny room, putting the table between them.

There were men — like his father — who preferred their lovers vulnerable and powerless. Who preyed on chambermaids and serving girls — women in difficult positions.

Like this one. It was an abuse of privilege, and it was wrong.

Since his first affair with an opera dancer at fifteen, Sparhawk had confined his passions to those who could not be hurt by a liaison. He took care to be certain that his lovers were financially secure and socially immune to censure. He bedded bored wives with open-minded husbands, carefree widows, and members of the demimonde who would not be thrown into the street by an angry father, jailed for immorality, or condemned to spinsterhood and destitution.

Sparhawk had always drawn this line between himself and his father, to prove that they were nothing alike. He had never found it inconvenient — until now.

On the deck above, holding him at gunpoint, Sarah had been aware that Sparhawk was handsome. Up close he was disconcertingly beautiful. She ought to have expected that. Rumor had it that he made too free with other men's wives. It would be easy for him, with his pale blue eyes and blue-black hair, bleached at the crown by the sun. Six foot aloft, he had the build of a fighting man but the face of a Bernini angel — or a fallen one anyway. His nose was slightly crooked. It had probably been broken at some point.

On deck, his beauty had made it easier for her to focus her anger — and her fear — on him, because he was as handsome as the man who had put her there. Easier to raise a pistol to his head and feel the smooth steel of the trigger beneath her finger.

Especially after seeing the captain's head torn off by a cannonball.

Sick with frustration at Molineaux's incompetence, she had been standing quite close when it happened, watching the *Wasp* overtake them. The ball had struck him and then the mast, exploding in a shower of blood and splinters and lodging in the heart of the hewed pitch pine. The impact had been so loud, it had temporarily deafened her.

She watched the top of the mast strike the water in eerie silence.

Then her hearing came back in a rush of sound, of flapping sails and shouts and the ring of axes. Mr. Cheap shook his head and pushed her down the hatch, ordering her to don her brother's clothes and tuck the sailing master's pistol in her sash and cover it with her jacket.

Then the British had boarded them, and found the gold, and tried to take Ned.

After she had faced Sparhawk down and they were well away, she knew she must confront him, this splendid naval officer with his glittering braid and buttons. She wished she could put herself on an equal footing with him, armor herself in silver lace and silk damask, but she had only her faded calico jacket and petticoat, the one she had worn to buy the French molasses and trade on her father's name in Saint Stash — Saint Eustatius, the Dutch free port in the Caribbean where anything could be had for a price.

She had entered the cabin expecting Sparhawk's haughty disdain, but he was outmaneuvering her with his kindness. He draped his soft wool coat, still warm from his body, around her shoulders.

"I kidnapped you," she said. "You needn't be so gallant."

"You did it to protect your brother," he replied, "and I cannot fault your motives. In the navy we celebrate the courage of our enemies. Without it, we would all be on half pay."

Handsome *and* charismatic. He was trying to charm her.

"I'm not your enemy, Captain Sparhawk.

Even loyal Englishmen find the press barbaric." The words carried slightly less dignity than she intended, because the *Sally* rolled again and threw her off the bunk.

Sparhawk caught her, his hands warm and reassuring around her waist, and replied almost without missing a beat, "It is how Britain has manned her navy for a hundred years. It is how she keeps your coast safe from French incursions. The press may be a trifle . . . callous, but it is legal, and you would not enjoy such security without it."

She had not been so close to a man since Micah Wild. And she had never been so close to a man like this. Sparhawk's face and form approached a heroic ideal, like an engraving she had once seen of a statue of Achilles.

The deck pitched again and she grasped him for balance. Her fingers discovered a lean, hard body beneath the fine tailoring of his uniform, and something hidden in his pocket. Her hand slid down. It was the briefest movement, disguised by the wild motion of the deck, and he did not appear to notice. "This is not Britain. And just because it is legal does not mean that it is right."

"Now you sound like a Rebel," he chided, but his hands were still around her waist, and his warmth was tempting her closer.

Sarah knew where such temptation led. With regret, she disentangled herself and stepped back.

"I'm no Rebel," she said. "You will want the name of the man expecting that French gold, which I can tell you, and you will require this as evidence if he is to be arrested."

Sarah held up the *Sally*'s log, which she had just picked out of his pocket.

He moved to pat his coat, then stopped, a self-deprecating smile playing across his lips. "That was very deftly done," he said. "What is it you want in return?"

"I want my father and the *Sally*'s crew cleared of any suspicion of treason. They are not Rebels, and they should not be treated as pirates. They knew nothing about the gold."

"Forgive me, but I am hesitant to trust the word of a woman — no matter how lovely — who has just picked my pocket. Where did you acquire such a skill?"

She blushed at the compliment, but she knew better than to answer truthfully. "Dame school," she said. Her father had been pardoned long ago, but some of the rogues in his crew had not.

"In between needlework and penman-
ship?"

"After music but before drawing. Will you
help us?"

"What you ask may be difficult. A hold
filled with French molasses is hardly a testament to your loyalty."

"*Everyone* smuggles. Even the admiral
drinks Dutch tea, for heaven's sake. That
does not make the man a Rebel."

"But treating with foreign powers does.
And someone aboard this ship most assur-
edly did."

"The *Sally*," she said, anger warming her,
"is my father's ship, but he did not hire the
captain, nor did he give the man his instructions."

"Then who did?"

"An investor," she said. If only Micah Wild
had been *just* that.

"And does your father take his business
affairs so lightly that he does not know the
character of his investors?"

"My father had no choice. We owed the
man money."

"He has embroiled you in treason. Tell me
his name, and I will do my best to bring
him to justice."

"British justice," she said, "extends no
farther than Boston these days. The Rebel

40

mob rules in Salem. If I cross this man without the Crown's protection, my family and I will lose what little we have left."

"I am sorry," he said. "I cannot give you the assurance you want."

"Then I cannot give you this." She slid the log into her skirt pocket. Sparhawk's eyes followed her hand, then lingered.

He took a step closer.

She took one back. "Don't even consider it," she said.

"I only want the *Sally*'s log."

"Liar."

"Fine," he said, and closed the distance she had put between them. "You're a saucy piece, and I'd like to have you too." His hand skimmed the silk of her skirt; his fingers slipped inside the opening at the seam, found the bare skin of her thigh, and stroked.

It had been so very long since a man had touched her, but her body remembered and ached with longing. She was no longer chilled. She was warm all the way through, heat radiating from the tips of his fingers dancing closer to the apex of her thighs.

And then he stopped.

His hand shot to the pocket tied around her waist and dove inside. "But I believe Mr. Cheap would have something to say about that, and what I *require*," he said, grasping the book in her pocket, "is the log."

She'd been a damned fool again.

The door crashed open. Ned stood panting and dripping on the threshold, and thankfully, he did not appear to notice that Sparhawk had his hand in her skirts.

Her brother gulped in air and words tumbled out. "You must come. Mr. Cheap would not furl the sail and the wind has fouled the spar, and the carpenter says that if he tries to run before the gale in this blow, her seams will open."

THREE

The skin of her thigh had been warm and silken. The responsive tilt of her hips had invited further exploration. He could not recall ever being so powerfully attracted to a woman. Closing his fingers around the slender book in her pocket had taken an act of will.

The child's interruption — the emergency — had been timely indeed.

With regret, Sparhawk pocketed the log and followed the girl up the ladder. His eyes were once more drawn irresistibly to her swaying hips. Until they emerged on deck and into a fierce maelstrom. It was a vicious little New England squall. Rain pelted his face and soaked through his coat almost instantly, replacing desire with sodden discomfort. His shoes filled with water. The wind whistled so loud he could no longer hear the boy shouting beside him, but he looked up to where the child was pointing.

The foremast was bristling with sail. Too much for the *Sally*'s slight build and far too much for this heavy weather. Cheap had left it too late. He couldn't blame the man. In the same position, he might have cut it too close as well. The *Sally* needed to put distance between herself and the *Wasp*, or risk recapture by another naval vessel.

Now she risked loosing her foremast and opening her seams. The topsail was the problem. It had to be reefed. Easier said than done. The mainmast had tangled the standing rigging when she fell. It would be tricky work and dangerous in such weather.

There was nothing else for it. He shouted as much to Mr. Cheap, who shouted back that he could not send a man up in such a blow, that it would be the death of anyone who tried. Cheap was, as Sparhawk had suspected, no captain. He would not order a shipmate to his likely death.

The alternative, Sparhawk knew, was that they would all die. The *Sally* was heeling and taking on water, and now was not the time for democratic decision making. Now was the time for blind obedience to orders.

"I'll go." A small piping voice.

Ned. Sparhawk had forgotten him.

"No!" The girl shook her head.

Sparhawk ignored her. "We'll both of us go."

The boy reached the top before him, proving himself, as Sparhawk had suspected earlier, a seasoned hand. It was the work of a few minutes to cut the sail free. Reefing her was harder. The boy did not have the strength of a grown man, and they did not make pretty work of it, but between them they got it done.

The descent was still more difficult. The schooner was settling, but there was still a wild motion in her. Hands that had been warm and nimble going up were cold, bruised, and numb coming down, and it was easy, so easy, to lose one's grip.

Then the *Sally* rolled and the boy fell. Not from a great height. Twelve feet perhaps, and if the weather had been still and the boy had been lucky, he might have hit the deck and broken a few bones.

The weather was not still and the boy was not lucky.

Sarah watched her brother plunge into the dark roiling sea.

Not this. Not this. She had already lost so much. *Not Ned.*

She ran for the side. There was shouting, but the words were lost in the wind and all she knew was that she had to reach the pale form that had fallen from the gray sky into the grayer water.

There was movement on the deck, someone dropping from the rigging and streaking toward the side, and then rough hands were grasping her from behind and dragging her back from the rail.

Sparhawk watched the boy fall. He was only a few feet from the deck. He slid down the rest of the way in time to see the girl running toward the rail. "Stop her," he barked over the howling wind. The crew was frozen, but Lucas Cheap acted. He grasped the girl and dragged her, kicking and screaming like a banshee, away from the pitching sea.

"Give me a line," he demanded. And now the crew was answering to him because Lucas Cheap had done so and they *wanted* orders. He took the line, kicked off his shoes, and dove over the side.

The water was bitingly cold. It sent a shock through his whole body, wet though he already was. It had been only moments since the boy had gone in, but every second counted. The cold would soon start to drag at him, make him clumsy and slow. Sparhawk saw a golden head break the water. Swam. Reached it. The boy was conscious and swimming. That was good.

He shouted, hoping his voice would carry above the wind, and felt the line begin to draw them in. They were only a few yards from the *Sally* when a wave picked them up and tossed them toward the hull. Sparhawk pulled the boy close and tried to take the brunt of the impact. His right hand connected with the hull, and pain lanced up his arm.

The boy, thankfully, had the good sense to grasp the line and begin hauling himself up. Another wave slammed into Sparhawk. He held his breath under water. His lungs ached. The churning sea receded, and he saw the boy scramble over the rail to safety.

His right hand was still numb from the impact. He could not make it answer. He wrapped his good hand around the rope and used his legs to lever himself up. An inch or two of progress, no more, and then another wave swamped him.

This time he didn't catch his breath. His lungs burned, his grip slackened, and he knew that he was going to drown.

The line jerked. His head broke through the water. The rope started to move, hauling him up in fits and starts until finally strong hands were reaching for him and lifting him over the side. They deposited him on the deck, where he stood swaying, the churn and tumble of the waves still echoing through his body and scrambling his senses. Even so, he could tell that the *Sally* was riding easier.

Sarah was hugging the bedraggled boy and yelling at him at the same time. Sparhawk could not hear what she was saying; the ocean still roared in his ears, but he imagined it was a litany of thanks to whatever iteration of the Divine they favored in Naumkeag and admonitions never to be nearly drowned again.

He envied the boy the harangue and the embrace. He could not recall a time when anyone had ever been that happy to see him alive.

The boy finally freed himself from her arms and began speaking urgently.

Sarah looked up and smiled at Sparhawk. The gratitude on her face warmed him. For a moment he forgot that he was bone tired and dizzy and soaking wet and that his arm hurt like hell. He forgot that she was a Rebel and a smuggler and that he was a naval officer and her captive. He tried to raise his battered hand to acknowledge her, but the cold made him clumsy and his aching fingers would not uncurl.

The girl's smile vanished. She pushed the

boy toward the hatch and came striding across the deck to Sparhawk. "Let me see your hand."

"It's nothing."

She cradled his forearm in her own and touched his wrist gingerly. It didn't hurt exactly, but it felt strange. Something looked wrong about it beneath his sleeve, but he couldn't quite tell what.

"Let's get you below," she said.

That sounded like an excellent idea to him.

He took a step, swayed, felt his knees buckle. The girl slipped under his shoulders to accept his weight, but she could not support him on her own. "Mr. Cheap!" she called out.

The sailing master came running and lifted Sparhawk's good arm over his shoulder. Together, Cheap and the girl got him down the hatch, across the deck, and into the captain's cabin.

His body felt not his own, and freed from it, he noticed things he had not earlier. The bed had been built for a bigger man than the dead captain. The chair as well. The bed curtains were a nice — if impractical — touch, with their fine blue needlework on a cream wool background. It spoke of a sort of permanence you could not expect in the navy. You commanded at the Admiralty's pleasure. You took what ships they gave you. You did not, as a rule, mistake them for a home.

They lowered him to sit on the edge of the bed. The sensation of waves tumbling his body slowed. Cheap took a good long look at Sparhawk's hand, grunted, and walked out, leaving the door pointedly ajar.

"Let's get you out of these wet clothes," she said. Her fingers were already lifting the hem of his shirt.

"Alas," he said, trying for a playful tone even as his head spun and a dull ache took up residence in his arm. "I suspect I am not fit for action."

She snorted. "Your vanity, at least, is unflagging. Lean forward."

He did so. She was deft and efficient pulling up his shirt, careful not to touch his injured arm any more than was necessary. It occurred to him that she had done this before.

"You're very calm in a crisis," he observed.

"I've had a fair bit of practice."

She peeled his sleeve off to reveal his injured arm. Broken, for certain. Crooked near the wrist, like a dinner fork. It was not the worst he had been hurt. He had seen enough broken limbs in the service to know that it was the good kind — nothing was poking through the skin.

"It will need to be straightened," she said.

"Is that one of your many skills?" he asked, hopefully.

"No, unfortunately not. I can make you comfortable for now," she said, feeling along his arm, "but I'm no bonesetter. You must see a doctor. Sooner, rather than later, or it will not set properly."

She bent to examine his hand, and he noted how long and slender her neck was, how dainty and pink the lobe of her ear. She pressed tentatively on his wrist. Pain shot up his arm.

"I think there is only one break," she said, "very near the wrist, and perhaps some smaller bones in the hand."

He was not squeamish about blood — or at least he had ceased to be after his first battle at sea — but the bent angle of his normally straight limb disturbed him in a way that blood did not, and to a degree that would not have been possible in the heat of a fight. When the guns were speaking and splinters flying, you lost all awareness of your own body except as it carried you back and forth across the deck or onto the enemy's vessel. He'd once been stabbed through the shoulder during a boarding action and not noticed until an hour later.

This, though, made him feel light-headed, and he did not want to faint in front of this brave girl. His attraction to her was maddening. Even cold, injured, and exhausted, his body stirred to her touch. "The bed curtains," he said, fixing his eyes on them, "are very nice."

"They're very old-fashioned. I made them when I was fourteen," she said. "And you're whiter than they are." So she was brave *and* perceptive. And she smelled like rain and soap and appealed to him like a hot bath on a stormy day. "Lie back and let me prop up your arm."

"I dismasted your ship and killed your captain — you needn't be so gallant," he said, echoing her earlier words, and hoping she did not notice his increasingly obvious condition.

"I'm not being gallant," she said, plumping a cushion. "Returning you to the admiral half drowned and crippled would hardly improve our situation."

She positioned a pillow for his head. He leaned back into the welcome warmth of the feather mattress, felt the cool linen sheet at his back, unexpectedly crisp and smooth. It steadied him, reminded him of the bedding his mother had painstakingly ironed for the trundle in their rude little cottage. It had been a luxury she had brought to the island from home. He had not thought of it in years.

Another cushion found its way under his elbow. That was nice.

There were captains in the navy with a reputation for high living, of course. He had never desired to be one of them. There had been a post commander in the Med who liked to entertain in his cabin, which was lined with Turkey carpets and crammed with exotic objets d'art.

This was something different. Not luxury. Comfort. Perhaps someday Sparhawk might have a trim little schooner like this, with a paneled captain's cabin, and bed curtains embroidered by a pretty girl. One who would not be harmed by his attentions, as this one would.

Ned entered the room, clothes dry but golden hair dripping, with a bundle under each arm — muslin and kindling, it appeared. He had a tankard in his hand, and Sparhawk's bedraggled blue coat thrown over his shoulder. He passed the bundles and the coat to his sister. "Mr. Cheap sent these," he said. Then he turned to Sparhawk. "Thank you for going in after me, sir. I brought you my ration of grog, if you'd like it." He held out the tin cup.

"I suspect Captain Sparhawk would prefer some of our late skipper's brandy, Ned," his sister said.

The boy looked crestfallen.

"By no means. Grog is just the thing. Thank you very much, Ned." He took the tankard in his good hand. "But from now on, when you're in the rigging, remember: one hand for the ship, one hand for yourself."

The boy nodded and beamed. "I shall, sir. I promise."

Sparhawk detected a whiff of hero worship. He supposed he had looked at old Captain McKenzie that way from time to time. Sarah only eyed him with suspicion.

As well she should. Despite his best intentions, he was trying to charm her.

Oblivious to his sister's disapproval, the boy went on. "Mr. Cheap says to convey his thanks as well, and tell you that he probably won't have you killed."

"Very kind of him, I'm sure," Sparhawk replied.

"That's practically a billet-doux where Mr. Cheap is concerned," the girl said.

"He's been threatening to kill Benji for years," Ned added.

"Who is Benji?" Sparhawk asked, sipping

his rum. It was dark, rich, and indeed quite warming. Better stuff than the navy bought and less liberally watered. Smuggled, no doubt.

"He's our older brother."

"And where is this older brother?" And why isn't he here looking after you?

"Away," said Sarah curtly. It was clear that she did *not* want to talk about this Benji. Interesting.

"He's in London," supplied the boy. "But he is coming back."

"And what was he doing in London?" Sparhawk asked.

The boy opened his mouth to speak, but his sister forestalled him. "That's enough, Ned. You mustn't tell the captain your name or anything that might help him identify us."

Ned looked uncertainly at Sparhawk.

"I already know your names, Sarah." It was the first time he had used it. He'd never thought the name pretty before. "I take it the *Sally* is your namesake. Is that what you prefer to be called?"

"No."

"Sarah, then."

"Altogether too familiar."

"I'm not some old retainer. I can hardly call you Miss Sarah."

55

"You may call her Miss Ward," uttered Ned, with a gravity beyond his years. "But you mustn't offer her any insult. Then I would be obliged to call you out, even if you did save my life." A very adult speech, Sparhawk thought. Then the boy added, "Though you would probably win. I am not the swordsman my brother is."

"Just as well," advised Sparhawk. "Fancy sword work is not much use in the navy. It's all hacking and slashing when you board the enemy."

"I believe we have already had this conversation, Captain. He won't be entering the navy."

"No. Not as a common sailor," Sparhawk agreed. "Although he is a very good hand." The boy beamed. "But he could go far as a midshipman. I did."

"You were not a colonial."

"I was an orphan." Or at least that was what the world thought. "I had no interest save that of the captain I served under." That part was true enough.

"But you were still English. It makes a difference." She gently lifted Sparhawk's arm and directed the boy to slide a length of muslin under it. Together they wrapped his wrist, using the wooden splint to provide stability, and when they were done he had to agree that he felt altogether more comfortable.

Too comfortable. She dismissed Ned, shut the cabin door, and placed her hands on Sparhawk's fall front.

He used his good hand to stop her. "There's no need," he said.

"I am *not* giving you my ration of grog, so to speak. Your skin is cold to the touch, and your wet breeches are soaking the bed. They must come off, and we must get you warm."

"Give me a blanket, then. An unmarried girl shouldn't have to do such a thing."

She raised one golden eyebrow. "There's no one else to do it, and you don't know for a fact that I'm not married."

"Yes, I do. Mr. Cheap is too old to be your husband, and no sane man would let his wife go to sea on a smuggler's ketch alone, particularly if she looked like you."

"Flattery does not sway me, Captain Sparhawk."

"It isn't flattery. You're a charming creature, and I have been on station for three months. The combination produces a rather predictable result."

His meaning penetrated. "Oh."

"It would be best if you left me to my own devices now," he said. "Unless you're going to offer me your ration of grog . . . so to

57

speak."

He was teasing, of course. His battered arm had claimed all of her attention up to that point. It was a bad break, but she had known better than to let him see that on her face. It must be set, well and quickly, or he would lose the use of his hand.

But he was as comfortable as she could make him now, and it was impossible to ignore the fine proportions of his body: the broad chest, defined pectorals, narrow waist, and strong, muscled thighs.

He was a very well-made man.

And inconveniently heroic.

It might at one time have been possible for James Sparhawk, master and commander of His Majesty's brig the *Wasp,* to take more than physical notice of fashionable Sarah Ward, heiress, but misfortune and her own mistakes had altered her prospects irrevocably. A man as accomplished and respected as Sparhawk, no matter what side Sarah took in the present squabble with Parliament, was forever beyond her reach.

She handed him the blanket. "No grog," she said, as much to herself as to him, because grog was the only thing they could share, and if she had been able to resist temptation before, everything would now be different. "But I am very grateful to you for saving my brother. Even if it is your fault that he was in the water in the first place."

She only half meant it. She knew that Sparhawk's actions had been necessary. It was what her father would have done.

"It seemed a great pity," Sparhawk said lightly, "after you turned pirate in order to save him, to let the boy drown."

He made light of his heroism, but Sarah was a mariner's daughter and had been bred to the sea. She knew the risk he had taken. Few sailors troubled to learn how to swim, because they understood it was unlikely to save them. Chances were that if you went into rough water, you drowned.

She fetched the *Sally*'s log from his be-draggled coat. "You have earned this, at least," she said, and laid it on the bed beside his good hand.

He let out a deep breath. For the first time since their escape from the *Wasp* she thought about what James Sparhawk would face when he returned to Boston. He had been separated from command of his ship. It was very possible he would be court-martialed.

In this country it is a good thing to kill an

admiral from time to time to encourage the others.

And heedless of the danger — both the immediate prospect of drowning and the looming threat of court-martial — he had braved the churning sea and saved Ned. There could be nothing between them. The gulf separating them was too wide for a legitimate connection, and a liaison would only drag her family further into disrepute. She could not give him what he — what *she* — wanted, but she owed Sparhawk something. "The man you want," she said. "His name is Micah Wild."

"Thank you," Sparhawk said. "This will make my reception in Boston a good deal more welcoming."

If Micah Wild learned of her betrayal, it would make her reception in Salem a good deal less so.

FOUR

Sparhawk slept deeply. It occurred to him only upon waking that he had done so in a dead man's bed.

His arm felt stiff and heavy. He was not in pain, exactly, but he ached. His body, clearly, needed more sleep, but something had woken him. That was when he realized that the *Sally* was riding at anchor.

The ship's log was still lying next to him on the bed. He had lost the schooner as a prize, but he could still return to the admiral with important evidence against the traitors who had been conspiring with the French. If the gold reached Boston, it would further mitigate the circumstances of his capture, and he might escape with only a reprimand. He ought to feel a measure of satisfaction. Instead, he felt unsettled about the girl.

The door opened. It was only when Lucas Cheap entered that James realized how much he had been hoping to see Sarah again.

The grizzled pirate had a brown coat and a crumpled hat in one hand and a jug of water in the other. "You'll get your fancy blue coat back, but for now you're to wear this."

Cheap left him to wash and dress.

The coat was threadbare copper velvet with tarnished gold lace. The wide gored skirts were thirty years out-of-date, and the lavish embellishment eclipsed the martial splendor of Sparhawk's uniform.

Unexpectedly, for he was not a small man, it was a trifle long and a whit roomy through the shoulders.

He tried the door and found it unlocked. He navigated the main deck successfully in the gloom, but the ladder was tricky with his bound hand, nothing in his stomach for twenty-four hours save seawater and grog, and six yards of figured velvet swirling around his knees. The coat, he fancied, demanded a certain swagger that was difficult to pull off with a broken arm. That he cared so much about his appearance while in the clutches of Rebel smugglers was a testament to the allure of Sarah Ward.

When he emerged on deck it was to a heavy morning fog. There were no lights, and the crew worked in disciplined silence. Sarah stood at the side, wrapped in a heavy wool boat cloak, her honey gold hair piled like silk yarn in the hood, bright against the tar black rigging.

Sparhawk had bedded more than his fair share of beautiful women; brought many of them aboard his vessels, either out of convenience or because his paramours pretended an interest in the workings of a man-of-war. Rarely did such interest last beyond their first faltering steps on deck. Never did the color of the sun filtered through canvas or the quality of light reflected off the water burnish their beauty more brightly. More often the roll and pitch of the ship robbed their bodies of grace and the wind disarranged their careful coiffures.

Not so with Sarah Ward. Aboard the *Sally* she was a jewel in a setting, shown to best advantage by wind-filled canvas and pitch pine spars.

Mr. Cheap observed Sparhawk studying the girl once more, but this time he did not flash his gold-toothed smile. Instead, he dug Sparhawk's silver gilt button out of a pocket and flicked it high into the air, then caught it. A little something to remember you by, Captain.

Sparhawk took the hint and looked away.

They were anchored beside a small island, low and rocky, with bursts of color — wildflowers, he presumed — and noble stands of trees. He turned back to Sarah Ward with what he hoped was an expression of polite interest rather than lecherous perusal. "Where are we?"

"Anchored off Misery Island, near Salem."

"It doesn't look particularly miserable."

"Try being stranded on it for three days in December, during a storm."

A brisk wind was blowing off the place. "The idea does not appeal." He buttoned his borrowed coat against the chill.

Her eyes fastened on his injured wrist, where his muslin bandages peeked out from the velvet cuff like a froth of antique lace. "I am sorry about your coat," she said. "But it would not be safe for you — or us — if you were seen in it. I promise you shall have it back."

Less one silver button, he feared.

The girl went on. "There is a doctor in town who is a friend. Ned will fetch him to our house."

"That will not be necessary," Sparhawk said. "Put me ashore in the ship's boat, and I will make my way to Boston and have the break attended to there."

"It cannot wait that long. And you cannot

ride or bounce along in a carriage — if you could find one — until the bones have been set."

"I am not as fragile as all that, Miss Ward. And you promised to release me."

"In one piece. Thanks to your heroics, I cannot do that without the assistance of a physician," she said, in the same steely voice she had used yesterday while holding a pistol on him. "If the wrist heals badly, you will be crippled for life."

"And if I delay, the admiral will want to know what I was doing, and whom I was with. He will want to know more about you and Mr. Cheap and Ned and the *Sally* than I am inclined to tell. You must let me go, for your own sake, Miss Ward."

Cheap, Sparhawk felt sure, was all for tipping him over the side and being done with him, but Sarah shook her head. "You saved Ned. We are in your debt. You will allow me to discharge it by bringing you to a doctor who can set your arm."

"Or you will order Mr. Cheap to break the other arm, I take it?"

"If necessary," she said.

And Sparhawk had no doubt the rogue would do it for her.

Cheap had called her a lady, but such a term only diminished Sarah Ward. Honor, in ladies, was defined by what they did not do. Honor, for Sarah Ward, meant keeping her word and paying her debts and protecting her family.

Cheap guarded Sparhawk with his pistol while Ned and Sarah climbed into the boat. Sparhawk got himself down with rather more difficulty and took a seat on the bench. He watched with fascination as Ned loosed the sail and placed the line in his sister's hand. Her other was already upon the tiller.

She piloted the little cutter with the ease of a born sailor. Sarah Ward looked the way Sparhawk often felt on the deck of the *Wasp* — in tune with the canvas and wind.

Cheap caught him staring again, and flashed that gold-toothed smile. Sparhawk turned to study the riverbank. He had never been to Salem before. He knew only that the port was firmly in the hands of the Rebels and that before the trouble it had been growing obscenely rich.

Rosy dawn light burned away the fog as the boat made its way upriver, and James saw that it was not a city of brick like Boston. The riverbank was crowded with brightly painted clapboard houses. The sky was a crazy jumble of rooflines ancient and modern, steep and shallow, cedar and slate, and the shore below bristled with a network of private docks and small boats that bobbed gently in the current. It reminded him, with the warm light, bright colors, and flowing water, of Venice.

A town built around the sea, and its commerce. Around domestic and foreign trade. With docks and warehouses handy for merchants who wanted to avoid customs duties.

Sarah had not exaggerated. The admiral *did* drink Dutch tea. Smuggling was a way of life in America. It had been for fifty years. The colonies would have failed without it. Parliament had been passing laws for decades designed to skim all the profit out of American trade, mandating that colonial goods could be sold only to British merchants — so that British merchants could sell them at a profit to the rest of the world — and that Americans could buy only British goods, cloth and copper and household necessities. At prices that would keep them in perpetual debt, beholden to the English mercantile agents to whom they were forced to sell their fish, their lumber, their abundant rice and grains. It was but a step removed from serfdom, and anyone who thought the colonists — Englishmen themselves — would stand for it was a fool.

For decades the Americans had for the most part been sidestepping these laws, bribing customs agents and sailing under false papers or into the Dutch free ports to trade their goods. It was a thoroughly corrupt system, grown out of corrupt laws, but it had worked. Sparhawk did not care for politics, but even he could see that suddenly trying to enforce crippling tariffs that had been largely ignored for half a century was madness on Parliament's part.

Here was the result. There was hardly an inch of riverfront unclaimed by private wharves — a smuggler's best friend — until a great empty expanse loomed up on the left. It was the first brick house Sparhawk had seen in Salem, and it dominated the waterfront. It was three stories tall, five windows wide, and capped by a gaudy copper roof; the green paint on the shutters still looked wet and fresh. An abundance of carved wooden ornament crusted the brick: pilasters and swags and flowers and pineapples, executed with the greatest skill, if not the most restrained taste. And that was just the back. He could only imagine how elaborate the façade might be. A wide manicured lawn and garden ran down to a pebbled beach — the stones white, regular, and carefully raked.

"Good God," Sparhawk exclaimed. "What nabob lives there?"

"Micah Wild," Sarah said tonelessly.

Ned opened his mouth to speak, but Sarah shook her head, and Sparhawk's earlier, disturbing suspicions became certainties. There was more to Micah Wild's treachery than a chest of French gold.

Sarah did not want to speak of Micah Wild. Even now, she could not look at his house — the house he had built for her — without feeling her chest constrict. She must have a serious word with Ned about the virtues of discretion. Their older brother's troubles and her relationship with her former betrothed were none of Captain Sparhawk's business. And pity was the last thing she wanted from him.

They reached their tiny dock before the river really began to stir. She dispatched Ned to the doctor and bustled Sparhawk into the house as quietly as possible. He was obviously in pain — though he refused to admit it — and she hoped that he was too exhausted to notice the condition of her home.

If he chanced to look in the parlor, he would see that the pale floors were scarred with nail holes and dotted with tufts of wool

69

from the missing carpets. The windows were naked, but damaged plaster marked where the cornices had hung. The pier glasses — sold, like everything else — had printed ghostly shadows on the walls. Only her bedroom and her father's were still properly furnished. Ned slept on a trundle in the keeping room.

Sparhawk did notice, of course. He could hardly fail to. Even the wallpapers had been stripped and auctioned, leaving the chilly hallway leprous and scabbed. He stopped her halfway up the stairs, placed his good hand lightly over her cold fingers on the banister, and said, "Sarah, what has happened here? You said you owed this man Wild money. This is more than debt." His eyes traveled over the naked walls and bald floors. "This is desperation."

"There are worse things than penury, Captain."

"Yes, but most of them take root there. It is shocking what you will do for a heel of bread if your family is starving."

He spoke as if from experience, but poverty was different for men. They could support themselves with the work of their hands, sign aboard a merchantman, load and unload cargo at the dock. Women had fewer choices, and if they were reduced to selling their labor outside their home or the confines of a family business, it was often assumed that they sold themselves as well. Still, Sarah would have taken work as a maid or a seamstress and been grateful for it; but thanks to Micah Wild, who had let it be known that he did not want to see his former betrothed scrubbing floors or taking in sewing, Sarah had no choices at all.

She longed to talk to someone about her situation, but there was no one who would understand. Micah hadn't just jilted her. He'd taken her best friend and confidante from her at the same time. Benji had been away; Ned, too young to comprehend; and her father, too ill to burden with her unhappiness. Her neighbors and friends and school companions were kind but distant, afraid, as well they should be, to put themselves on the wrong side of Micah Wild.

There were things she could not tell Sparhawk, but the bare outline of her story, at least, she could share. "When my father was appointed an agent for the East India Company tea, he thought he saw a safe and legal way to invest his money. A way to ensure my future."

"So he put his entire capital in the tea," Sparhawk guessed.

"Yes. When the tea was destroyed in

Boston, Wild and a gang of ruffians — they called themselves a Committee of Safety — announced that they would hang as traitors anyone who sold tea in Salem. It's in a warehouse — two shiploads bought and paid for by my father — down at the dock, rotting."

"The *Sally* is an extraordinarily fine vessel," Sparhawk said. "Your father could have leased her out to anyone. Why this Wild?"

"We had already borrowed money from him to keep ourselves afloat. My father would not sign the Rebel articles, so no one would invest in a new voyage with him. Except Micah Wild. He lent us the money to cargo her."

"And if I had not stopped you," Sparhawk said, "you would have come home with your musket flint and your French molasses and paid Wild off."

He was looking up at her with great intensity, his desire to be her champion plain on his face. He would not rise so quickly to her defense if he knew the rest of her story, but she was not obligated to tell it. There was nothing to stop her, just at that moment, from basking in the warmth of his regard.

"Yes," she agreed. "We would have paid Wild off." Their fortunes would have been restored, but her reputation could not be repaired.

"What will this man do?" Sparhawk asked. There was no mistaking the concern in his voice. It warmed her, though there was nothing he could do to help.

"Wild is a daring smuggler, and much admired in Salem. Only Elias Derby has more ships or money. And Micah is our own Sam Adams and John Hancock combined. The rich merchants and rabble on the docks love him equally well. He stirs the crowd with appeals to high ideals and common greed. They tarred and feathered a customs agent at his urging. And he has presided over beatings of Loyalists who will not sign the Rebel articles."

"And you fear what he will do to your family."

"No. You were right earlier. I fear what I will do to protect them."

The doctor, when he arrived, towed along by Ned, was surprisingly young. That was Sparhawk's first impression. A closer look revealed that Dr. Corwin — as Ned introduced him — was not so much young as youthful. He was probably near to Sparhawk's age, but with the sort of slight build and round boyish face that would preserve the illusion of youth well into middle age. He wore a very old-fashioned wig to counteract the effect, and carried a salt-stained bag that must have seen sea service. That, at least, was reassuring.

Corwin was more capable than Sparhawk expected. He ordered Sarah to take hold of Sparhawk's upper arm, while he himself manipulated the bone at the wrist. "We'll do this just like we did when Ned fell out of the tree, Sarah. You pull down and I pull up." The doctor smiled at her. Sparhawk saw in the expression a shared history — and possibly a shared future. To his surprise, that rankled. He could not recall ever being jealous about a woman before. Certainly not one he had never bedded.

He forgot all about such concerns when Corwin started to manipulate the breaks. It was a strange sensation, to feel his bones being pulled into place, and for about half a minute, it hurt like the devil. But then it was over, and the doctor was splinting and wrapping Sparhawk's arm in soft new wool. There were smaller splints for two of his fingers as well.

The short ordeal left him exhausted, but relieved. His arm no longer hung crooked at his side, and he could curl and uncurl his unbroken fingers, a good sign, or so the doctor told him.

"You won't feel like it," Corwin said as he tied the bandages, "but you should eat something. A chop or a beefsteak. Rare and bloody. Then rest."

"When can I travel?"

The doctor shrugged. "A week."

"I cannot stay here a week."

"If you could get a ship," the doctor said, "you could travel tomorrow. But you won't find a king's vessel in this harbor. You are lucky to have found a doctor. Our other sawbones in Salem is the brother of Joseph Warren, and just as radical. The Rebels ran the customs men out of town last September. They have sunk hulks in the harbor so that British ships cannot enter without a pilot, and the guns that Colonel Leslie failed to capture from the Rebels in February have been mounted on Juniper Point and Winter Island."

"By coach, then," Sparhawk said.

"The Wards and the Corwins are known Loyalists. The Patriots of Salem are unlikely to lend either of us a coach," said Corwin.

"I can get one," said Sarah.

Corwin shot her a speaking glance that Sparhawk could not interpret.

She ignored it. "But it can hardly drive up to our door in the middle of the day without

75

attracting attention."

"She's right," Corwin acknowledged. "We take a risk, both of us, helping you. Sentiment against the navy is running gallows high in Salem just now. Your squadron has been seizing men and cargo off Cape Ann ships with the abandon of buccaneers. The Port Act might have been meant to punish Boston, but it has kindled rebellion up and down the whole coast. In February, your Admiral Graves swept the Marblehead docks with a press gang and carried off twenty-seven seamen — husbands and fathers — crippling the fishing fleet. So when a box of candles intended for the admiral came their way, the selectmen there impounded it. In response, your admiral sent the *Lively* to Marblehead Harbor and threatened to shell the town."

"You sound," said Sparhawk, "as though you sympathize with the Rebels."

"We asked for the protection of government, for the king's ships and the king's soldiers to safeguard our property from the Rebels, not kidnap our young men and confiscate our goods to line their own pockets with prize money. If the Committee of Safety discovers you here, it will go hard — very hard — on Sarah and her father. Not to mention," he added, brightening, "that the Sons of Liberty will likely take you for a spy and string you up from the nearest tree."

His cheer, Sparhawk saw, was not entirely in jest. The good doctor did not like a fox in his henhouse.

James reminded himself that he could not have Sarah Ward. He was not his father. He would not seduce a vulnerable girl. An affair with a naval officer — and there was nothing more he could offer her — would be unlikely to improve her situation. Given the town's political climate, if they were discovered, it would only put her in greater jeopardy. And that would be a poor way to repay her care of him.

Yes, the good doctor was an altogether better choice for Sarah Ward.

"Beefsteak or a chop," Corwin repeated. "My wife has a rack in her larder. I am certain we can spare something for you."

Or perhaps not.

The doctor left. Sarah went with him, in search of a rig, and Sparhawk reclined on the four-poster and considered his prospects.

The door creaked open. Ned hovered on the threshold, looking nervously over his shoulder.

"It's all right," Sparhawk assured him.

"She has gone to find me a coach."

Ned came into the room. "She wouldn't like me telling you, but everyone in town knows, so I don't see why you shouldn't. And she likes you. I can tell."

She did like him. He could tell. And she mistrusted herself with him. He'd seen that on the *Sally* when she had become so brisk and businesslike after the allusions to her *ration of grog.*

A mutual attraction then, but not like so many of the others he had known, based entirely on physical appeal. "I like her too, Ned, but I'm not free to court your sister."

"Why not? You aren't married, are you? *Everyone* who likes my sister is married."

"No," he said carefully, "I'm not married, but I'm not free to marry either. I would, however, like to help her."

Ned's eyes narrowed, and he looked very much like his sister when she was suspicious. "So do all the married men who like her. She doesn't need that kind of help."

Had Sparhawk been so worldly at that age? He had known what his mother was doing with her visitors, but he hadn't really understood it, not until later.

"No," Sparhawk agreed. "She doesn't. But perhaps I can aid in some other way. Tell me about Wild."

"She was engaged to him," Ned said. "Until we lost all our money in that business with the tea. Then he married her best friend instead."

There was only one person in Salem who might lend Sarah Ward a carriage: Elizabeth Wild.

Dr. Corwin, of course, had been right. If Sparhawk was discovered in their home, the Sons of Liberty would hang him.

And punish the Wards for harboring a spy.

She had little choice but to apply to her friend and rival for aid.

Sarah had always believed that there was no better childhood than to be the daughter of a ship's captain. She had been born on the *Charming Sally* — though the schooner's name had been the *Sea Witch* then. She had taken her first steps upon its deck, to the despair of her mother, who worried about the prospects of a daughter with a sailor's rolling gait.

Sarah had learned to climb the *Sea Witch*'s rigging the way other children learned to climb trees, only trees were not peopled with sailors who spoke six different languages and knew where tea and pepper and ambergris came from and how to carve whalebone into a pie crimper with a picture of the king on the handle. And how to pick pockets.

Her playmates had been her brothers and the Sea Witches, and her chores had been those of a hand. She reefed sails and cooked porridge on a galley stove and got drunk for the first time in her life not on punch or brandy but on sailor's grog.

Until Sarah turned fourteen and her mother put a stop to it. Abigail Ward had sailed with Sarah's father, Abednego, a reformed pirate turned douce merchant, to Barbados and back for all the years of her married life, but she wanted her daughter to have a proper education, to become a fine lady, and marry a fine gentleman.

The dame school her mother chose educated the wealthiest girls in Salem and Marblehead. It was the first time Sarah had realized that not everyone thought being a pardoned pirate's daughter was a blessing. She found that socially, she ranked below almost everyone in attendance, except the daughter of a fisherman who owned a small fleet. Her money smelled of fish. Sarah's smelled of blood.

Evidently blood smelled nicer.

When she tried, earnestly, to ape the fine manners of the other girls, they called her Lady Frankland, after Agnes Surriage, the barefoot Marblehead serving girl who had gotten pregnant by a visiting English baronet at fourteen, and was spirited away by him to learn polish and manners — and deliver her child — in Boston. When Sarah failed, at anything, they called her Agnes.

Sarah hated the dame school and she hated the dame, until Elizabeth Pierce enrolled.

Elizabeth had a razor wit and she used it to cut people — particularly people who were unkind to Sarah Ward — to size. Their friendship was built on an equal exchange. From Elizabeth, Sarah learned to enjoy novels, needlework, and gossip. From Sarah, Elizabeth learned to navigate the docks of Salem, to cadge oranges and pineapples off the sailors, to wheedle ribald stories out of the tavern bawds.

From ages fourteen to twenty they were rarely out of each other's company. They determined together that if they could not captain ships and sail to great adventures themselves, then they could at least marry men who did.

And no one in Salem had sailed as far or dared as much as Micah Wild. Calvinist-leaning Salem regarded Wild's success as a divine endorsement. He had taken a small inherited fortune and made it a large self-earned one. Smuggling was the source of his wealth, cunning the source of his success. By the time he was twenty-five he owned seven ships.

Sarah had a fortune to rival Elizabeth's, but not an ancient family name, so when Wild entered their circle, she assumed his intent was fixed on her friend. When he cornered her outside the assembly hall between dances and kissed her, his tongue in her mouth and his hands on her body, she was surprised, but also elated. The thrill of desire was new to her, and intoxicating.

She found she liked his quick wit and the way people gravitated to him in a crowded room. He liked being able to talk hulls and hawsers with a woman. Abednego had never warmed to him, but when Wild sought Red Abed's permission, he gave it grudgingly, and Sarah embarked on preparations for her marriage.

Until the Wards lost all their money. And Micah decided to marry Elizabeth instead.

The two women had spoken only once since then. Sarah still burned with shame at the thought. She'd begged Elizabeth not to marry Micah. A true friend, Sarah argued, would not, could not do such a thing. But Elizabeth argued that the opportunity was too good to pass up, Wild's fortune and standing too great to refuse. A true friend, Elizabeth had believed, would encourage her to accept him.

That was when Sarah had lashed out, telling her that Wild was marrying her only for her fortune. She regretted it almost instantly, but there was no taking the words back.

Sarah knocked upon the door of that imposing brick house with as much dignity as she could muster. When she asked to see Mrs. Wild, the maid hesitated, and Sarah's heart sank. If Elizabeth refused to see her, if she did not find Sparhawk a carriage, if he was discovered in her home, their neighbors would punish them. And not just with the cool regard the Wards had endured of late.

The maid left her waiting in the hall, surrounded by the block-printed wallpaper Sarah had chosen herself, the bold geometric in blue and green that complemented the dove gray paneled wainscoting. The floorcloth she had selected was crisply executed in a marbled diamond pattern with a compass star. She wondered if Elizabeth knew that another woman had chosen so much of her home's decor, if she was reminded every day in her own house that she had been Micah's second choice.

Sarah had picked out all the furnishings

in the hall when she had been engaged to Micah, and now she felt poor and shabby amidst such elegance. She was relieved when the maid came back and led her not into the grand parlor with its Brussels carpets and damask sofas, but into the smaller sitting room at the back of the house. She did not know whether the choice of rooms was a slight or a sign of consideration, and she resolved not to care. Sparhawk's life, her family's safety — these things were more important than her pride.

The little parlor was dark, the blinds drawn, the chairs covered in cotton ticking for the summer heat. She had prepared herself to greet Elizabeth — to beg for the loan of her carriage — and plastered what she hoped was a look of contrition and conciliation on her face.

All for naught. The woman waiting in the lolling chair at the tea table was not Elizabeth Pierce Wild, the friend of her girlhood, but a very different lady. Older than both Sarah and Elizabeth by a decade, she was seated with a posture and poise that mimicked the straight backs of the chairs and called to mind the grace of a swan. Her gray sack gown was striped silk damask, the train suitable for a woman of leisure, and at odds with the lady's active, alert demeanor.

Sarah had seen her before. Angela Ferrers had appeared in Salem shortly before Micah Wild proposed the *Sally*'s voyage to Saint Eustatius. Stylish, sophisticated, said to be a widow of means, known to be political, and certainly no friend of government, the woman had quickly become a fixture at the town's fashionable gatherings.

An exodus of wealthy and influential Loyalists had followed close on the heels of her arrival, driven by threats, intimidation, and blackmail. The Wards, thankfully, had been spared. At the time Sarah had attributed their good luck to their poor fortunes. Now it occurred to her that the Wards might have been allowed to remain in Salem for another reason: because this woman wanted something from them.

"Won't you sit down?" said the lady, gesturing toward the other chair.

Sarah had to stop herself from treating the invitation as a command. There was cold steel behind the cultivated voice. It rang with the authority of the quarterdeck and carried with the borrowed vibrato of the pulpit sounding board.

"I am sorry, but I came to see Elizabeth," said Sarah.

"Not Micah?"

The question, if you knew Sarah's history,

as this woman surely did, was more than a little rude. And Sarah did not like the widow's knowing, arch smile, nor the way her shrewd eyes noted Sarah's faded jacket, frayed petticoat, and scuffed shoes.

"Micah Wild jilted me for my best friend, Mrs. Ferrers. What could I possibly want to discuss with him?"

"The whereabouts," said that lady, "of one hundred fifty tons of flint ballast, Salem's fastest schooner, and a fortune in French gold."

Sarah did not return immediately. Sparhawk knew from Ned that there were no servants, that she did everything herself, from carrying water to lighting fires to cooking, cleaning, and looking after their father. Ned had been oddly cagey about his father, but also decidedly proud. "My father could make Barbados faster than any captain in Salem. He was going to copper the *Sally*'s bottom. Hard to say what he will do with her now. He says we must hide her until she can be painted and repaired and that she can't be the *Sally* anymore. And that we can't sell our molasses in Salem because of Wild, and we can't sell it in Boston because of you."

Mr. Ward, unfortunately, was right. The crew of the *Wasp* and, more important,

Lieutenant Graves, would recognize the *Sally*'s colors — she had a lovely yellow stripe, bright, narrow, and very distinctive — and her name. Sparhawk hoped that Graves had not been close enough to get a good look at Sarah Ward before Cheap had felled him. If Sparhawk did not name her, she should be safe enough.

The doctor, it turned out, had courted Sarah, but his prospects had been dismissed as too limited. That was when Sarah had a great fortune in tea to bring to a marriage.

Ned had also spoken — much against Sarah's wishes, Sparhawk suspected — about the mysterious older brother. "He is overdue," Ned had said, with obvious concern. "He should have been home before the *Sally* left. Sarah says we must not worry yet, and Father says nothing at all. Although it was Father who said he must go to London to get it out of his system, and remain there if he could not."

Ned did not know what "it" was. Rebel sympathies, Sparhawk suspected. And damned selfish of him too, when his sister needed protecting and his father's health was failing. But Sparhawk kept that to himself. Ned obviously worshipped his older brother.

"All the girls always tried to dance with

Benji at the assemblies. And he could ride and fence and shoot better than anyone. And he can handle the *Sally* almost as well as Father. If he had been home, he would have had command of her, not Molineaux, and you never would have caught us."

The Ward family, it appeared, held a universally low opinion of the seamanship of anyone to whom they were not directly related.

The boy had scampered off soon after that, leaving Sparhawk staring up at the canopy and mulling his next move. The beefsteak was beginning to sound like a very good idea. His stomach gurgled, the sound loud enough to echo in the empty room. He watched the sun begin to set through the window — it would have been a pretty chamber when it was carpeted and papered — then decided to venture downstairs.

The house must have been older than it looked, because it was built to an antique plan with a central chimney. In front was a modern staircase in two flights, handsomely carved with twisted rope molding. The entire structure was one room deep on either side, and some of the fireplaces still sported fashionable paneling — though others had clearly been stripped of even that.

He arrived on the ground floor to find the

parlors chilled and dark, but light and warmth emanated from the far corner of what had once been the dining room, where a narrow batten door led into a service ell.

And there was music, of a sort: a low baritone rumble that started and stopped, the cadence, if not the tune, familiar; a sea chantey, but not one of the navy's.

The song drew him to the door, and when he saw through the crack that the chamber was unoccupied, into a kitchen with another door at the far end, from whence the singing came. There was no fire burning in the cooking hearth, but the room had a borrowed warmth from the chamber beyond. And a familiar air to it, something of his West Indian childhood — his real youth, not the manufactured tale of Shropshire summers that he and McKenzie had concocted — in the faint aroma of lime and molasses and the low-slung Campeche chairs beneath the window.

As he listened to the song drifting from the room beyond, and fingered the worn velvet of his borrowed coat, a suspicion stole over him, preposterous and at the same time, somehow inevitable.

He almost missed seeing the heavy-bladed cutlass propped in the corner. Someone had used it recently to bank the fire. It was blackened with soot and dulled by age, but there was no mistaking the tassel that hung from the guard: eight dark red ribbons strung with shark's teeth.

The girl's name was Ward.

Her father was a captain.

My father could make Barbados faster than any captain in Salem.

In a ship with a heavily tattooed crew.

Among whom was at least one pickpocket who had tutored Sarah Ward.

Mr. Cheap sailed with the Brethren of the Coast.

A name rose up out of childhood memory and bedtime stories, a bogeyman to put fear into the hearts of island children raised on soft breezes and sugarcane. A ginger-haired giant with a shark-tooth-tasseled cutlass.

"Red" Abed. Captain Abednego Ward.

Sparhawk had fallen into a nest of pirates.

FIVE

Sarah backed toward the door. Coming to Wild's house had been a mistake. This woman knew about the flint and the French gold, and now she knew that Sarah Ward and the *Sally* were back. Which put the *Sally*, the Ward family, and Sparhawk in terrible danger.

"I'll call on Elizabeth another time," Sarah said, feeling for the latch behind her.

"Very well," said Angela Ferrers. "I will interview your charming little brother instead."

Sarah froze. She did not want Ned anywhere near this dangerous creature in gray silk. Ned could not keep a secret to save his life — or Sparhawk's. If a Ward was going to match wits with this woman, it was going to be Sarah.

"How do you know about the gold?" she asked.

Angela Ferrers gestured once more toward

91

the empty chair at the table. Sarah took it. The young widow nodded with satisfaction and reached for the brown-glazed pot on the table, the kind the Dutch merchants sold, a delicate Chinese piece set in a scalloped gold mount. It had once been Sarah's, auctioned like so much else to fund the *Sally*'s voyage.

Beside it was a plate of ginger cakes, baked, Sarah knew, by Micah's cook, Mrs. Friary. They had been a favorite treat of Sarah's in childhood, when Mrs. Friary operated a bakery near the wharf. Knowing how much Sarah enjoyed the little delicacies, Micah had hired the baker to cook for the new house. Sarah's mouth watered at the thought of tasting one for the first time in years.

"Information is currency," said the widow, pouring a steaming ribbon of tea into Sarah's cup. Evidently the Rebel prohibition did not extend to the households of high Sons of Liberty like Micah. "And *currency*," continued Angela Ferrers, "of course, is currency, especially gold. It is welcome in every port of every nation and it is untraceable, melting back into the money supply after it has done its service." She passed Sarah a cup. The widow's hands were manicured, and she wore three dainty mourning rings crusted with pearls.

"The gold," said Sarah, seeing no point in dissembling now, "was captured by the British yesterday and will be in Boston by now."

"And you were on the same ship, yet here you sit. How is that?"

Angela Ferrers was far too well-informed. "They tried," she said, "to press my brother. So I took the captain hostage and ordered his men off the *Sally*. They had already removed the gold. I could not get it back without risking our freedom."

"Either you are a very singular young woman," said Angela Ferrers, placing a sugared brown cake on Sarah's plate — she could smell the ginger and molasses in it — "or that is the story you and Wild concocted to conceal your theft of the gold."

The spicy cake lost all appeal. "Why do you think *I* stole your gold?"

"You are penniless."

"Being poor is not the same thing as being a criminal."

"Please, Miss Ward, your father was a pirate. Criminality, or so it is said, runs in the blood."

"I doubt such traits are heritable," Sarah replied. "Neither of my parents could balance a ledger, yet I have a fine head for numbers."

A hint of a smile flashed over Angela Ferrers' face. "You are more intelligent than I expected, but the fact remains. You are a Loyalist, and Wild's lover. You had both motive and opportunity to plot such a theft."

"One encounter does not make a man a lover. Micah jilted me. And he is an ardent Patriot."

"And he was once your devoted fiancé. Until circumstances changed. Your head for numbers should lead you to a logical conclusion there."

She had never questioned Micah's political loyalties, only his romantic allegiances. "You don't trust him," she said.

"I trust Micah Wild to act in his own interest. I am here to discover where those interests lie."

"I am not Wild's lover. Credit me with some pride, at least."

"I begin to suspect that you have more than is good for you. What became of the flint?"

"The British threw that overboard."

"That is a pity. Flint is necessary to strike a spark."

"You mean it is necessary to start a war."

"Do not be fooled by the quiet, Miss Ward. War has already started. Formal declarations tend to come after the fact.

King George has said that the colonies must submit or triumph. Your countrymen have given him their answer. They are stealing cannon from their village greens and laying chain across their harbors."

"The ports have been at odds with the navy over the press and the customs acts for years. You cannot be certain that this time it will come to war," said Sarah.

"It is my policy," said Angela Ferrers, "to leave very little to chance. Congress is adamant that the colonies will not fire the first shot, but I will make certain that when that shot *is* fired, the American side of the story reaches London first."

"On a fast ship," said Sarah. "Like the *Sally.*"

"There is your talent for figuring again," said Angela Ferrers.

"But Micah has ships of his own that might serve." Sarah considered her former betrothed's fleet. "There is the *Oliver Cromwell,* though she may be too slow. Micah had her built with a deep draft and a false bottom for smuggling. My father advised him against sacrificing speed for concealment, and after today I would say he was right. Better not to be boarded at all. The *Conant* might be a better choice. Why not one of them?"

"That is the missing variable," said the elegant widow, refreshing Sarah's untouched cup of tea. "The *Oliver Cromwell* and the *Conant* are curiously absent from Salem Harbor, and not known to be under the command of a Cape Ann skipper. Their whereabouts interest me. I have found that Wild's business dealings do not add up, but his ambitions are easy arithmetic. The man who carries this story to London will rise high in the estimation of Congress, and they are about to have need of fast ships and bold seamen. America had only three working powder mills during the late war with the French. Today, she has none. She has no foundries to produce cannon. No factories to make muskets. It must all be imported. Before the war for America can be fought on land, the war for matériel must be fought at sea."

"And Micah wanted to carry the news on the *Sally,* to be the man Congress turns to — contracts with — for powder and shot and cannon, but she will be a week at least refitting." Sarah ran through the fastest Salem schooners in her mind. "Derby's *Quero* is almost as fast. Smaller too, and quicker to make ready."

"Just so," agreed Angela Ferrers. "It will displease Wild to be bested by Derby in this.

The *Sally,* though, could still be of great use. If you manage to keep control of her, you might restore your fortunes and your standing among your neighbors with a few successful powder runs to Portugal or Saint Eustatius."

"The *Sally* and my brother Ned barely survived one *unsuccessful* run to Saint Stash. Rebel machinations have cost my father everything we had. We can't afford to take part in your war."

"Neutrality is not an option for your family. You chose the Rebel side when you took up arms against an officer of the king."

"I did it to save my brother."

"Forget, for the moment, Micah Wild's rhetoric. This fight is not about abstract ideals or tea or tax. It is about the most basic kind of liberty — the kind you fought to preserve for your brother."

And which the Rebel mob and Micah Wild would take from Sparhawk.

"If I told you that I have brought another kind of cargo to Salem," Sarah said, choosing her words carefully, "something that might precipitate an incident that would not redound to your credit, what would you say?"

"I would say that I was interested, but that I needed more information."

"Information is currency."

"With which you hope to buy my help," the young widow said. "You came here to see the woman for whom Wild jilted you. You must have *needed* something, yes? What would you have used to purchase Elizabeth's aid?"

"Sentiment," said Sarah, honestly.

"A debased specie. You will find it buys very little from me."

"Then I will apply to Elizabeth," said Sarah, rising.

"Then I will send one of Micah's men for little Ned. Several, perhaps, if the formidable Mr. Cheap is still part of your household."

And Ned would tell Mrs. Ferrers everything. Sarah sat back down. "We brought the captain of the *Wasp* home with us as a prisoner. I fear that if Micah and the Sons of Liberty discover him, they will hang him."

Angela Ferrers raised a plucked eyebrow. "You are right to fear it. As do I. Such an incident might make a popular figure of Wild in the ports, but it would *not* redound to American credit in London. Not even Mr. Adams' talents for propaganda could cast the hanging of a British officer in a good light. What is it then that you propose?"

"I want to send the captain back to Boston, but he is injured, and I have no carriage."

Angela Ferrers made a study of the sepia mourning ring on her right hand. Finally she said, "I will have Wild's carriage sent to Judge Rideout's house at midnight. Rideout's man will drive your captain to Boston. But that is all I will do for you. It will be up to you to keep your captain safe and hidden until then."

James pushed open the door to find a cozy keeping room, appointed with rough-hewn furniture from the last century. Behind the painted tavern table sat a gentleman in an invalid's chair, a cane leaning against the arm. His hair might have been Sarah's honey blond in youth, but it was faded yellow shading into white now. On the table in front of him lay a model of the *Sally,* her mast unstepped. The old man held it in his gnarled hand. When Sparhawk entered, he stopped singing and put it down.

Abednego Ward had reportedly been a giant. Age had reduced him, but it had not robbed his eyes of light or his voice of mischief. He looked from Sparhawk's splint to the broken mast of the tiny *Sally* and chuckled with satisfaction. "At least she got a few swipes in at you as well."

He meant the *Sally*. "Yes," Sparhawk said. "If it is any consolation, I was quite sorry to be obliged to dismast her."

"Hah!" The old man reached for a jug on the floor beside him. "I'll warrant you were at that. Wanted to bring her in a prize all trim and neat. There are as many pirates in the British Navy as ever ravished the Spanish Main." He nodded at Sparhawk's blue coat, laid out on a bench by the fire. Someone had brushed it, he noted. "You didn't buy those fine buttons out of your pay, did you?"

"No." He hadn't. He'd always been lucky with prizes, until the *Sally*.

The old man slapped the table and laughed. "I thought not. Come all the way in and let me get a look at you."

Sparhawk complied. Abednego Ward studied him, and Sparhawk observed the old pirate in turn. He wore an old-fashioned coat with wide gored skirts and a silk waistcoat embroidered with gold wire. A white scar twisted from eyebrow to jawline down the left side of Red Abed's face, reminding Sparhawk of the man's checkered and violent past.

Abednego Ward huffed, set his jug on the table, and pushed it toward James. "My youngest son," the old pirate said, "thinks you're some kind of hero. My sailing master believes you're a seducer, out to ravish my daughter. And my daughter believes you are a wounded bird in need of her care. But she has notoriously bad judgment when it comes to men."

Sparhawk reached for the jug. "And what do you think, sir?"

"I think my old coat suits you, but you've yet to fill out the shoulders."

He was a canny old rascal. "I'm no pirate," James said. "I have been in the navy since I was eleven."

"The way my daughter tells it, you hailed our late and not particularly lamented skipper, and threatened him with a broadside. When Molineaux did not heave to, you dismasted the *Sally* and boarded her. And it was the *Wasp* that sailed away with the gold. If you don't think that's piracy, my boy, I suggest you make a closer study of the word."

When Sarah entered her house she was surprised to hear low voices coming from the kitchen. She had left Sparhawk resting in her bed and her father downstairs by the fire. Ned and Lucas were supposed to be readying the *Sally* to take her to Marblehead when night fell. The house should have been silent.

She hesitated at the door to the keeping room. Her father's voice she recognized, a bass rumble expressing interest and excitement. The other sounded familiar as well. She wished James Sparhawk's pleasing tenor did not make her pulse race. She had been foolish over one man. She must not be foolish over another.

At least not any more foolish than she had already been. Bargaining with a woman like Angela Ferrers for Sparhawk's life might cost Sarah her own. Carrying flint and French molasses had branded her a smuggler; kidnapping Sparhawk named her a pirate; dealing with Angela Ferrers made her a Rebel. If her actions were discovered, no doubt the navy would think it a pity it could hang her only once.

And she could not pretend that she had struck a deal with Angela Ferrers entirely out of a sense of obligation. The truth was that she cared for Sparhawk, thrilled at the way he made her feel — like the carefree girl she had been before Micah Wild jilted her.

She slipped inside the keeping room door. Her father and Sparhawk were crouched beside the table, scrutinizing the hull of the little *Sally* at eye level. The rum jug sat on the floor between them, and two dirty plates speckled with greasy crumbs — toast and cheese, no doubt — littered the table. They were so entranced by the miniature *Sally*'s timbers, so caught up in some scheme to copper her bottom and reinforce her decks, that they did not hear Sarah enter.

"You," she said to her supposed captive, "are meant to be resting."

Sparhawk stood and turned to face her. Unlike many sailors, he was graceful on land, even with one arm in a splint. "I got tired of resting," he said. "And your father is excellent company."

On the *Sally* he had been the picture of military splendor, his hair neatly clubbed, his collar starched, his cravat exactingly tied. Now his sun-shot hair hung loose about his shoulders, and he wore a soft linen shirt she had found in her brother's dresser, open at the neck, beneath her father's second-best coat. Even his once-polished shoes were now water stained from the squall aboard the *Sally*.

He was, if anything, even more appealing in dishabille.

She did her best to ignore his beauty. "And you," she said to her father, "are supposed to be in bed."

"As it happens," her father said, unfolding himself with obvious effort, "I am waiting for Mr. Cheap to return. I need a look at the *Sally.*"

"You're not fit for it," she said. "The damp will play merry hell with your joints."

"The damp finds me wherever I am. And the sooner I've seen her, the sooner we can fix her."

He should not go, but there would be no way to stop him. He bade them good night and ambled out, leaning heavily on his stick.

"Will he be all right?" Sparhawk asked, watching him from the window. Her father teetered over the lawn, his cane sinking deep in the earth, until Cheap met him at the dock.

"Mr. Cheap will see that he is as comfortable as he can be, but when he comes back, he will be crippled for days. He had the freedom of the sea his whole life, and now he is a prisoner in his own body."

"I am sorry," Sparhawk said. "He is a charming old rogue. Why didn't you tell me that your father was Abednego Ward?"

"Because having a pirate for a father casts doubt upon my character."

"It shouldn't. Red Abed was no ordinary pirate," said Sparhawk.

"We have our fair share of retired sea dogs

in Salem. Is my father's name really so distinguished?" she asked.

"Among men who have served in the West Indies, certainly. We abhor pirates, of course, except when they are British and colorful and know how to frustrate the French. Then we heap honors upon them."

"My father was no Morgan."

"Only for want of opportunity," said Sparhawk. "He was born fifty years too late."

"Would you have let Ned go if I had told you?"

"No. I could not make such an exception. It would set a terrible precedent. But we did, I recall, speak on *several* occasions after that."

"Would it have convinced you then that I had nothing to do with the gold and that my father was a loyal Englishman?"

"Your father, I daresay, has no love for the Rebels because he cannot abide being told what to do."

"That is a common malady amongst sea captains," she said.

He laughed. "So it is."

"My father will always put kin and crew before king and country, but that does not mean that he has no love for the king."

"I do not doubt his love for the king," said

Sparhawk. "On the contrary. Your father still has his royal pardon, rolled in a leather cylinder. I myself am the king's trusty friend, but he has never seen fit to sign a document with my name on it. Some Jack-in-office signed my commission on His Majesty's behalf."

He was being charming again. "Perhaps you don't cut a flamboyant-enough figure." And she was flirting with him.

He warmed to it, flicking the skirts of her father's old velvet coat. "No? Maybe it's that I haven't taken enough prizes. If I recall, Red Abed preyed mostly on the Spanish and French, but suffered occasional confusion when he saw British colors."

"And that is a common malady amongst pirates," she said.

"Your father made much the same argument." Sparhawk turned suddenly serious. "I wish I had not placed you in such a difficult position, but I am not sorry that I captured the *Sally,* however briefly. Micah Wild's French gold would have been used to buy powder and shot to kill sailors on British ships, many of whom are your countrymen, and one of whom, of course, is me." There was that charm again, damn him.

"Micah sees the pressed men as traitors,"

she said. "True Patriots would have chosen jail." She could quote much of his rhetoric. She had believed in it, once.

"You didn't tell me you were engaged to Wild, either."

She flushed with embarrassment. "No, I didn't. Ned shouldn't have either."

"You were jilted, Sarah. For mercenary reasons, it seems. There is no shame in that. It is Wild who was in the wrong."

"I have found you a rig and a driver," she said, changing the subject. "We must meet him at the home of our neighbor, Judge Rideout, at midnight."

"Sarah." He stepped closer. She could smell the soap on his skin, pine needles and juniper. She had fetched it from her father's washstand, but it was different on Sparhawk, deeper, earthier, like the forest floor in springtime. "I want to help you, if I can," he said.

He was so close to her now that the tips of their shoes met. She could feel the heat of his body. He was the kind of man she and Elizabeth Pierce had daydreamed about, the kind of man Sarah had thought Micah Wild to be: bold and brave and *honorable*.

She wanted him, even if only for one night, to feel desired by a man with integrity,

107

whose code was something more than personal convenience. To replace the shame and humiliation of her night with Micah Wild with something born of mutual respect and shared passion. But the danger to herself and her family was too great.

"That kind of help," she said, not troubling to disguise her longing, "sounds very appealing right now, but it would only leave me worse off in the morning when you are gone."

He could not recall a time since he had been ripped from his home and his mother's arms that he had wanted anything so much. Not food or drink or a woman, though he had been starving, parched, and deprived in his time.

He tried to muster all the reasons why he did not bed women like Sarah Ward.

He could not call them to mind. The room was pleasantly warm. There was a convenient trundle near the fire. He could see the red highlights in her hair and imagine the sweet taste of her mouth, the soft sound of her sighing. She wanted him as much as he wanted her, and he knew he could make it good for her, but that still did not make it right.

"Sarah, I realize that I have a certain

reputation when it comes to the fair sex, but I do have some principles. I don't bed girls like you."

Her nose wrinkled. She had a wonderfully expressive face, at odds with her fine features and porcelain complexion. Right now it was displaying indignation. He found the contrast enchanting.

"Why not?" she asked.

"Because of our difference in status," he said.

"You mean because you are my captive?"

She meant it as banter, but there was truth in it. Tonight, in this house, their positions were reversed. She held all the power and all the choices. If she did not want him, she had only to scream and her neighbors — Rebels all, it seemed — would come running to tar and feather him — or more likely worse. But tomorrow, things would be different. "I mean because you are, by your actions on the *Sally,* a criminal. And I represent the authority of the Crown."

"You don't look much like the Crown at the moment." She touched the bald velvet cuff of his coat. "And fool that I am, I'm not running away."

She wasn't. For Sarah Ward, desire had already overcome reason. And the invitation in her bright, dilated eyes and her moist open lips was enough to convince him to follow. One night, he reasoned, if they were careful not to make a child — and he had been careful all his life — would not harm her, so long as no one learned of it. There had been no seduction, no false promises on either side, only this powerful tide of desire, that would drag them both to the trundle, then wash them up on shore, panting and spent.

He leaned toward her. She was so close that her breasts touched his coat. Her breathing quickened. Rational thought fled and animal nature sprang to the fore. He reached for her —

Three brisk raps upon the front door, echoing through the empty house, shattered their intimacy.

"Don't answer it," Sparhawk said. If she did, the moment would slip from them.

"I have to," she replied, stepping away.

"Surely not. It's night, and you are alone with no servants. It could be anyone."

"But it *isn't* anyone. It is Micah Wild."

The knock came again, fast, sharp, demanding to be answered. Sparhawk did not like its tone. "How do you know it is him?"

"I went to his house today," she said. "To see his wife and beg the use of her carriage. Micah's servants will have told him I was there. He will know the *Sally* is back."

Sparhawk did not miss the tremor in her voice. "Cargoes are seized every day," he said. "Wild cannot blame you for his loss. Surely, despite the circumstances of our meeting, I have earned some little of your trust. What else is it you fear?"

"Without the flint you threw over the side, we cannot raise enough to pay Wild back."

Sparhawk should have figured it out sooner. But his attention had been fixed first on the gold, and making certain it did not fall into Rebel hands, and then upon Sarah Ward, in all her intriguing complexity. "The *Sally*," he said. "She was your collateral for the loan from Wild."

The knock came again.

"Yes," Sarah said. "That is why my father has gone with Mr. Cheap. Not just to hide the *Sally* from your friends in the navy. My father must hide her from Micah as well, or he and his Sons of Liberty will seize her and fit her out for their purposes."

The fastest ship in New England, probably. Abednego had shown him how easy it would be to make her faster and more maneuverable still, with a little money and a little time: new rigging, a copper bottom, and in the event that another ship sought to hinder her, reinforced decking for cannon.

A swift vessel, low in the water, able to outrun most of the navy's blockade ships. Ideal for powder runs to Lisbon or Saint Stash.

"I cannot allow that to happen," he said.

"*You* have a broken arm and are not supposed to be here."

"And you are asking me to behave like a coward," he said. It rankled — not just to shrink from his duty, but to do so in front of a woman he strongly desired.

"I am asking you to put the safety of my family ahead of your amour propre. Wild will break the door down if I do not answer it," she said, "to search the house for his gold. And the last thing he must find here is you."

Six

Micah Wild alone she could handle, but he had brought one of his longshoremen, a bandy-legged ruffian in rolled sleeves and nankeen trousers. She recognized the man from the docks, Dan Ludd. When the Salem customs agent had been tarred and feathered last October, Ludd had poured the tar. Sarah could still remember the stench of burning flesh.

Fortunately, she had convinced Sparhawk to hide. She had shown him the slender panel in the dining room, the one between the hearth and the china cabinet that disguised the hidden staircase. The join was invisible when closed, but behind the panel, a narrow flight, brick on one side, wood on the other, wound up the side of the chimney to the second floor.

"Why do you have a priest hole?" he had asked.

"We do *not* have a priest hole. This is New

England. You would be hard-pressed to find a papist to put in it. What a terribly gothic imagination you have."

"Your fair city inspires it. First you anchor us off Misery Island, and now you show me a secret passage."

"It isn't secret, or at least, it wasn't supposed to be. The oldest part of the house had a very large, very drafty fireplace. Father had it rebuilt, and the architect was at a loss as to what to do with the extra space, so he made this. It goes up to my room."

Sparhawk had eyed the cramped space dubiously. "Do you ever use it?"

"Not since I was a child. It's barely big enough for Ned. Now get in."

With some awkwardness and bent nearly double, he had angled his tall frame inside. "It would serve you right if I were to faint," he warned.

"Please don't." She gave him a gentle shove and closed the panel on his protests.

Then, her skin still flushed and her body aching with frustrated desire, she had gone to face Micah Wild.

Now he stood on her doorstep smiling, as though visiting his former fiancée in the middle of the night with a longshoreman in tow was a regular event.

"Sarah," he said, relief suffusing his handsome face, "you're home."

She had forgotten how musical his voice could be. And she had forgotten the power of his physical presence. Wild could afford to dress in embroidered silk waistcoats and diamond-buckled pumps, but he had adopted the *rage militaire* and wore buckskin breeches topped with a coat sewn from homespun linen. It had been cut to flatter his compact, muscular frame, and the muted color and slubbed texture set off his dark liquid eyes and curling brown hair.

She could not blame Elizabeth for accepting him. Even now, after all that had passed between them, when Sarah looked at him, she felt a pang of longing.

He crossed the threshold and caught her up in his arms. His touch was achingly familiar, but she had, only a few moments earlier, been anticipating that of another man, and taking refuge in Micah's embrace felt like a betrayal. She stiffened.

He noticed at once and released her.

"Sarah," he said, stepping back to examine her in the dim light of the hall, his honey voice ringing off the walls of the small chamber. "How are you come here by yourself? Where are the *Sally* and Captain Molineaux?"

"Molineaux is dead," she said. "Killed by

115

a British cannonball."

His dark eyes betrayed his shock and surprise. He drew her into the parlor. His man lingered within sight in the hall.

In a hushed voice that still managed to resonate through the empty room, Wild said, "Molineaux was carrying something for me. A chest."

"Of French gold. The British took it. It has gone to Boston aboard a brig called the *Wasp.*"

"Where did this happen and when?"

"Outside Boston Harbor. Yesterday just past noon." She knew he was making calculations of wind and weather and speed. They would bring him no comfort. The *Wasp* was in Boston by now. "The *Sally* barely got away. The navy will be looking for her. And she was cruelly mauled."

"Below the waterline?" asked Wild, sharply.

"No. But she was dismasted, and then we struck a storm. Two spars gone, topsails in shreds, and the standing rigging fouled."

Wild sighed. "That is . . . inconvenient." He shook off his disappointment and took her hands. "But the *Sally* can be renamed and repaired. And the gold was always a risky venture. The important thing is that *you* are home and safe. Your father should never have let you go on the voyage."

"If I hadn't gone, Ned would have been pressed aboard that British ship. And my father didn't know about the gold — and how much danger we were in — because *you* didn't tell us."

"I didn't tell you because you would have talked your father out of the venture — and your family needed the money. Where is the *Sally* now?"

"My father and Mr. Cheap are surveying her damage." Misery Island was one of the first places Micah would look, but her father and Mr. Cheap would be gone by then.

Wild pushed a straying hair off her face and tucked it behind her ear. The first time he had done it, a casual gesture of affection, in public, on his bustling wharf, had thrilled her. But he was married to Elizabeth now and would never touch her in public again. The thought still choked her with grief and anger.

"I don't want you worrying about the *Sally* or the debt," he was saying. "I'll see that the schooner is hidden safe and refitted good as new. The house I found for you is furnished. You will like it. The parlors have fine, large windows, and it is very near my wharf. I will be able to visit most days. You can bring Ned and your father with you. And everything will be just like we always talked about."

They had talked about making their home a center for thought and discussion, a birthplace of new ideas for the Salem mariners who ventured across the sea and the navigators who plotted their courses. They had dreamed of supper parties and salons where great voyages were planned and new discoveries revealed.

He had built her a home fit for it, and then, when her fortune had been lost, he'd bestowed it on her best friend instead. Now he was offering her a love nest, tucked out of the way, where no one with any character would visit her. She had been advised in the past to accept his protection, warned more than once that it was the best she could expect in the circumstances, that to ask for anything more from life would only ensure that she received less. But she burned with resentment at the idea that one youthful folly meant she was not entitled to a man who would love her alone.

"It can never be like we talked about, Micah. You married someone else."

"That is nothing to do with us."

"It is everything to do with us. You have a wife."

"I don't love Elizabeth," Wild said.

But Elizabeth, Sarah had realized on that terrible day when the two women quarreled, did love Wild. And that mattered to Sarah. "Then you shouldn't have married her."

"It is the way of the world. Marriages are made for property and money. Love rarely plays a part in such transactions."

"Then you threw away something rare, because I did love you."

"My feelings for you were and *are* the same, Sarah. That is why I want to take care of you and your family." He surveyed the scabby parlor. "You should have come to me long ago. I can't stand to see you live like this."

"You must. I will not live as your kept woman."

"Sarah," he said, in the ringing voice he used when he talked about tyranny and tax collectors. "The voyage was a failure. Your father is bankrupt. The *Sally* is mine legally, and without it, Abednego has no hope of rebuilding his fortune. This house has already been stripped bare. You are running out of options."

"If I accepted your protection, my father would feel compelled to violate his principles and hand over the *Sally*."

"They aren't *his* principles, Sarah. They're the ones you adopted when I didn't marry

119

you. Your father would have sided with the Patriots long ago if it hadn't been for your pride. Your brother is already one of us. Your father will relent when things are settled between you and me."

He meant once she became his mistress. "Even if my father took the Rebel side," she said, "he would not give the *Sally* to you."

"He's out in her now, isn't he? And tomorrow he'll be in agony. Do you want Abednego to come home to this bleak house in that condition? What will you do when the weather turns? You can't afford the firewood to warm his room. At the cottage you will have a servant. Ned will have a tutor. The doctor will visit regularly. Your father can live out his days in comfort. And we will be together, as we always hoped. We have waited long enough. I want you to move tonight."

Perhaps if she had not met Sparhawk, she might have been able to swallow her pride and accept Micah's offer, but now she wanted something better for herself and her family.

"No," she said.

He cast a glance at Dan Ludd, hovering in the doorway, and the longshoreman padded into the hall.

When she heard Ludd's feet upon the

stair, panic seized her. He must not find Sparhawk. "Where is he going?"

"To fetch your things. You cannot stay here by yourself. It isn't safe. They say shots have been fired in Boston, and that Graves plots to shell the ports. It is no time to be on your own. You're leaving this house tonight, even if I have to carry you out the door."

And he would do it too. There was no one to stop him, except Sparhawk, who would forfeit his freedom — and perhaps his life — if he revealed himself. She did not think for a moment that Wild would settle her chastely in her new home and leave her be, but she could cross that bridge when she came to it. The important thing was to get Wild and Ludd out of her house.

"I can pack my own things," she said. It would give her time to think of something. And then, "I do not want your man in my room."

Micah nodded and recalled Ludd, then followed her up the stairs to the bare little chamber.

She had hoped for a moment alone, an opportunity at least to open the hidden staircase door and whisper a warning to Sparhawk — and the direction of the judge's house — but Micah was not going to let

121

her out of his sight.

There was hardly anything to pack — a spare chemise and petticoat, a bed jacket, one gown. She laid them on the counterpane and dragged her sea bag from under the bed, trying to think of a way out. Micah came up behind her, trapping her between his body and the bed. He placed his hands on her shoulders and spoke in her ear. "At the cottage you will have better things, I promise."

She had never wanted the things, the house or its elegant contents, only what they represented: his esteem, his approval, his affection.

He kissed her neck, brushed his lips over the shell of her ear, and she felt the briefest flicker of desire, a shadow of what she had known when they were courting. And then the memory of that night swamped her.

She'd gone to the half-finished house with its wet plaster walls and sanded pine floors to tell him that the Wards were bankrupt; to release him from their engagement. Because she was not so unworldly that she thought things could be the same between them. And he had placed his coat on the floor and held her and kissed her and told her that he didn't care about the money, that she was his whole happiness, that they would be together.

And then he'd made love to her.

She'd exulted in the tangible proof of his affection, the intimacy. Afterward he had promised her that he would always take care of her and her family, and that was when she understood the place he intended for her in his life.

She had wanted to die.

Wild's hands plucked the first pin from the front of her stomacher.

"No, Micah."

"I have missed you so much."

"I don't want to do this here." She didn't want to do it at all.

"It's all right," Wild soothed, untying the laces of her jacket. "Dan will keep watch downstairs."

She fought an impulse to raise her voice, lest Sparhawk hear her and do something stupid and heroic. "No." She tried to arrest his hands, but he was determined.

"I'll make it good for you," he promised.

"That would be impossible."

He ignored her and plucked another pin.

She jabbed him with her elbow.

He cursed, the oath ringing off the bare walls; he ripped the lacing of her jacket, scattering pins across the floor.

The echo died, a door creaked, and the

distinctive sound of a pistol being cocked filled the silence.

"Let the girl go," said James Sparhawk.

Wild spun round and Sarah turned more slowly, holding her jacket closed.

Sparhawk was leaning negligently in the secret doorway, his broken wrist tucked into his pocket. It was a convincing pose, his bandages hidden by the wide velvet cuffs, a second pistol peeking as if by an afterthought from his embroidered pocket. Her father's tasseled cutlass hung at his waist.

He ought to have stayed hidden and safe, but he had exposed himself.

For her.

"Who the devil are you, sir?" asked Wild. Then, looking past Sparhawk's shoulder at the open panel, he added, "And what the hell were you doing in there?"

"My name is Sparhawk. Most recently, I commanded His Majesty's brig, the *Wasp*. Just now I am staying with friends. Perhaps you should let my friend go," he suggested.

Sarah didn't wait for Micah to comply. She moved out of his reach, then took a deliberate step toward Sparhawk.

She had never seen Micah Wild at a loss for words. He looked from Sparhawk to Sarah, and back again.

Finally, he said, "I see no uniform upon

you, sir."

"I am, as you find me, at my ease," drawled Sparhawk. "But the king's colors, I assure you, are downstairs."

"And whence come you, that you arrive without a king's ship?"

"I kidnapped him off the *Wasp*," Sarah explained, "to save Ned from the press."

"He does not appear to be a prisoner," replied her former fiancé coldly. "And he wears no uniform. I take him for a spy."

"These are the king's colonies, sir. I cannot be a spy, unless we are at war."

Micah smiled. "Then allow me to be the first to inform you, sir. Shots were fired at Concord two days ago." He drew a folded broadside from his pocket and tossed it on the bed. It was from the *Salem Gazette,* Mr. Russell's Whig paper, and the headline read "BLOODY BUTCHERY BY THE BRITISH TROOPS." Two rows of black coffins decorated the top.

Sparhawk didn't take his eyes off Wild. "That is as may be, but even so the fact remains that I am in a private home, and I have not appeared in public without my uniform."

"Only because you are here in secret," replied Wild. "Your presence must be reported to the Committee of Safety."

Sparhawk cocked his head. "Is that the body that authorizes you to assault young women, or do you undertake that on your own authority?"

"The lady and I have an understanding."

"I fail to comprehend it," said Sparhawk.

A floorboard creaked. Wild's man, Dan Ludd, appeared in the door, hand on his truncheon. He looked darkly at Sparhawk and sent a questioning glance at Wild, who shook his head.

"You have me at a disadvantage, sir," said Micah Wild. "It will not happen again."

Sparhawk gestured toward the door with his pistol. Sarah watched him follow Wild and Ludd down the stairs, her heart seeming to beat in time to his feet upon the risers. She gathered her pins from the floor; listened to the door open and close, the latch click, the bolt slide home, feet upon the stairs again. By that time she had managed, hands trembling, to pin her jacket to her stays. The ribbon she would have to mend later. Then Sparhawk was back, one of her father's pistols still in his good hand.

"You heard everything, I suppose," she said.

"I heard enough."

"I am not crying," she said.

"Of course not." He laid the first pistol

atop the chest, but left it loaded. He drew the second out of his pocket and placed it there as well. Then he came to stand in front of her. Close enough that she could rest her head against his chest.

The velvet of his coat felt cool upon her cheek and when, after a moment of hesitation, he closed his arms around her, she began to cry in great racking sobs. She had not felt so safe, so understood, so cared for, in two long years.

He stroked her hair, rubbed small circles across her back, and whispered soothing nonsense into her ear. The words were not so different from the things her father had said to her: that Wild was a selfish bastard, that she deserved better, that none of it was her fault. Not true exactly, but reassuring to hear all the same, and somehow more satisfying coming from this man she had known barely more than a day than from her own father.

When she had no more tears left, she looked up at Sparhawk and said, "You have been very kind, but you must go. Micah will be back with his friends."

"I'm not leaving you alone. I will wait until your father and Mr. Cheap return."

"You cannot wait for them," she said, wiping her tears with the back of her hand.

"Now that I know what Micah intends, I can protect myself. The carriage will be at the judge's house at midnight. It may be your only chance to escape. You cowed Micah and Ludd with your ruse, but if they had known you had only one good hand, they might have taken you. If they *do* catch you, they will drag you to the common and try you. It is the kind of street theater Micah excels at. As a king's officer, your chances of survival would have been slim at best, but now that you have wounded Micah's pride, I would put them at null."

He considered a moment. "Then come with me," he said.

"What do you mean?"

"Come with me to Boston. Your father and Mr. Cheap cannot guard you day and night. If you remain here, you will end in Wild's keeping. I want to help you. I am offering you, in every sense of the word, my protection."

"Oh."

"My terms will sound altogether too like Wild's, but there are, I flatter myself, important differences. I have money to keep you. I could get Ned a place on a good ship, your father perhaps a pension. Lord knows he deserves one. He captured more pirates than the navy did in those days."

"You forget," she said. "I took you captive. I will be wanted in Boston for piracy."

"An American *boy* will be wanted for piracy. No one on the *Wasp* saw your face."

"Your lieutenant may have," she said.

"But he is a lieutenant, and I am a captain, and I will swear it was not you."

"And how," she said carefully, "would this differ from Micah's offer?"

"Well, for one thing, I am not married. For another, I think you actually like me." There was his damned charm again. "I would offer you more, if I could, but I cannot."

"That is what Micah said, the night he told me he was going to marry Elizabeth."

"Granted, the effect upon you is similar," he admitted, "but I swear to you that I have better reason in this than Wild. I cannot offer you my name because I was not born 'Sparhawk' and I was not christened 'James.' I'm an imposter."

SEVEN

Sparhawk owed Sarah Ward some measure of the truth. She had risked her family's safety to bring him here and save his hand, and tried to fight off her former fiancé on her own to save him from discovery. She was staring up at him expectantly, and he knew that if he did not tell her now, she would always regard it as a betrayal.

"James Sparhawk," he said, "does not exist."

"The bullion on your coat looked real enough," she said, a note of challenge in her voice.

"My rank," he said, "is real. Earned without interest or advantage of birth. But I did not enter the navy a midshipman and rise to captain like other young gentlemen. I was kidnapped from my home as a boy and pressed aboard a ship bound for Bombay as a common sailor.

"My father," Sparhawk said, choosing his

words carefully, "was the second son of a country gentleman, with no great expectations. What property there was would go to his elder brother. The navy seemed a natural choice. His father approved, and he went for a midshipman when he was not much older than Ned is now.

"He met a girl, a parson's daughter, while he was on leave visiting the West Country and eloped with her against the objections of her family. His father would not give him money, and he could not keep her snug in England on a lieutenant's pay, so he brought her and their infant son — myself — to Nevis, where his ship called frequently, though not frequently enough to keep him out of other women's beds. He was young and feckless, and he forgot to send her money as often as he forgot his marriage vows. He never took the trouble to introduce her to society in Nevis, and most of the English there doubted she was really his wife."

They had called him a bastard, and his mother a whore.

"My father's visits and his financial support became increasingly irregular, and my mother began taking in mending and washing to make ends meet. For a time, it was enough to keep us. Then his money stopped coming entirely, and the letters started to arrive. My father's uncle and elder brother had died in quick succession, leaving him the heir to an ancient barony in Cornwall. Scrubby land. Poor for farming but rich in metals, if someone had the capital to mine it. But the estate was drowning in debt. My father needed money, fast, and hoped to acquire it in the time-honored way of his class — by marrying it. Unfortunately, he already had a wife.

"But the union, he decided, had been irregular. A hole-and-corner affair, contracted when they were both too young to be held responsible, never recognized by their families. He presented this view to my mother, who rejected it out of hand, not necessarily for herself — but for me. She was raising me on the little money she scraped together, to be a gentleman."

On Tuesdays and Wednesdays he had gone to the Jewess for Hebrew and mathematics. Thursdays and Fridays to the English parson for Latin and Greek. An old Spaniard tutored him in *destreza,* the true art of the sword. A bookish child, small and weak, he varied his route each day, hoping to avoid the island children who threatened and bullied him.

"My father attempted to buy my mother's silence with his future wife's money — he already had a candidate in mind, some plantation owner's daughter whose family were eager to secure a title for her — but my mother would not acquiesce. She even vowed she would write to his intended and reveal him for a bigamist. So he turned to threats. Rumors were rife on the island that my mother accommodated men. For money."

By then the rumors were true. The first time he had awakened to the sound of the bed ropes creaking, he'd thought his father must be home — an unexpected visit, but welcome. Peering into the darkness, he had seen the shape straining over his mother, distinctly that of another man, thicker and fairer than his darkly handsome father. He'd been stricken with a deep feeling of dread, a sense that something was profoundly wrong, as chilling as if he'd seen a ghost or a monster.

"My father finally condescended to return to Nevis to speak with her. They quarreled. She told him she had already written to his intended, and sent the proof of their marriage lines. We were living in such squalor then that all I could think as I looked at him was how he glittered with gold, how the braid and buttons of his uniform could have fed us for a year."

His father did not stay in the cottage that night, and in the morning, his mother discovered why. His fiancée and her family were aboard his ship. He was to fete them that night with a grand party, to introduce his betrothed to English society on Nevis. Sparhawk's mother had sobbed and raged, gut-wrenching grief alternating with helpless anger. Then she had taken his hand and led him down to the docks, and spent one of their precious coins to have them rowed out to his father's ship.

There were musicians playing prettily as they came alongside, and paper lanterns hung from the rigging. Tropical flowers dripped from the rails, and their heady scents disguised the fug of bilge water, hemp, and tar. His mother had climbed awkwardly up the side, as foreign, he recognized at the time, to that wooden world as the colorful blooms trailing over the side. He had followed, watching in horror as she caught sight of a tall, lithe young woman in green silk and made straight for her. His father intercepted her, and, bellowing in a voice Sparhawk had never heard him use before, he ordered his marines to drag her from the ship. He watched his father turn his back on his mother, and on him, forever.

"A few nights later, five men broke down

the door to our cottage. Two of them carried me to the docks. Their instructions were to drown me, but sailors, even the worst of them, are a superstitious and sentimental lot. They pressed me aboard a brig bound for Bombay. Later, I learned that my mother had been taken to the magistrates and imprisoned for debt and prostitution. I was never again to see her alive.

"I was not, as you might imagine, a midshipman, and I learned — at the wrong end of a cat — to obey orders. The captain of that brig was a tyrant with a taste for boys, and I suffered accordingly."

The details, to the daughter of a seafaring family, would be easy to guess.

"I was two years on that unhappy vessel until the Admiralty replaced our vicious captain just in time to forestall a mutiny.

"I was more fortunate in my next commander. He guessed that my origins were not as they'd been entered in the ship's muster — I could read Latin, Greek, and French — and he invited me to study with the midshipmen. When I confessed my true identity, he cautioned me not to reveal myself to anyone else, lest my father learn that I was not dead and send men to finish the job. And in any case I had no proof of who I was, and my status, in the navy and thus in the wider world, was the lowest of the low.

"So we bided our time, and when one of the midshipmen, always sickly, and now consumptive and unlikely to live, was transferred to shore, I accompanied him as a servant. This boy — the real James Sparhawk — had no living family. When he died, the captain helped me to assume the boy's identity, and I remained ashore to 'convalesce' until the crew was changed out. When I returned, not a man but the captain had known me, nor the dead Sparhawk.

"Under my new name, I passed my lieutenant's exam at fifteen, captained my first prize at sixteen, achieved a command of my own by eighteen. I have worked these past twelve years to assemble the proofs of my true identity, and my father's crimes. I do not have them all yet, but I will shortly. That is why I requested service in North America. I have tracked to the Massachusetts Bay the cleric who married my parents on Nevis and tutored me as a child. If I can find him, I hope he can be persuaded to swear out a statement validating their marriage and my identity. But from the moment I step forward and declare myself, my life will be in danger — and so would that of any woman

I married, who might be carrying an heir to the title and fortune my father was willing to kill to secure."

Sarah did not doubt a word of his story. Men had done as much and more when great titles and fortunes were at stake. The Annesley case had still been dragging its way through the courts when she was a girl — and James Annesley, the heir to the Earl of Anglesey, who had been kidnapped by his uncle and endured ten years of indentured servitude in America, and nineteen years of litigation in pursuit of justice, had died of natural causes before he could regain his birthright. But not before surviving two attempts on his life.

On the *Sally,* Sparhawk had shown himself to be brave, but Sarah was stunned, momentarily, by the determination that must have carried him from Bombay to the quarter-deck of his own brig.

"I am tempted by your offer," she said. "But I cannot leave my father and Ned without a word. And you must go tonight." Abednego Ward had run his family the way he had run his crews, democratically. Everyone had responsibilities, and everyone had a say.

A smile quirked the corners of Sparhawk's perfect mouth. "Miss Ward, does that mean that if you could confer with your family, you would consider accepting my offer?"

"Would you really take me with Father and Ned in tow? And possibly Benji, whom you have never met, as well? We are a passel of rogues, and unlikely to advance your naval career."

Sparhawk laughed. "I will reserve judgment on Benjamin until I have met him, though I am disinclined to like this brother who leaves you to the mercy of men such as Wild. Ned, however, has promise. And your father would make me a sought-after dinner guest in naval circles. There is nary an admiral save perhaps Old One-Foot-in-the-Graves who would not like to pass the port with Red Abed."

It was not, to conventional thinking, an honorable offer; yet she thought it the most honorable offer she had ever received. Sparhawk was not interested in her money, because she did not have any. He was not lying to her or holding out false hope of marriage, because there was none. He was being completely honest with her. He was offering friendship and physical pleasure and financial support. She had lived too long without all three.

"Then yes," she said. "If you would welcome my family, I will consider your offer."

She rose on her tiptoes and kissed him on the cheek. The close contact, the way his body tensed and hers hummed, promised future passion. But tonight, with the memory of Micah's hands on her, she could not contemplate more.

Nor did he press her for it. "Will they take you in at this judge's house, until your father returns?" he asked.

"The Rideouts are old friends, and despite pressure, loyal to the king. If they have not been driven out of town yet, it is only because the judge is bedridden and too ill to go — and he has nothing but daughters."

"Who aren't handy with a pistol," Sparhawk replied.

"We were at school together. They are obedient, genteel creatures," Sarah admitted.

"Thank God," said Sparhawk. "If there were more such as you in Naumkeag, Miss Ward, the sea-lanes would not be safe for the British Navy."

Together they descended to the hall. She reached for the latch on the door, but before her fingers touched it, Sparhawk pulled her back and motioned for silence. He angled his body to peer out the sidelights, then beckoned her to do the same.

There were men in the street. Dan Ludd.

And others. Ranged in front of the house. Cutting off Sparhawk's escape. Ready, no doubt, to drag him to the common and hang him.

In this, she was determined that Micah Wild should not get his own way.

Sparhawk had just acquired a mistress.

Sailors tended to collect things on their travels. His bosun kept a small box stuffed with plant seeds from foreign ports, a whole future garden *in potentia;* his carpenter kept a bag of heathen votives and shrunken heads. Curiosities, both natural and artificial, were difficult for wandering seamen to resist. One of the hands on Sparhawk's first snow had found a giant clamshell on Fiji and brought it aboard. When his shipmates quizzed him on what he planned to do with it, he said he hadn't the slightest idea — but he knew that he should regret leaving it behind.

Sparhawk had not expected to find a mistress in the cold waters off Boston Harbor, but Sarah Ward was a natural curiosity herself, and he knew that he should regret leaving her behind.

She barred the front door of the house and led him back up the stairs and into a disused bedroom that looked out over the roof of the service ell. The window was small — the relic of a previous century — and narrow, but it rose with a soft hiss in smooth channels. Sarah climbed out onto the cedar shakes and motioned for him to follow.

It was tricky with his arm in the splint, but he managed. From there she led him over the shingles to another lower roof, this one a shed in a neighboring yard that rubbed close up to the Ward house, and from there she dropped to the ground in someone's vegetable garden.

He placed his faith in her and followed, landing softly in a bed of cabbages.

"You've done this before," he said.

"Of course," she whispered. "Benji and I used to sneak out of the house to meet Elizabeth and drink rum in the *Sally*'s jolly boat when the schooner was in port."

"Your father," he replied as quietly, "does not seem like an easy man to sneak past."

"He wasn't. When we were old enough that we no longer had to sneak out, we realized that Mr. Cheap used to follow us."

She was leading Sparhawk through a maze of low wooden fences, narrow alleys, and neat kitchen gardens, negotiating them with the skill of long practice. "Very intrepid of Mr. Cheap," he remarked.

They picked their way through a dark passage between two long narrow houses, breathing the distinct aroma of molasses and rum. A distillery. Then they reached the mouth of the alley and a broad street, and Sarah peered cautiously out.

She drew back at once. "There are men in the street."

"They could just be out for a stroll," said Sparhawk hopefully, edging toward the opening with a hand on his pistol.

They were not just out for a stroll. It was the beginnings of a mob. There were groups at both ends of the street, the town's main thoroughfare by the looks of it. They were sailors, mechanics, dockside ruffians. Old capstans had been rolled up from the shipyard to serve as barricades, and the toughs congregating around them held torches, buckets, and pillows.

Tar and feathers, no doubt.

One of the sailors carried an ominous coil of rope over his shoulder.

"Is there another way round?" Sparhawk asked.

"No. It is the manse directly opposite."

"Very well," said Sparhawk. It was a pretty house, gambrel roofed but larger, by far, than the Ward home, surrounded by a painted wooden fence carved with swags and urns, with a brick enclosure and carriage house behind. Built on a high fieldstone foundation, with stout shutters without and within, it would be a veritable fortress.

And impossible to reach without being seen by the mob.

They would have to make a run for it, and pray someone stood by the door at the ready to let them in. Sparhawk cocked his pistol. Sarah nodded, that same flinty expression in her eyes that she had worn on the *Sally* when she'd taken him prisoner.

He could not think of a man he would rather have at his side than Sarah Ward, who was of course not a man at all. It was the highest form of compliment, in one sense, and in his experience of women, unlikely to be taken as such. He refrained from speaking it.

They ran, Sarah taking the lead and Sparhawk following with his pistol at the ready. They were spotted almost immediately, a pockmarked sailor with a length of wood closing the distance faster than Sparhawk would have liked.

Then they were up the steps and Sarah was hammering on the door. A gust of candle-scented air met them, and they were through with a rush.

The door slammed behind them. After the *Wasp* and the *Sally* and the bare Ward house, the Rideout mansion overwhelmed the senses, all polished mahogany and satinwood and glittering ormolu and gilt. There was the distinct aroma of beeswax from the fine tapers, of brandy from the crystal that littered the glassy surface of the long table in the dining room. Continental landscapes hung above the sideboard and fireplace; carved mirrors between the windows; the famed wealth of New England's codfish aristocracy on proud display.

Before Sparhawk could take it in, he was surrounded by a flock of females who led him into a large double parlor, cooing and fluttering in a rustling cloud of silk and lace. They called him "dear" and "brave," and forced him into an ancient and uncomfortable chair. It was hard and oak and straight as a mast, and Sparhawk suspected it had come to the New World on the first boat from England. It had pride of place in an otherwise perfectly classical scheme, and Sparhawk could only presume it was some sort of Puritan heirloom.

He had not marked Sarah's faded jacket or frayed hem before, but beside these fashionable creatures in their brightly colored silks, she looked like a ragamuffin.

No powder, no paint, no art to the dressing of her honey gold hair. And yet she drew the eye like a sail on the horizon.

She would be the first woman he noticed in any room.

The flock settled, and Sparhawk spied a lady standing a little apart: tall, graceful, dressed in a gray sack gown closely molded to a lithe, athletic body. Her calm too singled her out. She was not one of the Rideout sisters. Sarah was watching her warily.

"The carriage," said this unusual lady, "is waiting in the enclosure. The judge's coachman, unfortunately, is inebriated. You will need to sober him."

This she had addressed to Sarah. Now she turned a cold, assessing eye on Sparhawk. "I know your face," she said.

He rose and bowed. "Captain Sparhawk, madam. At your service."

"I think you rather at the king's service, which is a pity, as I have heard of you, though Sparhawk is not the name that your face brings to mind."

Three sharp raps on the door were followed by a demand, in the honeyed voice of Micah Wild, to send the British dog out. There was no need to put the implied threat of fire into words — the torches dancing beneath the casements spoke for themselves.

The Rideout sisters paled. Sarah's lip curled. And the singular lady in gray silk raised one plucked eyebrow and said, "I believe it is about time for the captain to leave."

Judge Rideout rose from his bed and bought them a little time by addressing the mob. Now that he was seventy-two years of age and ailing, his oratory was not the equal of Micah Wild's, but he had built the smallpox hospital on Winter Island and paid for the inoculations that had saved so many lives — though not Sarah's mother's — in '72. They were bound to hear him out.

While that worthy man spoke, Sarah poured coffee into the coachman. She had brewed it strong, and when Phippen balked at swallowing the sludge in the bottom of the cup, she threatened to make more.

He swallowed it.

The widow and Sparhawk muffled the horses' hooves with blankets. Then they were out in the walled enclosure behind the house with the widow dictating instructions to the judge's not-quite-sober man and Sparhawk checking the powder in Abednego Ward's pistols.

"I shall send them back to you," Sparhawk

said, "with money for the trip to Boston. Enough to keep you until I return if the *Wasp* and I are not in port." Then, suddenly hesitant, he added, "Say you will come."

She had not seen him look so vulnerable before, even lying injured and half drowned in her father's bed on the *Sally*. She wanted to say yes, without condition or qualification, but she had her family to think of, and could not. So she said, "I shall speak with my family."

And then she kissed him. She had to grasp his shoulders and rise on tiptoe to reach him, but when she brushed her lips against his, she realized with a shock that it was the most intimate she had been with this man whose protection she had so blithely accepted.

He froze and she feared she had misjudged him; that a man who was so used to command would not welcome such forwardness. Her doubt lasted only a moment. Sparhawk slid his good hand around to the small of her back and pulled her close, then deepened the kiss. Fierce desire, long dormant in her, woke.

She felt a pang of loss when he climbed into the carriage, and a sudden, giddy elation when he stopped on the running board and turned to her. "The Three Cranes in

Charlestown is where I stay. The landlord there knows me. I have money banked with him. If I am not in port, he will extend you credit on my account."

She nodded.

"The Three Cranes," he insisted. "Say it so I know you will remember it."

Sea captains, she knew from experience, could be very trying. "I am *not* one of your midshipmen, to repeat orders and say, 'Aye, aye, sir.' "

"I understand that you take orders from no one, but the last time I parted with a woman in dangerous circumstances, I never saw her again."

He meant his mother.

"The Three Cranes," she said.

Sparhawk smiled. There was a boyish, hopeful light in his eyes. On impulse, she reached out to stroke his hair. He caught her hand and pressed it to his lips. The coach jerked forward, breaking them apart. With a rueful smile he climbed inside and took a position at the window, resting a pistol on the sill. Phippen struck up in earnest, and the carriage thundered out of the enclosure.

It was only when Sarah had shut and barred the gate that she realized the widow was no longer in the yard. Nor in the parlor.

A sound drew Sarah up the rope-carved staircase and to the open casement, where Angela Ferrers stood looking out, the barrel of a long hunting rifle in her hand. In the moonlight, Sarah noted ink stains on her fingers, and she recalled the printed broadside with its row of black coffins.

Sparhawk's carriage emerged from the alley at the end of the street.

The mob stirred. Those nearest saw and gave chase. A few shots rang out. A man climbed onto the running board.

Angela Ferrers braced a shoulder in the window frame to the open casement, raised her rifle, sighted, and fired.

The man gave a cry and fell off. The carriage broke free of pursuit and disappeared around the corner.

The widow nodded. "And they are away."

Sarah watched as the man the widow had shot climbed unsteadily to his feet, grasping his shoulder. Sarah recognized him — a sailor from one of Micah's regular crews.

"Thank you," Sarah said.

"Don't thank me, Miss Ward. I didn't do it for you or your captain. The rumors in the street are true. The British fired on the militia at Lexington. They bayoneted old men and children in their homes. That is the tale printed in the *Gazette,* and that is the tale that must reach London and be taken up by our supporters in Parliament. The hanging of a British captain in a New England port would tarnish that story. We have been allies tonight because our aims converged. Tomorrow we will be enemies again."

"Are politics the determinant of all your actions?" Sarah asked.

"Is sentiment the determinant of all of yours?"

"Not sentiment," Sarah said. "Loyalty."

"A scarce commodity indeed," said the widow. "Spend it wisely, Miss Ward. And if you can spare a little for your country, seek me out. I could make good use of your knowledge of the ships and seamen of Cape Ann."

"I'm not free to play politics with you, Mrs. Ferrers. My elder brother is abroad, and my father is no longer young."

"Your brother Benjamin has been in Boston these three months. He understands what you do not. Cleaving to the authority of the Crown will not protect your family. It didn't protect your brother Ned from the press. You did. Those who lie down meekly in a civil war are always the first to be trampled."

■ ■ ■ ■

They got the judge back into bed and waited out the riot that ensued, the Rideout sisters clustered on the settee and Sarah and Mrs. Ferrers in the chairs opposite in the pretty gold and green parlor, listening to the tumult outside: the shouting and sounds of destruction as the mob took its frustrations out on the Rideout home.

Micah's followers ripped the ground-floor shutters off the windows and hurled rocks through the transom lights. Then, when it became evident that the Rideout house was too stoutly constructed to tear down, the rioters began on the fence, hacking the urns from their balusters and pulling the posts out of the ground.

The violence lasted the better part of an hour, and then ended when there was nothing fragile enough left to break. A little while later, when the street was finally empty, Angela Ferrers took her leave, a muff pistol concealed in the folds of her cloak, and Sarah and the Rideout sisters breathed a collective sigh of relief.

Sarah herself set out half an hour later — unarmed, and all the more cautious for it — and picked her way home through the evening's wreckage.

There were broken bottles littering the gutters, paper wrappers, discarded items of clothing, and here and there a bit of stray vandalism had occurred: a broken shutter on one house, a shattered transom on another, lanterns smashed to cover the actions of the mob in darkness.

She had spent two days in nearly constant company with James Sparhawk, and the impulse to turn and share her thoughts with him now was ingrained, but of course he was not there. Sarah longed to discuss the enigmatic widow, Micah's oratory, the antics of the Rideout sisters, with a mind that ran on a parallel course with her own.

She'd felt a similar sense of loss when Benji left for London, but there had been nothing she could do about that. This was different. There was something Sarah could do about this.

She could join Sparhawk at the Three Cranes in Charlestown. She could take a lover. Become a mistress. Keep house for a man she desired and who desired her. Matters had to be settled with the *Sally* and her family first, but for all Mr. Cheap's surliness and her father's caginess, they liked Sparhawk. And Ned, of course, already worshipped him.

The damage to the Ward home was remarkable in its thoroughness. There wasn't a single intact pane of glass, not even on the third floor. The mob had gone to some effort — Micah's doing, no doubt. The front door was hanging on one hinge and mud spattered the bare floors inside, along with other less pleasant fluids.

Sarah did not want her father or Ned coming home to this. It was bad enough that the house had become a shadow of the home they had once enjoyed. She drew a pail of water and began washing the worst of the filth. Lucas would have to help her rehang the door. They could board up the third-floor windows — no one slept up there anyway — and perhaps use oilcloth on the lower floors until they could afford glass.

No. Without the *Sally,* they would not be able to afford glass. And the house must be sold to keep the *Sally* out of Micah's hands.

A door creaked open at the back of the house. Her father and Ned had returned. She wished she'd been able to put at least the kitchen to rights before they saw it, but she was heartsick over Sparhawk and wanted nothing more than to see the people she loved best in the world.

She rushed into the kitchen and stopped dead in the middle of the room.

It was not her father, and it was not Ned.
It was Dan Ludd and three other men.
The first held a bale of straw.
The second a bundle of rags.
The third carried a bucket of pitch.
And in Dan Ludd's callused hand was a
burning brand.

EIGHT

Sarah opened her mouth to scream. Ludd punched her in the stomach — a merciless jab, with no concession for her size or sex. She doubled over in pain, breathless and mute, unable to resist as he dragged her out of the house.

He did not plan to burn her. That was a relief — until he grasped her wrists and wrenched them behind her back. She tried to call for help. Nothing but spittle and wind came from her mouth.

It didn't matter. These were Micah's men. Her neighbors would not dare to cross them. And she had sent away the one man who would.

Before she could get her breath back, he tied her hands, gagged her with a wad of cloth and a piece of rope, and bound her feet as well. For a moment she thought she would suffocate. Then her lungs filled painfully with air. He gripped her under the arms and thrust her into the shadows behind the boatshed.

Ludd reached down to tighten the gag, and his coarse features went suddenly slack. The point of a sword burst through his corded neck, and blood shot down the steel to pool at the tip. He fell atop her, heavy as ballast.

She looked up into the dawn light and beheld the longed-for face that was a more angular reflection of her own: Benji.

Her brother touched a finger to his lips. *Quiet.* Then he dragged the corpse off her and knelt to remove the gag and cut her bonds.

Three of them — inside, she mouthed.

He nodded and stood. Blood dripped from his gory blade as he turned toward the house. She watched him pad quietly in stocking feet over the grass and disappear into the open door of the kitchen. Flames already flickered in the parlor windows. The house, she knew, was lost.

Her brother came out a few minutes later, as silently as he had entered, their father's model of the *Sally,* wrapped in Wild's "Bloody Butchery" broadside, tucked under one arm. He knelt to wipe his rapier on the grass. Then he helped her to stand. There was blood speckling his fawn breeches, and more staining the lace of his shirt cuffs. "I could not find Father's pistols or his cutlass," he said.

For all the polish she had gained in dame school and in the company of Elizabeth Pierce, Sarah was still a pirate's daughter. She knew bad men. Dan Ludd and his cronies had been worse. Fire, in a neighborhood so crowded, was wanton murder. She could not mourn them.

"The pistols and cutlass are elsewhere," she had said. "Safe." She hoped. Along with Sparhawk.

And then she flung herself into Benji's strong arms, bloody though he was. He was her brother, and he was home.

Together they dragged Dan Ludd into the kitchen. They worked wordlessly and efficiently, their actions a macabre parody of childhood exploits. Ludd's men had used pitch in the parlor and the dining room, and the dry timbers of the old house were well ablaze, but Benji had closed the kitchen door to slow the spread of the fire, and the service ell, newer and not as flammable, was still untouched. Outside once more, she told him as quickly as she could about Wild and the *Sally* and Sparhawk.

By that point she had been up all night, escaped a mob, parted with a man who had revived, however hopelessly, both her native desire and her interest in romantic love, and lost the few possessions she had left. Benji, thankfully, took over from there. He found a boat for them and rigged it, then raised the cry of fire for the sake of their neighbors, and had them away down the river before anyone knew they were gone.

She asked him when and how he had reached Salem.

"I came on the *Desdemona* from London. She was bound for Salem, but she was carrying sailcloth and salt beef, and the navy impounded her — rapacious bastards — and diverted her to Boston." He did not say he had been in the city for three months, nor what he had been doing there.

She told him about Sparhawk's offer, although she did not share the story of the captain's dangerous past.

"I can see why you accepted," said her brother, "and I am sorry you were driven to it, but that's hardly necessary now. I am home, the *Sally* is still in our possession, and we can repair our fortunes."

"I did not accept out of necessity," she replied.

"You may be all grown up, Sarah, but you are still my little sister. Do I really want to know the rest?"

"No, probably not."

"I have heard of this Sparhawk. You deserve better than to be some rake's amusement."

His censure stung. "It was not like that. He behaved with nothing but honor."

"An offer of marriage would be honorable. An offer of protection is an insult."

"It is the least insulting offer I have received since Micah jilted me."

"Wild might have harmed your prospects in Salem, but there is a wider world beyond Naumkeag. When we have money again, no one will care about what happened with Micah."

He was wrong about that. People would care. If the Wards became rich again, there would be men willing to overlook Sarah's folly for the sake of her money, the way Micah had overlooked her humble origins for the sake of her fortune. The idea did not appeal. And Sparhawk had wanted her for herself, and been willing to take on the whole piratical Ward clan to have her.

"We have a hold of French molasses we cannot sell on the North Shore because of Micah Wild, and we cannot sell in Boston because the *Sally* is wanted by the navy. Even if you repainted her and ship-rigged her and managed to fool the customs men, we have no funds to buy a new cargo. Even Father could not trade air, Benji."

"Father would tell you that there are ventures for which an empty hold is no impediment."

So, she suspected, would Angela Ferrers. Sarah said, "So long as I have a say in her, the *Sally* will carry no more contraband. No more flint, no more foreign gold, and certainly no powder from Saint Stash. We cannot afford to take any more risks."

"*Any* move we make now is a gamble," Benji replied. "At least smuggling is a gamble we're good at. And the greater the risk, the greater the reward. Father terrorized the Main and earned a fortune doing it."

"You are not Father. And that was a different time," she said. "Red Abed was lucky not to hang in Port Royal like Calico Jack."

Benji shrugged. *"Fortes Fortuna adiuvat,"* he said. "It is why you fell for Wild. His daring. But Elizabeth was always the better choice for him."

Sarah had missed Benji terribly, but no one irritated her quite as much as her brother. "Why? Because her father was only a smuggler, not a freebooter?"

"No. Because she is an opportunist, just like Wild. And you, dear sister, are not. Elizabeth Pierce will bend to circumstances. She's a flower that will always grow toward the sun."

"And what does that make me?" she asked sourly.

"Heart of oak, my girl," he said, redeeming himself entirely. "Heart of oak."

Marblehead was not a grand town of wide streets and graceful mansions like Salem. It was a scrappy little fishing village, and its timber frame houses clung to the steep harbor streets like barnacles. There were no copper or slate roofs here. Just weathered cedar shingle, green and mossy with the damp. Salem smelled like hemp and tar and pine and oak and, when the ships were in, tea and spices. Marblehead smelled like cod.

Abednego Ward had friends in Marblehead. Smugglers, to be sure, old buccaneers, some of them, but honest men after a fashion who would refit and repaint the *Sally* and swear before God and the magistrates alike that she was not the ship they were looking for; she had never touched Salem Harbor. The *Sally* would disappear in Marblehead's forest of masts, just another sleek little schooner in that fast fishing fleet.

But the Wards, it was decided at a family conference held in the smoky lean-to of an ancient house hard by the water, could not blend in so easily. Not with the Ward hair. And not in such a small, close-knit community. The *Sally* would be a week at least refitting, and if they stayed with her, Micah Wild would hear of their presence.

Cape Ann was too dangerous for them. Their only choice was to seek the king's protection in the Loyalist strongholds where Wild could not touch them: Halifax in the north, or Boston in the south.

"Boston," Benji said.

"The port is closed. No work there," said Mr. Cheap.

"I have friends there."

"What kind of friends?" asked Mr. Cheap.

Benji didn't answer.

"I vote for Boston as well," said Sarah, ignoring a pointed look from Benji.

Abednego asked once again if they were certain the house was burned. His mind kept returning to it.

"It is gone," Sarah said.

Her father looked tired. "It was the last place I saw your mother," he said. "The last place I heard her voice. The last place I lay with her."

There was not enough money for a coach, so they set out in a cart loaded with stockfish. Sarah and Abednego rode on the back and Benji, Ned, and Mr. Cheap walked alongside. Their guinea gold Ward hair was hidden beneath broad-brimmed country hats, Sarah's bound tightly under an unflattering cap.

They had gone five miles before she stopped looking over her shoulder for pursuit. By that time, the news was everywhere. Acting military governor General Gage had sent a column of some seven hundred regulars to investigate reports of a Rebel arms cache at Lexington. The local militia had formed up on the green and the British had fired on them, then cut a bloody swath home to Boston, burning farms and bayoneting old men and children in their homes.

"It is not a false alarm, like the last time," Sarah said to her brother. "Is it?"

The last time had been Charlestown in September, when Gage had seized the powder in the storehouse there, and rumors had flown about shots fired and blood spilled. They had proved untrue.

"I don't think so," Benji replied. "There are too many specifics, too many eyewitnesses. Names and places."

Sarah observed that everywhere they stopped, Benji asked questions, gathered information, and once they were on the road again, made notes in a journal he kept tucked in his elegant waistcoat.

The closer they got to Boston, the more armed men they saw: militia units mostly, but also ad hoc bands. These were not the opportunists of the Salem mob, out-of-work sailors and caulkers bent on vandalism. These were farmers and brewers and shopkeepers and even artisans and lawyers who had put down their pens and plows and answered the call to defend their homes from the British as they once had done from the Indians or the French.

And they were angry. The Wards were stopped repeatedly by militia and asked from whence they came and where they were headed. The farmers and innkeepers who bought salt fish off the cart questioned them sharply as well.

Benji talked them past every time, dropping names of Patriot leaders and gathering places with knowledgeable authority. By the time they neared the city, Sarah was fairly certain she could guess with whom, if not exactly how, her brother had spent the last three months.

Boston was almost an island, a one-square-mile peninsula connected to the mainland by a slender isthmus. Normally a ferry ran from Cambridge, but the Rebel

militia occupied the college and the riverbank, and now the only way to reach Boston
by land was over the narrow causeway
known as the neck.

General Gage, they heard on the road, had
made a bargain with the militia. He promised to allow Rebels out of the city with
their possessions if the Americans allowed
Loyalists in. But everyone entering or exit-
ing must surrender their weapons to the
British. Neither Benji nor Mr. Cheap liked
the sound of that. And the militia would let
no supplies through, so the Wards were
forced to leave the fish cart behind and walk
the final mile to the gates on Boston Neck.
Given the state of Abednego's joints after
two days on the open road, they liked that
even less.

The narrow isthmus was choked with traffic: carts piled high with household furnishings; wagons laden with trunks bound in
leather and studded with brass. The yellow
chariot in front of them had an upturned
tea table tied to its roof, ball and claw feet
reaching into the sky like the corpse of a
mahogany gryphon. A clutch of green baize
bundles were stuffed between the legs, and
from one of them peeked the spout of a
dragon-headed silver teapot. The early-
morning sun burnished the silver to gold,

165

which glittered off the water lapping at the causeway.

"It's like the bloody road to Bethlehem," swore Benji.

"No need to blaspheme," said Lucas Cheap.

"I have heard you call General Gage a Pontius Pilate, Mr. Cheap," Sarah pointed out.

"That's different," said Mr. Cheap, with the affronted air of a man who has made a solemn study of biblical oaths.

They reached the guard post just as the sun peaked overhead. The gates, Benji told her, had once been a tumbledown pile of bricks manned by the town watch, but the army had been busy. Now it was a white-washed fort with guns mounted on the walls and cannon flanking the portal. Sarah could almost taste the cool air beneath the looming arch that offered a narrow slice of longed-for shade. Here was safe harbor at last from the mob in Salem, from Micah Wild, from the surly armed men on the road.

The ensign who asked them for their pass was young and earnest and apologetic, but he could not let anyone in who did not have one. They might, for all he knew, be Rebel spies, or saboteurs. Sarah asked how they might obtain a pass, and the young man had the good grace to look embarrassed when he said that they must apply to the governor in person, which of course they could not do since they could not enter the city.

Benji asked to see his commanding officer. This person, a humorless captain from the 47th, took one look at Mr. Cheap and Abednego and ordered the Wards searched.

"Wolfe's Own," muttered Benji. "The heroes of Quebec. Searching Englishmen."

Mr. Cheap was relieved of two pistols, three knives, and a collection of evil-looking Chinese brass implements. They took Benji's sword, which Sarah noted was inlaid with mother of pearl and a diamond. When the sergeant approached Sarah, the captain shook his head and the man refrained.

Their weapons were impounded and they were refused entry. Only the friends of government were welcome in Boston. Suspected spies, Rebels, and instigators were not.

Benji looked ready to argue, but Mr. Cheap had been observing the way the unsmiling captain had been eyeing Sarah. He put a hand on Benji's shoulder and turned the Wards back the way they had come.

The apologetic young ensign ran to catch

up with them at the end of the causeway. Sarah, the ensign told them, out of breath from his sprint, might enter on her own, but — and now he looked around to make sure there was no one to overhear — he did not recommend it. He was delivering the message for his captain, who had taken an *interest* in her welfare.

"He must be married, then," said Ned.

Sarah kicked him.

Mr. Cheap smiled his gold-toothed smile, and the ensign nodded and backed away, because the ensign was intelligent and intelligent men did not turn their backs on Mr. Cheap.

When he was out of earshot, Sarah, who had Mr. Cheap's sword pistol under her hip roll, Benji's practical hanger in her petticoats, and Ned's favorite knife tucked into her pocket, laughed.

Mr. Cheap sighed. "We need to get Red inside."

"Sparhawk would help us," Sarah said, looking back the way they had come. "He told me to go to the Three Cranes in Charlestown. The landlord there will extend us credit in his name."

Cheap nodded. Benji cast her a baleful look, but he shouldered his pack and led the way back down the isthmus, and on to

Charlestown.

Sparhawk sat waiting in the wardroom of Admiral Graves' fifty-gun flagship, the *Preston,* anchored at Boston's Long Wharf. The journey from Salem had taken a day and a half and carried him through a hostile countryside furiously preparing for war.

He had been forced to abandon the carriage the last few miles, as the roads were choked with militia, but wearing Abednego's old brown coat, he had been able to pass their lines unmolested.

More than unmolested. The country people had assumed his injury to have been acquired in their cause. A pretty young girl, no more than seventeen, had rushed out of a whitewashed farmhouse as he walked by and given him the handkerchief from around her neck for a sling. Her mother had given him sausages.

Sparhawk had spent the last twelve years defending the lives and property of Englishmen, but no one had given him sausages for it.

He had not been a spy in Salem, but here, on the road to Boston, with his uniform folded neatly inside the pack Sarah Ward had given him, talking to the Americans and taking their salt and eating their bread, he most certainly felt like one.

Every village he passed through offered him hospitality: a glass of cider here, a loaf there, even a chicken from a farmwife who told him that his country was proud of him and bade him look for her man when he got to Cambridge, where the militia were massing.

The wives and daughters he passed wished him well, told him to fight bravely, clucked over his arm, and pressed handfuls of bullets on him, still warm from their molds. When he stopped between villages and sat down under a tree to eat, he opened a napkin that he had assumed contained a pasty, only to discover a bundle of cartridges. Very well rolled they were too.

His instinct, when he reached town, had been to report directly to the admiral. If Graves had been a fighting officer like McKenzie, a man of action, that was what James would have done. But Graves was a seagoing bureaucrat, enamored of protocol, and Sparhawk knew that arriving at the *Preston* in a buccaneer's coat covered in the dust of the road and smelling of sausages would not aid his cause or lend credence to his story.

And he would need all the help he could get with Graves, because two years ago in

Portsmouth, when Sparhawk had not foreseen a day he might serve under this admiral, he had carried on a dalliance with the
man's pretty, bored young wife.

Such liaisons had offered physical satisfaction free of emotional entanglement that
might divert him from his goal. There would
be no such freedom with Sarah Ward. She
had engaged him from the start, elicited his
curiosity and admiration before his desire,
though desire, when it struck him, had been
all the more potent for it. While he was on
the road to Boston, through a countryside
bristling with rebellion, his mind had returned to her over and over. Sometimes he
imagined what they might have done on the
trundle in the keeping room had Micah
Wild not interrupted, but other times he
pictured them gathered together — Sarah,
Ned, Abednego, even Mr. Cheap — and
himself, at the table or beside the fire, listening to the old pirate's stories. And this
surprised and intrigued him.

He had always thought that a mistress
would be an encumbrance, would slow his
progress toward proving his identity. He had
never considered that a woman might be a
partner and an ally in his quest, but then he
had never met a woman like Sarah Ward.

He would find her a house in one of the

seafaring neighborhoods of Boston, convenient for him when the *Wasp* was in port, and where the Wards would feel at home. It would need to be something big enough for Ned and Abednego and Mr. Cheap. The sooner the better, lest Micah Wild make another attempt to force her into his keeping. But first, he must report to Admiral Graves.

He begged stockings, a shirt, and a neck cloth off the landlady at the Golden Ball. It was not his usual tavern, but he dined there when he was obliged to be in Boston. He washed and shaved and did the best he could with his salt-stained shoes. He also wrote a note to his prize agent instructing him to reimburse the landlady if Sparhawk was unable. With Boston almost surrounded, and the harbor to defend, every officer would be needed, and it was possible Sparhawk might be required to report directly to the *Wasp* from his meeting with Graves.

Now he sat on the other side of the bulkhead from the admiral's great cabin, in his borrowed shirt and stockings, his hair brushed and tied at the back of his neck, observing the messengers who arrived nearly every quarter hour with fresh dispatches.

Finally he was summoned, the admiral's secretary ushering him into the pretty paneled cabin with its carved pilasters and long row of windows, the view of Boston Harbor with Castle William, stark on its island, in the distance.

The admiral, it appeared, had just finished dining. A joint of beef lay half carved on the table, along with the remains of a pie and an untouched dish of bright green peas.

Sparhawk had passed the market at Faneuil Hall on his way to the Long Wharf and observed the effects of the Rebel siege firsthand. The tables had turned on the British in the blink of an eye. Their blockade had been meant to deprive the rebellious city of commerce and luxury. It had only constricted the flow, not stopped it. Boston Harbor was too riddled with smugglers' coves and narrow inlets. The whole North American squadron was not equal to the task of patrolling her, let alone the six ships the admiral had on station.

Not so the land route, which the Rebels now controlled. Fresh produce had disappeared almost overnight. Half the stalls were shuttered. The rest sold only flour and salt meat. The situation was worse among the poor, which included the soldiery, and Sparhawk had seen more than a few deserting regulars on the road. It was impossible to blame the ones with families. Civilians attached to an occupying army would be the first to starve if the siege dragged on. And while the army, unlike the navy, was mostly made up of volunteers, these individuals had not volunteered to fight Englishmen.

The admiral's table was not affected because the navy still controlled the harbor and Graves had begun foraging hay, fodder, livestock, and produce off the islands — at the ends of his guns — months ago, from Loyalists and Rebels alike. It had not made him a popular figure in town. Now he was studying a map of the local coastline. The chart lay on the dish-strewn table, pinned down at the corners by the port, the salt, the relish, and the untouched peas.

Someone had added notes in a fine flowing hand showing the positions of the Rebel batteries from Salem to Providence, as well as the obstructions they had sunk in those harbors, the hulks and chains and chevaux de frise. Boston Harbor was as yet relatively unmarred, only a few batteries dotting Cambridge. As for obstructions, the Rebels needed none. Boston Harbor, a warren of hidden shoals and ever-shifting sandbars, was tricky to enter even at high tide with the best of pilots. It did not help that the best pilots were American.

"Well," said Graves, looking Sparhawk up and down, "what do you have to say for yourself, sir?" His eyes settled on the spot where one silver gilt button was conspicuous by its absence. "You look like a vagabond. And where in Hades is your hat?"

"I am lately come from Salem, sir, where I was taken by the smugglers" — not Rebels, he owed Sarah that much — "who abducted me. With the help of Loyalists in that town, I made my escape. My hat, I presume, is still aboard the *Wasp.*"

"You lost your ship, sir. On the eve of war, when we have need of every vessel."

"But I sent the Rebel gold safe to Boston, with your nephew." He knew, from the admiral's secretary, that the *Wasp* had made Boston Harbor the evening Sparhawk had been captured.

"The gold," said Graves, "is none of your affair."

"I believe that to be for the prize court to determine," said Sparhawk.

"Do you, by God?" said Graves, upsetting the salt as he rose. "Granny Gage has made a shambles of the powder affair at Lexington. Hancock and Adams have escaped. Gage could not even manage to bribe the

175

popinjay smuggler with a title or the impecunious demagogue with a fortune. Now we are besieged by fifteen thousand Rebels, and that man sits idle, unwilling to do his duty and chastise these misled violent people, for fear of offending his American wife. He has four thousand soldiers but will not bestir himself to employ them. If he allows the Rebels to dig in at Charlestown and Roxbury, we will be completely cut off. Everything, firewood, fodder, hay, meat, will have to be supplied by the squadron, and we do not have the ships to do it. And you, sir, dream of Spanish gold and make light of the loss of your brig."

"I do not make light of it," said Sparhawk, trying to rein in his own temper, because he knew that Graves was incapable of doing likewise. "I merely said that the disposition of the gold was for the prize court to determine."

"You will see a court-martial before you will see a prize court, sir. Since you gave up command of the *Wasp* so lightly, I have turned it over to my nephew."

It was a blow. Sarah Ward had been right — the *Wasp* was a lubberly brig — but there were few enough seaworthy ships in the squadron, and none to spare. Unless an American vessel was captured and lawfully bought into the service — unlikely, cash-strapped as Graves was — Sparhawk might sit out the next year on half pay.

"Not so lightly as all that, sir," said Sparhawk. He produced the *Sally*'s log from his pocket. He had hoped not to need it, as the Wards were named, but neither did he wish to spend the winter in the cells beneath Castle William. "I forbore engaging the smugglers in a fight on their schooner's deck to avoid an incident that might lead to war."

Someone on the green at Lexington had not been so careful.

"But I did not return empty-handed. The schooner's log records the voyage's investors. Some are innocent Loyalists. I can mark them out for you. Others, including Micah Wild of Salem, are not."

Sparhawk laid the book on the table.

Graves ignored it. "I do not have the time to chase after Rebels in the hinterlands. We must strike a blow before the Americans take steps to fortify the harbor. They have intimidated most of the local pilots and are building batteries to turn upon our shipping. If you wish to have a command again this year, you will proceed to the *Somerset* and bring her guns to bear on Charles-town."

The hair on the back of Sparhawk's neck prickled. The skirmish at Lexington had occurred less than a week before. Only Parliament could declare war, and it would take six weeks at least for word to arrive in London and a reply to reach Boston.

Still, to disobey a direct order — lawful or not — was dangerous. He could be hanged for it. "Am I directed and required to do so?" Sparhawk asked, invoking the language of the Admiralty, in which lawful orders were always framed.

"Do you dare to question me?"

The *Somerset* was a seventy-gun ship of the line, beyond Sparhawk's reach. La Cras had command of her. If La Cras was not commanding her guns, there was a reason for it.

The action was not lawful. The man who carried out such orders would be sacrificed, like poor old Byng, if it all went wrong and the Admiralty wanted someone to blame.

And it *would* go wrong. "I have just traveled fifteen miles through the Rebel lines. The people are angry about Lexington. Burning Charlestown," he said carefully, "would only further inflame them."

"You have carried out similar operations before. This is no different."

"Boston Harbor is not the Barbary Coast."

Charlestown, in fact, was much like Salem, a busy little port town, just across the water from Boston, full of homes and warehouses and workshops. It contained the livelihoods not just of Rebels but of loyal British subjects and law-abiding colonists too stretched by hardship to play at politics. "Charlestown is not a North African slave port."

"No?" said Graves. "And who, pray, brewed your coffee this morning, sir? These people talk of liberty and keep a tithe of their population in chains. They are damnable devious hypocrites, the lot of them, and Gage has coddled them for too long."

"I am not certain I could with conscience burn a British port. Have I leave to consider the proposition?"

"You have leave, sir, to find a new hat. You will report to the *Somerset* tomorrow, you *will* fire hot shot, and you will burn Charlestown to the ground, or face trial," he said, invoking the words that had condemned Byng, "for failing to do your utmost against the enemy."

NINE

Charlestown was half abandoned. The British regulars had retreated through the tiny enclave on their demoralized march from Lexington, and taken their frustrations out on the colonists by looting the larger homes. The further threat of a naval bombardment had driven anyone whose business could be relocated to flee.

The Three Cranes was housed in an ancient, rambling structure that claimed to be the first governor's mansion in the colony. The main building showed three overhanging gables to the street, like a flight of birds, Sarah supposed, if you were in a fanciful frame of mind. She was not. Tired, hot, and hungry, she wanted only to find the landlord, draw on Sparhawk's credit, and get her father a soft bed and a hot meal.

Piles of broken furniture and smashed tableware, indicating that the house built for John Winthrop had not escaped the retreat unscathed, flanked the entrance. Inside, the taproom was cool and dark. The furnishings were sparse — no doubt a product of the looting — but it was the sort of place sea captains liked: old-fashioned and unfussy, with its Turkey work chairs, sanded floors, and green baize curtains.

The inn remained one of the few lively centers of urban life. The patrons were an uneasy mix of naval officers, Redcoats, and locals. No one, at that moment, was certain exactly to whom the town belonged. Except the landlady, Mrs. Brown, whose ideas on that subject were fixed.

"If Captain Sparhawk had an arrangement with my husband, then you must take that up with him," she said when Sarah asked for credit on his account.

"And where might I find your husband?" Sarah asked.

"Canada," said the landlady. "With our serving maid. He said he was fleeing the king's troops, but the truth is that he got the girl with child and decamped. If you plan on seeing him, you may bring him his shirts. He wrote asking for them. And you may tell him he'll have nothing else out of me or this house."

"Where," put in Benji, "might we find Captain Sparhawk?"

The landlady shrugged. "I've not seen him these three months."

Sarah felt a prickle of unease. Sparhawk should have reached Boston before them.

Benji drew her into a corner, out of hearing of their father and Ned. Mr. Cheap trailed after them, his gaunt face a study in bland neutrality.

"Father must have a bed tonight," Benji said.

Sarah knew it. The Wards had slept rough the past two days, and her father's hands were curled into rheumatic claws. He needed a soft mattress and a warm drink, and they had no money for either. Their last meal had been breakfast the previous day. That had been only apples and cider, quickly soured in an empty stomach.

"How bad is our situation?" she asked. The fact that Benji had considered turning to a man who had offered his sister protection indicated that things were dire indeed. Now that the man was not to be found . . .

"There is a connection I can call upon," said Benji tentatively. "A naval officer I knew in London. We are not on the best of terms at the moment — politics, don't you know — but if I can slip across the river and find him, I believe he would help a friend in distress. There is only one complication."

"What?" she asked.

"I did not come directly home after the *Desdemona* docked. I spent some time in Boston."

She had figured that much out already. "Tell me."

"I was working with the printers."

"You? Printing?" She had a difficult time imagining her dashing brother with ink on his fingers.

"Good Lord, no. Smuggling. Parliament has been urging Gage to make arrests. The general, it seems, is too temperate for his masters in London. But we could not afford to lose the presses if he decided to act. I helped Edes and Gill and Thomas and that lot to move their equipment out of the city. Along with a couple of British cannons that used to defend the North Point. Somehow Gage got wind of the business and raided Edes' shop. Several of us managed to get out. Those who didn't are in jail on charge of treason and sedition. Gill and Thomas got clean away for certain. Edes has fled to the countryside. His son had more nerve. He's taken the small press and gone underground to keep on printing. It is possible, though, that the British have got my name.

If I am wanted for treason, my friend will have little choice but to do his duty and arrest me."

"Then you cannot take the risk," Sarah said.

Benji turned to look at Abednego, huddled on a bench in the corner. "I would not suggest it if there were any other way. I promise I shall do my best not to get hanged."

"Go, then," interjected Mr. Cheap, who had been listening in silence. "Red'll not last another night in the open."

Benji nodded to Cheap, pecked Sarah on the cheek, then strode out the door.

Sarah turned to look at the corner where her father sat huddled on a hard bench. That such a tower of strength had come to this. He should be comfortable, painting his models and plotting improvements to his ship. Not shivering in a drafty corner with nothing in his belly for two days. A private room, a hot drink, a cushioned chair — if only she could give him these things. Micah had offered them. Out of pride, she had refused. And her father was the one to suffer.

"I could take Ned over to the market and get us some bread, maybe a jug of something for your father," Mr. Cheap suggested.

"By 'get' you mean 'steal,' Mr. Cheap. No."

"Why not?" Ned asked.

She had not noticed him approach. "Because picking pockets is a charming sleight of hand if you are rich, but it will get you thrown in jail if you are poor."

Cheap nodded. "Then I'll head down to the docks and try to turn an honest coin with a few hours' work."

Work would be difficult to find. The harbor had been blockaded for a year, with nothing but the most necessary supplies coming in or out. No trade, no cargo, no work. And the few jobs that were available were taken by the soldiery in their spare time.

Mr. Cheap left. Sarah sat down next to her father and worked on mending the hem of her skirt. She did her best to avoid the notice of Mrs. Brown, but the woman scowled every time her eyes fell on the raffish Wards. The hours passed. Her father scarcely stirred. Ned made forays into the street a few times, to see if Benji or Mr. Cheap might be on the way back, and the crowd changed several times over.

First there had been the tradesman in the morning, wearing homespun and wool, breakfasting or talking business — which everyone agreed was bad — over coffee. Next had come the gentlemen in silk waistcoats and clocked stockings, merchants and traders, discussing their ransacked homes and warehouses and the likelihood that Governor Gage would indemnify them for the damage his hooligan Redcoats had done. The taps were open and flowing by late afternoon, and the common room slowly filled with army and navy officers — and quickly emptied of locals.

And still neither Benji nor Lucas Cheap returned.

Sparhawk went directly from the *Preston* to Province House, where the colony's acting military governor, "Granny Gage," resided. It was a massive antique structure, much improved over the years, but the steep slate roof and elaborate brickwork told of its Tudor origins.

James did not know Thomas Gage personally, though he had been introduced, recently, to his beautiful American wife, whose exotic good looks were said to come from a Turkish grandmother. It was she whom he asked for, gossip be damned, when he discovered the hall of Province House crowded with petitioners, the long row of chairs against the left wall occupied by army officers in red and the row on the right by local merchants in sober suits of worsted. Some of the officers were injured. Those who could not find seats paced the tiles.

Sparhawk joined them. He ignored their outraged looks when a servant appeared a few minutes later and led him up the wide branching staircase and into a long reception room graced with a Dutch tiled fireplace and appointed in matching green and cream upholstery.

The woman who entered, who had rebuffed his overtures with regal grace the last time they met, was as beautiful as he remembered, with her high clear brow and fine skin. And she was as elegant in her striped peach sack-back gown as the pretty chamber. He was only surprised to discover that her glamour had no effect on him; it could not displace the appeal of Sarah Ward.

Margaret Gage cast a skeptical eye upon Sparhawk. He bowed and said, "Forgive me, but I craved admittance to your husband's presence, and had no appointment. I have presumed upon our acquaintance, but I believe that the nature of my business will persuade you to forgive me."

"That will depend," said Margaret Kemble

Gage, "on what you mean to tell my husband."

It was a betrayal: of the confidence of his commanding officer; of the service; and because he knew the consequences of his actions, it was a betrayal of Sarah Ward, whom he might be in no position to help.

But not a betrayal of his country; he was certain of that. "Admiral Graves has ordered me to take command of the guns on the *Somerset* and burn Charlestown."

Ned returned from his latest exploration of the neighborhood surrounding the Three Cranes, looking warily over his shoulder. "A man offered me money to go down an alley with him," he said. "I think he might have followed me back."

This was all they needed. "Sit down beside Father," Sarah said, "and stay there."

A few minutes later a tall man in a gray silk suit came in the door and scanned the crowd. He spotted Ned, and began to cross the room. Sarah stepped in front of him. "I believe you are looking for my brother," she said.

The man considered. "The little towheaded urchin? I might be, depending on the price."

Her revulsion was instinctual, but she

knew better than to make a scene. The landlady was looking for an excuse to throw them out, and they must not give her one, not now with the sun falling and men like this prowling the streets. "There are no terms," she said. "My brother is not for sale."

The man merely shrugged. "Then he shouldn't wander the docks at this hour." He took in Sarah's travel-stained silk dress, at odds, she knew, with her accent and deportment. "Refugees, are you? I could buy the boy a meal. There would be something for you as well."

Her stomach turned. She had been raised in a port town, befriended by women of negotiable virtue when she was a child — and too young to be in danger when she ran wild on Salem's safe and familiar docks. She had been the daughter of Abednego Ward, once the terror of the Caribee, and the sister of Benjamin Ward, the quiet, dangerous boy who sailed as his father's apprentice and was known to have a sharp sword and a short temper.

But she remembered the lessons those women had imparted, when she had thought that their world could never touch hers. About choosing men from the better taverns and cleaner ships, because they were less likely to give you a pox. About having your own room to take them, safe, with friends in earshot, or else servicing them as close to a public place as possible, so they could not demand more than they had paid for or refuse to pay at all.

It is shocking what you will do for a crust of bread if your family is starving.

"No," she said. "But thank you for your *kindness.*" She suspected it was the only sort they would be offered.

After that they stayed inside. The evening crowd changed again, all save one man, a naval officer she had spied in the corner while she was fending off Ned's would-be seducer. She had noticed him earlier because he had striking black hair with a gilded crown of sun streaks, like Sparhawk. For a moment she had thought it might be him, but that had been wishful imagining. This man was equally tall and gracefully proportioned, but nearer forty than thirty, though it was hard to tell with sailors and their weather-beaten complexions. He sat nursing a glass of claret and reading first a book and then a newspaper. Finally the publican's wife brought him dinner.

Sarah tried not to stare at the food, but it had been a day and a half since she had eaten anything but apples, and the brown roasted bird, the crusty bread, the soft pungent cheese, and the steaming sage dressing were impossible for her to ignore. The meal was so fragrant she could almost taste it.

And still no sign of Benji or Mr. Cheap.

The landlady brought him pudding and coffee as well, then crossed the crowded room to Sarah Ward and said, "The tap closes in an hour. You can pay for a private room, or leave. If you don't go then, I'll call the watch." Then she bustled back into the kitchen.

Sarah made a quick check of the street outside. The curfew meant that law-abiding Bostonians were safely at home. With her father unwell and Mr. Cheap gone, they would be prey to the most unscrupulous element. "Ned," she said quietly enough that her father did not hear, "stay with Father. If anything goes amiss with me, wait for Benji and Mr. Cheap to come back. Do you understand?"

Her younger brother scowled at her. "Yes. But I don't approve."

She took a seat well away from Ned and Abednego, and studied the room. The mechanics playing backgammon in the corner were sober New Englanders in plain-cut clothes. They were wary and suspicious,

191

casting surreptitious looks at the table of loud army officers next to them. None of these local men were drinking enough to be a safe mark. Her skills were not of the same caliber as Mr. Cheap's, and she knew it.

The little table of army officers was a different matter. There were four of them. They were young — "callow" was the dame school word that sprang to mind — and drinking too much for their own good. They were talking in loud, braying voices about the action at Lexington, the "despicable people" of Massachusetts, and the indecisive policies of their commanding officer, "Granny Gage."

One of them described, in detail, how his men had come upon a farm in Menotomy. The Rebels had refused to come out. The regulars had stormed the house and put the whole place to the torch.

He spoke without regret or remorse, in the same tones with which he described the uneventful remainder of the march. Sarah could still feel, when she thought about it, the heat of the flames that had consumed her home.

The hour grew late. The mechanics departed, emptying the taproom and leaving a sudden quiet behind in which the voices of the young army officers sounded startlingly loud, even to themselves.

Sarah watched them wake up to the emptiness of the room and reach for their purses. She took note of whose was fat and whose was slim, where they tucked them — in a boot, a knapsack, a vest, a coat pocket.

She picked her mark, a tawny-haired fusilier captain she judged to be just out of his teens whose gold braid and lace cuffs indicated he could afford to spare a few shillings.

She had never stolen anything of value before. A candy stick from a sailor's pocket, glasses from the reverend's waistcoat. Things she meant to — and always did — return. Her actions had never gone beyond parlor games.

This was different.

Sarah crossed the room. She did not look directly at the captain, but kept track of him out of the corner of her eye. She slowed her pace so that just as he crossed her path, she collided with his right shoulder — and slipped her hand into his left pocket.

He looked right, as she had hoped, as Mr. Cheap had told her a mark always would. Bump right and dive left. Her fingers curled around the strings of his purse. He didn't feel it. She drew her hand up, smooth and quick, the way Mr. Cheap had taught her.

Too quick. The strings snapped. The purse plummeted to the floor and burst open, sending coins scuttling across the boards.

The fusilier, dull with drink, stared down at the floor. Then he looked at Sarah. "She's picked my pocket."

Sarah stepped back. "You are drunk, sir."

Out of the corner of her eye she saw Ned tense — and then remember his promise to stay out of it.

"Call the watch," suggested the stockiest, an ensign with a high-pitched child's voice and a public school accent.

"I did not touch his purse." She used the older-sister tones that always worked on Ned. "It fell out of his pocket when he walked into me."

"It did not," said the affronted officer.

"Call the watch," repeated the ensign. "Let them put her in the stocks."

"Yes," said Sarah. "Call the watch." Given the emotional climate of the city, they'd take her word over that of the regulars.

And then because they were staring at her with the same haughty dislike she had endured in school, because she was an Englishwoman and a friend of government and entitled to the benefit of doubt — and because they had burned a house like hers, she added, "The watch will enjoy teaching clumsy Redcoats manners."

A mistake. She knew it at once. The fusilier captain bristled. The ensign curled his child's lip.

And the tallest of them, the boy who had bragged about the brutality of his men in Menotomy, stepped forward and said in cool, clipped tones, "Don't call the watch."

Sarah met his cold, glittering eyes and knew real fear.

He plucked a coin out of his purse and tossed it to the ensign. "Speak us a room, Harry," he said.

"What for?" asked Harry, catching the coin and turning it over in his palm.

"This girl," he replied, "needs a lesson the watch won't teach her."

TEN

Sparhawk watched Margaret Kemble Gage's pretty face lose all color.

A few minutes later he was shown into a smaller paneled study. Dark and cool, the chamber smelled of wet dog, no doubt from the three muddy spaniels lying on the carpet. Thomas Gage rose to greet him and introduced his brother-in-law, Stephen Kemble, who also, Sparhawk knew, happened to be his chief intelligence officer.

They were both polite but wary. They did not know Sparhawk. He was a man with a certain reputation where women were concerned, and he had obtained entry by using the general's beautiful wife. And the general had lately quarreled with Sparhawk's commanding officer.

James stepped over the dogs to take the chair offered, sat, and related his interview with the admiral.

Gage and his brother-in-law listened attentively.

When he was done, the general sighed and said, "I thank you for telling me this, Captain. It obliges me to remonstrate with the admiral. I am sorry to say that if you do not report to the *Somerset* tomorrow, I can do nothing to protect you from his wrath."

Sparhawk had feared as much. He had come anyway. So he plowed on. "Graves is right about the squadron," he said. "It cannot supply the city if the Rebels tighten the siege. Charlestown and Roxbury must be taken, or Boston will starve."

"The point," said Gage, "has not escaped me. However, they are fifteen thousand, and they have more veterans among their militia than I have among my four thousand regulars. I have already warned the selectmen of Charlestown that if they allow the militia to dig in on their hills, I will be forced to fire upon the town. It has so far sufficed as a deterrent."

"Graves will not wait for them to dig in," Sparhawk said. "He is determined to burn Charlestown to the ground now. *Somerset* has the guns to do the job in an hour. The population should be ordered to evacuate. My refusal is only the inevitable delayed. If I do not report for duty tomorrow, the admiral will find another, more agreeable captain to do his bidding."

"You see how these people have reacted to a skirmish in the woods," said Gage. "Imagine what they would do if they believed we were plotting to destroy one of their towns."

"But we are — or the admiral is, at any rate."

"The army can barely hold Boston," replied Gage. "The Rebels are led by shrewd propagandists. If Adams or one of his ilk got wind of this business, they could instigate a riot we do not have the men to quell."

Kemble leaned forward in his chair. He had his sister's keen gaze and dark good looks. "Do you mean to report to the *Somerset* tomorrow?"

If he did, he would be free to make good on his promise to Sarah Ward, to enjoy her company at his table and in his bed all summer long and longer. If he did not, she would end in the keeping of Micah Wild. The thought turned his stomach.

"I have an obligation," he said, "to a lady. If I am arrested, I will not be able to keep it. Her family are Loyalists, hard-pressed in Rebel Salem. They helped me escape. I would like to send her a message. And money. Along with her father's pistols."

"Write her a letter," said the general, rising. "I have a mind to send a scout into those parts. He will deliver it for you, along with any funds you entrust to him."

"He will find the countryside up in arms," said Sparhawk, and described his troubling journey to Boston.

"Our scout is a resourceful man," said Kemble.

No doubt their resourceful man was a spy.

Sparhawk knew better than to try to leave Boston for his usual rooms at the Three Cranes — he suspected he had already been followed to Province House by a sailor off the *Preston* — so he gave the general his direction at the Golden Ball. On his way out of the house, Lady Gage stopped him and drew him into the privacy of her sitting room.

"You met with my husband," she said.

"Yes, thank you."

"My brother noticed that you are injured."

Sparhawk had taken pains to hide his splint beneath the lace of his cuff, but he doubted that Stephen Kemble missed much. "I broke my arm escaping from the Rebels," he said. It was almost true. "But I received excellent care from the friends of government who helped me escape." And that was technically not a lie.

"Even so," she said, "I would like to send

199

my doctor to look at you. May he call on you this evening?"

"There is no need."

She insisted, and since he was under an obligation to her and her husband, Sparhawk agreed.

At the Golden Ball he did his best to put his affairs in order. When the general's "scout" — Sparhawk was certain the man was a spy — called, he was ready with his letter, a purse of gold drawn from the funds he kept with his prize agent, and Abednego Ward's pistols and cutlass.

The man's name was DeBerniere, and he was in appearance the single most forgettable person Sparhawk had ever encountered.

He asked Sparhawk to describe the mood in Salem.

"I discovered similar conditions in the towns to the west the last time I ventured out of the city," said DeBerniere. "You were lucky to escape with your life. How on earth did you manage to stay hidden?"

"A secret staircase, if you can believe it," replied Sparhawk. He described the Ward house so that DeBerniere might find it.

"Very common in these older dwellings," said DeBerniere. In a few strokes he sketched, from Sparhawk's spare details, an amazing likeness of the Ward place. Sparhawk said as much.

"It is a useful talent," replied the spy. "How did you journey safe through the Rebel lines?" he asked.

Sparhawk wondered if the fellow disguised his speech when he traveled among the Americans. The man had an aristocratic public school accent that would betray him if he opened his mouth. James found he rather missed Sarah's Yankee twang.

"The Rebels," Sparhawk replied, "thought I had been injured in their cause." He sloughed off his coat to reveal his splint.

DeBerniere smiled — a crafty expression — and Sparhawk suspected that tomorrow this utterly forgettable man would be sporting something similar.

A little while later the spy left and Sparhawk ate a meal, such as it was, prepared by the Golden Ball's kitchen. Cabbage and salt pork. Almost as bad as the fare on the *Wasp*. It was past seven when someone scratched at his door and a gentleman in a velvet suit with a pale blue silk embroidered waistcoat and sleeves dripping with Mechlin lace introduced himself as Lady Gage's doctor. He was quite the most exquisite physician Sparhawk had ever encountered, and he did not give his name.

Sparhawk admitted him, then apologized. "I fear you will regret taking the time to call on me. My arm is giving me very little trouble, apart from dressing."

"*That* is about as useful to me as my professional opinion on rigging would be to you," said the doctor, insufferable as most physicians. "Though in truth I have come about your other difficulties. I take it, sir, you are a friend to America."

Sparhawk did not reply all at once. He was the dispossessed heir to an English barony, but he had been born in the New World, and not set foot on English soil until he was fifteen and a midshipman. "I am an officer of the king," he said finally.

"One who will not burn an American port."

"One who will not burn a *British* port. It is my duty to protect the king's subjects and their property." If it was determined that the Americans were no longer the king's subjects, Sparhawk was less certain how the king would feel about their property — and where his own loyalties would lie.

"But you do not wish to see Charlestown burned."

"Neither does General Gage," countered Sparhawk.

"No, but Gage will not be able to stop the

admiral if he can find an officer willing to carry out his orders. That is why I have come. Graves will not risk the careers of his nephews on such a gambit. That is three of his captains accounted for."

"Four," amended Sparhawk. "He has given my Wasp to Francis Graves."

"Four, then," said the doctor. "We must know if there are any other officers in the squadron who might be inclined to carry out the admiral's orders."

"By 'we,' I presume you do not mean the general and his staff."

"No," said the doctor.

"You are asking me to commit treason."

"You strike me as a thoughtful man, Captain Sparhawk. Britain has broken the bonds of loyalty that tied America to her. Your admiral has done likewise with you. He would use you for his purposes and see you hang if his superiors censured him."

"I have served under bad commanders before," said Sparhawk. "They are not the navy. And I would not see any of my brother officers assassinated."

The doctor bristled. "You insult me, sir."

"That was not my intention," said Sparhawk. "Your colleagues in Salem threatened to burn an old man and his daughters out of their house in pursuit of me."

"As you say, bad officers are not the navy. And Micah Wild is not America."

There came a scratch at the door, followed by the voice of Sparhawk's landlady. "There is a party of marines in the street below, Captain Sparhawk. They demand I let them in."

"Are they here for you?" Sparhawk asked his unnamed guest.

The doctor considered. "Possibly. Or perhaps Admiral Graves has already learned of your visit to the general. In any case, it is time I took my leave."

Sparhawk's visitor turned to the window and raised the sash.

"Dr. Warren," said Sparhawk, pleased when the man turned and confirmed his guess. A Rebel, and a famous one, he was the man behind the Suffolk Resolves that had so moved Burke. He was also the orator, just that March, whose theatrics on the anniversary of the Boston Massacre — he'd arrived at the meetinghouse dressed in a toga — had so enraged the army. Their dislike of Warren had risen to a fever pitch over the stunt. He was, by their lights, a damned seditious bastard. He would be mad to take the field against the king's troops now. Yet Sparhawk had never heard anyone impugn the man's honor.

"Moore and Mowat," Sparhawk said, naming two officers in the squadron. "They are hotheads. Moore is not fit to command a tender, and I doubt Graves would trust him with the guns of the *Somerset*. Mowat is another matter altogether."

Warren considered a moment, then said, "Men of such temperaments often have difficulty with supplies, misunderstandings with merchants and such, that can interfere with their duties and delay their sailing or entangle them in civil proceedings for days, if not weeks on end."

"Yes," said Sparhawk, relieved that his estimate of Warren had been correct. "I believe that to be so."

James heard feet upon the stair, the clank of cartridge boxes and bayonets.

Warren nodded, climbed out onto the roof, and paused. "You might come with me. Talent, not interest, determines a man's rank in America. And we have need of a man with your talents."

"Good evening, Dr. Warren," said Sparhawk. He closed the window and drew the drapes, and by the time the door burst open and the marines stormed in, there was no sign he had entertained a visitor.

Unfortunately, they had not come for the American.

Eleven

Sarah took a step away from the blond Red-coat with the cold eyes, but the fusilier whose pocket she had picked moved to cut off her retreat.

"Leave the girl alone," said a voice resonant with the unquestioned authority of the quarterdeck.

Sarah turned toward the speaker and saw that it was the naval officer she had earlier observed taking his meal and reading his paper. He was standing in front of his table now, his posture relaxed, but it was a deceptive stance. His hand rested lightly on his hanger sword, an implied but not overt threat.

"Your purse fell out of your pocket when you mauled the lady," he said. "I suggest you apologize."

"I will not," said the fusilier captain.

"That is Trent," said the boy with the cruel eyes, the one who had wanted to teach

Sarah a lesson. A note of caution had entered his voice.

But the fusilier didn't hear it. "I don't care who the devil he is. He can go hang. She's a pickle pocket. A pock picket. Pox on it, you know what I mean."

"Pickpockets do not dress in travel-stained silk petticoats and lace," said the man called Trent. "*The lady* is one of the Loyalists the army is in Boston to defend. *You,* sir, are three sheets to the wind, and dropped your purse. Apologize and we will say no more of it."

A space formed around the fusilier officer. He looked to his friends for support but found none. Finally, he muttered, "My mistake."

That was good enough for Sarah, but she didn't move. She did not know where, just yet, to run.

"Good night, gentlemen," said Trent. His tone was not unfriendly, but he spoke with a remarkable formality, such as only sea captains and other tyrants like the Grand Turk or Great Mogul could project.

The fusilier's friends took the hint and filed toward the door, but the captain could not resist a parting shot. "Thieving little slut," he said under his breath.

Steel whispered softly against wood. The

sound stopped the soldiers in their tracks. They turned to observe this Trent, whose blade, sharp and well oiled, was now half unsheathed.

"For the love of God, Fairchild," urged the cruel-eyed boy, "*apologize*. Again. Trent has killed seven men in duels. He has never lost."

A look of sick realization passed over Fairchild's face, as detail triggered memory. "I misspoke," he said. "Apologies."

A moment later the taproom was empty save for the Wards and their mysterious savior.

"Thank you," Sarah said.

"Not at all. Forgive me if I am taking a liberty, but you and your family appear to be in some distress. May I offer my assistance?"

"You already have," she said. "And my older brother will be back shortly. He has gone in search of a friend, a naval officer," she added, hoping it might afford her some protection from further offers of *charity*.

"Then perhaps you and your father and the young man will do me the honor of sharing some small repast while you wait."

It might be an innocent offer, but she could not, under the circumstances, take the risk. "No, thank you."

He cocked his head. "Why do you assume that my intentions are less than honorable?" he asked, genuine curiosity in his voice.

"Because you said that the lieutenant dropped his purse, but you know he did not."

"Ah. Yes. And you suspect that I only saved you from rape so I could blackmail you into my bed."

"Something like that."

"I flatter myself there are easier ways to get a pretty girl under me."

He was rich and handsome, so that was very likely true; yet she was still wary. "Perhaps you have sordid tastes," she said, unable to help herself. It was the first real kindness she had been shown in two days, and she spurned it like a beaten dog.

"Or perhaps I saw you defend your brother from the pederast earlier and have spent the evening hoping for an opportunity to make your acquaintance. And offer you my aid, without insulting you with my charity." He smiled. "If so, it seems I overplay my hand. I'd rather you take me for an officious philanthropist than a crafty seducer. By and large."

She wanted to believe it. She had been awake for more than a day and a night, and had eaten nothing in forty-eight hours; and there was her father huddled in a corner suffering the pains of his rheumatism.

If she accepted this man's offer and Benji and Mr. Cheap did not come back — and the chances were looking smaller with each passing hour — she must also accept his advances. She could not pretend naïveté and cry off, not after attempting to pick pockets in front of him.

Such an act, even born of desperation, would put Sparhawk out of her reach forever.

The flexible ladies of Salem would tell her it was a good bargain. He was not only clean, he was handsome. Slighter perhaps than Sparhawk, whose perfection had printed itself in her memory, but just as well-proportioned and just as lean. Rich, almost certainly, to judge by the embroidered silk waistcoat and clocked stockings, and quite senior in the service to judge by the amount of bullion he wore. He was older than she, but his exact age was impossible to determine. There was no silver in his thick black hair. He wore a signet ring on his left hand, but it was the only jewel on his person. He had the robust physique of youth but the sun-crinkled eyes of a seaman. He might be a weathered thirty or a youthful forty.

If the circumstances were different, she expected she would find him attractive.

"Allow me to propose this," he said, breaking into her thoughts. "I have a chamber spoken for upstairs — don't look so alarmed. I had intended to repair there and take my dinner in private, but did not. Perhaps your father, who appears to be a seafaring gentleman of some years, might enjoy resting there for a few hours. There is a good bed and a fine chair for the young man. And you and I can sit here in the taproom and await your brother."

She longed to accept. If she did so, if Benji did not return, and this man propositioned her later, she would be in no position to refuse. She must make her decision knowing this.

Appearances, of course, could deceive. Micah Wild had been wholesomely handsome and selfish as sin. James Sparhawk had been too gorgeous to be good; yet he had treated her with nothing but affection and honor. The man before her was as striking as James Sparhawk, if not as sublimely beautiful, and he projected an aura of confidence and command.

It occurred to her then that there was a certain freedom in poverty and obscurity. Micah's machinations had been about her money and the *Sally*. There was nothing she had to offer a rich and powerful man now besides her body, and there was only so much use one man could make of it in a single night.

She made her decision. "Yes. That would be acceptable." Not the most gracious of thank-yous, she conceded.

"You still don't trust me," he said. "Is it customary in these parts for a man to proposition a lady with her father in the room?"

"Yes," she said. "Quite. It is called a betrothal."

He laughed out loud. "So it is. Landlady," he called. "Ah, Mrs. Brown. Please help the gentleman . . ."

"Captain Ward," Sarah supplied.

"Captain Ward, up to my room. His son will assist you."

"Very good, Captain," she said through clenched teeth, plastering a false smile across her face. Abednego stirred only briefly as they led him to the hall.

Sarah turned to confront her dubious benefactor. He pulled out a chair for her and she sat. It was cushioned, unlike the bench along the wall where she had spent most of the day, and she could not resist sighing with pleasure at the very feel of it,

212

molding to her bones and curves.

"You have a lovely smile," he said. "I am glad to be the cause of it."

"The cushion is the more direct cause," she said, "but I have you to thank for that, Captain."

He pursed his lips. It would be a woman-ish gesture on anyone less masculine, but his square jaw and wide, expressive mouth were undeniably male, and undeniably appealing. After her experience with Wild, she had thought her appetite for physical passion forever extinguished. She had been wrong. James Sparhawk had brought desire roaring back to inconvenient life in her.

And now he was missing.

"We have not been properly introduced," said her rescuer. "My name is Anthony Trent."

"I'm Sarah Ward, Captain Trent."

"Alas, I am commander of nothing bigger than this table at the moment. I brought the *Charybdis* over from Portsmouth, but the navy yard fitted her out so shoddily that we had three men at the pumps at all hours, and when we dropped anchor in Boston, her keel split. The Americans will not sell Admiral Graves the necessary lumber to repair her, and she is, I fear, a lost cause. That is my sad story. What is it that brings you to Boston?"

"Rebels confiscated our cargo of tea and burned our house down," she replied baldly.

"I am so very sorry," he said. "In England it is believed that all the trouble is in Boston, that these riots are instigated by saucy boys and slaves and city rabble, and that the country people are not infected with sedition. And that it will take only a firm hand, a little hardship, to bring them to heel. This is what Parliament believes, because no one in Parliament has ever been to America. It is a peculiar notion, that a people who have tamed a wilderness should be so much softer than native-born Britons. Ah, Mrs. Brown." The publican's abandoned wife had returned. "Will you bring Miss Ward some supper?" Trent asked. "And a glass of brandy. Or would you prefer small beer?"

"Tea, if they have it," Sarah said. He had proved himself an observant and dangerous man. She must keep her wits about her.

"I'm so sorry, Captain, but we're done serving. There's nothing but bread and butter." *For the likes of these,* her tone indicated.

"There was rabbit on offer at dinner. She will have some of that. Hot. And a pudding. The brown one that you served earlier, with cream. And the same for her father and the boy," said Trent. His tone brooked no argument.

"Of course, Captain," said Mrs. Brown, with a smile that told Sarah he would be charged double for it.

The rabbit, when it arrived, was hot and succulent, the meat falling off the bone into a puddle of rich buttery sauce. The pudding was cornmeal scented with nutmeg and cloves and sweetened with molasses that lingered on her tongue.

She licked her sticky lips, and Trent shifted in his chair. He intended to seduce her then. The pudding, she thought with giddy resignation, might just have been worth it. Mrs. Brown cleared the dishes and brought the brandy. Trent poured her a glass and pushed it across the table.

"Go ahead," he said. "You need it."

"I don't think that would be a good idea," she said.

He smiled. "If it had been my aim to debauch you, I would have approached you earlier, when you were tired and hungry and afraid for the boy and your father. It would have been easy then, to press a glass on you, and other things."

He was right. She drank the brandy.

To her surprise he did not take the opportunity to move closer to her when they repaired to the bald velvet wing chairs by the fire, nor did he pour her a second glass. Instead, he asked her about what kinds of books she liked to read — novels, she admitted — what her house in Salem had been like — old but well loved; her eyes watered when she described the keeping room and parlors, gone now — what Ned's schooling had been so far — Latin, mathematics, geometry, a little Greek — and if he would go for a sailor.

She discovered that Trent had been married and widowed, had no living children, was somewhat older than she had estimated — forty-four, in fact — and feared he might not get another ship in North America, as there were no seaworthy vessels to be had in the squadron.

Then there was a ruckus at the door. Mrs. Brown had locked it for the night. When she lifted the bar and opened it a crack, Benji burst through in an agitated state, bellowing for his sister. He took one look at Trent, Sarah, and the empty brandy glasses and reached for the sword that no longer hung at his hip.

The conclusion he leapt to made her angry. Her stupidity with Micah Wild colored even how her own brother saw her.

"The captain was kind enough to offer Father his room and intervene with the innkeeper when she might have thrown us out," Sarah said. She had no intention of mentioning the Redcoats or her attempt at petty thievery. She hoped Trent wouldn't either.

He didn't. Instead he said, "It is your sister who was kind, to keep an old salt company through a dull evening. Allow me to introduce myself. I am Trent."

Her benefactor offered Benji his hand.

Sarah saw recognition in her brother's keen eyes — though none of the fear those young officers had exhibited — and something else: calculation.

"I thank you, then, for your care of my sister," Benji said. "I had gone to find my friend, Ansbach, but his ship, the *Hephaestion,* is anchored out in the harbor, and it took me all day just to discover this."

"And will he help us?" Sarah asked. They were in desperate straits if he would not. They could not get into Boston to seek the king's protection from Micah Wild and the Rebels. Sarah had just antagonized yet more of the king's officers, and they were defenseless and friendless in a half-abandoned town where only predators roamed at night. They had no safe place to lay their heads.

"I paid a fisherman to take a message to him, but I did not receive a reply," said Benji. "I fear there is no help for the widow's son."

He said it pointedly, as though Trent should take some meaning from this doggerel, and evidently, Trent did.

"Charles Ansbach is like a brother to me," said her rescuer. "I am certain that he would wish me to open my home to you, and that he would do the same if he were to encounter friends of mine in distress."

Trent arranged rooms for them for the night in the Three Cranes, as everyone agreed that Abednego should not be moved until morning, and there was the matter of passes to be obtained from the governor. And Sarah still held out a faint hope that Mr. Cheap would return.

Her room at the Three Cranes was clean and private with a stout lock on the door, but she could not sleep that night, worried about what had become of Sparhawk and what Trent might expect from her in exchange for his kindness. But in the morning, seeing her father already much restored, she quelled her own misgivings about the sort of man who would invite a pickpocket into his home. If she had not spurned Micah's advances, their own home would still be standing.

A bright yellow carriage with black lacquer trim called for the Wards just after breakfast and carried them over the neck and through the gates of Boston, past the waiting carts and long line of supplicants from the countryside.

Their benefactor had rented a house on the Common that was almost as fine as the Rebel Hancock's abandoned mansion next door. Finer, in one sense, as the pretty white fence with its swags and urns was intact here, whereas Hancock's had been hacked to pieces by angry army officers returning from the fight at Lexington. Trent's home was three stories, brick, and elegantly trimmed in granite, with a marble entrance hall and double parlors on both sides, receiving rooms and bedrooms upstairs, and French wallpapers, English carpets, and silk drapes throughout.

Sarah's room was papered in pale blue and green stripes alternating with flowers on a cream background. It was carpeted in the same colors in a pattern of cascading cubes, and all the furnishings were upholstered in silk damask with cotton ticking covers for the sticky summer heat. There was a gilt mirror over the fireplace, and a washstand inlaid with yew and satinwood.

The ewer and bowl were Chinese brown glaze ware, like the teapot she had been forced to sell in Salem.

The view had no doubt been more pleasant when cows grazed the Common instead of Redcoats. Their tents stretched in long unbroken lines from the top of the hill down to the mudflats of the Back Bay. When Colonel Leslie's column of regulars had marched to Salem in search of Rebel arms last February, and turned back at the drawbridge after a long negotiation with the Reverend Bernard, she had fumed at the injustice. Now she thought Naumkeag might have had a narrow escape.

All of it — the carriage; the house; the peaceful, orderly soldiery — felt curiously unreal to Sarah. She had arrived after a sleepless night at the Three Cranes in a dreamlike stupor, and when she sat down upon the feather bed with its dimity curtains and canopy, her heartbeat slowed and her eyes fluttered shut; the next thing she knew it was evening and she had slept ten hours in her tattered clothes.

During that time a maid had come and gone, leaving water and soap for washing and a pile of clothing. The clothing turned out to be respectable, practical garments borrowed from one of the better servants.

There was a linen petticoat, tack-hemmed to about the right length, a pair of wool stockings, a linen chemise, and the roomy kind of jacket she often wore about the house, although hers, when they had money, had been cotton and silk. This was the homier sort of homespun, with an unfortunate accumulation of slubs in the weave at the elbows.

If Trent was fitting her out for seduction, he had prosaic taste indeed. She was both relieved and amused.

She went downstairs to discover her father in the parlor with Captain Trent replaying the battle of Quiberon Bay with the tea dishes. A night's rest and a decent meal had much restored him.

The housekeeper replaced the cakes and the tea periodically. In the afternoon, Trent took Ned to the Common to watch the army drill. Benji, she noted, was absent all day.

Mr. Cheap turned up just before supper with a cut lip. Sarah threw herself into the grizzled sailing master's arms and received one of the gruff bear hugs he had not dispensed since her childhood. Relief washed over her. If Mr. Cheap was back, perhaps Sparhawk would appear as well.

Trent endeared himself to Sarah by inviting Mr. Cheap to share brandy and tell his tale in the parlor.

The sailing master had offered his services unloading a boat of rice from the Carolinas. A press gang had swept the docks with a party of marines who meant business. No billy clubs or fisticuffs — they had taken him and thirty others at the points of their bayonets. He'd spent the night locked in a warehouse on the docks, but when the marines attempted to move the Americans to their boats, Cheap had instigated a general riot and escaped.

Trent promised Mr. Cheap papers of immunity from the press, thus rising a little higher in Sarah's estimation.

In the evening, a new servant appeared, a crisp cheerful woman not much older than Sarah, with a husband in the navy, and two children who went to her mother during the day so she could earn extra money. Prices were rising daily in the city. She straightened Sarah's room, carried water for Sarah's bath, and left an enormous parcel on the bed before disappearing to the kitchen.

The parcel on the bed did *not* contain sober respectable garments. There were two silk petticoats with tape waists, obviously from a mantua maker's ready — but very expensive — stock. They had been hemmed to match the length of the tattered garments in which she had arrived. There were two polonaise gowns in coordinating colors with laced fronts and pinned stomachers. They were slightly snug through the shoulders, breasts, and hips, but the silk had some give, and the gowns had obviously been constructed by an expert hand. And there were two pairs of silk shoes and a rainbow of clocked silk stockings.

Unless she wanted to wear the clothes on her back indefinitely, she must accept the gowns and the stockings and petticoats. She could not go down to dinner in her servant's linen jacket now without offending Trent. And she would not risk her father and Ned being turned out on the street. But as she drew the chemise over her head and felt the silk whisper over her body, she knew that she could not go to Sparhawk now, not dressed in finery provided by another man.

After dinner, Sarah cornered Benji in the little Chinese parlor with its pagoda-papered walls and fretwork sofas.

"The gifts worry me," she said.

"We arrived in rags. The man is widowed. And rich. He's a baron, actually — the arms on the carriage should have told us as much — though you are not to call Trent 'my lord.' Ansbach tells me that *Lord* Polkerris

223

does not like to be addressed as such. He gave Ned and Father new suits as well. It is generosity, nothing more."

Someone had given Benji new clothing as well. He wore an embroidered waistcoat trimmed in silver lace, and a diamond pin in the folds of his neck cloth. His knee buckles glittered with a fire that did not come from paste.

"Linen is generous," she said. "Silk is profligate."

"Linen is suitable for servants. Silk is suitable for a young lady. And *that* is what you are, Sarah."

She could not say, *Trent knows I am not; he saw me pick a man's pocket.* But she did say, "It is convenient for you, isn't it? To live under the roof of a naval captain who talks freely about the state of the squadron and its disposition. Do you write it all down in your little book?"

"Has Trent made any demands on you?" he asked, deflecting her question.

"No." But Trent had told her, sitting at that table at the Three Cranes, how easily he might have done it.

"Nor will he," said Benji. "Our English lord provided help for the widow's son. That means he is a Mason, Sally. And as such he will not seduce the wife, mother, sister, or

daughter of a Brother, which is what I am
— in this regard at least — to him. I am
sure you are quite safe from forcible seduction. Any other sort is entirely your own
lookout."

"It is the other sort that worries me."

"He bought you gowns and petticoats.
When he buys you gossamer night rails,"
Benji said, "that is when you may worry."

A week later they were still with Trent.
With his ship a hopeless wreck and no
prospect of a new one, he was put on half
pay and had the leisure to devote to enter-
taining the Ward family. In the mornings he
provided unflagging good company to her
father, with whom he shared a surprising
number of disreputable naval acquaintances.
At noon he tutored Ned in astronomy and
navigation. After lunch he took Sarah for
walks on the Common and through the
nicer parts of town.

It was difficult to keep her guard up
against him. They shared an interest in
geography and exploration, and he had
visited most of the ports that were technically closed to American ships. He brought
her to a mapmaker and to a shop that sold
instruments of navigation, and he bought
Ned a fine sextant, wood with brass fittings.
They spoke about hull design and those

American innovations the British Navy refused to adopt, the merits of pitch pine spars, and the British obsession with oak.

Benji came and went from Trent's house freely, dressed stylishly, and spent most nights out, always returning well after the curfew, often not until dawn. Sarah wrote to the landlady at the Three Cranes twice asking after Sparhawk, but received no reply. Benji's inquiries, made grudgingly at her insistence, yielded no word of the missing captain. Her brother urged her to forget about him, but she could not.

At the end of a month, Trent announced that he had gotten Ned a place aboard the *Preston,* Admiral Graves' flagship.

"It is not," Trent admitted, "an exciting post. The *Preston* is a floating office. She's too big to be of any real use in Boston Harbor. But your brother will learn gunnery and navigation and the traditions of the navy; and for the purposes of becoming a midshipman, it will count as time served at sea. Real time. Not 'false muster,' with his name entered on a ship he has never even seen from the dock. The practice, shamefully, is widespread, much to the detriment of the service. In any case, Ned will be close to home for the start of his career. I thought that should please you."

He told her this in the little Chinese parlor that looked out over the Back Bay.

"It is very generous of you," she said, "but Ned is an American, and he does not have the interest to make a career in the navy."

"It is true that peacetime promotion relies on patronage. Wartime, however, is another matter. And Ned will have my patronage," said Trent. "Before you protest, I will say that I have no one else to lavish it on. My son died when he was Ned's age. I have helped other promising young men, without debauching their sisters. And I like to think it balances somewhat the nepotism of Admiral Graves, whom I must call on tomorrow. Perhaps you and Ned would like to accompany me."

It was too generous an offer to refuse. Sarah knew they must accept it, for Ned's sake. She was coming to believe that Trent's kindness was genuine, or at least that if he intended to seduce her, he also intended to reward her for it. She wondered if barefoot Agnes Surriage had been similarly maneuvered into accepting the attentions of Harry Frankland, or if she had been the one doing the maneuvering. Had she welcomed his advances, or felt as Sarah did, guilty because she was pining for another man?

She and Ned did accompany Trent to the

admiral's flagship. Ned, naturally, was much taken with the *Preston* and the fanfare with which Trent was piped aboard, so different from the democratic workings of an American merchantman. The *Preston*'s first lieutenant welcomed them all very cordially, and no sooner did her brother express his admiration for the ship than a midshipman quite close to Ned's age appeared and offered to show him over the whole vessel.

Sarah and Trent were led to the wardroom. A few minutes later, Trent was called into the admiral's cabin. He left Sarah in the care of the first lieutenant, who made polite small talk with her about the navy and encouraging remarks on the prospects and training of young gentlemen on a fifty-gun man-of-war.

Trent had been closeted with the admiral for half an hour when a young man, fair-haired and lightly built, stormed through the wardroom, cursing with great vehemence but little imagination. Sarah's heart skipped a beat when she recognized him: Lieutenant Graves, from the *Wasp.*

The *Preston*'s first officer rose hastily to intercept him, and Sarah was thankful that his back was turned while she composed herself. Lieutenant Graves had not seen her face on the *Sally.* She was almost certain of it. But her hair was distinctive, and if he saw Ned, he might connect the two blond children of the *Charming Sally* with the Wards.

"You cannot go through," said the *Preston*'s first lieutenant to young Graves.

"You're a bloody officious toady, Jeffries," said Lieutenant Graves.

"There is a lady present," that officer replied icily.

Graves cast a contemptuous eye over Sarah Ward. She was ready for it. She smiled her best hen-witted lubberly smile, and attempted to look nothing like a woman who had spent most of her life on ships and among seamen — and nothing like a certain ship's boy.

She needn't have worried. Graves was wholly intent on gaining admission to see his uncle. "I won't stand for it," he said. "It is enough to vex any officer who cares at all for his character."

"Guarding the livestock on Noddle's Island is vital to provisioning the city," said Jeffries.

"Do I look like a swineherd?" asked Graves.

"I wouldn't care to comment," said Jeffries.

Before Graves could reply, Ned came flying into the room, vibrating with excitement, full of praise for the lofty heights of the fighting top — where one of the marine sergeants had shown him how to load and aim a musket in a stiff wind — and the staggering spread of canvas possible on a fifty-four.

Young Graves scowled. He did not like having his tantrum interrupted. Then he took a second look at Ned, furrowed his brow, cursed, and said, "That little brat is a fugitive from the press."

TWELVE

Sparhawk counted himself lucky. When the marines had turned him over to the guard at Castle William, the grim island fortress guarding Boston Harbor, he had feared being thrown in one of the cells beneath the thick stone walls. They were airless, windowless storage chambers for powder that a man might survive at the height of summer, but which would almost certainly prove deadly in the winter. Later he learned that such had been the admiral's orders. But the fort was under the control of the army and the military governor, and General Gage had anticipated Sparhawk's arrest.

On Gage's orders James was not placed under the authority of the castle's military commander, but in the charge of the fort major, a retired reverend and veteran of Louisbourg, who lived with his family in an apartment within the walls. Major John Phillips was the castle's former military commander and had been accustomed to an income of two hundred pounds per annum, plus twenty or thirty guineas a year in let-passes for the shipping, and of course bribes.

The major, it transpired, had been unjustly ejected from his post in '70, when he was in his sixth decade of life, and could not be expected to find new employment. Such was the ingratitude of the last governor, Hutchinson, that Phillips had been named fort major only after the most strenuous efforts of his friends. That he had been reduced to living on a mere hundred pounds per annum meant that he could not entertain James as befitted a king's officer, but that he was amenable to allowing the importation of any little luxuries that James might require, or the procuring of them, for a small commission.

James was given a room in one of the guardhouses in the yard, on a corridor occupied by a customs inspector and an agent for the East India Company tea, along with their families, who had fled Boston and the Rebel mob when the trouble started and still dared not go back for fear of their neighbors. This was another indicator that General Gage's hold upon the city was fragile indeed.

Sparhawk's chamber was sparsely furnished, but the tea agent's wife lent him
linen, and Lady Gage sent him a basket of
fresh food and other necessities, with her
compliments . . . and no doubt Dr. Warren's.

During the day Sparhawk had the freedom
of the yard. At night his door was locked —
a formality only. Castle Island was an
impossible three-mile swim to the mainland
through frigid water. Pressed sailors had
done as much to escape naval service, but a
man would have to be desperate to attempt
it.

And Sparhawk was not desperate — yet.
He had known the consequences of refusing Graves' orders: a trumped-up charge
and no doubt an unpleasant court-martial,
the threat of which was meant to bend him
to the admiral's will and induce him to burn
Charlestown.

He would not do it.

Graves could not prosecute him for failing
to obey an unlawful order, but such was the
wonder of the King's Rules and Admiralty
Instructions and the Articles of War that
just by carrying out his duties as an officer
with a modicum of common sense, he was
almost certainly guilty of something for
which he *could* be prosecuted.

Sparhawk's best hope was that his sin of

losing the *Sally* as a prize would be mitigated by his perspicacity in sending the French gold home to Boston, because there was nothing an Admiralty Court liked better than cold hard cash.

James had expected word of Sarah Ward from Gage's spy by the end of the first week, but had still heard nothing at the end of the second. It was possible that DeBerniere had been captured, of course, but Sparhawk expected that in such circumstances he would have heard from General Gage himself.

Graves could hold him for only so long without a trial. In the meantime, Sparhawk decided on optimism. He undertook to arrange his affairs to make room in his life for Sarah Ward and her family. The tea agent and the customs inspector still conducted business from their refuge, and a boat came every day to ferry their correspondence back and forth to the city. Sparhawk wrote to his man of business instructing him to find a house suitable for a family, with access, but not too close to, the waterfront. He directed that it be furnished and provided with at least a maid and a cook. That, on account of Abednego's least surprising confidence: *She cannot cook worth a damn, my Sarah, but she packs a sea chest tight as an oyster and stitches a sail something pretty. Talks French and Latin too, but that was her mother's doing.*

And Sparhawk took up the line of inquiry he had come to Massachusetts to pursue, and wrote letters attempting to ascertain the direction of the parson who had married his parents.

In the middle of Sparhawk's third week at the castle, without warning, the utterly forgettable DeBerniere appeared in Sparhawk's room, sitting in the chair by the table and amusing the customs inspector's children by sketching them and doing a very good impression of the sergeant drilling in the yard downstairs.

DeBerniere sent the children back to their mother, and Sparhawk spied the oilcloth package laid on his bed. He did not need to ask what it was. Red Abed's shark-tooth tassel peeked from the folds.

"You were not able to find them?" Sparhawk asked.

"I am so very sorry," said DeBerniere.

It was warm in the room, but Sparhawk felt suddenly very cold.

DeBerniere had traveled north up the coast on foot, stopping in all the port towns of Cape Ann. He had discovered the shipyards hard at work refitting American vessels "for defense." Recruiting for such rebellious enterprises was open in the waterfront taverns, more circumspect in the finer public houses where skippers were looking for skilled men such as doctors and carpenters.

DeBerniere had found the Ward place easily enough. The central chimney, with its curious hidden stair now exposed to view, was all that was left. Fire had consumed it and two other houses in the neighborhood on the night of the riot.

Four charred bodies had been discovered the next day.

DeBerniere described the scene with an artist's eye for detail, but in his mind Sparhawk did not see the smoking ruin of the Ward house. He saw Sarah standing on the deck of the *Sally* in that storm, smiling at him; and felt the sense of home and welcome she had kindled in him so briefly.

For a moment he could not draw breath; then the world came rushing back, and he realized DeBerniere was still speaking.

"A local feud," said the spy. "Some kind of long-simmering dispute over a schooner, I was given to understand. The kind of private murder that is so easily cloaked by a civil war. They did not want to talk about it in Salem, or in Marblehead." He produced two glasses and a bottle of something quite like whisky. "The schooner itself, naturally, has disappeared."

Sparhawk disliked whisky but drank it anyway. DeBerniere nodded toward the cutlass laid out on the bed and said, "What was he like? Red Abed?"

She was remarkable. Loyal and brave and beautiful as a ship under sail. We ran through moonlit gardens and defied an angry mob.

"I spent an afternoon with him," Sparhawk said. "He was old and frail, but he had forgotten more about the sea than I shall ever know."

And I will mourn his daughter all my days.

Ned, God bless him, put on his most convincing expression of innocent puzzlement, the one he used when the last of the cream had disappeared or when a book was left lying open on its spine or out in the rain. Sarah forced herself to laugh, to smile, to put a hand on Ned's shoulder, look young Graves in the eye, and say, "Don't tease him, Lieutenant. He has been threatening to run away and sign aboard a king's vessel as a common sailor if we do not let him go for a midshipman."

"He was the ship's boy that started all the trouble on the *Sally,*" insisted young Graves.

The door to the great cabin opened. A portly, jaundiced, and solemn man who had to be Admiral Samuel Graves emerged, with Trent at his shoulder. "What the devil is going on now, Francis?" the admiral demanded.

Young Graves could not contain his indignation. "That child should be in irons. He's a pirate."

"Francis," said the admiral in a warning voice.

"You must be mistaken," said Anthony Trent. "Edward is the son of a family friend and has been in school this past year."

Ned beamed. Another dubious demigod for his pantheon.

Young Graves took a second, less certain look at Ned. "Do you know that for a fact?"

"Have you some reason to doubt my word?" asked Trent, in the same polite, edged tone he had used in the Three Cranes. And Sarah had no doubt that now, as then, he knew that the Wards were liars.

"Of course he doesn't," said the admiral, whose own family was as much trouble. The Graves nephews were in another mess at the moment, with two of them embroiled in feuds with Boston merchants and one of them suspected of an illegal duel with a romantic rival. Graves himself was at odds with General Gage, their wives were not on speaking terms, and the admiral had antagonized more than one of the Loyalist merchants by seizing their cargo for naval use. Samuel Graves could not afford another affair of honor right now; certainly not a quarrel with one of his own officers; especially not a known duelist like Trent.

"It was an honest mistake, I am certain," offered Trent.

Francis Graves was hotheaded but not stupid. He saw his way out, and he took it. "As you say," he agreed. "A mistake. It was the uncommon hair," he added. Then he looked at Sarah. "Honey gold," he said. "The pair of you."

His eyes lingered, and she knew he was comparing her size and shape to that of the boy on the *Sally.*

Trent made their farewells and guided Sarah and Ned down the gangway.

When they reached their carriage, he put Ned up top with the coachman and closed the windows despite the heat, so that he and Sarah could be private.

"Now what was all that with the admiral's idiot nephew?" he asked.

There was nothing to be gained by concealing the truth from Trent, who had already embroiled himself in the matter, and

Ned was in too much danger.

"Lieutenant Graves was right," she said. "He did recognize Ned. He tried to press him earlier this summer. We were homeward bound on my father's ship when the *Wasp* overtook us. We were carrying French molasses, flint for ballast, and a chest of foreign gold. I took the captain of the *Wasp* hostage and traded the gold for our freedom. I am sorry, but Ned cannot serve aboard the *Preston.* If Lieutenant Graves questioned him closely, he would have the truth out of him."

She held her breath, waiting for his reaction.

Trent leaned forward. "Sarah," he said, "are you certain the gold was put aboard the *Wasp?*"

Considering that she had just confessed to an act of piracy, it was the last thing she had expected him to ask. "Yes."

"How?"

"I carried it." In answer to his raised brow, she said, "I was dressed as a ship's boy when we were boarded. Mr. Cheap thought it a wise precaution. Why do you ask?"

"Because the captain of the *Wasp* has been arrested and will shortly stand trial. He is accused of colluding with the American smugglers to steal the French gold. That is why Admiral Graves called me here today. He needs three captains willing to serve as judges. The story circulating is that this Sparhawk conspired with the Rebels to send a chest full of flint to Boston, then buried the treasure somewhere on Cape Ann."

"That is nonsense," said Sarah. "Captain Sparhawk was our prisoner. And if my family had stolen a chest of French gold, we would not have come to Boston on a fish cart. The gold was on the *Wasp*."

"I do not doubt it. In the last several months Admiral Graves has made a number of expensive purchases — including a vessel for one of his nephews to command — and carried out extensive repairs to the squadron. It is not unusual for an officer abroad to advance his own funds for such purposes, or if he does not have such sums, to use his own credit, in expectation of reimbursement. But there is always the danger that the Admiralty will disallow the expenses. Especially when there is an indication that they were undertaken less for the good of the service, and more for the advancement of a particular officer's career. In this case that of Thomas Graves, one of the admiral's nephews, who has received the *Diana*. The admiral has boasted that he bought her from a Marblehead merchant and that she is the largest schooner in the service — one hundred twenty tons. She has an unusually deep draft."

"She would," said Sarah, recognizing the characteristics. "She has a false bottom." In answer to Trent's questioning glance, she added, "She is not a Marblehead schooner. She is a Salem vessel." And Sarah knew whom Graves had bought her from.

"I bow to your knowledge," Trent said. "She certainly has distinctive lines. And she definitely cost more than the admiral could absorb himself, if, as seems almost certain, the Admiralty denies the expense. The *Diana* alone was seven hundred fifty pounds. Repairs to the squadron could have run several times that. If he undertook them on credit, the merchants will demand payment. If they make their case directly to the Navy Board, Graves will be ruined."

"You think he has taken the gold from the *Wasp* to cover these expenses."

"It seems quite likely. And Sparhawk, the unlucky bastard, will hang for it."

"No," Sarah said. "I can testify that I carried the gold aboard the *Wasp.*"

"And you would hang alongside him; he for gross theft and you for piracy. You cannot go anywhere near this thing, Sarah. And Ned must take his place aboard the *Pres-*

ton. He is old enough to learn discretion, and needs must. If he does not report for duty, Lieutenant Graves' suspicions will be confirmed. And you will be arrested."

He was right. She knew that. But it did not explain his behavior. "Why are you so willing to lie to protect us?" Sarah asked.

"I think you know the answer," said Trent.

She had suspected as much. She ought to be pleased and flattered. A month ago, she would have welcomed his interest. But now all she could think of was Sparhawk. "I am very grateful —"

"Now is not the time for me to make a proposal. You might accept out of a sense of obligation. And I have not yet had the opportunity to broach the topic with your father, though I believe the canny old sea dog suspects my intention. But I ask that you will consider that we might become more than good friends."

If she had never met Sparhawk, the answer would have been yes. But she *had* met him. James had done nothing to her and her family but that which his duty required. And he had gone beyond duty to rescue her brother. "This is my fault," she said. "Sparhawk would not be on trial if I hadn't kidnapped him."

Trent reached across the carriage and took

243

her hands. "Your sense of honor does you credit, but there is nothing you can do for him. This will not be a fair trial. If Admiral Graves means Sparhawk to be his scapegoat, then Sparhawk will hang. Graves has kept him at Castle William for weeks, with no outside contact. He will be transferred tomorrow to the *Hephaestion,* Charles Ansbach's frigate, to await trial, but it is already too late for him to prepare a defense. And there is no defense that would save him, because Samuel Graves *is* the Admiralty in North America."

Sparhawk's words on the *Sally* came back to her. *Dans ce pays-ci, il est bon de tuer de temps en temps un amiral pour encourager les autres.* "In this country," she said aloud, "it is a good thing to kill an admiral from time to time to encourage the others."

"I am sorry," replied Trent, "but it is true. He will go the way of Byng."

Thirteen

Sarah sat up waiting for Benji in the parlor of Trent's house, long after the clock in the hall had struck midnight and the household had all gone to bed. It gave her precious time alone to think.

A little after four she heard the brass key turn in the lock and her brother's heels upon the marble tile.

"Do not," she said, "go upstairs."

He stopped, turned, and padded lightly into the parlor, the pale blue silk of his coat and breeches shimmering in the candlelight. He wore knee bands embroidered with pink and yellow flowers, a waistcoat embellished likewise, and a diamond pin in the folds of his neck cloth. His cologne tonight was different, bergamot and bitter orange layered over his more familiar sandalwood.

"You knew," she said. "About Sparhawk."

Her brother took the seat opposite and crossed his legs. The diamond buckles on his shoes sparkled. They had not come from Trent.

"I only learned this week, when it was announced he would be transferred to Ansbach's ship, but Sparhawk's fate is none of our affair," he replied smoothly.

"The man saved Ned's life."

"And you repaid his bravery by returning him to his people. The matter must end there," said her brother. "Even if," he added, "you repaid him in other ways. If the man has any fondness for you whatsoever, he will agree with me."

"He probably *would* agree with you," Sarah replied. "That doesn't change his need of my help. He is in the dock because I put him there, and if he hangs, it will be my fault."

"No. It is Admiral Graves and a corrupt government that have fit Sparhawk for the noose. You cannot become involved in this affair, or you will incriminate yourself, Ned, and Father in a hanging matter."

She looked him straight in the eye and said, "You have already incriminated us in a hanging matter, Benji."

His golden brows, as pale as her own, shot up in disbelief. "Are you trying to blackmail me, sister mine?"

"Yes."

He laughed. When she didn't, he fell silent.

"Help me to save James Sparhawk," she said, "or I will tell Trent about the papers in your desk."

"My desk," he said, "is locked."

"Was locked," she corrected. She held up the set of thief's picks she had borrowed from Mr. Cheap.

"Of course," said her brother. "I had forgotten whom I was dealing with. Salem's own Anne Bonny. I suppose you have already enlisted Mr. Cheap in this escapade."

"And Father too," she said. "But we cannot do it without you."

The next morning, Sarah instructed Mr. Cheap to take her to the King's Head tavern in Cornhill. Benji had tried to talk her out of it. He'd unlocked his desk himself this time and showed her a half-finished mock-up of the "Bloody Butchery" broadside, the nameless black coffins marching across the top. It was all rhetoric, devoid of details, but the date in the corner told its tale.

"April eighteen," Benjamin Ward had said. "The day before the skirmish. This Angela Ferrers is no ordinary revolutionary," said her brother. "She is a Machiavelli, like Adams, and she gets people killed."

But Sarah was determined, so he had

drawn out another paper, an ink-stained map of Boston with a wordy advertisement for the King's Head, a public house that sold looking glasses, tea tables, china ware, English and Dutch toys for children, by wholesale or retail. Its location, only a block removed from the seat of the provincial government, the Town House, with its gilt lion and unicorn on top, was conveniently and prominently marked with a pointing hand.

The taproom of the King's Head was bright and modern, with tall windows and fashionable silk drapes. In the room behind the stairs Sarah found the promised mirrors, china, toys, and all manner of maps, prints, and engravings as well as carved and gilt frames and stacks of pamphlets and books. The pamphlets were tepid sermons, the toys had a dusty, disused look, and the chamber itself, positioned at the back of the building overlooking a small garden, well away from the bustle of the taproom, was hushed and quiet.

A bespectacled publican in an apron came and asked her if she wanted to purchase anything, and she replied that she had hoped there might be a lady who could help her. The barkeep considered a moment and decided that there might be a lady who could help her, if Sarah could be persuaded to wait. He offered to bring her a shrub. She asked for a glass of punch instead.

While she waited, she pretended to examine the maps for sale. She was alone for a few minutes before she detected it, a consistent thump beneath her feet. Sarah, born aboard a schooner, was used to feeling the motion of the *Sally* through her deck. But land, in her experience, tended to stay still.

She ventured into the hall where the vibration died entirely, lost in the competing clamor of pots and dishes and the liquid sounds of the taps and kettles. Back in the room it was unmistakable. It was not the clip-clop of a horse or beast of burden or the click-clack of shoes across tile, but the steady mechanical rhythm of a loom or saw, over and over again.

Curiosity drew her out the back door into a yard where a set of stone steps descended to batten cellar doors. Latched from the inside. It was the work of a moment to fish her whalebone busk out of her stays, slide it between the doors, and lift the latch.

The tannic smell of a printing press, of linseed oil and urine, met her on the threshold. A boy in an ink-stained leather vest was setting type while a black child stood by with leather swabs. Stacks and stacks of pamphlets, decidedly not for sale upstairs, *Letters from a Pennsylvania Farmer, The Rights of the Colonists,* and more of those "Bloody Butchery" broadsides, black coffins across the top, were piled on every available surface.

"Miss Ward."

Sarah turned. Angela Ferrers stood silhouetted in the doorway. Her Salem silks were gone. The dun-colored petticoat and jacket she wore, pinned over a homespun shift, would have attracted no attention at the market or in the tavern upstairs. A plain cap hid her hair. Even the rings on her fingers, genuine mementos, Sarah had somehow felt sure, were missing from her hands.

It was not a disguise so much as it was transubstantiation. Sarah was certain that Angela Ferrers knew how to set type as well as she had poured tea in Micah Wild's parlor; the way that Sarah knew both how to repair a torn sail and stitch an accomplished sampler. Abednego Ward's daughter moved in two worlds. Angela Ferrers, Sarah suspected, moved in many more.

"Unless you prefer being hanged for sedition to being hanged for piracy, we should speak upstairs," said the widow.

"Is it wise to operate a press so close to the Town House?" Sarah asked.

"It is not *wise* to operate a press anywhere, just now," replied Angela Ferrers. "But the noise is easier to conceal in a busy place than a quiet one."

Sarah followed her to a private parlor on the second floor. The older woman closed the door, then the shutters. In the resulting gloom she turned to face Sarah and said, "Now, what brings you to see me?"

"Admiral Graves has arrested James Sparhawk."

Angela Ferrers shrugged. "A rather predictable outcome. You did relieve him of his ship."

"I am responsible for his predicament, but he is not on trial for the loss of the *Wasp*." She related the story of Graves' appropriation of the gold.

"Where did you hear this?"

"From a credible source," Sarah hedged.

"You will have to do better than that."

"From Anthony Trent."

For the first time in their acquaintance the widow betrayed a flicker of surprise. It humanized her. "How do you know Trent — Lord Polkerris?" she asked.

"We are staying with him, in his house near the Common."

Angela Ferrers' manicured brows lifted fractionally. "Does Sparhawk know this?"

"No. I have not seen him since the night he left Salem."

"If you are determined to rescue Sparhawk, then I suggest you do not tell him of your connection with Polkerris. There is, I suspect, a rivalry there."

"Over a woman," Sarah guessed. She had no illusions about either man.

"In a sense, yes. Polkerris," she said, "is a powerful protector. A better catch than Sparhawk. You would do well to forget all about the young captain, and reel in the fish that you have. Landing him would make you a regular Lady Frankland. She went from a Marblehead tavern girl to baronet's wife. The leap is no greater from pirate captain's daughter to baroness."

"Thank you for the advice," Sarah said dryly. "But it is my fault that Sparhawk became embroiled in the affair of the gold. And it is my obligation to get him out of it. I need evidence against Admiral Graves, and I believe you can get it for me."

"I have a talent for obtaining such things," the widow admitted. "But this time, you will need better coin than sentiment."

"Information, you once told me, is currency," said Sarah. "I have found Micah Wild's missing schooner, the *Oliver Cromwell*."

■ ■ ■ ■

After spending a month at Castle William, Sparhawk was transferred to the *Hephaestion* and given to understand that his trial would take place within the week, two at the outside.

He was glad of it. When he had first arrived in Boston, the wild coast of New England had struck him dumb with its fierce beauty. The sight of her trim little schooners plying the choppy waters had stirred him. Like Sarah Ward. Now that she was gone, he could take no pleasure in any of it. He had not slept a night through since DeBerniere's visit, could not close his eyes without seeing the flames that had consumed the Ward house, and Sarah Ward with it.

Now he wanted only to be done with the admiral's trumped-up charges, and pursue some measure of justice against a villain as bad as or worse than Micah Wild. He did not think his fellow officers would deal too harshly with him because they might find themselves in the same position if they served any time on the blockade. He would receive a reprimand or be docked some pay, and then he would be returned to service or put on half pay and be free to find the parson who had married his parents. Once he had the man's sworn testimony, he would apply what interest he had and get himself recalled home to England, where he would place his evidence before the courts.

Aboard Charles Ansbach's frigate he was treated as a guest, not a prisoner, and allowed the freedom of the wardroom and assigned a cabin suitable for an officer. No doubt some poor lieutenant had been turned out of his quarters, but Sparhawk could not be sorry for it. There was precious little privacy to be had aboard a man-of-war, and he was wise enough to cherish it.

Ansbach's surgeon, a weathered but genteel Scott, examined Sparhawk's wrist and pronounced it healed, though he warned him that it might be weak and stiff for the first few days after the splint was off.

Time passed pleasantly aboard the frigate. Sparhawk had served with Ansbach in the Med and found him to be a capable fighting officer. He needn't have been. As Princess Caroline's royal by-blow, he might have risen on interest alone. Instead, he had carved out a reputation for himself as a fine sailor with a talent for gunnery. He had another sort of reputation as well, but it was the kind best politely ignored because of his exalted connections.

He invited Sparhawk to dine most nights, sometimes on his own, and other times in company with the ship's officers. He did not probe the subject of Sparhawk's melancholy, and for that James was grateful.

Initially, Sparhawk had been surprised to find Ansbach in Boston Harbor at all. "I heard you refused to serve in America," James said over the port the first night they dined alone.

Ansbach inclined his burnished head. He had the leonine mane of an Alexander, chestnut brown sun-shot with gold, and fine, classical features. "My uncle is sadly deluded about the situation in America. I refused to bolster his fantasies. The problem is not confined to Boston, and bottling up the harbor will not solve it."

His uncle was the king. And such, after three months' blockade duty and several weeks' imprisonment, was James' assessment as well. "But you came anyway," he observed.

"Just so," Ansbach replied. "I came anyway, because my uncle has lost faith in Admiral Graves and the First Lord of the Admiralty will not remove him. I am here to report on the admiral. Of course, Graves knows this, and so the only seaworthy frigate in his squadron" — he gestured at the graceful contours of his cabin — "is anchored off Castle William playing the role of prison hulk."

"It is an extraordinarily comfortable prison," said Sparhawk. "I thank you for it. I only wish I were better company."

"From what I have observed," replied Ansbach, "half the officers on the blockade have been court-martialed at one time or another. When they are not running aground on the blasted shoals of this miserable excuse for a harbor, they are running afoul of the locals, who beg for our protection in one breath and then complain of our presence in the next. I ask only that when it is my turn to play prisoner, you return the favor."

He would not be able to return the favor quite so lavishly. Sparhawk had made himself comfortably well off in the navy — capturing smugglers brought prize money, convoy duty the gifts of grateful merchants; transporting currency paid captains a generous percentage — but Ansbach was rich. He kept a fine table, and like many wealthy officers, he bought his own powder for gunnery practice to augment the Admiralty's stingy provision. Drilling the gun crews provided Sparhawk with a welcome daily distraction. In the afternoon the tea agent and the customs inspector had themselves rowed out from the castle to join him in the wardroom for cards.

The customs inspector, Sparhawk had long since discovered, cheated, but they played ombre for small stakes and the company prevented James from brooding, so he ignored this lapse in judgment.

The door opened and Ansbach's servant, Hobbs, put his head in. "Begging your pardon, gentlemen, but there is a lady to call on Captain Sparhawk."

The tea agent smirked. "Old One-Foot-in-the-Graves' would-be widow, I'll wager."

James did not find the gibe amusing. He regretted his affair with Graves' wife more than ever. He had no doubt it had played into the admiral's malice toward him. But Sparhawk, at least, had been discreet. That the tea agent knew of it indicated that *she* had not. "I am not receiving ladies."

Hobbs hesitated. "It is not *that* lady, sir."

Now the customs inspector, who had frowned at the tea agent's remark, turned toward the door with obvious interest. An admiral's wife was dangerous game, but opportunities for amorous sport were limited at the castle, and less politically risky ladies were always of interest.

"Then what lady is it?" Sparhawk asked. General Gage's American wife might just plausibly visit him, but he was not altogether certain it would be safe to receive her. She was playing a deep game, with her Rebel doctor friend.

"*Lady* was more in the way of a courtesy, sir. Or what I might call a euphemism. I think she's a trollop. But a fine, expensive one."

"Show her in," said the tea agent.

Hobbs looked to Sparhawk. He did not take orders from landsmen.

"Tell the *lady*," Sparhawk said, "that I have been losing to a certain gentleman" — he nodded at the customs inspector — "and as he is now in funds, he may be inclined to engage her if she will wait outside until we have finished our game."

Hobbs remained half inside the door, and now he abandoned discretion in favor of directness. "I would not have let her aboard, sir, but she said she knew you. That you had sent for her and would pay the boatman. A very dubious-looking character, if you don't mind my saying. He's still waiting. I did question the lady, sir, and she described you to a tee."

The customs inspector laughed. A clever trollop, at least. No doubt she had gotten his description from the landlady at the Three Cranes. Vexed but at last interested, Sparhawk threw down his cards.

"Show her in, then." It was either a joke played by some fellow officer, or a ploy by an enterprising harlot. He would soon see.

Ansbach's man disappeared. The game continued another hand. The customs inspector slipped a card up his sleeve, the door opened, and a breeze blew in, carrying with it the scent of ambergris and neroli. An expensive lady indeed. Nothing had stirred his carnal appetite since he had learned about the death of Sarah Ward, but this woman's perfume was calculated to arouse hunger.

Sparhawk's back was to the door, but he resisted the urge to turn and look. The tea agent, however, had an excellent view of their visitor. "Don't be shy, sweetheart," he coaxed.

Out of the corner of his eye Sparhawk saw the woman stiffen. Finally he turned to look at her. She was wearing a short red cape of watered silk with a wide, pleated hood that shadowed her face but fell open to reveal a tantalizing expanse of full breasts thrust high by expertly molded stays. Her gown was cream chintz trellised with roses and trimmed with box-cut ruching, hitched into a high polonaise that barely covered her calf. The entire effect was reminiscent of a sugared confection with a cherry on top.

She looked, in a word, delicious.

"Come here and show us your face," crooned the customs inspector, in a tone Sparhawk had never heard him use with his wife. The man patted his lap. The girl hung back. The customs agent leaned across the small room and reached for her.

The *Hephaestion* rolled with the onslaught of the evening tide. The woman stepped neatly around the table and out of range. It was a difficult maneuver in a tiny, crowded room on a pitching deck — executed with arresting balletic grace.

For an instant, Sparhawk's heart stopped. The gown might belong to any woman with money and a certain taste. The scent was expensive but hardly rare. The finely turned ankles would not be uncommon out in the country. The dramatic curves beneath the cape could belong to a countess or a courtesan.

But he had met only one woman who could move like that on a swaying ship.

The moment stretched. His mind, out of habit, denied the evidence of his eyes. For so many years he had held out hope that he would see his mother again, had fought a war within himself to deny fantasy and accept reality. A war that had been won before he ever saw his mother's grave. The impossibility of it had come to him in, of all places, Drury Lane. McKenzie had taken him to the theater to celebrate his promotion to the rank of lieutenant. The play, Steele's *Conscious Lovers,* had been amusing enough, if mawkishly sentimental, until the climactic scene when the heroine was reunited with her long-lost parent.

The falseness of it had struck him to the core. He'd vomited in the street afterward, sickened by his own weakness and gullibility. McKenzie had put it down to drink, but it was the spectacle of his most fervent desire turned into popular entertainment that had soured his stomach and made him see the truth: his mother was dead.

Not once since learning of Sarah Ward's death had he allowed himself to imagine her alive, to imagine such a moment as this.

He put down his cards. "I am afraid I must ask you to leave," he said.

"If you don't want her," the customs inspector said, "I'll take her."

"I do not think your wife would appreciate such a guest," Sparhawk said. "My apologies, but the game is over."

The merchants looked at each other, muttered something wry about sailors, time, and tide, and got out.

And Sparhawk was alone with Sarah Ward.

FOURTEEN

Sarah had not seen James Sparhawk for a month. He was more handsome than she remembered. But different. This was not the same man who had talked hulls and hawsers with her father in Salem, who had almost kissed her in an empty parlor and challenged Micah Wild.

This man was every inch the naval officer. His hair was combed and queued, his satin waistcoat smoothly pressed and pin neat, his linen snowy white, his shoes polished and buckles sparkling.

And he was staring at her with dangerous intensity. Instinct told her to defuse it.

"Your wrist has healed," she said.

"Yes, so it has. Coming here, like this," he said, his eyes raking her ensemble, "was risky and stupid. What if Hobbs hadn't shown you directly to the wardroom?"

So much for defusing the tension. "I'm dressed too expensively for an ordinary sailor to proposition," she said. She had faced down *Captain* James Sparhawk once before. She could do so again. Of course, she had been holding a pistol at the time.

"You are barely *dressed* at all. And for that reason — among others — some might not bother with a proposition."

"I told the captain's servant that you had sent for me."

"But I didn't. What if I hadn't admitted you?"

"The steward would describe me. Mr. Cheap said that after four weeks' confinement, you were unlikely to turn down a shapely trollop. It seems he was correct."

"No, he wasn't. I was going to give you — *her* — money to go away."

"Mr. Cheap suggested that would only happen if you'd found yourself a pretty wench among the crew's women." She'd seen them plying their trade between the gun carriages as Hobbs had led her through the main deck, most pleasant but plain, one of them winsome as a Fragonard, bent over a cannon and being tupped silly by a bellowing Yorkshireman. The earthy carnality of the scene had made her pause and flush.

"Mr. Cheap is no doubt an expert on trollops, but I did not engage one," Sparhawk said, closing the distance between them.

"Not even after I was told you were dead."

The door was already at her back. There was nowhere left to retreat. And suddenly she knew that coming herself had been a mistake, that she should have sent Benji, taken the risk that Sparhawk might not believe a stranger, because she did not have the power to resist this man.

Sparhawk touched her cheek with the hand he had broken saving her brother, trailed his fingers down her throat, between her half-bare breasts, to rest at the top of her stays. His expression was that of a man who had been in an open boat for a week: parched.

"My shade would have been touched by your forbearance," she said, removing his hand and taking a step to the side. "How is it that I am supposed to have perished?"

He did not pursue her, but his expression told her he was undeterred. "In a fire," he replied. "When I suspected I might be detained, I sent your father's pistols and his cutlass — along with money and a letter — north with one of Gage's *actual* spies. He went to your house, or what was left of it. I knew he had the right place when he described the hidden stair. That and the chimney were all that remained. There were bodies. I thought you all murdered."

Dan Ludd and his friends. She had not considered that their bodies might be mistaken for the Wards. Micah, of course, would know better. "I am sorry. I never intended you to think me dead. Wild did not want us selling the house to repay his loan, so he sent his creatures to burn it."

"And your father and Ned?"

"Safe," she said.

"Thank God. But, Sarah, that was a month ago. Why did you not write to me?"

"I only discovered your direction a few days ago, and by then, what I had to say could not be entrusted to a letter."

"If you had only waited a few more days, this blasted court-martial would be done with and we might have spoken on dry land. I have always intended to honor the offer I made you in Salem. I bought a house in the North End and put it in your name. There is room for Ned and your father. I am told it is a little old-fashioned but that it gets good light and is very snug."

She had indulged in a fantasy very like it on the road to Boston: a snug house, her father and Ned with her, Sparhawk a regular visitor. He would share their table and her bed. In Boston no one would know her. She would not be Abednego Ward's daughter, no better than she ought to be, or Micah

Wild's jilted lover. She would just be Sarah, and he would just be James, the two of them against the world.

It would never happen now.

"I have come to warn you," she said, the words sticking in her throat, "that your life is in danger. Your court-martial is set to be a farce. Admiral Graves stole the gold from the *Sally*. And he intends you to swing for it."

She had come to him like Cleopatra rolled in a rug, this pirate's daughter with the dead-shot aim, a heroine out of schoolboy fantasies. Before DeBerniere's news, he had imagined her in his arms, in his bed, on dry land, a world removed from the dreary confines of Castle William, the martial routine of the *Hephaestion,* and the petty malice of Admiral Graves.

Her words were difficult to fathom. He felt them sink in at last, like a mast being stepped into place. "Tell me."

"The admiral wrote to the First Lord asking for money. He did not hear back, but he was certain, given the circumstances, that he would receive funds, so he purchased two new ships for the squadron, and commissioned repairs for the worst vessels in his fleet. And borrowed the French gold to do it. He thought he would be able to pay it back before anyone noticed it was gone."

"But the Admiralty did not accommodate him," Sparhawk guessed.

"No. The king has been disappointed with Graves. The First Lord does not want to replace him — that would be admitting he chose the wrong man for the job — but he cannot justify sending the admiral funds, which critics would view as reward for his failures. And it is too great a sum for the admiral to make up out of his own pocket."

"It is gross theft," said Sparhawk. "The kind the service does not take lightly. A share of that gold was owed every man on the *Wasp*. But how, exactly, does this touch on my affairs?"

"Admiral Graves and his nephew claim that the chest you sent to Boston on the *Wasp* was filled with flint, and that you conspired with the American smugglers to steal the gold and bury it on Cape Ann."

It was, if you knew the facts, absurd. If you didn't, it would be all too plausible, a tale worth telling — complete with buried treasure. Boston's North Shore had been the haunt of pirates for a hundred years, almost every inlet and harbor a supposed hiding place for their loot. Blackbeard's silver was rumored to be buried somewhere in the Isles of Shoals; the hoard of Quelch in a cave at Marblehead; that of Veal in the Lynn Woods. The American Main was the stuff of pirate legend.

"What of witnesses?' he asked.

"Your first officer, the admiral's nephew, naturally. And the marines from the *Wasp.* Bribed, of course."

"And these American smugglers? Are they named?" If they were, Sarah and Ned would also be in danger.

"No," she said. "But we are suspected. A friend of the family found Ned a place as a young gentleman aboard the *Preston*. The gesture was well meant, but it has proved disastrous. Francis Graves recognized him. I cannot testify to the real events on the *Sally,* or I will implicate my brother and myself in resisting the press and the kidnapping of a British officer. In piracy. But I can help you escape."

He was touched. She had been brave just to come warn him. But escape was impossible. "I think you will find the *Hephaestion* more difficult to carry than the *Wasp,*" he said gently.

"No doubt. That is why I have enlisted help."

She was serious. "What kind of help?"

"My brother Benji."

"The same brother who left you and your family to the tender mercies of Micah Wild?"

"He doesn't much like what he has heard about you either."

"Escaping from an armed frigate is no frivolous caper."

"My brother is not a frivolous man." The hollow note in her voice told him not to press for details.

"If I flee," he said, "it will be taken as proof of my guilt."

"If you don't, you will hang from the *Preston*'s yardarm. Your judges have been chosen to deliver the verdict Graves desires. But the admiral is not without vulnerabilities. He has bought ships, cannon, shot, cordage, clews, hawsers, and spars. There are receipts, ledgers, and witnesses who can reveal the admiral's dealings and the scope of the 'personal' funds used in payment. But you cannot prove your innocence from the grave."

"I won't be able to prove my innocence at all. I will be a fugitive hunted by the law."

"Fugitives are notoriously difficult to track in America. The law never caught up with Whalley and Goffe. They died of old age."

"That was a hundred years ago," replied Sparhawk. "And the regicides of Charles the First were aided and abetted by a roundhead populace."

"You will find local sentiment little changed today. The lady who enabled your flight from Salem and her friends have gathered enough evidence to vindicate you. They will see that you reach London with the papers."

Sparhawk had suspicions of his own as to who that lady might have been. She was not someone who gave her help — or her other favors — for free. "And what do this lady and her friends want in return?" he asked.

"The *Sally*," said Sarah Ward, looking him straight in the eye. "For a powder run to Spain. Under the command of my brother. That is the price of their aid. He will land you on the English coast with money and the papers. I can get you off the *Hephaestion*, but I could not lay hands on the evidence needed to prove your innocence, and I could not get you all the way to England. So I made a bargain with the Rebels. You must decide if you can live with the terms. I have already made my choice."

If the elegant lady of Salem was in fact the Merry Widow, the agent who sometimes worked for France and sometimes for Spain and always against British interests, Sparhawk had no doubt she could lay hands on the evidence to clear him. And that she would require more than just a run to Spain with the *Sally* in return.

Sarah Ward was willing to tangle with forces like this for him.

"I wondered," he said, "after I left Salem, if you felt as I did. Or if you would wake the next morning and decide that our attraction had been a hothouse flower watered by proximity and danger." He took a step closer. "But you are here, now, when you could have stayed out of it."

"You saved Ned, and you stood up to Micah," she replied. "Honor demanded I come."

"Merely honor?"

"If you were hoping for more, I am sorry. The last time I made such a declaration to a man, I regretted it."

"But you don't deny that there is something between us."

"No, I don't deny it."

"Then come back to my cabin with me now."

He was so near she had to tilt her head back to look up into his pale blue eyes, and she was struck once more by his beauty — and how very much she wanted him.

"This isn't the time," she said.

"If anything goes wrong with your plan," he countered, "it may be all we have."

"I thought the prospect of hanging was supposed to concentrate the mind."

"In the navy, they shoot officers. It is pirates and common sailors they hang. But the effect is the same. It concentrates the mind on the advantages of feeling alive."

He leaned closer, and she felt his pull like a compass needle.

"I can't go to bed with you."

"The bed is rather cramped." He placed a hand lightly on her waist, tugged her closer. "I was intending to bend you over it."

She flushed, her mind returning to the pretty Fragonard strumpet. She tried to banish the image, to rein in her racing pulse and speeding breath.

"You want to," he said.

"I want to, but I can't."

"I will be careful," he said. "I will pull out." And the image *that* conjured, of Sparhawk rearing back from her, rampant, was almost enough to undo her resolve.

She shook her head to clear it. "It isn't that."

"What, then?"

"Please let me go."

He did. Because he was nothing like Micah Wild. Then he retreated to the other side of the room, because he was enough like her former fiancé that he did not trust himself within reach of her.

"Was it so bad with Wild?" Sparhawk asked, shoulders flush with the paneled wall, his body taut as a bowstring.

"It's not that either." Although she might have been better off if it had been awful, if her night with Wild had quelled her ability to feel passion. Then she might not have been so susceptible to Sparhawk. "It is only my pride that Micah misused. I know it can be good."

He cocked his head. A slow smile spread over his face. "And how, exactly, Miss Ward, do you know that?"

"I am surprised a notorious rake cannot work that out for himself."

He laughed. "We will take the question as asked and answered, then. But perhaps a rake knows something you don't. It's even better if I do it for you. With my hands," he said, pushing himself away from the wall and prowling toward her, "if time is short, or with my mouth, if we have the leisure to explore each other."

The thought made her pulse speed. She sidestepped him once more, but he tacked and followed her new direction, until she put her hands out. "I cannot . . . ," she said with a sigh, the euphemism bathetic but apt, "give you my ration of grog. I have a suitor."

He checked his advance. "Ah. Your sense of honor again. Is it truly a greater betrayal of your suitor to lie with me than to save my life?"

She had known this would not be easy, but she had not suspected how hard it would really be. "I have already betrayed this man with you a hundred times in the privacy of my own mind."

"And was it any good?" he asked, a mischievous glint in his eye.

"It was very good," she said baldly, though she had not imagined the things he might do with his hands. Or his mouth. And she was doomed to think of them now. "And that is why it would be a very bad idea to make fantasy into reality."

"Unless reality failed to live up to fantasy. I suppose I could promise to disappoint you."

"As a seduction technique, that leaves something to be desired."

"My apologies. Even I have limited experience wooing lady pirates. Why don't you tell me what would please you?"

Your hands, your mouth, your well-made body, covering mine. The snug little house, and sometimes, a place at your side on board ship, like Abigail and Abednego.

Impossible, all of it.

"Be ready tomorrow night a quarter of an hour before the watch changes, and follow Mr. Cheap's sage advice for such situations. Run, and don't look back."

FIFTEEN

Sparhawk had awakened to find a marine guarding his door. That was new.

And inconvenient.

The day passed more quickly than any since his arrest. He was not invited to practice with the gun crews, but instead sat listening to the familiar rhythms, the bells and watches and work songs that had replaced hearth and home and been his whole world for fifteen years.

He was not allowed to join Ansbach and his officers for dinner. Ansbach himself appeared a little after the meal hour, equal parts apologetic and angry.

"It is an insult," said Ansbach, "and Graves knows it. To send his marines aboard my ship. To suggest that we cannot guard one prisoner, who is in any case a gentleman, and only under the most nominal arrest. I must warn you not to stir from your cabin. They have been given orders to shoot you upon sight, as though you are a common criminal."

His arrest was not as nominal as all that, Sparhawk now knew. He hoped that the guard was only a precaution on Graves' part, and not a response to Sarah's visit. If anyone knew of their meeting, she and Ned would be in even greater danger.

And Sparhawk was both more and less than the gentleman Ansbach imagined him. He accepted Ansbach's apology, and felt ashamed.

After Sarah's visit the previous night, he had been invited to a particularly fine dinner with Ansbach and his officers. There had been fiddle music during the meal and a bottle of port later, but he had eaten with treachery in his heart. The men of the *Hephaestion* had included him in their good fellowship, and now he was planning to break his parole to participate in an escape that might bring disgrace to their ship.

Confined all day to his cabin, Sparhawk could not stop thinking about Sarah Ward. She had risked a great deal to warn him, and she was risking more to help him escape. He should not presume upon it. She had a suitor, a man who could offer her marriage and repair the damage Micah Wild had done to her reputation and her amour propre.

He ought to leave her alone.

He could not pretend that he was rescuing her from Micah Wild, not if another man was offering her the far more permanent protection of marriage. But Sparhawk still wanted her. And his desire for her he recognized as entirely selfish. No matter that his feelings for her were more than simple lust, that they included tenderness and a regard for her family, a desire to be part of that roguish Ward clan. Pursuing her now would make him no better than his father.

Something struck his door and slid down it, interrupting his thoughts.

The latch rose. The door swung open. The man who entered was almost Sparhawk's height. He had Sarah's gilded hair and he might have had her delicate coloring, but his skin was deeply tanned and any freckles he had were obscured. He was dressed in somber dark colors from shoes to collar, but his coat had the subtle sheen of silk and his tailor had been gifted with genius.

With a nod at the unconscious marine on the floor without, Benjamin Ward said, "Is he the only guard?"

"No. And the watch is about to change."

Ward dragged the marine inside the cabin.

"Come quickly, then."

Sparhawk turned to get his bag.

"Leave it. The less you carry," his rescuer said, "the faster we move."

"It is your father's pistols, and his cutlass." The copper velvet coat was packed as well. No one had asked for it back, but Sparhawk had kept it all the same.

Ward stopped him on the threshold. "I know what you did for Ned and my sister while I was gone, and I am suitably grateful, but I am home now. Sarah has already suffered at the hands of one rake. I cannot kill Wild for her, because despite all that the man has done, he is married to the dear friend of her childhood and she forbids it, but if you toy with her affections, I *will* kill you."

"Mr. Cheap said much the same thing when we met."

Ward flashed him a crooked smile he must have learned at the knee of Lucas Cheap and said, "Well, you're still alive, so that is a point in your favor."

They crossed the main deck and reached the ladders without attracting attention, though it was impossible to do so without being seen. But common sailors at their duties were not obliged to worry about the comings and goings of gentlemen. Sparhawk and Ward climbed on the deck to find night fallen, and a voice boomed, "You there!"

Sparhawk turned. It was one of Graves' marines.

"This way," said Ward.

They ran. Sarah's brother indicated a point on the rail where a line had been rigged.

Sparhawk grabbed the rope and climbed over the side. Ward was right behind him. Then a cultured voice Sparhawk recognized cried out from the darkness in surprise and alarm. "Benji!"

Ward turned. Sparhawk spied two of the admiral's marines in the forecastle. Moonlight glimmered off their musket barrels. Sparhawk saw the flash, heard the shot ring out.

Sarah's brother staggered, pitched back, and fell over the rail.

Sparhawk caught him — just. For a moment they hung like that, Sparhawk clasping the rope with one hand, and gripping Benjamin Ward's silk collar with the other. Then Ward grasped the rope, and the strain across Sparhawk's shoulders eased.

"Go," Sparhawk said. "I'll follow you down."

James took one last look at the *Hephaestion*'s deck, where Charles Ansbach, his face a mask of horror, was ordering the admiral's unwelcome marines to stand down. Then Sparhawk followed Ward down the rope to the waiting boat.

"We must row smartly," said Ward, tight-lipped. "I cut away their boats, but they can still fire upon us." He could not contain a hiss of pain as he reached for the muffled oars.

Sarah had been right. Her brother was indeed a capable man. Cutting away the *Hephaestion*'s boats was the first thing Sparhawk would have done. And Ward had disabled the guard with ruthless effective-ness. He had not, unfortunately, foreseen that Admiral Graves might send a detail of his own marines aboard the *Hephaestion.*

"Put pressure on the wound," said Spar-hawk. "And let me row. Ansbach will hold off pursuit."

"A friend of yours, is he?"

Loyalty, it seemed, was a Ward family trait, but the truth had been plain to see on Ans-bach's face. "I suppose, but that hardly signifies," Sparhawk said. "He's your lover."

Ward paled. Canny old Abednego. He had sent his son to London in the hopes that he would "outgrow" it. Perhaps he was not so canny as all that after all.

"You have insulted me, sir," said Ward,

jaw clenched. "And I will meet you to settle the matter as soon as I am able."

"I am not interested in your affairs, or Ansbach's for that matter, except where they touch upon my own. In this case I must ask you, are you on such terms that he will further delay pursuit?"

Ward looked right and left, as though there might be someone to overhear him in Boston Harbor. Sparhawk pitied him. He knew what it was to hide one's true self; he had probably been doing it for as long as Ward. Caution was a necessary habit. Finally Ward said, "There will be no pursuit. Though there is likely to be a reckoning."

"Ansbach did not know of your plan?"

"Of course not. He is the king's nephew. Asking him to aid in your escape would have placed him in an impossible position. It's bad enough that I have sided with the Rebel cause."

"You would take their part, even after what Wild did to your sister?"

"I am a Ward. I will always put my family and the Sallys first, just as Sarah does. That is why I have taken the American side: I want Ned and Sarah to enjoy the rights of Englishmen, to live without the fear of search and seizure and arbitrary arrest, and the violence of press gangs. The cause is bigger than the failings of the men who lead it. Now we must row for the creek. The *Sally* is hidden behind Noddle's Island. The navy does not patrol the channel because it is so shallow, but she will be stranded if we do not make the tide, and we must reach the meetinghouse in Chelsea before daybreak to collect the evidence the Rebels have assembled for you."

This last was said in a quiet, tight voice that worried Sparhawk. "Did the ball pass through, or is it lodged in the wound?"

"It is lodged within."

Sparhawk looked out at the dark water and the freedom that beckoned. Ansbach might be able to hold back the marines on his own ship, but eventually he would have to report Sparhawk's escape to the castle. In a few hours, Boston would be crawling with searchers. To enter Boston now would be to risk capture, and the outcome of his trial now that he had fled was certain to be execution. He could not have made it easier for Admiral Graves to condemn him.

"I don't suppose you have a surgeon on the *Sally*?" Sparhawk said.

"Mr. Cheap is handy with a needle."

A needle would not serve. The ball must come out. And preferably on land. Extractions were tricky to perform at sea. A man did not want a surgeon poking about in his guts on a moving ship.

And this man was Sarah's brother. She had sent Benji into danger, for him.

Sparhawk turned the boat toward the nearing docks. "We row to Boston."

"I promised my sister I would get you away."

"Loyalty is an admirable Ward family trait," Sparhawk observed. "But I daresay she did not expect you to do so at the cost of your life. You are bleeding profusely. We need a surgeon." He set a brisk pace at the oars.

"If we are discovered in Boston, they will hang you as a deserter, trial be damned. And you will never find a doctor in the city willing to call upon a fugitive and a Rebel."

"More likely they will shoot me, but I think I would prefer the firing squad to facing your sister if you expired. And I believe I know a doctor who owes me a favor," said Sparhawk.

"The risk is too great. Row for the *Sally,*" insisted Ward.

Sparhawk shipped his oars, and the boat drifted. "You do it," he said.

Ward gamely reached for an oar, cursed, and slumped over the bench.

"I thought not," Sparhawk said, taking up

the oars once again.

"If you had any prospects at all," Benji gasped, "I should say you and my sister deserved each other."

"My prospects may not be all so grim if I can prove my case against the admiral," Sparhawk said.

"If you live that long," said Ward. "Those marines were not firing warning shots."

Sparhawk had thought of that. There was a more expedient — though riskier — method for silencing him than a trial. Shot — trying to escape. Since Sarah's visit, he had kept the pistol loaded and the cutlass handy. "You think Admiral Graves would prefer me safely dead to tried?" asked Sparhawk.

"I think you are lucky to count my sister and Mr. Cheap your friends."

Sparhawk docked the boat in pitch-blackness at one of the little wharves in the North End. A single skiff more or less would not be noticed in such a jumble of small craft. Ward had been quiet and contained for some time, and he leaned heavily on Sparhawk as they made their way in silence up the quay.

Sparhawk had never seen the little house he had purchased, but his man of business had sent him the keys and a goodly description. He need only find a three-story dwelling, green, with two dormers, on an alley, in the dark, while dodging the city watch and the Redcoats who vied with them for authority over the townspeople. This, when supporting an injured man roughly his own size and weight.

His man of business had further informed him that the North End was a nest of wickedness and sedition, inhabited by Rebels and smugglers; but it was also a neighborhood of sailors and carpenters and caulkers, and Sparhawk had thought the Wards would feel at home there. Certainly tonight the choice was proving fortuitous. The North End was one of the oldest parts of the city, a warren of twisting streets, blind alleys, and overhanging second stories that cast deep shadows.

The house, when they found it, was one of those peculiar, narrow gambrel-roofed structures built side to the street. Sparhawk opened the gate as quietly as possible, and discovered an empty garden plot, freshly tilled, with the rich, earthy smell of loam, and a neat classical façade. The brass key turned smoothly in the lock, and at last they were inside and, for the moment, safe.

He had asked his man to engage a cook and a maid and see that all the little details that would please a young lady were attended to. In the moonlight that filtered through the transom, he could see that the floor in the hall was brightly painted and cheerful, and if the furnishings were somewhat out-of-date, with their turned legs and exuberant Tudor carving, the upholstery was good new Russia leather and the cushions were fine — if mismatched — damask silk.

The pine floor in the parlor had been spread with sand and brushed into a zigzag pattern. He spoiled it now by half carrying, half dragging Ward to the daybed beneath the window.

"Dare I ask who owns this place?"

"I bought it for your sister," said Sparhawk.

"Then you'd do best to let me bleed out on the floor, for I shall never let her occupy it."

"For the children of a freebooter, you are both shockingly inflexible. I was going to take care of her generously."

"But without name, or honor."

"Hold that unflattering thought," said Sparhawk, "while I send for a doctor. I fear if you go on, I will take you up on your offer of martyrdom."

On the other side of the staircase Sparhawk found another parlor, fitted up as a dining room with a plank table, high-backed chairs, and a menacing sideboard on bulbous legs. Beyond that was a narrow service ell. He discovered the cook, a neat but plain middle-aged woman, asleep in a chamber at the back of the house, and her ten-year-old son on a trundle beside her.

The child seemed bright enough and the mother sensible, so he made the boy commit two messages to memory. The first was for Lady Gage at Province House; the second was for Sarah Ward, whose direction he received from her brother.

Sparhawk was determined to find a doctor for Benji, but a belly wound was always serious, and if things turned for the worse, Sarah must be there. Sparhawk's mother had died friendless on a dirt floor. Such a fate, he believed, was no better on a silk cushion.

He sent the boy into the night, found a bottle of rum and two glasses in the well-stocked kitchen, and returned to find Ward sitting up. James handed Sarah's brother a glass. "You'd best drink," he offered. "It's never pleasant, letting the sawbones fish for lead in your belly."

Ward did not reach for the glass. "I want you to understand that I am not a moralist or a prude. I know my sister is partial to you. And you might make her happy for a while. But Micah Wild's betrayal left a mark on her. I don't mean the gossip. She doubts her own worth. Your esteem is not enough to restore her. Nothing less than a man's name and fortune will make her whole."

"I did not offer your sister my protection because I think her unworthy of my name. Quite the opposite. If I were free to consider marriage, I would, but I am not."

And he told him. The whole story. The things he had not told Sarah Ward. About what Slough had done to him on the *Scylla*. How he had fought the first time and then, when Slough ordered him tied to the gratings and lashed, discovered that he preferred being defiled to being beaten. How someone at the jail on Nevis had been paid to pour lye down his mother's throat so she could never tell her tale, and then sold her into indentured servitude on a plantation where she had died of overwork and starvation.

Sparhawk told him everything, because he was privy to this man's secret, and Ward had risked his life for him.

"My father is a ruthless man. You must see that once I step forward with proof of my identity, any woman tied to me by marriage would be a threat to him. And he would deal with such a threat as he has in the past — ruthlessly."

"All the more reason," said Benjamin Ward, "that if you truly care for my sister, you will leave her alone. You and I have only just met, and here I lie waiting for the sawbones with a ball in my belly."

He was right. Sparhawk's encounters with the Ward family had not been to their benefit. He had destroyed their hopes of escaping poverty, driven Sarah to an act that could get her hanged as a pirate, and nearly seen Ned drowned.

Ward finally reached for the glass at his side. "Sarah cannot leave the safety of Boston because of Micah Wild. He has made it known that the *Sally* is his property, and Sarah along with her. Admiral Graves suspects her of piracy. I am suspected of treason. General Gage may have me taken up at any time. My sister needs a protector here, who can shield her if I am arrested. She forbade me to speak of it to you, but it is no secret that she is about to receive a very good offer. From a man of property and standing, who is a friend of government. You should encourage her to forget about you, and take it."

"She is only helping me to satisfy her overdeveloped Ward sense of honor," said

291

Sparhawk, remembering her rebuff on the *Hephaestion.*

"If you believe that, you are a fool. Honor demanded we help you escape. It did not demand we bargain with the Rebels for proof of your innocence. A month ago my sister vowed the *Sally* would carry no more contraband. Now she directs me to pick up a cargo of Spanish gold for the Merry Widow, a very dangerous woman. Sarah would be safely betrothed, she and Ned secure and beyond the reach of Admiral Graves now, if she did not hold out some hope of you."

"In a few days' time," Sparhawk said, "the point will be moot. We will sail for England, and it is unlikely that I will return to America. If I survive Graves and the Admiralty Court, I will have my father and a case in Parliament to contend with."

"Then tell her," said Benji. "Tell Sarah you are leaving and you are not coming back. That there is no future to be had with you, so she can accept the one waiting for her."

Sparhawk could imagine a great many things with Sarah Ward, but delivering such a speech was not one of them. Still, he resolved that he would do it, tell her that tonight's meeting would be their last.

The boy returned from his errand a few minutes later and reported to Sparhawk.

His trip to Province House with its marble floors, silk-hung rooms, and haughty servants had been daunting, but he had persevered. "I spoke to the lady alone, as you told me, and to no one else. She said she would relay the message to the gentleman, but that she did not know if he would come."

It was the best he could hope for under the circumstances.

"And the other lady?" asked Sparhawk. "What did she say?"

"She said a word I'm not allowed to use."

Benjamin Ward laughed, then groaned in pain. "At least you can be certain he spoke to my sister."

James gave the child a coin and sent him back to his mother.

An hour later, Sparhawk answered a soft tap on the door and admitted a man who should not have been in Boston at all. Joseph Warren was dressed far less flamboyantly than when he had visited Sparhawk a month ago at the Golden Ball. Tonight he could pass for a mechanic in plain brown breeches and an old leather waistcoat.

"I learned of your predicament a few days ago," said Warren, "and hoped that you might call on me."

"In truth," replied Sparhawk, "it is the physician I sent for, not the Rebel."

Warren gave a wry smile. "My colleagues in Congress do the same. When I have completed my errand of mercy, though, will you hear me out?"

Sparhawk agreed and led Warren into the parlor.

Benjamin Ward took one look at the newcomer and cursed. "Dr. Warren should not be in Boston. The army will hang him if they find him here."

"Then they had best not find me," said Warren pleasantly. "Close the shutters, please, and muffle the cracks with cloth. Then bring me a light. Spermaceti for preference."

It was, as Sparhawk had foretold, an unpleasant business, but Ward was almost silent throughout, save for the moment Warren plucked the ball free with a distinctly liquid sound.

"There," he said with satisfaction, dropping the gory bullet into Ward's hand. "A token of King George's affection."

Ward rolled the bloody slug around in his palm. "I was there at the meetinghouse in March when you gave the Massacre Day oration," Ward said, taking a deep swig from the rum bottle as Warren began to sew the wound closed. "I saw that fusilier captain in the first row reach up and offer you a handful of bullets."

That was a part of the story that Sparhawk had not heard. It was the clearest message that if — *when* — fighting broke out in earnest, Warren would not be treated as an honorable enemy. Benji was right. The doctor was mad to be in Boston. But it was the madness of Edward Hawke and Francis Drake, and Sparhawk could not help but like the man for it.

Warren tied off his neat line of stitches. "The British think we will not fight," he said. "That we are bumpkins and cowards. But I mean to return the fusilier's favors, by and by."

A little while later, in the old-fashioned dining room with its elaborate sideboard and conspicuous Bible box, Sparhawk listened to the Rebel doctor's offer.

"The Provincial Congress will pay you handsomely for intelligence about the disposition of the squadron, the draft, armaments, and manpower of the ships stationed in the harbor, and Graves' immediate plans." Warren named a large sum. "More, if you will accept a commission. There is also the promise of an excellent farm in

Cambridge, with a fine house."

"Confiscated from a Loyalist, I presume."

"A regrettable necessity," said Warren. "It is not possible to leave strategically situated land in the hands of the friends of government."

No doubt Micah Wild had justified the burning of the Ward home in much the same way, and Henry Tudor the dissolution of the monasteries. "That is a very martial proposal from a physician," Sparhawk observed.

"The day is coming when the only way to save American lives will be to take British ones. Some will see it as a betrayal of my Hippocratic oath, but I mean to trade my scalpel for a sword."

Like the farmers and farriers and innkeepers on the road to Boston; the caulkers and shipwrights in Salem; and the maddening, beguiling Sarah Ward. Every effort the Crown made to force obedience pushed another American into open rebellion.

"If I aided or joined your cause," Sparhawk said, "it would be taken as proof of my guilt. And I do not relish the thought of spending the rest of my days as a wanted criminal."

"Do you really believe that Graves will allow you to walk into the Admiralty and present your evidence?"

Sparhawk didn't. If he had truly been a Shropshire gentleman's son making a naval career, his chances of reaching the marble steps of the Admiralty building alive would have been poor. But he had survived Slough and the docks of Calcutta and half a dozen other port towns that were as bad or worse. He knew when he was being followed, and could defend himself against an attacker.

"The *Sally* is fast," said Sparhawk. "Barring misfortune, we should reach London ahead of any pursuit." And he had other matters to attend to in England: his father, his inheritance, a measure of justice at last for his mother.

Warren got up from the table and walked into the hall. He closed the door to the little parlor where Benjamin Ward lay sleeping off the effects of rum and surgery, then returned to the dining room and closed that door as well.

"At the risk of being indelicate," Warren said, "I was given to understand that you were connected to an American lady. She has risked a great deal to free you. For her part in this affair, Graves could hang her. I confess that your desire to leave surprises me. You do not strike me as a man who uses women callously. Does the lady's danger mean nothing to you?"

He was speaking of Sarah Ward and the deal she had struck with the Rebels for the evidence to free him.

"It means a great deal to me," replied Sparhawk. "And that is why I am parting with her. Because our connection has brought her nothing but misfortune, and to continue it would only place her in greater peril."

Warren gave him a wry smile. "When a man says that he is parting with a lady for her own good, it is often self-serving, and yet it is almost always true."

"In this case," said Sparhawk, "to remain with her would be the selfish choice. And she has better defenders than I to keep her safe from the admiral." Lucas Cheap and Benjamin Ward would see that no harm came to Sarah Ward. Sparhawk could not have sailed if he believed her to be unprotected and in danger.

Warren sighed. "I am in a poor position to argue with you. My own dealings with the fair sex are tortuous. I am to be married again shortly, to a woman with the soul of a poet and the fortune of a pasha."

"My felicitations," said Sparhawk.

"Thank you," replied Warren. "Unfortunately, I have also gotten my children's governess pregnant, and because I am providing for the girl, my intended has discovered it."

It was of a piece with what Sparhawk had seen of the man so far: honorable, but danger-loving and reckless. Few men would risk the affections of an heiress to dally with a governess.

"I presume you will not cut the girl off to placate her."

"Of course not," said Warren. "Women are shockingly unforgiving of one another, but Mercy will come around. She is not passionate herself, you see, so she does not understand how I can love her but still consort with the governess. If you have found a woman who can stir both spirit and body, sir, do not give her up lightly. Do not. The alternatives can be damnably complicated."

Sparhawk had found such a woman, and he was not leaving her lightly. "I am sorry," he said, "but my mind is made up."

"I wish your answer were different," said Warren. "I do not believe that you will receive justice from a government that I know to be unjust, but I pray and hope that I am wrong. I wish you Godspeed, Captain Sparhawk."

They shook hands like civilized Englishmen, in the full knowledge that they might meet again as enemies. The doctor checked Ward's condition one last time and slipped out into the night.

Sparhawk was sitting in one of the caned chairs in the dining room when he heard the scratch at the window. He let Sarah Ward, followed by Mr. Cheap, into the house he had bought for her.

He was glad to see the sailing master at her side, not just because the streets were dangerous at night, but because he did not want to be alone with her. Warren had been right. She stirred him, body and soul. He had been tempted to violate his own principles and seduce her aboard the *Sally,* and he had been on the verge of it again in her father's keeping room. He would have consummated his desire yesterday on the *Hephaestion* if she hadn't had the good sense to refuse him. One look at her face tonight, the worry and tension written clear across her piquant features, told him that any encounter alone between them in such a charged atmosphere would end in something more than a heated embrace.

But not with Mr. Cheap present.

"Your brother is out of danger," Sparhawk said.

A little of the color returned to her cheeks.

Cheap grunted and pushed past her into the parlor. He bent over the chaise where Benji lay resting.

"Holed below the waterline," clucked Mr. Cheap, with the disapproval that fathers reserve for mortal sins.

Benjamin Ward turned his eyes, bloodshot with rum and pain, on that forbidding countenance. "I failed to follow your advice, Mr. Cheap," he confessed, in as solemn a manner as a pint of Jamaica's best would allow. "I looked back. Never look back. You and Father always say."

Cheap sighed. "You must have made a great wide target of yourself too, to get belly shot so."

Sarah Ward crossed to her brother's bedside, removed the rum bottle from his hand, and raised a plucked eyebrow at the last few ounces sloshing in the bottom. "I'm not sure I approve of the medicine, but at least someone has done a nice clean job with the stitchwork."

Mr. Cheap turned to Sparhawk. "He won't be getting to the *Sally* on his own two feet tonight, and there'll be no moving him quiet enough to sneak past the watch at this hour."

"He cannot stay here," said Sarah Ward, turning to Sparhawk. "The regulars are

301

already out, searching for an escaped prisoner and his Rebel accomplice."

Cheap nodded. "Best chance is to join the morning traffic on the wharf. I'll find us a cart and lie low until dawn."

It was the most sensible course of action, the surest and safest way to get Benjamin Ward, injured as he was, and Sparhawk, a wanted man, marked by his height and coal black hair, out of Boston. It should work. They had only to play the part of sturdy fishermen in the murky predawn light, to traverse less than a half mile of twisting streets. If they were stopped, it was unlikely to be by a large party of soldiers — Gage's forces were spread too thin guarding the city to conduct a proper manhunt — and Cheap and Sparhawk, even encumbered with an injured man, ought to be able to fight their way free to the boat.

The devil of it was that this sure and sensible plan left Sparhawk in the one circumstance he did not feel equal to: alone with Sarah Ward.

Sixteen

Sarah stood frozen in the hall, looking up at James Sparhawk.

She had not expected to see him again after the *Hephaestion,* but tonight Mr. Cheap had come to her, up the floating back staircase of Trent's manse, quiet as a mouse despite his hulking size, to say that Benji and Sparhawk had not made their rendezvous with the *Sally,* and that boats were passing between the castle and the admiral's flagship.

Sarah had grown up in a town with more widows than wives, and when the *Charming Sally* was overdue, she had learned to follow her mother's stoic example of staying busy and keeping her fears and her doubts to herself. She was fifteen, three years in the clutches of the dame school, when she hauled up her courage to confront her mother and ask how she could remain so calm when her husband and son were six weeks past due from London.

Her mother's answer had been simple and sensible and more difficult to master than Latin or Greek or needlework: "Do not catalog the terrors of the sea in your head. Do not imagine them drowned, crushed by a spar, or thrashing with fever. Do not, when it is your beau instead of your brother, imagine him in the arms of another woman. Picture him in the privacy of your mind on his deck, with a clear sky, a good wind, and calm seas, and there at least, it will be so."

Sarah had tried to envision her brother and Sparhawk, escaped, hiding on one of the harbor islands perhaps, but her treacherous mind had painted them captured and killed a thousand ways; she had seen Molineaux's head explode and blood run past the toe of her shoe on the deck of the *Sally*.

And she had thought of Sparhawk's proposition on the *Hephaestion* the day before — and wished she had accepted it.

He could not marry her. There was no security in being a man's mistress. She had been sensible to refuse him.

She would regret it for the rest of her life.

She busied herself brewing coffee that Mr. Cheap surreptitiously tossed in the fireplace when he thought she wasn't looking, and toasting — or to be accurate, charring —

bread that he slipped behind the sofa cushions.

Then the boy had arrived and told her that she must come quickly.

Mr. Cheap had not liked the sound of it. The North End was a tough neighborhood. He'd wanted to reconnoiter on his own first and report back, in case it was a ruse. She had insisted on going, in case it was not, and had finally prevailed.

Now she was here, alone with Sparhawk, in a meeting she had neither anticipated nor prepared for. She had found his beauty disconcerting in the close confines of her father's cabin on the *Sally* and in her Salem home. She had steeled herself against it for her visit to the *Hephaestion*. Since then she thought she had become inured to it, but tonight, confronted with his startling physicality and conscious of the service he had done her, she could not ignore his glamour.

She stalled for a few minutes, rechecked her brother's temperature, which was normal, his pulse, which was strong, and the rum bottle, which was empty. That was just as well. He was deeply unconscious now, and would likely sleep through the night; the best thing for him. When there was nothing else she could fuss over, she closed the door on her brother and found Sparhawk waiting for her in the hall.

"I am sorry to have alarmed you," he said. "I sent my message when I did not yet know if I would be able to find a doctor, or how your brother would fare."

"There is no need to apologize. You brought him back, when you might have cut and run."

"There were moments when I was tempted," he replied. "Your brother is brave and capable . . . and irritating as hell."

"Now imagine growing up in the same house with him," she said. Then a question occurred to her. "Whose house is this?"

"It is yours, actually. I bought it and put it in your name."

"Oh."

"Sarah," he said, taking a step forward and then stopping himself. "I have acted wrongly in all regards toward you from the moment we met. My comments about pressing you on the *Sally* were thoughtless. My advances in your father's cabin were ungentlemanly. And in your father's house worse still. I regret the proposal I made yesterday on the *Hephaestion*. It was selfish and ungrateful. I am sorry, for all of it."

The lady her mother had hoped she might become, that the dame and the dame school had trained, would have accepted his apology with a condescending nod, and made a graceful exit, but Sarah Ward was not that lady, and never, she was coming to realize, would be.

"I wish you had not dismasted the *Sally*," she said honestly, "and that you had not been arrested, but otherwise, I am not sorry for any of it. And I am not sorry to be here with you now."

"Our meeting here like this" — he gestured to indicate their closeness in the hall — "was unintended. I meant to call at Chelsea for the papers your Rebel friends prepared for me and sail for England with your brother. I still mean to do that, to do the right thing, to leave you alone," he said.

She took a step forward. "*That* isn't what I want. *That* I *would* be sorry for."

"Your brother is in the next room."

"My brother is unconscious."

"Mr. Cheap will return," said Sparhawk.

"Not for several hours."

"Then it would be wrong to abuse the trust he has placed in me," said Sparhawk.

"Mr. Cheap trusts that you will not force yourself on me. And that I am old enough to make my own choices."

"But it is as you said in Salem. What you want — what we both want — would leave you worse off in the morning."

"Not if we were careful," she said. Her mother and the dame might have been disappointed before. They would be positively horrified now.

Sparhawk wasn't. He was tempted. She could see it in the stiffness of his posture, in the way he held himself as far back from her in the tiny hall as he could manage. "I never meant to be anything else with you," he said.

They were dancing around it, but she must be certain they both held the same understanding. "You must pull out," she said, feeling her face flush. She had received a graphic and thorough education in the matter. Not from the dame, of course, but from the well-meaning trollops on the Salem docks. Now, as then, her cheeks colored and her tongue failed to form the words. She was a pirate's daughter, but Micah had been her only lover, and they had not discussed anything beforehand.

"Micah did not," she said. And afterward, it had only deepened her humiliation. When he started talking about settling money on her, buying her a house near his wharf, making her his mistress, not his wife, she had realized her folly. She'd told him she would never consent to being his mistress. "You won't have any choice if you are pregnant," he'd replied.

He'd been right. The Wards were too stretched already. They could scarcely support themselves, could not bear the loss of even a fraction of Sarah's labor, or afford to feed and clothe a child. She had spent the better part of the next month in anxious misery. News of her broken engagement raced through town on the wind of gossip, but she seemed to move through the days between her night with Wild and her next courses like a ship becalmed.

For two years she had raged at the way Micah Wild had robbed her of her ability to chart her own course. She had struggled, ever after, to remake her future. Tonight with Sparhawk, not only could she change her future; she could also change her past, dislodge Micah Wild from his place in her history as her only lover, as her logline for passion and intimacy.

Sparhawk took a hesitant step forward in the hall. "Before you arrived, I resolved to part with you, for your own good."

"I know you fear acting the part of the rake and seducer, but here, tonight, you are not the authority of the Crown, and I am not the fugitive from its justice. Only our sexes make us unequal, and that is a distinction of bodies, not of spirit."

She had demolished all his arguments. Sparhawk had known Sarah Ward to be his equal in spirit from their first encounter on the *Sally;* he knew he would not meet her like again.

He took her hand in his. It was small but capable, softer than it had been on her father's schooner, a delicate gold bracelet circling the wrist. He lifted it to his lips, and she came lightly into his arms as he pressed a kiss in the center of her palm, then over her pulse point, and again on the downy inside of her forearm.

His heart beat faster, and the last of his misgivings fled. He was sorry her first lover had been Wild, but he was also glad she was not a virgin. He had never deflowered one, never known the responsibility of setting the pattern for a woman's future passions. He was glad of that as well. He had not understood, until now, that first encounters were more than physical experiences. Wild might not have hurt Sarah physically, might even have given to her generously of pleasure and attention. It was *himself* he had withheld.

Sparhawk would not make the same mistake.

Sarah felt the last of Sparhawk's resolve crumble. He pulled her close and his mouth descended; his lips covered hers; his tongue sought entry and gained it. His mouth tasted molasses sweet with the rich dark rum he had shared with her brother, whose life he had just saved.

He backed her to the wall until his taut body met every inch of hers. She felt the cool plaster against her shoulders through the thin cotton of her gown. Her center of gravity shifted. Weight pooled between her legs. His body responded, thick and urgent against her belly.

She had been land bound in Boston for so long that the tang of sea and salt in his hair, on his skin, thrilled her senses and made her want to drown in him. The familiar textures beneath her questing hands, the soft snowy linen of his shirt, the starched white cotton of his neck cloth, the soft wool of his fawn breeches, were made startling and new by the presence of his hard muscular body beneath.

He stepped back and looked down at her, eyes wide with wonder. She shared his excitement. "Upstairs," he whispered, his inflection at once hungry and solicitous.

She nodded and took his hand, as eager as he was for this thing that was unfolding between them.

They climbed the first two steps, but when they reached the bend in the stair, he stopped and turned to her to kiss her lips, her eyes, her hair, and whisper her name over and over. She could feel the beat of his heart in his chest, setting an insistent rhythm that her own body echoed.

They were as close as they could be with layers of muffling cloth between them, but it was not enough. She needed him. Flesh to flesh. Skin to skin. She raised her knee and hooked it over his hip, bringing them closer together *there.* He moaned and grasped her buttocks, then lifted her and turned to mount the next stair.

She locked her ankles at the small of his back, kissed his throat where his tanned skin was bare above the ruffle on his shirt, opened her mouth and flicked her tongue against the pulse in his neck.

That undid him. He staggered and set them down, locked together, on the stairs.

"I meant for you to have a bed," he whispered.

"I don't need a bed," she said just as quietly, still dimly conscious of her brother sleeping downstairs. "I just need you."

The stairs were dark, but there was enough moonlight coming from the landing above for her to see the expression of sensual intent that suffused his face.

He reefed her skirts, neat as a foretop-man, folding each layer of cotton back until there was only the gossamer silk of her chemise covering just her knees. This he reefed as well, carefully, almost reverently, until she was completely exposed to him.

"Beautiful," he said, stroking the thatch of blond curls with the backs of his knuckles. She was already slick and ready for him, but he took his time to please her anyway, and she came very near knowing just how good it could be if he did it for her before he stopped.

Then he opened his fall front. He stroked his shaft to spread the moisture beading at the tip. There was nothing preening or self-conscious about the gesture, just a pure carnality that freed her to embrace her own.

He knelt over her. She grasped a banister and leaned back. The risers of the second flight bit into her back, but she didn't care. His hardness was stroking her slickness, back and forth, a prelude to the joining she hungered for, and when she raised her hips and he lowered his, they slid together in a perfect fit, a dovetail joint.

She had a little leverage, with her feet upon the stair below, her hand upon the banister, to move with him, to arch and meet his thrusts and find for herself that which she had passively waited for Micah to give to her. And that discovery made the moment, with Sparhawk, wholly new.

Right as her body went slack, his tensed. He gasped, stilled, and pulled out, just in time.

He rested his forehead against hers. She could hear his deep-drawn breaths, feel his heartbeat reverberate through her whole body.

They climbed to their feet, whispering endearments, straightening each other's clothing, kissing, touching, smiling at their own impatience. Together they crept up the stairs, like errant children sneaking back to bed.

They discovered three chambers on the second floor. The first two were small and sparsely furnished with simple low beds and practical straw ticks. The third was obviously meant to be the great room, and like the rest of the house, reflected the taste of a previous century. The bed was heavy oak and paneled, the posts carved in a frenzy of stylized floral motifs. No doubt it had been quite grand once, but age had darkened the wood almost to black, and much of the fine detail was lost. It did, however, boast the plumpest feather mattress Sarah had ever seen.

"I asked my man of business to buy and furnish a love nest," Sparhawk said, by way of an explanation.

Sarah flounced on the edge of the cloud-like mattress, and a feather floated up. "It would seem he has a very literal mind. At least the bed is roomy and there is no need to bend me over it."

His eyes widened fractionally, and he tensed with what she now recognized as desire held in check. "Need . . . ," he said, considering her assertion, then shaking his head, *"no."* He crossed the room, drew her to her feet. "But what is a necessity at sea may prove a pleasing variation on land. And *need* is a matter of perspective."

Sparhawk lay staring up at the canopy of the great bed. Sarah Ward was curled beside him, her honey gold hair spread across the pillow. She radiated happiness and content-ment. Over and over again as they had moved together, he had thought, We are made for each other.

After the first time on the stairs he had experienced a sense of discovery that recalled his very first affair, a liaison with a Venetian opera singer named Marcella. McKenzie had introduced her to him, part of the gruff old Scot's effort to broaden a young officer's horizons.

Marcella had been thirty, experienced, beautiful, and kind to a fumbling youth. He'd come so quickly the first time that he'd expected to be thrown out of her bed, but instead she had roused him again and shown him, patiently, how to stop and start and prolong his pleasure to ensure hers. After a mutually satisfactory second performance, and then a third that met with not only her approval but her praise, he'd lain back on her gilded bed, surrounded by grinning putti, and seen the world anew. So long as he was considerate of his lovers, and did not repeat the mistakes of his father or the brutality of Slough, he could enjoy *this* anytime he was in port.

Making love to Sarah Ward on a darkened staircase had filled him with a similar sense of revelation. They'd climbed to the second floor and laughed over the ludicrous old bed, and he had shown her how a man enjoyed a woman in the confines of a crowded ship, bent over a cannon or a narrow berth. He had described to her how much he wanted to have her that way when he had a ship again, his words, as Marcella had taught him so long ago, painting pictures to drive both their passions higher.

When they were spent, melancholy had washed over him, and self-loathing such as he had not felt since the first time he had given in to Slough. He had told Sarah Ward that he loved her, implied with his heated talk that they would share a future together.

She reached out to stroke his shoulder. He felt her fingers, feather light, tracing over the linen of his shirt, which he had kept on to hide his scars. They were not the sort of thing that refined ladies liked. Her hand traveled lower and he tensed. Then her fingers reached the hem and met the ridged flesh of his back.

She did not shrink from the contact, did not take her hand away. "If you asked me, right now," she said, "to come with you tonight, I would."

He was as bad as his father. She had a future within reach, safe from the horror of imprisonment and execution, and he had compromised it. Even now her brother slept downstairs with stitches in his belly — a tangible reminder of the danger in which this affair placed her.

He rolled over and pushed her questing hand away. It felt like amputating his own.

"Your brother told me that you are about to receive an offer," he said, the words tasting like bile in his mouth. "On terms I cannot match."

"Indiscretion," she said, "is a Ward family failing."

"He also pointed out to me that ours is a dangerous association, one that could get you hanged."

"My older brother is a hypocrite."

It had not occurred to him that she might be aware of her brother's affairs. "You know?" he asked. "About Benjamin?"

"He told me when he was seventeen and I was fifteen," she said. "The girls at my dame school, including my best friend, all adored him. I asked him why he didn't take any of them into the garden during dances at the assembly hall. I thought I was so very worldly then, but he had to explain it to me, the way men loved other men. I knew I mustn't tell anyone, although I think Father suspected early on. But I didn't understand what it would mean, the danger it might place him in, until later. And now he has a lover who is rich and royal, and who can do as he pleases. And if they are found out, it is Benji who will suffer."

"Ansbach held the marines back after Benji was shot," said Sparhawk. "I will not

318

say that your brother has chosen an easy path, but Charles Ansbach is an honorable man, and the fact that the streets were not teeming with soldiers hours ago is a testament to the affection in which he holds your brother."

"I thought the navy took a dim view of sodomy," she said.

"When it is discovered, yes. But between consenting adults, on most ships, it is more often ignored than prosecuted."

"And on your ship?"

"Your brother has nothing to fear from me," said Sparhawk. "And he is right about us, about our prospects."

"My brother," said Sarah Ward, "is the last man on earth who should lecture another about dangerous entanglements."

"Nevertheless, he is right. And prosecution for sodomy is rare, whereas arrest for piracy, smuggling, and treason is epidemic at the moment."

"I am not afraid of Admiral Graves or his odious nephew."

"You should be. Your testimony could condemn them both. And now Benji is implicated as well. He was seen on the *Hephaestion*. Ansbach restrained the marines, but not before he called out your brother's name. It would not take much for an alert informer — and both sides have their share — to put two and two together and realize that Ansbach and your brother were acquainted in London. That will give the admiral greater leverage over you. And as you pointed out, Ansbach is royal and inviolate. Your brother is not."

"Do not presume to lecture me about the risks my brother takes."

"I am sorry," he said. "That came out ungracious and ungrateful. I am conscious of the great service you and your family have done me, and would like to repay you. I can instruct my prize agent to sell the house and forward you the money."

She stiffened. He felt it through the feather mattress. "That is very generous of you," she said in an icy voice, "but I don't require payment for my services tonight —"

"That is not what I —"

"And we don't need the money. The Rebels will pay us for the use of the *Sally* and Benji's services as captain."

She was brave and loyal and tenacious, and that was why, for the first time in his life, he was in love. And that was also why he must now act like the man he despised above all others — his father — and abandon her.

He got up and paced to the washstand,

where he completed a quick toilette in silence. He could feel her watching him, knew he had hurt her, and was about to hurt her more. He buttoned his breeches, tied his shirt closed, reached instinctively for the blue wool coat that he was no longer entitled to wear, then left it where it lay on the chair. Finally he turned to her. She had drawn herself up on the bed, pointed chin held defiantly in the air.

"Your brother may be a hypocrite," he said, knowing his words would lash her like a whip, "but Benjamin's assessment of your predicament is correct. If you come with me, and we are overtaken, you will be at the admiral's mercy. He must try *me* as an officer, but the Port Act means he can arrest *you* and hold you indefinitely, without trial. And I very much doubt, since you know the truth about the French gold, you would survive long in his custody. I cannot take you with me. I sail on the tide for England, alone, and I will not be coming back."

She would never learn.

It was impossible to stay after that, in the pretty little house he had bought her with its sturdy antique furniture and sanded floors, where they had made love. Her heart broke again when he didn't try to stop her.

A few blocks away, the cook's son caught up to her carrying a lantern and a kitchen knife and looking solemn and scared, whether of Sparhawk, the regulars, or common criminals, she couldn't say. He walked her the rest of the way home.

He needn't have bothered. The streets were no longer empty. Carters and drovers were already stirring, bringing their scanty produce, their precious eggs, their dear butter, the fish that the admiral only occasionally allowed them permission to catch, to market.

But she was glad of the boy's company, because alone she might have broken down and started crying. When Micah had jilted her, the humiliation, the public tallying of her worth, had been crushing, but in the months that followed, she had been able to tell herself that money and Wild's mercenary nature had played a role in her rejection.

There would be no such comfort with Sparhawk.

Inside Trent's manse it was cool and silent, the stairs dark. She longed for the enveloping cocoon of her dimity bed curtains, where she could lay her head on the feather pillow and stretch her body, sore from its exertions, over the smooth fresh sheets.

She saw the light under the door: her father would be waiting up for her, eager for news of the escape he had helped plan, of Benji and Mr. Cheap and the *Sally;* the sort of exploit that harked back to the escapades of his youth. He would be able to read her face, and offer his bottomless understanding. She only wished she didn't need it quite so often.

She pushed open the door and hesitated on the threshold. It was not her father. Trent sat in one of the slipcovered chairs flanking the paneled fireplace.

"Come inside and close the door, please," he said. "Your father finally has gone to bed and the servants are too well paid to gossip."

Sarah stepped inside the room and shut the door.

"Thank you," said Trent, with the brittle politeness she recognized from his confrontation with the fusilier at the Three Cranes, and his more recent meeting with Lieutenant Graves. She had known, of course, that he was a duelist and a dangerous man, but lulled by his kindness to her family and the gentility of his home, she had lost sight of the fact that he could be dangerous to her.

"I was called to the admiral's house near the battery this evening," he said. "It seems

Sparhawk has escaped."

She wished she had the poise of Angela Ferrers, the widow's practiced ability to conceal her thoughts and feelings, but she did not.

"I know," she said. "Benji and I helped him."

Trent did not answer at once. He had taken his blue coat off in deference to the warmth of the night. He was dressed from head to toe in faultless cream linen and gold lace, but now, as the silence stretched, she noticed that his sword lay across the arm of his chair, and that he had placed two pistols on the table beside him.

Finally he spoke. "That is . . . unfortunate. This Sparhawk has used you badly. If he takes his case before the Admiralty, and can muster even a shred of proof, Graves will try to find another scapegoat for the theft of the gold, and he has one near to hand, in you."

I am not afraid of Admiral Graves or his odious nephew.

You should be.

Here was the danger Sparhawk had warned her about. And abandoned her to.

"You must be sorry you took us home from the Three Cranes," she said.

"No. I'm only sorry that you did not heed

324

my warning and stay out of this."

"I could not let Sparhawk die. He had saved Ned's life, and he was innocent."

"But you are not," said Trent. "To prove you innocent of theft is to prove you guilty of piracy. Either will see you swing from the *Preston*'s yardarm. We have a little time, I hope, to take steps to protect you from that fate."

She considered her options. Salem was closed to her because of Micah Wild. She might appeal to Angela Ferrers, but she had nothing to bargain with now.

Trent seemed to read her thoughts. "You cannot run. Graves has transferred Ned to the *Diana,* under one of his nephews, Thomas. It has been done in the guise of patronage, with Ned made midshipman, but he is a hostage; do not doubt it."

"What, then?" she asked.

"Admiral Graves knows you live under my roof. No doubt he assumes that you are my mistress. He is a man of limited imagination and will not suspect that I might wish to make you more. I am a baron. It is not a great name or beautiful estate, but with it come certain privileges. Peers and peeresses can only be tried in Parliament. Such trials are very public, and the truth about the gold would be almost certain to come out. At least as damning allegations. Not what the admiral wants at all. Marry me, and Graves and the Admiralty Courts will have no authority over you."

He was offering to save her life, by joining theirs forever. She could not play this man false. "I have had lovers."

"So, as it happens, have I," he said.

"That is different."

"Only if you think of women as commodities, to be bought and sold, their value dropping with use. I have been a mariner long enough to know that maiden voyages are generally full of unhappy surprises. Better a seasoned ship that's had a taste of the wind and settled into her frame."

"How can you be certain that I'm not a shoddy old tub like the *Charybdis*?"

"Because I have come to know you, these past weeks, and your father shared with me the circumstances of your disappointment."

There were other, more recent circumstances as well. But they did not matter. What mattered was that she had a family who loved her and a man who esteemed her and was prepared to shelter them from harm. She felt tears prickle her eyes. "Did he also tell you I am a bad cook?"

Trent smiled. "Yes, as a matter of fact he did."

■ ■ ■ ■

Cheap returned just before dawn, pushing a briny cart. Benji was still unconscious. Sparhawk and the Wards' sailing master made a bed for the injured man out of tarps, and concealed his presence with oyster nets and baskets. Sarah's brother barely stirred until they reached the dock, and fortunately by that time he had recovered a little of his sangfroid, enough to remark on the persistent smell of oysters and to pluck a handful of swamp roses growing between the stones of the rough-hewn quay. He inhaled their elusive scent, then tossed the flowers into the waiting boat and climbed stiffly down after.

They rowed, oars muffled, north toward Noddle's Island where Mr. Cheap had concealed the *Sally,* staying as far from the *Somerset* and the *Glasgow,* their guns trained ominously on Charlestown, as they could manage in the narrow channel.

When Sparhawk chanced to look back at the *Preston,* he spied an unfamiliar sail behind her.

Ward looked as well. "Ah," he said, plucking the petals of his mallow roses. "Behold the *Cerberus,* the Atlantic plow. Her pre-

327

cious cargo — Burgoyne, Clinton, Howe" — Sarah's brother awarded each a petal over the side — "Bow, wow, wow. Or so the papers say. She came in yesterday, bearing three new major generals. Parliament's answer to the present troubles. More soldiers. And a promotion for Samuel Graves, to vice admiral of the white."

"Flag officers advance when the rank above them becomes vacant," Sparhawk said. The system always sounded ludicrous when it was explained to civilians. And yet, like the press, it was an integral part of the most powerful navy in the world, and for the most part, it worked.

"Graves will celebrate his elevation tomorrow, with all the ships in the squadron dancing attendance on him," said Ward. "There is to be a grand ceremony on the *Preston,* with the high Tories invited to partake. My sister will be there," he added pointedly. "With her beau."

Mr. Cheap snorted.

Benjamin Ward sighed. "Mr. Cheap does not think anyone is good enough to marry my sister, but I am inclined to say that she can make do with a lord."

"Lord or no, it doesn't sit right," said Mr. Cheap. "A Ward marrying a navy man."

"I did not realize he was a fellow officer,"

said Sparhawk. Although after tonight, he was probably no longer an officer himself. In his mind he ran through the other captains in the squadron.

"Trent is only lately arrived in Boston Harbor," said Benjamin Ward.

The day promised to be warm, but Sparhawk felt a chill wind. "Trent is in the Med." Sparhawk knew where he was at all times, made it his business to know.

"The *Charybdis* came in while you were at the castle," said Ward. "Evidently, she was so badly damaged by the crossing that her keel split."

"Sarah cannot marry him," said Sparhawk.

Ahead the dark shape of the *Sally* peeked out from behind Noddle's Island. And beyond her, the Atlantic. But all he could see in his mind's eye were another harbor, another ship, rails dripping with tropical flowers, a splendid figure in blue and gold bellowing from the quarterdeck, Sparhawk's mother being dragged, screaming, to the side.

He could not leave Boston now.

"Do you know him?" asked Sarah Ward's brother.

"I have not laid eyes on him in fifteen years," said Sparhawk. "But he is a rake, a villain, and a murderer."

Cheap stopped rowing.

Ward dropped his flowers.

"How do you know that?"

"Because he is my father."

SEVENTEEN

It was midmorning when Sarah woke. The room was cool and dark, the shutters closed against the beating summer heat. One of Trent's pistols lay on her bedside table. He had left it there when he said good night, as a precaution. He believed she would be more valuable to Graves alive, as a scapegoat in a show trial, but it was impossible to be certain how the admiral would take Sparhawk's escape. And it would be all too easy to conceal a private murder in the actions of a Rebel mob.

She washed and dressed in one of the smart cotton jackets Trent had bought her when she had expressed a longing for clothing simpler than the fashionable gowns that now filled her closets. There was such a thing, she had explained to him, as too much luxury, particularly when it came in the form of unforgiving silk over stiff reed stays. After the night she had just experienced, a pair of soft leather jumps and a roomy caraco jacket offered simplicity and comfort, and she needed a little of both.

She was surprised to find the routine of the house unchanged when so much else, including she herself, felt transformed. Her brother had sailed for Portugal, Mr. Cheap with him. Ned was on the *Diana.* She had gone to bed with Sparhawk, and she could still feel the print of his hands on her body.

She had consented to marry Trent.

They could not speak of it yet, must move quietly and quickly so that the admiral did not learn of their plans to put Sarah beyond his reach. But Trent had agreed that they must speak with her father, and promised that he would do so first thing in the morning.

And then he would go out and begin to make delicate inquiries. A marriage outside the church might be open to legal challenge. A marriage inside the church required a license. They did not want the bans read. Nor did they want the admiral to learn of their plans. King's Chapel was out of the question: too gossipy, too closely tied to the Loyalist community, too likely for word of their scheme to reach Samuel Graves.

"I hope to have a license in hand by the end of the week," Trent had said. "If I cannot find a sympathetic cleric in Boston, then I will find one outside of Boston who can be persuaded to come to us."

The Rebels, of course, held Cambridge and the college, but passes, as Sarah had discovered, were easy to obtain if you were rich.

Trent was already gone by the time Sarah came downstairs, so she went in search of her father and found him at the table in front of the windows in the Chinese parlor. The celadon damask upholstery and pale green walls glowed softly in the sunlight sparkling off the waters of the Back Bay. The model of the *Sally* lay on its side, a pot of gum and a pile of tiny copper foil plates, such as a goldsmith might use, beside her. Abednego's paints and brushes held down the corners of an inscribed letter sheet, a receipt for ten ounces of copper, with the compliments of one Paul Revere.

"I presume your brother, Mr. Cheap and all" — and by "all" he meant Sparkhawk — "got well away last night," said her father, not troubling to look up from his paint-brush.

"Benji got himself shot, but Sparhawk found him a doctor." She felt a pang of the misery she had known walking home last night. "The bullet came out clean, and they are well away."

He would not take me with him.

Her father looked up from his model. He had already laid a row of copper plates over the keel. "I was surprised when Trent spoke to me this morning. When you did not come right back last night, I thought you might have gone with James Sparhawk."

Her father was too perceptive by half.

"Don't you like Anthony?" she asked.

"I like him better than Micah Wild," said Abednego Ward. "And he is well cut to be a husband."

And Sparhawk, she knew, was not.

Sarah had discovered early on that there was very little to do in Trent's well-ordered household. The cook might have welcomed the interest of a skilled chatelaine, but she had politely banned Sarah from the kitchen when she had seen what passed for toast in the Ward family.

Now, with Benji and Ned gone, there was even less for Sarah to do, so she turned to needlework, one of the genteel accomplishments of the dame school, to keep herself busy.

Embroidery had come easily to her in school. She had already known how to sew neat, even stitches in canvas, and how to tie complex sailor's knots. Silk and wool, she had learned, were far easier to manipulate than tarred hemp. The preliminary sketches that stymied the other girls, copied from the dame's precious collections of engravings, posed no challenges for Sarah. The Sallys had taught her how to transfer the images they found near to hand, playing cards and newspaper illustrations, onto far more difficult material like wood and whalebone. Sarah's samplers, pillows, chairbacks, and fire screens had exceeded those of her classmates in design and execution.

There was a frame and a worktable in the large parlor looking out over the Common. Recalling Trent's warning, she brought the pistol downstairs with her and stashed it in her sewing bag.

She drew Trent's coat of arms from memory on a sampler canvas. Pleased with the result, she began selecting thread and making a list of colors to purchase at the market.

She'd run the first thread through the canvas when she heard the carriage in the street. The day was warm, but she felt chilled when she looked out and saw it come to a halt in front of Trent's manse. Larger than the rig her host rented, it was black with gilding, drawn by a matched set of four. The servants who rode on the back were sailors in uniform.

The officer who alighted was a stranger to her, but his epaulets and the cockade in his hat told her he held the rank of captain, and she could think of no good errand a naval officer would perform at her house the night after she had helped Sparhawk escape.

Her maid appeared a few minutes later. Charles Ansbach, captain of the *Hephaestion,* hoped that she would receive him.

He was Trent's friend, her brother's lover, and until last night, Sparhawk's jailer.

From the street she had seen that he was simply and soberly dressed, his shirt, breeches, and waistcoat cut from practical cream linen. No silk or gold-wire embroidery. His coat was dark blue wool with cream lapels, the gold lacing around his buttons narrow and discreet. Not one of the navy's peacocks, then, like Sparhawk or Trent.

When he entered the room, she observed that he was handsome in a bluff and hearty way, with deeply tanned skin and blond curling hair. She tried to detect some resemblance to portraits of the monarch or George's sister, Princess Charlotte, but found none.

He removed his hat and bowed low.

The dame had been a font of knowledge on protocol, on the correct way to greet everyone from one's future mother-in-law through the royal governor. Sarah did not know, exactly, where Charles Ansbach fell on this spectrum, but she curtsied prettily as the dame had taught her and waited.

Ansbach received this stiffly, then shot an anxious glance at the door, where Sarah's maid stood waiting. And Sarah realized something: Ansbach wanted to be alone with her.

Sarah sent the maid for coffee and closed the door.

"Thank you for receiving me," said Charles Ansbach. "Your brother and I were acquainted in London. You and I should have met before now, but I was detained by duty in the harbor."

"My brother," she said, "has told me of your friendship."

"Did he? I am glad of it. I was to dine with Benji today, but he did not appear at the appointed time, so I thought perhaps I had mistaken the place or the hour, and came here to inquire for his direction."

That was an obvious lie.

Sparhawk had told her that Ansbach had seen and recognized Benji, and held off the marines on the *Hephaestion*. If this man had intended to expose her brother's part in Sparhawk's escape, he would already have done so. He would not have delayed the pursuit last night. And he would not have come here today on his own.

All well and good, but that did not mean she could trust him. Charles Ansbach might be willing to shield her brother from Admiral Graves and the justice of the Crown, but that did not mean he was willing to do the same for her or James Sparhawk.

"My brother has gone to Portugal on family business," she said. It was true.

Ansbach stiffened. "He said nothing of this to me."

Her brother had refused to embroil Ansbach in their scheme to free Sparhawk from his ship. That she had understood. But his connection to this man was of some duration; yet Benji had planned to leave the country for six weeks — possibly longer — without telling him.

Sarah resented the danger this man placed her brother in, but she had not intended to drive a wedge between them, had not considered that it would be impossible for her brother to tell Ansbach that he was making a powder run to Lisbon for the Rebels.

"I am sorry," she said, at a loss. "I believe he felt the nature of the business might compromise your loyalties."

"It vexes me to hear it. I have tried to tell your brother that I am not unsympathetic to American grievances, but I cannot support open rebellion. It is not only the navy that constrains me, but also family loyalties. You must tell me," Ansbach said, no longer bothering to hide his distress. "Did you see your brother before he sailed? And was he well? I have reason to believe that he might have been . . . that is to say, I think his health may have suffered a blow, when last I saw him."

That explained Ansbach's anxiety. He knew that Benji had been shot; he was not, perhaps even now, certain that he lived.

"He did receive an injury, and that is why, I am certain, he did not write to you. He was out of danger when he embarked, but also dead drunk."

Ansbach's relief was palpable. "That does sound like Benji. Whatever else he may be up to, I am very glad to hear that he is well. And it may be for the best, this trip of his. If you write to him, you might advise him not to land in Boston, and to avoid, if he can, encountering any of the ships on this station." He paused, then added, "Even mine."

"I will do that," she said.

Ansbach smiled. "Thank you." He seemed at last to take in his surroundings. "And I am very grateful to Lord Polkerris for extending his hospitality to you and your family. Your brother and I are . . . very good friends . . . and it has distressed me that I was not able to come to your aid when your house was burned."

"Trent has been most kind to us," she said. Without thinking, she glanced down at the embroidery canvas.

Ansbach followed her gaze. "Forgive me," he said, "but it seems that perhaps a closer connection between your families is imminent."

She must make a decision, whether to risk trusting where her brother had not. Benji had been forced to learn the habit of caution, to hide his affections, whereas Sarah had only ever been hurt by concealment. "Trent is marrying me so that Admiral Graves cannot hang me. It would be poor payment for his hospitality if you were to let anyone know of our plans, as the admiral would see me shackled in quite a different way."

It took Ansbach a moment to adjust to her candor. Then he said, "I am certain that is not the only reason that Trent is marrying you. And you are nothing like I thought you would be."

"Really? Is it the embroidery?"

"In part," he replied. "There is also the setting. Your brother described a tomboy who climbed rigging like a monkey, and here I find a very proper Boston lady ensconced in her fashionable parlor with embroidery silks and a sewing bag."

"I have a pistol in the sewing bag, if that helps."

"Good Lord, is that what women put in them? No wonder they're so heavy."

"Will you keep our secret?" she asked.

"I shall not breathe a word about pistols in sewing bags," he said gravely. "Nor the other confidences you have vouchsafed me."

She gave him coffee, and poured as she had been taught in dame school. He hesitated when she passed him his cup, no doubt forewarned of her handicap by Benji. "Don't worry. Someone else brewed it," she said.

He accepted the cup, and ate the entire plate of ginger cakes while they talked. She learned a little more of this man who had kept her brother in London for two long years. He was kind and gallant and amusing and knew ships and seamen. It was impossible not to like him, and equally impossible not to wish that Benji had never met him;

341

that her brother might have come home and settled into a comfortable — if not wholly fulfilling — *safe* life.

"I am sorry your house was burned," Ansbach said again, "but I am glad that you met Trent. He deserves a little happiness. His first wife died too young, and his second marriage was hell. He has spent the last fifteen years looking for a fight he could not win, and failed to find it. But he is different since he met you."

She had known that Trent was widowed, but not that he had been married twice. She filed the information away for the future, when she could ask him more about his family.

Ansbach left just after noon, and a little later Trent returned.

"I have put our plans in motion," he said, reading the letters that had arrived while he was gone. "This," he added, passing her an opened missive, "will help us to fend off Graves in the meantime."

It was an invitation, of all things, to dine that afternoon with Lady Frankland, whose name still caused Sarah to flinch. "I thought Lady Frankland lived in Hopkinton," she said.

"She has a house in the North End as well," said Trent. "I knew her and Harry in

Lisbon. And I understand that she is sailing for England soon. She does not believe that Gage will be able to put an end to these troubles."

"Must we go?" Sarah asked.

"We should. Even if Lady Frankland believes you are my mistress, she will not scorn you. Not only do you share a common childhood on the North Shore, but she was Harry's mistress long before she was Harry's wife. Now, of course, she is a respectable widow, and attending on her together will remind Graves that he cannot touch you without provoking me."

"In dame school," Sarah said, "the girls used to call me 'Lady Frankland,' because they thought me as uncouth as barefoot Agnes Surriage. Pregnant at fourteen with a bastard in her belly and no better than she ought to be."

Trent's black brows rose. "Do you know how barefoot Agnes Surriage got Harry Frankland, baronet, to marry her after ten years as his mistress?"

"No." She had never thought to ask.

Trent smiled. "It is a tale worth telling. They were in Lisbon in 'fifty-five. Sir Harry had paid Agnes off with jewelry, intending to leave her in Portugal to find a new protector. He was on his way to the church to marry an English girl from a good family when the great earthquake struck. His horses were killed instantly, and Harry was buried alive in the rubble. His driver ran off. Agnes knew — as the discarded mother of his child, how could she forget? — where he was going that day, and she ran through the streets searching for him. She found the carriage, and not knowing whether Harry was alive or dead, with no thought to her own future, she used the jewelry Harry had bought her — her entire fortune, really — to induce the locals to dig him out. Your Marblehead serving girl was a heroine of sorts — certainly Harry's. He married her the next day. And I will lay odds that not a single one of the sharp-tongued harridans who treated you cruelly in school has since traveled as far or lived as boldly as barefoot Agnes Surriage."

She had never thought of it that way.

Lady Frankland's home in the North End was a far grander structure than the modest house Sparhawk had bought her, but such was the motley heterogenous character of the neighborhood that it was only a few twisting blocks away. Three stories with a dormered fourth and a slate roof, it had to be one of the largest homes in Boston.

Lady Frankland herself was difficult to

imagine as the saucy serving girl who had beguiled a baronet, though Sarah thought she might detect some of the fortitude of the heroine of Lisbon in her forthright manner. Near fifty, plump, and upholstered in an expensive but unflattering silk damask that made her look like a sofa, she was nothing if not comfortable in her skin. She ribbed Trent for not calling on her sooner, quizzed Sarah on their possible Salem and Marblehead connections, and complained mightily about the ungrateful Rebels of Hopkinton, who neglected work on her plantation and thought nothing of leaving their labor to play at revolutions.

"My income," said the old lady, "is quite halved. I cannot live on it. There is no one left to plant at Hopkinton. And they wanted my butter and my beef for their ragtag army, but why should I sell it to them when General Gage will pay double for it? Of course the rabble will not let me sell to General Gage, and they threaten to take my property from me if I try to do so."

"Rebels burned Miss Ward's house down," said Trent, by way of commiseration.

"They confiscated my nephew's house," said Lady Frankland, not to be outdone. "No small property either. You would know it, if you are from Salem, Miss Ward. A fine brick manse with much ornamental carving. Fourteen rooms, and every one of them with a fireplace. A very industrious young man. I did not even know of the connection until the poor boy turned up on my doorstep, with barely the clothes upon his back. These madcaps speak of the rights of Englishmen and then trample the right to the one thing they hold most dear: property. The local 'Committee of Safety' took his home and ships from him. All because he sold one vessel and a few spars to the admiral."

Sarah knew before the door opened who this long-lost nephew must be.

Micah Wild was much as Sarah remembered him, and it was easy to see how he had charmed an old lady into believing him a relation. He had abandoned the Rebel *rage militaire* in favor of a silk suit in a becoming shade of cocoa, cut to flatter his compact, muscular frame. She took some satisfaction in his split lip and the cut on his cheek that he had tried to conceal with a strategically rolled curl.

If Trent recalled the name when Lady Frankland introduced her nephew, he gave no sign of it. Micah murmured something polite and noncommittal about knowing Miss Ward's family. And Sarah nodded and

346

murmured something equally civil and noncommittal about being sure that was so.

Lady Frankland told them how the Rebels had seized the powder and musket she had brought with her for protection while traveling, and professed her intention of trying to buy another off the starving soldiery, who were said to be selling their weapons to feed their families. Trent advised her against it. She waved this away and begged his counsel on how best to pack her household for the sea journey. He agreed to accompany her out to the barn, where her goods from Hopkinton were stored.

Naturally he offered the old lady his arm, and just as naturally she took it. Which left Micah Wild offering Sarah his arm. She was loath to suffer the contact, thought they should repel each other like two magnets — she and this man who had burned her house down — but they did not, and together they followed Trent and the former Agnes Surriage out into the muggy afternoon.

"Are you really her nephew?" she asked, when it became apparent the world would not stop spinning because his hand was at her elbow.

"Almost certainly, in a manner of speaking. Fifteen families settled Naumkeag. Go far enough back and we are all related."

"That does not make every rich old lady north of Boston your aunt."

"There are parts of India where any older woman in the village may be addressed as 'Aunt' as a sign of respect. An admirable practice we might do well to emulate."

"Does Elizabeth call her 'Aunt' too?"

"Elizabeth went home to her family. It was her father who got wind that I'd sold the *Cromwell* to Admiral Graves."

Sarah had given the information about the *Cromwell* to Angela Ferrers, knowing that Micah Wild would be hurt by it politically and financially. She had not considered that it would hurt Elizabeth Wild and their marriage as well — not fully considered, at least.

"I am sorry, Micah."

"Don't be. The Pierce family has excellent business sense. If I prosper with the friends of government, Elizabeth and her money will no doubt return. And if I don't, she'll divorce me, and I'll be free to marry some Tory heiress. As you, it seems, are free to be passed from hand to hand around the fleet."

It was galling that he still had the power to hurt her, but she would not be baited. "And how exactly do you expect to prosper with no ships, Micah?"

"Ships have a way of multiplying. I will have the *Conant* back within the week. She was only leased to Admiral Graves, and the lease has ended. In return for keeping quiet about the extraordinarily familiar gold he paid me for the purchase of the *Cromwell,* he has given me a letter of marque to recover the *Sally.*"

"So now you will be an open brigand," she said, "rather than a covert one."

"*Privateering* is perfectly legal, and in the case of recovering the *Sally,* the very purpose for which it was invented. Marque and reprisal. To take back that which is yours. The *Sally* has been mine since your father defaulted on his loan."

"And what, assuming you can find the *Sally,* will you take her with, Micah? A pair of swivel guns and the power of your voice?"

"The *Conant* is no more a toothless merchantman," said Micah Wild. "Admiral Graves returns her to me much improved, with reinforced decking, six four-pounders, and berths for forty men."

Any sea voyage was dangerous. Storms, disease, the navy, and pirates all preyed on New England's scrappy little merchant vessels. But being hunted by an armed marauder was an entirely different matter. Sarah had grieved after parting with Sparhawk, over the life they would never share in that snug little house. She had hoped in her most secret heart that he might be delayed by poor winds or a contrary tide, have time to rethink his decision, and send for her. Now, though, she prayed he had cleared Salem Harbor and reached the open seas, because if the *Conant* was armed and hunting her, the *Sally* could not sail far and fast enough.

The *Sally* had been refitted since Sparhawk saw her last. Her smart yellow stripe was gone, repainted bright blue. Her broken mast had been replaced, her standing rigging restored, and her gunwales pierced for cannon, though she carried nothing but her two rusted swivels at the moment. She rode a little lower in the water, hidden by the grassy slopes of Noddle's Island, probably because her deck had been reinforced to withstand the recoil of her as-yet-theoretical guns.

Sparhawk remarked on these changes to the convalescent Benjamin Ward, who ordered a hammock strung for himself on deck and refused to retire to occupy the captain's cabin until he was capable of taking command.

"Admiral Graves is pressing any vessel he can get his hands on," said Benji. "We must buy guns in Lisbon. Without them, we might as well hand her over to the navy with our compliments."

Which begged the question of what they would do if they encountered a naval vessel *on the way* to Lisbon.

"Outrun her," said Benjamin Ward. "We sail in ballast. With no cargo, we can outsail anything big enough to outgun us. You only caught the *Sally*," said Benjamin Ward, echoing his sister's words on that occasion, "because Molineaux was a fool."

Sparhawk could not argue with him.

Sparhawk checked the *Sally*'s provisions, her salt beef, her water, her peas, her little supply of powder and shot for the swivels, her spare cordage and spars and sails. Most of it was better than what the navy yard provided the king's ships. Once he was satisfied that their stores were sufficient for the voyage to Lisbon, he left Benji in Mr. Cheap's capable hands and rowed himself to the Winnisimmet ferry landing for his delayed meeting with the Rebels.

The admiral, James knew, had been routinely raiding Chelsea and the nearby Noddle's and Hog islands for provisions for weeks. Now the landing was guarded by a company of militia under an elderly but formidable American, a Captain Sprague, who carried a Brown Bess of French and Indian

War vintage and a wicked-looking club of polished maple inlaid with wampum that might easily have belonged to the Indian leader, King Philip, himself. Sprague declared Sparhawk's pass from the Provincial Congress to be in good order and detailed two sturdy farmers with fowling pieces to conduct him to the meetinghouse.

He also, as it happened, admired Sparhawk's velvet coat.

"Got married in one just like it," said Sprague.

Which was probably sometime in the forties, thought Sparhawk. No doubt Red Abed had been quite the dandy.

The countryside, even to a sailor with an untutored eye for such things, was admirable. Lush marshes filled with game marched alongside well-watered fields, and a cool harbor breeze mitigated the summer heat. Sparhawk's polite inquiries about the hunting, the fishing, the cattle raised there, and the general situation of the island were met by stony silence from the local militiamen, who did not relish the sudden interest being taken by the world at large, and the navy in particular, in their little paradise.

The meetinghouse was a simple, antique structure, clapboard, with a massive central chimney. The interior was cool and dark, and it took a moment for Sparhawk's eyes to adjust. At the end of a long aisle formed by rows of rough-hewn benches, standing in a shaft of sunlight streaming through the pulpit window, stood Angela Ferrers, the Merry Widow. Her costume was at odds with the austere building, an elegant robe à l'anglaise cut from oyster satin and trimmed with wide bobbin lace *engageantes.*

"New England houses of worship are known for the thunder of their oratory," she said, gesturing to indicate the ax-hewn timbers. "Not the splendor of their architecture."

The wonder of God's creation, Sparhawk could not help but observe, was indeed more manifest in this woman's face and corsage than in the rude chamber. It was a studied effect — like a jewel against a square of plain black cloth.

"I understood that their preachers were ranked on the length, as much as the thunder, of their sermons. Seeing the furnishings, I would hold the shorter the better."

"As a naval man," said Angela Ferrers, "you must be used to discomfort."

"I am used to discomfort with purpose."

"And you have no purpose for the Divine."

"On the contrary. I make use of his designs

every day. Of the stars he has set in the sky and the angles and cosigns of his geometry. I find evidence of his works all around me on the open sea, but I see no sense in looking for him in a place like this. It is more secular evidence, against Admiral Graves, that I hoped to find here today."

Angela Ferrers nodded. "We had expected you to meet us here to collect the papers last night. There was, I am credibly informed, some difficulty during your escape. Young Captain Ward has been injured."

"Benji was shot by one of Graves' marines. The ball is out and he is recovering."

"Recovering, but not *recovered*. How soon will he be able to command the *Sally*?"

"You would have to speak with his doctor. But then, I believe you already have."

"Just so," admitted Angela Ferrers. "Dr. Warren tells me Benjamin Ward is unlikely to be fit for command for several weeks. A powder run to Lisbon was our condition for handing over the evidence we have gathered. It appears that condition will not be met."

He had known nothing would be simple with this woman. "A delay of two weeks hardly signifies," said Sparhawk. "A storm might add as much or more to the journey."

"The army of the United Colonies has powder for twenty cartridges per man. We outnumber General Gage four to one, but if he learned of our situation, and broke out with his four thousand, he might destroy our force in an afternoon. Every day, every *hour* counts for us now. And you, sir, are more than capable of commanding the *Charming Sally.*"

"I am, but the navy frowns upon its officers making powder runs for its enemies. Even those on half pay."

"It also frowns on fugitives from naval justice," she replied coolly. "Your loyalty to the service has proved somewhat elastic. Tell me what would convince you to stretch it in this matter."

He had already been tempted to stretch it when he saw the *Sally* again. In the navy, ambitious captains sidestepped promotion to flagships and ships of the line, the dull steady march toward empty rank and emptier pockets, in favor of smaller commands and the promise of action and prizes.

Schooners and frigates were what you wanted, small and fast, but there were precious few to be had, and often you chose a ship with more guns over a better sailor. The *Sally,* once she was armed, would offer no compromises. From the first time he had seen the trim little schooner with her lovely sharp lines, he'd wanted her. The thought of commanding her, of feeling her sails belly and stiffen and her hull thrum in answer to his orders, filled him with a desire similar to what he felt for Sarah Ward.

"Very well," he said. "Get Sarah Ward away from Anthony Trent, and I will take command of the *Sally* as far as Lisbon. Sarah's brother should be sufficiently recovered by then to oversee dealings in the port and command the return voyage."

Angela Ferrers shook her head. "That would not be in our interests. Lord Polkerris is so deeply embroiled in the treasons of the Ward family, he is ripe for blackmail, and too well placed to lose as a possible source of intelligence."

"He is a murderer," said Sparhawk. "A monster. And it is Sarah's life at hazard."

"There are more lives in the balance than that of one sea rogue's daughter. But I am not unsympathetic, Captain. If you are determined to spirit her away, you may find ample opportunity tomorrow, while the admiral celebrates his ascension to the white — and while we remove his naval stores, his hemp, his tar, his sails, and all the cattle and fodder from Noddle's Island."

"You mean to take on the British Navy in Boston Harbor?" Sparhawk asked, incredulous. "With Captain Sprague and a company

356

of grandfathers?"

Angela Ferrers smiled. "I daresay Captain Sprague has a little life left in him yet."

Sparhawk recalled the briskness of Sprague's step and the war club hanging at the man's hip, and decided she was probably right.

"Captain Sprague," said Angela Ferrers, "will fight to protect his home and his family. If you are not willing to do the same for Sarah Ward, then she is better off with Anthony Trent."

"You are determined to see me branded a Rebel," said Sparhawk.

"I am determined to show you where your best interests lie. Step into the light, please," she said.

He was not in a mood to indulge her, but his concern for Sarah overrode his resistance. He took a single step.

"Yes," said Angela Ferrers. "I was right. The resemblance is not obvious, but it is there. You are Lord Polkerris' missing son. He searched for you, across the Indian Ocean and through the Med, for two years."

Sparhawk felt the old sick fear in the pit of his stomach. McKenzie had been right. His father *had* learned of his survival, and tried to finish the job. More than once he thought he might have been followed, that

357

ordinary footpads might have had deeper designs against a teenage boy on the streets of Portsmouth, in the stews of Calcutta — and he had been right.

"If you know of my existence," said Sparhawk, "then you also know of his crimes. He is a seducer, a bigamist."

"To you," said Angela Ferrers. "But to the world he is a decorated naval officer and a baron with a comfortable income who risks his life in the service of his country. Even his renown as a duelist — and what is dueling but private murder cloaked in ritual? — is admired by his peers. He is a generous philanthropist and a beloved friend of the king."

"He killed my mother. He tried to kill me."

"He did what privilege allowed him to do. You think your quarrel is with an individual man, but it is with an empire. One that uses nations the way Trent used your mother. The way Trent *will* use Sarah Ward. He has taken her under his roof. How long do you think it will be before he has taken her into his bed?"

The thought turned Sparhawk's stomach. "I will save her from him." As he had not been able to save his mother.

The widow looked pleased. "There will be

an opportunity for you to reach her tomorrow night. I can tell you both the place and the hour. But know this: if you pit yourself against Trent, then you pit yourself against British rule in North America. Deprive him of his prize, and he will use all of the power at his disposal — including the king's forces — to get her back."

Angela Ferrers was almost certainly right, but there was no other course open to him, so he spoke the words she wanted to hear: "Tell me where to find Sarah Ward."

EIGHTEEN

At eight bells on a slightly overcast morning
Admiral Graves raised his white pennant on
the *Preston*'s yard-arm for the first time.
His flagship received a thirteen-gun salute
from the vessels of the squadron in the
harbor: the *Somerset,* the *Glasgow,* the *Bri-
tannia,* the *Mercury,* the *Hephaestion;* and,
of course, those ships, the *Diana* and the
Wasp, under the commands of the admiral's
two nephews, Thomas and Francis Graves.

The salute was heard as far away as
Cambridge, where the students of Harvard
College had been sent home from the
theater of war, and the American commanders counted their powder barrels, then
counted them again, hoping they might
discover some hidden error in their calculations, or at least a few extra ounces hidden
beneath the floorboards.

It was heard at the meetinghouse in
Chelsea, where old Captain Sprague had

marched his company to join Colonel Stark's six hundred militia for a cattle raid.

And it was heard by Sarah Ward as she tried to put together an ensemble that would withstand twelve hours of dining, drinking, and dancing in the sticky summer heat. As Trent had no ship, they had been spared the early-morning salute, but they would be expected to attend breakfast on the *Preston,* which was intended to last all morning, and where General Gage would *not* appear, because his wife was not on speaking terms with the admiral's lady.

From there they would proceed to dinner at the home of Mr. Williams on Noddle's Island, where his wife and her cousin, Mrs. Martin, would be feting the newly arrived major generals Clinton, Burgoyne, and Howe, and the Gages, who *would* attend so long as Admiral Graves and his wife did not.

Once, Sarah would have celebrated the arrival of these three commanders as the other Tories in Boston did, with a naive expectation that they would, in Burgoyne's words, "soon make elbow room," and send the Rebels packing. But she could no longer see British military intervention in American affairs as anything but dangerous interference. Trent's description of the officers in question did nothing to change her opinion.

"Clinton," he said, "is a shy bitch. Awkward and unsociable. Burgoyne fancies himself a wit. He is only occasionally correct. And Billy Howe is every bit as sentimental about America and Americans — his eldest brother died at Ticonderoga in the Rebel general Israel Putnam's arms — as Gage."

Breakfast was lavish, served under canvas awnings on the deck of the *Preston*. Sarah scrutinized the cabin boys who came and went among the tables, hoping that Ned might have been detailed to the flagship for the occasion, but she caught no glimpse of her little brother. The admiral's cook was French, and quite possibly skilled, but unused to the sticky New England summer, and the elaborate jellies and aspics decorated with bright flowers and cut fruits quickly melted into sad puddles on the silver.

There was a fracas sometime after noon on deck when word reached the admiral that Rebels were rustling cattle on Noddle's Island. He dispatched Thomas and Francis on the *Diana* and the *Wasp* to deal with the trouble, and firmly assured the generals that their dinner on the island would not be interrupted.

It was late afternoon by the time the major

generals, Trent, Sarah, and the other guests left the *Preston*. The little flotilla of three whaleboats waiting at the Long Wharf to ferry them to Mr. Williams' house on Noddle's Island had been rigged thoughtfully with sailcloth canopies, which provided welcome shelter from the slanting summer sun.

Later, Sarah could not say exactly how they became separated, she from Trent, her boat from the rest of the flotilla. It began with the suggestion that the ladies should have the boat with the cushioned benches, and that the gentlemen should embark first, as the boat intended for the ladies was last in the queue for the gangplank and the whole party would be delayed if the time was taken to reorder the little flotilla.

It was further suggested that since the gentlemen would now arrive first on the island, they could help the ladies debark, which would be the gallant thing to do. Sarah thought this idea might have originated with the boatmen. No mention was made of who would help the ladies to *embark*. The jug the gentlemen began passing around was definitely given to them by the rowers, and declared to be very restorative in the heat. No doubt it contributed to the agreeable mood with which the gentlemen left the ladies behind.

Sarah had no trouble maneuvering her cotton polonaise and petticoats into the boat. She had dispensed with a hip roll for the occasion, knowing they made travel in small craft more difficult than necessary. Two of the ladies had worn panniers and required a bench apiece.

General Gage's wife, who had but lately joined them, had dressed as so many fine ladies chose to be painted, à la turque, in a purple silk robe bound with a golden girdle, and she climbed in with grace and agility.

Elizabeth Loring, "the Sultana of Boston," known for her gambling and her extravagant costume, wore cream silk embroidered with gold wire and, true to her reputation, was careless of her riches. The beauty settled on her bench and draped one arm over the side, sleeve ruffles trailing in salt water and ruining a fortune in gold lace.

Lady Frankland was wearing a quilted petticoat with crewelwork, despite the heat, and required the assistance of four boatmen to lower her down. Once seated, she demanded the awning be rolled back over her bench so that she might take the sun, which she believed, against all evidence, preserved her youthful complexion.

By that time the gentlemen were well

ahead of them. It seemed to Sarah that the ladies' vessel was being rowed at a markedly slower pace, and she itched to take up an oar and propel them at greater speed.

The distance between the boats widened. Then, just as the two vessels carrying the gentlemen came within hailing distance of the dock at the Williams mansion, Sarah saw their rowers slip overboard, splashing into the water — with their oars — and swim for the marsh to the east of the house.

The gentlemen began to drift.

The ladies' boat, rowed with new vigor, shot right, away from the Williams mansion and the dock. The gentlemen shouted. The ladies, for the most part, were dumbfounded. Within minutes their little canopied whaleboat had disappeared into a creek hidden by tall marsh grasses.

Silence closed in around them. Lady Frankland castigated the boatman nearest her and began to belabor him with her fan. He ignored her. One of the ladies in panniers started to cry. Margaret Kemble Gage leaned across her bench and slapped her. For the first time all afternoon Elizabeth Loring looked less than bored. And Sarah wished she had brought the little muff gun Trent had given her, and not worn her mother's necklace. She was a pirate's daughter, and she could well guess the purpose of waylaying a boatload of bejeweled women in a marsh.

The tall grass thinned, a rocky beach appeared on their right, and two men, their faces obscured by kerchiefs and broad hats, stood waiting, pistols in hand.

One of them wore a copper velvet coat. The other had tried — and failed — to hide his honey gold hair in a tightly wrapped queue.

Too late, too late. Sparhawk had come back for her, when she could not possibly go with him. When Ned's life hung in the balance. When saving herself meant sacrificing her little brother. Trent had cautioned her the night he had proposed. She must do nothing to provoke the admiral, nothing to suggest that she might speak out against him, or attempt to reach London with her damning testimony, or Ned would pay for it. To press home his concerns, Trent had not spared her a recitation of Admiral Graves' threats. Ned would suffer as Sparhawk had suffered as a boy. He would be lashed with the cat until he passed out, then be allowed to recover, then lashed again. Thinking of it now made her light-headed.

The oarsmen disembarked and dragged the boat up onto the rocks.

The golden-haired brigand who was her older brother tossed a sack into the boat. "Place your jewels and your purses in the bag," he said, his voice muffled by the cloth, but familiar all the same. He would enjoy this piratical masquerade, her daring brother. But he did not know that Ned's life was at risk. She looked away so she would betray no hint of recognition.

The ladies were more anxious and excited than afraid. The masked men — after all — were the very picture of dashing highwaymen.

"She weeps if but a handsome thief is hung," thought Sarah.

When the bag came around to her, she put her earbobs and her purse in it alongside Margaret Gage's diamond earrings and Elizabeth Loring's paste, but she could not part with her mother's gold chain, could not bear the thought of removing it from her neck.

The sack was collected.

The tall brigand in the familiar copper velvet coat shoved his pistol in his pocket and waded down to the boat.

"You ladies may row back to the farmhouse," said James Sparhawk through his silk kerchief. Then he pointed to Sarah Ward. "But she comes with us."

He reached for her and she shrank back. "No."

Her name was on his lips, she could tell, even with his eyes veiled by the hat and his mouth hidden behind the neck cloth, but he stifled his impulse to speak it. "You have my word that I will return you to your friends unharmed, in the morning," he said, echoing the words she had spoken to him when she took him prisoner on the *Sally.*

He addressed the rest of the ladies in the boat. "Provided, of course, that everyone stays inside the manor tonight, and no boats are sent to the fleet or to the mainland."

If she did not go, she risked Sparhawk or Benji giving himself away, but she was determined to be back long before morning. Determined to afford the admiral no cause to punish Ned.

Sarah stood up carefully in the tiny boat and gathered her skirts to climb over the side. Margaret Kemble Gage put out an arm and held her back. The governor's elegant wife looked up at the masked thief and said, "Shall I relay your compliments to my husband, Captain Sparhawk?"

He should have guessed that Margaret Gage was in league with the Merry Widow. They were all connected: Warren, Angela Ferrers,

368

the governor's beautiful wife, who sat staring up at him with a smug expression. As well she might. Angela Ferrers had been determined to maneuver him to the American side: to brand him not just a thief and a fugitive, but a Rebel and a pirate.

Margaret Gage had succeeded. Her pronouncement, to a boatload of wealthy beauties and an old woman sure to live on scandal and gossip, meant that he was no longer James Sparhawk, the naval officer who had fled court-martial, his guilt an open question; but by virtue of committing robbery in the waters of Boston Harbor, he was now James Sparhawk, pirate.

Later, he would have to consider what argument could be made to the Admiralty about the necessity of waylaying a skiff full of aristocratic Boston ladies in a marsh.

Just now he had to get rid of said boatload of aristocratic ladies so he could talk with one pirate's daughter.

"You may tell your husband whatever you like, Mrs. Gage," said Sparhawk, removing his kerchief and his hat. "It will not get you your diamonds back."

He lifted Sarah out of the boat and carried her to a path above the beach. The militiamen who had rowed the boat pushed it back into the creek, and the ladies began paddling furiously, the old besom in the bow urging them on. They were soon out of sight.

Benji's vigor had lasted long enough for the show, but now he was sitting on the ground looking pale. Sarah knelt beside him to examine his bandages.

She looked up at Sparhawk. "His stitches have pulled out. He needs to lie down and rest."

"Not here," said Sparhawk. "We are too close to the house. The *Sally,* though, is not far."

Sparhawk dismissed the militia, who had muskets and powder horns hidden in the grass — but not before he fished Sarah's earbobs out of the bag and tossed the remainder of the loot to Captain Sprague's equally elderly lieutenant. "By way of a thank-you," said Sparhawk.

"You are supposed to keep the jewels," grumbled Benji. "You have no talent for this at all." But after that, on the path through the field to the cove, with Sarah and Sparhawk supporting him, he was silent.

Mr. Cheap was waiting for them on the white beach, armed with his sword pistol, brass knuckle rings, two hangers, and something quite like a sickle hanging from his sash.

"Miss Sarah," he said, "in you go first" —
he gestured to the boat — "with your pretty
white skirts. Then I'll push her out."

"Benji first," she said. "He needs stitching
back up, Mr. Cheap."

Sparhawk watched, astonished, as Mr.
Cheap nodded and picked up all six feet of
Benjamin Ward and lifted him into the boat
as if he were a newborn. Next he beckoned
Sarah, but this time she shook her head and
stepped back.

"I'm not going."

Cheap looked from Sarah to Sparhawk,
uncertain what to do.

James had parted badly from her at the
house in the North End. Her reluctance was
natural, but untimely. "We must go now,
Sarah," said Sparhawk.

She turned to him. "You should not have
come back," she said. "Micah Wild has
switched sides and received letters of
marque from the admiral. He has six four-
pounders and twoscore men."

"On what?" scoffed Mr. Cheap.

"On the *Roger Conant*," said Sarah.

"Ah," said Mr. Cheap. Apparently the *Conant* was a ship to be reckoned with.

"I am not afraid of Micah Wild," said
Sparhawk. He would manhandle her into
the boat if he had to. "We can talk on the

Sally."

He reached for her.

Mr. Cheap cocked his pistol. "I have grown to like you, Captain," said Cheap. "Truly I have. But Sarah comes of her own free will, or not at all."

Sparhawk should have considered that. It was the first thing he had observed about Lucas Cheap: his loyalty to Sarah Ward. There was no arguing with it. "Very well, Mr. Cheap. Take Benji to the *Sally.* I'll signal for the boat when we are ready."

Sarah's expression told him there would be no "we."

They watched Mr. Cheap push the boat out into the water and climb in.

Sparhawk turned to Sarah Ward. He had never seen her face so bleak. It was his fault. A lifetime of avoiding entanglements, of keeping the women he bedded at arm's length, had left him ill-equipped for this moment.

"I love you," he said.

The words did not banish her despondence. They did not light her eyes with the fire he remembered from the deck on the *Sally,* when she had leveled her pistol at him, or kindle the excitement she had betrayed in her father's keeping room before Micah Wild's untimely interruption. But

372

there was nothing keeping them apart now, if only he could express himself with some eloquence.

"I am sorry. My education was cut short at an early age and I have spent much of my life among seamen, and very little of it in salons. I do not have the wit to do your qualities justice, the poetry to describe what I feel when I watch you walk across a deck or sheet a sail or, God help me, aim a pistol. I should have said all this before we parted, but I was determined to give you up, to cut you loose from this mess I am in and see you safe in another man's keeping. You possess every quality I admire in a woman, or for that matter in a man, and I will find no happiness on this earth without you."

Tears brimmed in her eyes. It was not the reaction he was hoping for.

She shook her head. "It doesn't matter now. Admiral Graves has Ned hostage aboard the *Diana.* I have to marry Trent, or the admiral will have Ned lashed and then he will arrest me."

"Sarah, you cannot marry Trent. He is my father."

For a moment the world spun around her. Then Sparhawk's arms were steadying her and he was lowering her to the ground, the coarse sand and small pebbles rough against her back.

"Wait here, Sarah," said Sparhawk. "I'll send for the boat."

She sat up carefully and shook her head. "No boat." She tried to fathom what he was saying. "It cannot be. Trent is —"

"Trent is forty-four," said Sparhawk. He ran to the water's edge to dip his kerchief in the surf and returned to drape it, cool and soothing, around her neck. "I am twenty-eight," he continued. "Trent was fifteen when he married my mother, sixteen when I was born."

It had to be a mistake. Sparhawk's father had been a monster. "He cannot be the same man. Trent is everything kind and generous. He has fed and clothed my family. He shielded Ned and me from the admiral. He has offered me marriage."

"He is very good at making himself agreeable to women. Much like Micah Wild."

"Trent is nothing like Micah Wild."

"Past experience indicates that you are not the best judge of character."

"No," she said coldly. "Apparently I am not."

"Sarah, even if you will not have me, you cannot return to Trent. In Salem I did not tell you everything he did. Some things were too painful to speak of, but I will speak them now, even the ones that shame me, because I cannot bear to see you in his power. You have felt the scars on my back. That is what Slough did, when I refused to service him. He broke me, so that I got on my knees willingly for him, to be spared the lash. That was Trent's doing. My mother suffered worse. When she was in jail, she begged her guards to take a message to the island parson who had married her to my father. The guards held her down and poured lye down her throat so that she might never tell her story again. The magistrates declared her a debtor and an indigent, and they sentenced her to indentured servitude on a plantation, where she died from abuse and neglect. This is what Trent did to the woman he loved, whose only sin was to refuse to collude in bigamy with him. Imagine what he might do to you if he learned of our connection."

Sarah's whole life had been a succession of happy worlds stolen from her. The freedom and adventure of the *Sally* had been exchanged for the constrictions of the dame school. The heady thrill of her engagement to Micah Wild had been traded for the liminal status of a half-fallen woman, used goods. The promise of Sparhawk's little house in the North End had been exchanged for the secure certainty of marriage to Trent, which now appeared far less safe. "You were abducted on an East Indiaman. You were half a world away. How do you know what happened to your mother?" asked Sarah.

"Once I had my own ship, I requested service in the Caribbean, and tried to find her. I was naive enough to think she might still be alive. The cleric who married my parents had long since left the island, but the Spaniard who taught me swordplay and the Jewess who tutored me in Hebrew were still there, and I was able to piece together some of the story. Trent, though, covered his tracks well. The magistrates who tried my mother were dead. Killed in duels manufactured by my father. Along with the plantation owner who had bought her indenture. Two of the slaves remembered her and how she had died, and, in exchange for their stories, I bought and freed them."

Sarah took a step away from him.

It was too neat. It had the elegant simplicity of one of Ned's stories, of a hero and a villain locked in mortal enmity. And life, as she knew from her experience with Micah Wild, was not like that. The man who had jilted her was no stage villain. He had not

376

climbed in her bedroom window, had not, like some rake's progress, made fast the lock upon the door. *She* had gone to *him,* been complicit in her own seduction. She had flung her innocence at his feet to bind him with obligation when their mercantile ties unraveled. When it all went wrong, she had hidden behind the mask of victim, held her father and their fortunes ransom to the narrative of the scheming Rebel villain, and the cost — their home, the *Sally,* Ned's freedom — had been too dear. The cunning rake and the naive virgin might make a better story, but that did not make it true.

"I do not doubt that these things you experienced happened," she said. "That you have suffered and that an injustice has been done you. But you were twelve years old when all this occurred. Younger than Benji is now. Your understanding was not that of an adult. The testimony you heard was second- and thirdhand, and in the case of the slaves on the plantation, bought from desperate men who would say anything to escape their servitude. Even if everything you believe is true, even if Trent is a murderer, I will marry him, and gladly, to keep Ned from suffering as you did. I should go now," she said. "I do not think Trent will be content to wait for my return, no matter what threats Mrs. Gage repeats. And they must not find the *Sally* and Benji."

"Sarah." Sparhawk's voice was tinged with panic. "If I could get Ned off the *Diana,* if he was safe, would you leave Trent?"

"Please don't try," she said. "Take the *Sally* and Benji and leave. Ned is safe for the moment, and Graves will not be able to touch him or me if I can marry Trent before the admiral learns of our plans."

"I cannot sail so long as you remain under that man's roof."

"He has not touched me," she said. "Not once. Though he has had every opportunity. He saved me from a gang of soldiers the night we came to Charlestown, when we were looking for you at the Three Cranes. Mr. Cheap and Benji had been gone for hours. We were tired and hungry, and my father was at the end of his endurance. I would have given myself to Trent out of gratitude, and he knew it, and he did not press his advantage."

Sparhawk shook his head. "If he spared you, it was only because he plays some deeper game. Do you know how many men he has killed in duels?"

"Seven," she said. "He almost fought one to save me. I tried to pick a Redcoat's pocket, but I was not so deft as on the day I picked yours on the *Sally*. The fusilier caught me. And his friends wanted to have their pound of flesh. They would have done too, but Trent stopped them."

"That makes him fastidious, not noble," spat Anthony Trent's son.

"If you will not see reason, then leave," she said. "You endanger Benji's life by staying. Mr. Cheap's as well."

"If you know your family, then you will realize I did not have the power to delay the *Sally*'s sailing on my own. Mr. Cheap and Benji both voted to come back for you."

"But they will not make me come, and they will not let you force me to come."

"No," he said. "They will not, but chances are they will be all for rescuing Ned. The *Diana* sailed past Noddle's and up the creek this afternoon. If she engages with the Americans, there is a chance we will be able to get Ned off."

She hesitated, then said, "If you can get Ned away from the Graves family, I will have more freedom to consider my course of action."

"That is not the assurance I was hoping for," he said.

"It is the best I can give you under the circumstances."

He did not try to stop her from leaving.

She took the path he showed her, up over the headland. She could smell smoke on the air, thought she might hear guns firing, but the dense growth on the island muffled sound and confounded her ability to decide where it was coming from. North, perhaps. At least if the *Diana* was involved in a skirmish with cattle rustlers, Ned would be relatively safe. The Americans did not have ships that could match fire with a British man-of-war.

She had wanted to go with Sparhawk so badly, her chest hurt. It felt as if a line were wrapped around her ribs, growing tighter every second, tied with a clove hitch knot to the *Sally.*

I love you. Too late. He had not said it the night they made love, but even then, she had been prepared to go with him. His company, his wit, their mutual attraction, would have been enough for her. She had already resolved in Salem to take what life offered her, to put aside the dream of that elegant brick house and the status it would have accorded her, all false lures and vanity. With Sparhawk she might not have had the respect of her neighbors, but together they would have shared all the things that really mattered, and devil take the gossips.

Now that was impossible. And she had

only her pride to blame once more. She could have argued with him that night, and if that had not worked, begged, or broken down into tears. She could have simply demanded to be taken aboard the *Sally,* and Mr. Cheap and Benji would have obliged. But she had not, because she would not allow Sparhawk to see how much he had hurt her.

The manor house was brightly lit, with candles blazing from every window. Music floated on the air, and the smell of food — more appetizing than the admiral's breakfast — drifted through the night. She had not eaten, she realized, all day. She reached the manicured lawn just as the sun was setting, and she discovered an old-fashioned, formal knot garden and a long parterre, which led to the steps of the landside façade.

The house was old and stoutly built, part fieldstone fortress and part country manor. The doors were open, and she entered the starburst marble hall and surprised two sleepy footmen who did not expect guests to come from that direction. Sarah hesitated on the threshold of the dining room when she saw her hosts seated in the place of honor at the center of the broad polished table: Mr. Williams, Mrs. Williams, and their *cousin,* "Mrs. Martin," who was, without a doubt, Angela Ferrers, wearing pale blue silk, the pearl-crusted mourning rings on her long elegant fingers sparkling in the candlelight.

One of the ladies in panniers looked at Sarah and shrieked. Mrs. Gage got up smoothly from her chair and emerged from the room to sweep Sarah up the stairs and into the chamber where Trent was closeted with Generals Gage and Howe.

Trent's relief was evident on his face. They all asked her, of course, if she had been hurt. Howe thundered something about getting horses and chasing down this devil, Sparhawk.

"They are gone," said Sarah. "And Mrs. Gage's earrings with them."

Trent's eyes, she saw, settled on her neck, where her mother's gold chain still circled her throat.

Then General Gage asked gently if Sarah wouldn't like to speak alone with Mrs. Gage about anything that might have happened, and Sarah thanked him for his kindness but said plainly that she had not been offered any insult.

Howe was all for action, but Gage soothed him. If the rascals had a schooner, they would be well away by now. No one had been hurt, little of value had been stolen, and because the ladies had been waylaid, however briefly, turning a supper party into a manhunt would suggest that something far worse had happened to them.

The point was moot, because Sarah was not able to remember which direction she had come from, nor where the schooner was anchored. And just in case Billy Howe could not be dissuaded from riding into the night, she added, "I saw smoke and heard fire coming from the north." Which would take pursuit in the opposite direction from the *Sally,* away from Sparhawk and Benji.

Billy Howe's ears perked at this, but Thomas Gage shook his head. "It is a cattle raid by the Rebels. Nothing more. They want the beasts and hay off the islands, and it is, after all, their property. Admiral Graves lays some claim to the cattle, but has not paid for them yet, and he keeps his naval stores here, without paying rent to the landowners, so it is his responsibility to pursue the thieves. I warned him of their intention two days ago when Margaret's brother got wind of it."

Howe pointed out that warships did not have the men to chase cattle raiders across miles of territory.

"Then the admiral," said the governor, "should take care not to become involved in disputes over livestock. I have kept the peace in Boston," said Gage wearily, "for nigh on a year. Parliament will not send troops, only provocation. Bills and acts designed to drive the mildest yeoman farmer into open rebellion. They play into the hands of Warren and Adams and the demagogues who hunger for war, and try to taunt us to rash and bloody action. They had their day at Lexington, their 'Bloody Butchery.' I will not give them another excuse to expand this rebellion beyond the Massachusetts Bay."

Mrs. Gage voiced her agreement. Billy Howe appeared shocked to discover she had a voice at all. Until she said something he liked, which was that Mrs. Loring had been asking for him. She made no mention of Mrs. Loring's husband, who seemed an unusually broadminded gentleman. Howe decided that perhaps the best thing — for Sarah, of course — was that they should continue on with the evening.

The Gages and Howe rejoined the party, leaving Sarah alone, for the moment, with Trent. Somehow, with only the two of them, the chamber seemed smaller.

"Are you really all right?" he asked.

"Yes."

"I should have spoken with you earlier, but I have secured a license, and a willing parson, albeit a radical one, from the college. I am arranging the passes now. He will not enter Boston, for fear of arrest, so I have suggested that he meet us in Charlestown, and perform the ceremony at the Three Cranes."

I will marry him and gladly. Here was abstraction become reality, and she found she was not glad of it, not with Sparhawk so near, but out of reach. "How do you know a radical divine?"

"He married my first wife and me, and he took an interest in her and my son when I was away at sea."

This, then, was the cleric Sparhawk had come to Boston to find. That he was willing to perform another marriage for Trent argued that Trent could not have arranged the arrest of his first wife and murder of his son.

He crossed the room to her, and she took a step back. Her shoulders touched the door behind her. Trent stroked her neck where the fine gold chain lay close against her skin.

"Sarah," he said, continuing to stroke, his hand moving lower now with a practiced, skilled sensuality. "Have I made a mistake with us? Left this" — he dipped his head to press a kiss against her neck, making her skin tingle and her nipples tighten — "too late?"

His hand dipped into her stays, found a nipple, squeezed it into a tight bud. His knee pressed into her skirts and up until it met her sex through the silk, and friction kindled the inevitable response.

He was Sparhawk's father.

"Please don't," she said.

He stilled immediately and stepped away.

"I am sorry," she said. "It is nothing to do with Sparhawk." It was everything to do with Sparhawk. "My brother was with him. They came back," she lied with near-convincing smoothness for the first time in her life, "so that I would know Benji was all right."

Regret played across Trent's handsome features, so very like Sparhawk's, now that she looked for the resemblance. But she had always known he was a seducer. It did not mean he was a murderer.

"I am sorry," he said.

But it was her fault. It was not his touch that had unnerved her, but her unsettling — and unexpected — response.

NINETEEN

Sparhawk was determined to remove Ned from the *Diana*. Mr. Cheap agreed that it was the likeliest way to get Sarah away from Trent. Sparhawk still thought the likeliest and most direct way was to tie her up in a sack, but the infuriating Ward family and their amanuensis would not hear of it.

But there was a chance, given the sound of the guns and the smoke rising to the north, that if the *Diana* was still engaged with the Rebels, there might be an opportunity to spirit one small boy off that British man-of-war.

Cheap and Sparhawk made their way around the island, seeing everywhere evidence of the Rebels' success: burnt barns, dead livestock, trampled grass indicating the passage of great herds of beasts. They followed this path of desolation to the creek separating Noddle's Island from the mainland at Chelsea and found the tide out and the Americans fled across the shallows. Cheap and Sparhawk crossed in their footsteps, followed the sounds of fighting, of ship's cannon, and surprisingly, fieldpieces, to the west.

The scene they found at the mouth of the sandy creek north of Noddle's Island beggared imagination. The Americans, some six hundred of them, were massed on Chelsea beach, near the ferry landing. They had two fieldpieces with them, and were firing upon the *Diana.*

She did not return the American volleys with her sixteen guns. She did nothing at all, because she was stuck fast in the mud, her draft too deep for the shallow creek, the angle of her deck too steep for her guns to be of any use. The tide was ebbing more with each passing minute. She had six boats out in the shallows, their crews rowing furiously to pull her off, but the Americans were peppering the British sailors with small-arms fire and they could make no headway. The *Diana* was Gulliver caught fast by the Lilliputians.

Every once in a while a ball hurtled out of the darkness from the hill on Noddle's, where a handful of British marines had set up two of their own fieldpieces, but the Americans were undaunted.

Sparhawk scanned the *Diana*'s deck for some sign of Ned, but there was not a head to be seen above the schooner's tilted rail, and when so much as a pennant moved in the breeze, an American discharged his rifle with astonishing accuracy.

Under heavy fire, one by one the boat crews, trying to pull the *Diana* off, cut their lines, and once freed, shot toward the safety of the British guns on Noddle's Island. Sparhawk could not blame them.

The last two boats became caught in a race to hack themselves free, their crews knowing the final vessel tethered to the *Diana,* heeling hard as the schooner was, would be lashed by the recoil of the rope.

The second-to-last boat got free. The sailors in the final shallop took turns sawing at the rope while the others crouched low to escape the fire of the Americans. Finally, with a loud snap, the cable broke. The rope whipped wildly through the air. The little boat capsized, and her sailors stood up in waist-deep water and splashed desperately toward the shore.

A voice Sparhawk recognized as belonging to Thomas Graves, older brother to Francis, excoriated the fleeing sailors in the strongest terms, but the effect was somewhat spoiled when he raised his head above the rail and had his hat shot off. It fell into the mud with a splash and stayed there.

A few minutes later, the *Diana* followed its example. For one hopeful moment the outgoing tide lifted her up over the sandbar that had snared her. Then she settled and rolled with unexpected grace onto her side, beached like a whale.

The Americans on shore were silent at first, the spectacle of a British naval vessel helpless and impotent almost impossible to believe. There was something indecent about the sight of her keel above water, like a forbidden glimpse of a woman's knees, and the men lining the beach were uncertain how to react.

Until one fellow let out a whooping Indian war cry and the others took this up, Mohawks all now that the *Diana* could not level her guns at them. Then the most uncouth American Sparhawk had ever seen, gray, round, and wearing a coat even older than Abednego's, waded up to the stranded schooner and offered the captain of the *Diana* and his crew quarter in a bellowing voice.

Graves refused to surrender.

A cannonball hurtled out of the night from Noddle's Island and passed between the gruff American's legs.

"That would be Old Put," supplied Mr. Cheap.

Old Put — Israel Putnam — ignored the ball and laid out his terms. The British could abandon the *Diana,* or the Americans would burn her, and every man in her, including Sarah Ward's little brother Ned, to the waterline.

Sarah woke with a start in the predawn hours to the sound of thunder. She listened for rain but heard none. The rest of her sleep was fitful, disturbed by traffic in the street below and voices — the soldiery drilling far too early — on the Common.

She tried to return to sleep, but every time she closed her eyes and allowed her mind to drift, it returned to Trent and his hands on her body in that small chamber. At the borders of sleep, her body replayed its response to his skilled, calculating touch. Then she would come awake with a start, awash in a sea of guilt.

Because she loved Sparhawk.

She had lived under Trent's roof and accepted Trent's protection, knowing that a physical relationship — congress — could and now *would* be the inevitable result. But she had always shied away from imagining it. There had been so many excuses: her ill-fated encounter with Wild, her abandoned promise from Sparhawk, Trent's own delicacy where such matters were concerned following his candor the night they met.

Somehow she had thought that once they married they would be able to become lovers with a safe distance between them, one that preserved her tenderness for Sparhawk, whom she now knew to be his son, without cheating Trent of her whole affection.

Now she understood that it would be impossible to be the focus of Trent's singular passion and remain unmoved; that she had always, even from the start, been drawn to him. Their age difference, smaller than that between many couples, particularly when one partner was widowed, had never concerned her. This was in part because of his youthfulness and vigor and in part because her own father was so much older than Trent, having been nearly fifty when she was born. She did not see Trent as belonging to her father's generation.

If Sparhawk had meant nothing to her, she might have married Trent with no impediment. It was not that she and James had gone to bed together. It was the unalterable fact that Sparhawk was the man she wanted to share her troubles and joys with, whom she wanted to amuse with the eccentricities of Lady Frankland and turn to for comfort when she worried about Ned.

She could not marry Trent.

When she finally gave up on sleep and dressed and went down early to breakfast, she found Trent drinking his coffee and writing letters while his servant stood by.

"This to the admiral," said Trent, handing off a sealed letter. "And this to the general at Province House. And this, by whatever means you can contrive, to Israel Putnam with the Rebel army at Cambridge."

"What has happened?" she asked.

"The *Diana* is taken, burned to the waterline. The Americans say they killed three hundred British last night, the navy says it lost no one, but the crew of the *Diana* is not to be found."

Sarah sat down heavily in one of the dining room chairs. Trent knelt in front of her. "Do not think it. There is no reason to believe Ned was among those, if any, killed. The Rebel numbers smack of exaggeration; the *Diana*'s whole complement was barely sixty men. I will find him for you, and Graves or no, I will bring him back to you."

She nodded dumbly. "Don't tell my father," she said. "Not yet. Not until you have to."

"I have already instructed the servants to

bring no newspapers to Abednego. His brushes and paints usually consume him of a morning. By midday, I hope to be back, with news."

He left. She remained seated in the chair. The servants brought coffee and laid dishes on the table and left her, no doubt on Trent's instructions, to herself. It was only when she felt a tug on her sleeve that she realized she had been there for too long.

She looked up into the scrubbed face of the cook's child from Sparhawk's house — her house — in the North End.

"He has a message for you," said the child.

She knew who *he* was.

"He said to tell you that Ned is safe. And that he wants to see you. He asks if you will meet him at the house."

He had told her he loved her, and she believed him. She understood love, not because she had shared it with Micah Wild, but because she had a family that loved and infuriated her in equal measure. After twenty-seven years in a loving, maddening family of roguish mariners, she could predict Sparhawk's next move.

And because she loved him in return, she wrote not one reply, but two. The first she addressed to Mr. Cheap, and filled with precise instructions. She closed it with her father's seal. The second she wrote to Sparhawk, appointing a time to meet, and this one she closed with Trent's seal.

Sparhawk was used to giving orders, not debating them. The Ward family, unfortunately, did things differently. At least in their little democracy everyone cast an equal vote, and Ned was now his devoted ally.

Sarah's younger brother had boarded the *Sally* and run straight to Benjamin Ward with the tale of how Sparhawk had rescued him from the beached *Diana*.

"The Rebels were going to burn her to the waterline," said Ned to his older brother, who lay in a hammock, favoring his wound.

"They were only threatening to burn her," said Sparhawk. "They wanted the stores off her, the powder and cannon and swivels. They would not put her to the torch so long as there was a hope of plundering her."

"Quite right," said Benji.

"They *did* burn her," said Ned, who wanted to tell his tale. "Later. But Captain Sparhawk got us off first. Well, Dr. Warren got us off, but it was Sparhawk's idea. The doctor waded up to the *Diana* — not so far as Old Put, who just stood there while the cannonballs whistled through his legs — but close enough for all that. He said that he knew the *Diana* was holding pressed men, Americans, and that the Rebels would stop their fire if any of us wanted to come off. Two men jumped. Then Captain Graves said there were no more Americans on board, only Englishmen. Then Captain Sparhawk whispered in Dr. Warren's ear and Dr. Warren began calling out names, saying they had a list of pressed men on the *Diana*. It was no one's name that I knew, but one of the tars, who was an Irishman and no American of any kind, leapt up and answered to Ezekiah Martin of Malden, and another from Glasgow to Giles Fitch of Boston. I did not know what they were about, but the Irishman took me by the collar and told me that it was better to be a live American than a dead British sailor. Half the crew deserted. Captain Graves did not have the men to defend her after that. His boats came back and took him and the rest of the crew away under the cover of the guns on Noddle's. And then I found Mr. Cheap and Captain Sparhawk. And we got the *Diana*'s cannon."

At this Benjamin Ward sat up. "How many?" he asked.

"Not all of them," said Sparhawk. "I agreed to help Old Put bring the guns and their carriages off in one piece if he would give me two swivels and six four-pounders for the *Sally*. It seemed a wise precaution, given Micah Wild's designs."

"If we have guns," said Benji, "there are nearer and more profitable sources of powder than Lisbon."

There might very well be. The whole harbor knew that three supply ships had set sail from Portsmouth at the same time as the *Cerberus*. They had become separated during the crossing and were now overdue.

"The *Diana*," said Mr. Cheap sensibly, "was a fluke. It's not likely another ship will oblige you by grounding herself in a creek."

"Not," said Benjamin Ward, "without help."

"You are forgetting the more immediate problem of your sister," said Sparhawk. "She is living under the roof of a murderer."

Benji and Mr. Cheap exchanged looks.

"Captain Trent?" asked Ned. "He's not a bad fellow. He bought me a sextant."

He had bought Sparhawk a sextant too. It had been smashed to pieces the night the men came for his mother.

"I do not doubt your word," said Benji. "Perhaps the man was once a monster. But he is not now. He has been good to Sarah, and Ansbach also says he is a fine fellow."

Sparhawk knew he was not.

"And you cannot *make* my sister do a thing against her will. I have twenty-seven years of experience in the matter and know it cannot be done."

"There are other, confounding factors that would make a marriage between them an abomination," said Sparhawk.

Ned's brow furrowed. Mr. Cheap looked away. And Benji said, "When I am up to it, remind me to call you out and kill you."

Trent returned in the late afternoon. He looked tired, and Sarah did not doubt that he had called upon every ounce of interest he possessed to discover news of Ned.

He took the parlor chair opposite her. "There is reason to hope," he said. "The Rebels offered the pressed Americans on the *Diana* their freedom. That is why the admiral is claiming no casualties. He does not want it known that half the crew of his nephew's ship, which had no Americans besides your brother, deserted him. As best I can tell, only Thomas Graves was seriously injured in the affair. Burned quite badly, I'm told. He tried to get back aboard her after she was set afire, devil knows why. I will cross to Cambridge myself in the morning and try to find Ned among the Americans."

"There is no need. I've had word. Ned is safe."

Trent looked equal parts relieved and concerned. "How do you know this?"

"I received a message this afternoon."

"Thank God. Where is he?"

"With Sparhawk," she said.

Trent's expression darkened. "Sarah, Ned cannot remain with Sparhawk. This man is a fugitive. He presumed upon your obligation to him and embroiled you in his escape. With Ned in his power, he can prevail upon you again. You are already a hairbreadth from the gallows. Further association with this man could hang you."

"He will not prevail upon me again. He is in love with me. And he is your son."

Trent became perfectly still. The clock in the hall chimed. A carriage passed in the street. The silence in the room stretched. Finally, he leaned forward and said in a low, deadly voice, "Who told you this?"

Her mouth felt dry. She had not been afraid to broach the topic, but she was afraid now. "Sparhawk did," she said, summoning her voice and her courage. "He says he was born on Nevis, to your first wife, and he believes you have done him a terrible wrong."

Trent considered, then sat back and

smiled. "He is an imposter. My son is dead."

His certainty was chilling. Sparhawk had warned her that Trent would kill to protect his secret. She had not taken the threat seriously until now; she found that she was too frightened to press his claims of murder and imprisonment. "There is a resemblance," she said.

"No doubt. Most, though certainly not all, of the imposters who have attempted to blackmail me have held claim to a passing resemblance, but dark hair is not so very uncommon, and it is no secret that I searched for two years for the child of my first marriage, who I believed, wrongly, had died on Nevis. What is less well-known is that I found him."

Her stomach churned. "Where?" she asked.

"Buried. At Portsmouth."

It did not *directly* contradict Sparhawk's story. "As he tells it, that is the grave of the real James Sparhawk, the midshipman whose identity your son took."

Trent smiled again, but it was a cold expression, with no light in his eyes. "That is a very clever twist on an old refrain. I give the boy credit. But I can assure you, Sarah, that he is not my son, and any congress you have had with him will be no impediment to our marriage."

"But the fact that I love him will be."

A muscle in Trent's jaw twitched. "This man is a known rake and seducer, Sarah. He has deceived you."

"He says much the same about you."

"No doubt he would. The tricks men play on gullible women, the tricks *I* once played, have changed little over the years. You are young and have led a sheltered life in a small port —"

"Until Wild jilted me, and the navy tried to press my brother, and the mob burned my house down. I am not a child, and I have not been gullible for a long time. I cannot marry you, Anthony, because even if you are right and I am wrong, *I* believe Sparhawk is your son, and he has been my lover."

"What," said Trent, "must I do to prove to you this man is a liar?"

If she was right she could restore Sparhawk to his father, heal wounds that went deeper than the scars on his back, and enlist a powerful ally to fight with them against Admiral Graves. "This parson who is to marry us, do you trust him?" she asked.

Trent considered. "For many years after my wife died, I paid Reverend Edwards the rent from the living at Polkerris. He stopped accepting it around the time of the business with the tea, out of conscience. He is honest to a fault. I do trust him."

"And do you believe he would recognize your son?"

"Tristan is dead," said Trent. She had never heard his name before, thought it might have suited the boy she imagined James Sparhawk had once been, but found it hard to reconcile with the man.

"But if the Reverend Edwards declared James Sparhawk your son, then you would accept him as well?"

The muscle in Trent's jaw twitched again. "Yes."

If she was wrong, she was placing herself in the power of a murderer. She had to take the risk. "Then you must meet with him," she said. "You must do it, for me."

The muscle in Trent's jaw twitched again. His answer was long in coming. But at last, he replied simply, "Yes."

Sparhawk pondered his choices. He had spent years assembling the evidence of his identity, planning his revenge against Trent. He might, even now, if he took the *Sally* to Lisbon for Angela Ferrers, be able to clear his name with the Admiralty and pursue his long-held goal.

If he left Sarah to Trent's mercy.

He could not do it. He had to get her away from the bastard and take the surest route to keeping her safe: killing Trent. He now knew he could not call upon the Wards for help spiriting her off. If he brought Sarah Ward aboard the *Sally*, Mr. Cheap and Benji would simply release her again. Not even Ned had been willing to join in his plan.

That left him only one option. Taking her and holding her somewhere long enough to execute his father. Public vindication was vanity, and Sarah's life was more important than Sparhawk's reputation.

The cook, he suspected, would not like it, but she had been hired to manage house in a love nest and would be used to exercising discretion. Money, no doubt, would help. He had brought a length of soft rope. Though he shrank from the idea of binding and gagging her, he did not know any other way to hold her silent and secure in a neighborhood like the North End.

He arrived early, at dusk, to the meeting she had set with him, and used his own keys to let himself quietly into that snug little house. The sand had been spread once more over the floors and brushed into chevron rows. He had not seen it from the street because the shutters were closed, but a light already burned under the door to the parlor.

He lifted the latch and pushed the door open. Sarah Ward was seated on the daybed where Joseph Warren had extracted the bullet from her brother's belly. She held a pistol in her hand, and she was aiming it at Sparhawk.

"Come in and shut the door," she said. She did nothing so foolish as gesture with her pistol. Someone had taught her well.

"I'm not convinced you will shoot me," he risked saying.

"Nor am I," she replied. "That is why I invited Mr. Cheap."

The Wards' worthy sailing master stepped out from behind the door. He had a long blade in his hand, and Sparhawk had no doubt whatsoever that he would use it.

"Empty your pockets," said Cheap. "Onto the table."

He did. Out came the pistol, a necessity for a wanted man, the knife, a practicality, and the soft rope, which was damning evidence of his intentions.

"Very nice," said Mr. Cheap. "We brought hemp cord for you."

"I was going to keep you here for your own good," said Sparhawk to Sarah as Mr. Cheap lashed him to one of the room's ladder-back chairs.

"You were going to keep me here because

you love me," she said.

"I believe that is my cue to exit," said Mr. Cheap. "I shall be in the Green Dragon Tavern."

TWENTY

"Thank you for saving Ned," said Sarah Ward.

"I suppose you came early and suborned my servants," said Sparhawk.

"They're my servants, in point of fact. You put the house in my name and paid them a year's wages in advance."

"I did, didn't I? What happens now?"

"We come to an agreement and I set you free, or we fail to come to an agreement, and I hold you here indefinitely."

"I will never agree to let you marry Trent," he said.

"I don't want to marry Trent."

"Because you know he is a monster."

"No, because I am in love with his son."

No glib response rose to his tongue. He had heard sacred oaths and slavish endearments from women in the throes of passion, but in fifteen years, no woman had said she loved him. All at once the ropes and his chest felt too tight. A sense of worth filled him. Sarah Ward loved him. She was remarkable. Brave and loyal. And she did not bestow her affection lightly. If a woman like this could love him, his father's scorn and Slough's abuse no longer mattered. Together, they could remake the world, start a new and better family, one in the mold of Sarah's roguish clan of pirates, where treachery like Trent's was unthinkable.

He was afraid, just yet, to believe it. "I thought you had sworn off such declarations."

"I find them easier to make with a pistol in hand. I love you. That is why I am offering you the chance to prove your identity, and to find out the truth about your father. The parson you are searching for, the one who married your parents, who was living on the island when you were abducted and your mother was arrested, is a cleric at the college in Cambridge. He will be at Three Cranes on Saturday. Trent believes he will declare you a liar and imposter. I know you are not."

She placed the pistol on the table alongside his weapons and bent to kiss him. It was a light peck on the cheek, but more sensual than he expected. He could not move at all, and his predicament focused all his attention on the smooth skin of her lips, the soft velvet of her cheek brushing his, the warm caress of her breath in his ear.

He hardened instantly, like a randy boy, and strained against his ropes, the chair groaning in protest.

She drew back and looked at him, understanding lighting her loved features. A sly smile spread across her face and she kissed him again. This time she peeled back his neck cloth and brushed her lips against the hollow of his throat, her tongue flicking out, warm and wet, to taste him.

He groaned as loudly as the chair. "Untie me," he said.

"That was supposed to be my line."

She straddled his lap, resting her weight on his thighs. Her hands slipped into his coat pockets, drawing out the items Cheap had deemed harmless and unworthy of confiscation: a boat whistle, a slab of candy he had bought for Ned, the letter she had written him setting this assignation. She tossed them on the floor and slipped her hand, fiery hot, down his breeches.

And stroked.

There was too much clothing between them. Waistcoats and petticoats and stays and his velvet coat and her cotton round gown all separating him from the sweet spot at the juncture of her thighs.

"Please," he begged, though he wasn't sure exactly what he wanted her to do.

She worked him with her right hand in the tight confines of his breeches until there was barely room to move, and then she popped his buttons with her left.

He sprang free, and she left off stroking him to push his coat down his shoulders, unlace his cravat, untie his shirt, unbutton his waistcoat, and bare him neck to navel. She ran her hands over his chest, tweaking his flat nipples and pressing wet open kisses over his collarbone.

It was too much and not enough all at once.

And wicked thing that she was, she knew it. She leaned back and untied the sash that held her round gown closed, and began gathering her skirts up, instinctively coy as the most experienced demirep. He swallowed hard when her pale thighs and pink center came into sight and then watched with fascination as she held her skirts aloft like a curtain at the theater and engulfed him with her sweet flesh.

She rode him, holding up her gown so that he could see their connection. He could not tear his eyes away until her cries became urgent and then he wanted to watch her face, as he had been too consumed to do the last time.

"Sarah," he begged, "let me free. Let me touch you."

She shook her head. "Later."

Later she did let him touch her, after she had convulsed and cried out and helped him, with her hand, to his own conclusion. Then she had cut his bonds, and they lay tangled in each other's arms on the narrow daybed.

"If I'm right about my father," he said, stroking her silky blond hair, "will you come away from the Three Cranes with me?"

"Where will we go?" she asked.

"I don't know. England if I can get the evidence against the admiral from Angela Ferrers. The Dutch free ports if I cannot."

"And your inheritance? Trent's money? The title?"

"I have never desired them for their own sake, only as a means of obtaining justice. Say you love me again."

"Pass me the pistol."

"I have a better idea."

Sarah saw little of Trent that week. The burning of the *Diana* was taken by the admiral as a personal affront, and he had every available officer scouring the harbor in whatever craft he could lay hands on. He issued general passes for fishing boats to land their catch in Boston Harbor, and then confiscated any vessel foolish enough to accept the invitation and pressed it into service patrolling the channels.

In the mornings Sarah sat with her father in his study while he worked on the model of the *Sally*. In the afternoon she made visits and received callers. She accepted an invitation to tea at Province House from Mrs. Gage, and when she arrived was surprised to discover a large gathering. Lady Frankland was there in the long, cool room with the Dutch tiled fireplace, along with the panniered ladies and several women Sarah had never met.

Margaret Gage showed herself a skilled hostess and *raconteuse* when she regaled the company with the tale of her abduction by whaleboat pirates. She made certain to refer to Sparhawk by name, and when prompted, related the story of that naval officer's fall from grace. It was an almost irresistible fiction: the rakish young man lured by a Rebel seductress and the glitter of gold, stealing the navy's hard-won prize and burying it in a secluded cove. That Sparhawk and the American jezebel had made love atop the mound of riches was a particularly nice touch.

If she still thought of herself as Micah Wild's jilted lover, used goods, she might have found the notion of herself as the Rebel seductress uncomfortable, but considering her recent night with Sparhawk, and remembering how she had ridden him to completion in the parlor and then later again upstairs, she decided with some amusement that the tale might have a little truth in it after all.

Then Saturday arrived and Trent's carriage was waiting and Sarah knew a moment of real trepidation. She had not left Boston, save for the whaleboat trip to Noddle's Island, in more than a month. If the parson of Sparhawk's youth confirmed his identity and Trent's treachery, she would go away with James and become his mistress, embark on an uncertain future with Sparhawk's affection her only fixed star.

But if the parson proved him an imposter as Trent expected, she would have to make a decision. To tether herself to a man she could never be sure of and run from the danger Graves represented, or take Trent's offer of safe harbor and allow the parson to marry them, putting her forever beyond the admiral's reach.

There was no one on the causeway this time. Their carriage rumbled out of the gates on the neck unimpeded. The Loyalists in town had persuaded General Gage to stop issuing any passes at all. They feared that if all the Rebels fled and only the friends of government remained in town, there would be nothing to stop the Americans from putting Boston to the torch — nothing, reflected Sarah, but the fact that they were Americans and Boston was their city. That the Loyalists could contemplate the burning of the place meant to Sarah that they did not think of themselves as Americans at all.

Charlestown was more deserted than the last time she had seen it. Homes were empty and boarded up, and many showed obvious signs of looting. Someone had taken it in mind to steal most of the copper drainpipes on one street. A house with particularly large fine windows showed only empty sockets to the street, the sashes removed and curtains left fluttering in the breeze. Only a few businesses hard by the water still plied their trade.

The Three Cranes put on a brave front amidst the squalor, as though the farther Mrs. Brown's fortunes fell — runaway husbands, pregnant maids, and looting notwithstanding — the harder she clung to her livelihood. The yard out front had been swept clean. Too many shutters, it seemed, had been damaged to present an orderly façade to the street, so all had been removed. Inside, the floors were sanded, the curtains washed and mended, the bar freshly scrubbed.

It made no difference. The taproom where Sarah had tried to pick the fusilier's pocket and Trent had come to her rescue was empty. Mrs. Brown greeted them warily and led them up to the private room Trent had requested. It was not the spacious chamber he had spoken for Sarah the night they met, nor was it the well-appointed suite where her father and Ned had slept. This was a mean little room with no fireplace and a low, bare timbered ceiling at the back of the house. The stuffy garret had only one window, no connecting door, and nothing but rushlights on the table.

The choice surprised her, and it must have shown on her face, because Trent said, "This is a private matter. Hardly something one discusses in a taproom."

And a more comfortably appointed chamber, she thought to herself, settling on a loose and sagging chair, would have implied some measure of respect for their guest.

Trent took up a pose beside the window. The frayed rush seat prickled through her silk petticoat. Fortunately they did not have to wait long. There was a scratch at the door. Then the latch rose and James Sparhawk entered. She had not seen him for a week, but the way her spirit lifted to be near him, she knew that whatever happened in this room tonight, she would leave with him.

He was not dressed as the splendid naval officer of the *Wasp* and *Hephaestion,* nor the raffish blade of Salem and Noddle's Island. Tonight he wore a simple suit of black silk with narrow tailored sleeves over an equally subdued waistcoat subtly embroidered, white on white. His stockings were fine and new, his shoes polished, the buckles plain but good silver. His hair was brushed and queued in a faille ribbon. It gave him the air of a scholar or a jurist, and for the first time she wondered what James Sparhawk might have become if he had not been pressed into the navy. Only the practical sword at his hip with its well-worn scabbard betrayed him as a military man.

Anthony Trent stood up and scrutinized Sarah's lover. Trent's face took on a quizzical aspect. "I commend you, sir," said the cold, distant Trent, who had faced down the fusiliers in the taproom. "It is a far better impression of my youthful self than I am usually treated to."

"You can be forgiven for thinking me dead," said Sparhawk balefully, "since you paid good money to have me killed."

Trent put his hands together and clapped slowly. "Righteous indignation, worthy of the theater. You are a veritable Garrick, but your flair for blackmail is sadly lacking. When a man is about to marry, you threaten him, not his new bride, with revelations about his dark past. I have dealt leniently with others who sought to traffic in my secrets, but your deviltry has endangered Sarah. That I cannot forgive."

Trent drew his sword.

"Anthony," said Sarah.

"Go downstairs and wait with Mrs. Brown," he said coolly. He had spoken to her, but his eyes were fixed on Sparhawk.

Sparhawk drew his own blade and looked left and right. "We should leave Sarah up here and take this downstairs where there is more room."

"No need. I have more than sufficient scope to kill you," said Trent pleasantly, and lunged.

His reputation as a duelist had not been exaggerated. Trent moved in a straight line, and there was nothing that Sarah could see that telegraphed his intentions, just the point of his sword flying toward Sparhawk,

416

who, damn him, still had his eyes on her.

Sparhawk danced right just in time, in a circular path, and Sarah dove into the corner to get out of his way.

Trent retreated, his sword held casually. He cocked his head to study Sparhawk's posture. She saw what Trent saw. James held his sword high, his body in profile.

Trent looked intrigued, and as though testing a theory, he darted forward once more with a savage thrust. Sparhawk's body continued to move in a circle, but his blade remained in the path of Trent's and met it. Sparhawk twisted, and the strongest part of his blade kissed the weakest span of Trent's. With a movement that began in his shoulder and rippled down his arm, Sparhawk used his leverage to bind and deflect Trent's blade. The maneuver laid the older man's right thigh open, for a fleeting moment, to a riposte, but Sparhawk either failed to see, or to capitalize on, the opportunity.

Surprised but undeterred, Trent disengaged, then lunged again. Sparhawk moved in an arc once more, neat as a figure in a mechanical clock, but the irregular shape of the room hampered him, and this time Trent's blade scored his shoulder and came away bloody.

A terrible suspicion stole over Sarah.

Sparhawk was not the swordsman Trent was.

She had watched her brother practice when they were teens. He had sparred often against Mr. Cheap, who fought with terrifying strength but no finesse at all, and against Micah Wild, who had the best fencing master money could buy. She recognized real skill when she saw it, such as Micah had acquired from his paid tutors, and Benji had taught himself by observing Micah.

She watched, heart in her throat, these two men fence now, and her suspicion grew into certainty.

Trent was skilled indeed, as well as talented. He moved with absolute economy, indulged in no showy flourishes, followed no pattern. Instead, he attacked cleanly again and again, the tip of his blade drawn like a magnet to the most vulnerable point of his opponent's body, flickering, feinting, and thrusting, but always seeking avenues past his foe's guard and outside his expectations.

Anthony Trent fought opportunistically, like her brother, because he meant to kill.

Sparhawk did not. He meant to win, yes. To injure or maim perhaps, but only incident to his goal, which was an abstract notion of justice. He meant to spit his father's black heart, and his goal was a fixed point in Trent's chest.

He darted forward and danced aside at the same time, putting the point of his blade through Trent's sleeve, and snarling it.

Sparhawk was going to die. His sword was caught; the way was open for Trent to slash him across the body, a killing blow.

Sarah cried out.

Trent hesitated.

There was a knock upon the door. Mrs. Brown's voice came through the thin wood, clear as a bell. "I know you said to admit no one, my lord, but there is a reverend here who insists on coming in."

Trent's brow furrowed. "But I did not send for him."

He had always planned to kill Sparhawk, Sarah realized. She was, in fact, a terrible judge of men.

"No," said Sparhawk, "but I did."

The door swung open. The cleric who filled it was a New England divine of the old school, dressed even more soberly than Sparhawk, his neck cloth starched like a drainpipe. His presence made you feel like a sinner in the hands of an angry God.

He was no longer young, and his tall, angular frame moved stiffly. He took two steps into the room, narrowed his eyes upon Sparhawk, and spoke in a voice ravaged by too many years at the pulpit. "Almighty God is merciful. Tristan, you live."

Sparhawk heard his father's sword clatter to the floor. He looked away from the cleric to see Anthony Trent stumble back against the wall, shaking his head. "It cannot be," he said. "I saw your grave."

Sarah stepped to the center of the room. Sparhawk had forgotten for a moment that she was there. She addressed the parson. "You will swear it? That Sparhawk is Trent's son?" she asked.

"Yes," said the parson. "He is Tristan. I saw the boy every day of his life from the hour he was born. I knew him as well as his own mother." He turned to Trent. "It is he, my lord, and no other."

She turned to Trent. "You agreed to accept his judgment," she said.

Trent nodded numbly. "I think I began to suspect the truth myself, a few moments ago. *Strutting and circling.* I should never have entrusted my son's introduction to the blade to that dropsical Spaniard."

"And will you confess," asked Sparhawk, standing upon a precipice, "to bribing the magistrates, to ordering my death?"

"Is that what you thought? Why? In God's name, why?"

"You threatened my mother with arrest for prostitution, and three days later she was taken to jail."

Trent closed his eyes. "I see. Yes. You are right to blame me. I didn't order it, would have given my life to stop it, but I *am* the cause of your mother's death. And of everything that you suffered."

Sarah shook her head. "No."

"Poor Sarah," said Trent, smiling faintly. "I was going to make up for everything — by saving you."

Sparhawk swallowed. "If you didn't order it, then who did?"

"My wife. My second wife. Or more accurately, her family. And I brought them to Nevis. On my own ship," said Trent. "Like some biblical plague."

Sparhawk felt the anger that had sustained him on the *Scylla* returning. "My mother died on a dirt floor in rags like an animal, and you have slept on silk sheets these past fifteen years."

"Yes," Trent said. "It was my fault. I was young and selfish and arrogant, and I thought your mother ought to bend to my whims. I loved her, passionately, as a friend and partner. I wanted to have her, and money besides, and I saw a way to get it. Flora Milton was passably attractive and came with a hundred thousand pounds. Enough to make Polkerris both solvent and profitable. I envisioned your mother kept snug in a nice cottage on Flora's money. One woman a rich, unloved dupe, the other a cosseted pet. It might even have worked, had I chosen another heiress for my scheme, but the Miltons were more ambitious and ruthless than I understood.

"I thought that if I could speak with your mother in person, I could get her to fall in with my plans, so I stopped in Nevis on my way home with the Miltons aboard. They were a planter family, rich off sugar and slaves, and eager for the advantage that a titled connection at court would bring.

"You were in the cottage that night, when your mother and I argued. She threatened to write to the Miltons and tell them that I was already married. And fool that I was, I told the Miltons. I lied to them, of course, but I had half convinced myself it was the truth. I told them that your mother had been a youthful fancy of mine, that I had tricked her into thinking a form of marriage had taken place, and that she had no real legal standing. I even tried to pass myself off as an honorable gentleman who had done the right thing, and set her up with money for your keeping.

"I was twenty-eight and thought myself clever and worldly, but I was a fool. The Miltons did not believe my tale of a sham marriage, but they were the very picture of warmth and understanding. Flora's brothers explained that it was a simple matter to make the problem of my first wife go away."

Sparhawk dreaded what he would hear next.

"They told me not to worry, that all would be taken care of, and that I was to think nothing more about the matter. I protested, of course, but I realized, sitting there listening to these two men casually talk murder on the veranda, that I had to get your mother away."

"No," Sparhawk said. "I saw you throw my mother off your ship the next night."

"Yes," said Trent. "A few hours after Flora's family had plotted your mother's murder on the veranda. I had had no opportunity to warn her, dared not betray any sign to the Miltons that I would not fall in with their plans. She had come to the ship because the cottage had been broken into, and all of her papers stolen. The Miltons, I realized, but I could not tell her that then. So I returned to the cottage the next day. You were out studying with the Jewess."

Trent closed his eyes and went on. "The

Miltons had money and influence in the islands. I had none. Edwards" — he turned to the parson, who had been sitting quietly — "agreed to help her get away."

The Reverend Edwards took up the tale in his reedy, high voice. "We feared that once Anthony broke things off with Flora, the Miltons might take revenge on you and your mother, so we determined to hide you on one of the neighboring islands. Your mother did not want to tell you, did not want to frighten you. It was going to take a few days to arrange, to be sure that your refuge would not be easily discovered."

"And I," said Trent, "fool that I was, thought that by sailing with the Miltons aboard, I had removed the immediate danger. But men like the Miltons do not do their own killing, and they had already hired the sailors and bribed the magistrates."

Sarah, Sparhawk realized, was weeping silently. He had no more tears, only a sick grief clawing his chest.

"When I went to fetch your mother for the journey," said Edwards, "I found the cottage broken open. Everything of value taken. I went to the magistrates, of course, but they had been bribed to jail her, and such was the Miltons' sway on the islands, there was no one to gainsay them. Of you I

424

could find no trace. I managed to bribe one of the guards to let me in to see her, but afterward . . ." He trailed off.

"They poured lye down her throat so she could not tell her story to anyone."

"I thought she was safe," said Trent. "That she would be waiting for me when I returned."

"And yet you married Flora Milton," said Sparhawk. He did not know how his father could have done it.

"When we reached London, I tried to break it off with Flora, but her brothers told me that you . . . had already been taken to the harbor and drowned, and that your mother had been indentured to one of their plantations. Her life, they explained, depended on my good behavior. The Milton brothers had the letters I had written your mother, suggesting that we put aside our marriage, no doubt taken when the men they hired broke into the cottage. They had our marriage license and lines. Flora made it plain — very plain — that if I did not marry her, she and her brothers would make those letters public, and your death and the degradation of your mother would be laid at my door. I felt I had no choice. I married Flora and maneuvered the Admiralty into sending me to Nevis at the first opportunity.

But by that time, it was already too late. Your mother was dead."

"How did you discover I was not dead as well?" Sparhawk asked.

"With you and your mother lost to me, there was nothing to stop me from taking revenge on the Miltons, but first I decided to deal with the men they had hired to carry out their designs. I found the merchants who had sworn out accusations against your mother, and the magistrates who had been bribed to sell her indenture, and I killed them.

"With like purpose, I searched for the sailors who I thought had drowned you, and found one of them: an old tar who had once served with me and who swore that he would never hurt a child. That he had pressed you aboard an Indiaman and that, God willing, you lived still. Then I set out to find you. I had been directed to cruise the Caribbean, so could hardly go direct to Bombay, but I returned home and wrote letters and begged favors and accepted the leakiest brig afloat with a dispensation to survey the China Sea."

"We would have been recalled by the time you got to Bombay," said Sparhawk.

"Yes. And once I got there, I was ordered to stay. When I finally returned to Plymouth, Slough had been put on half pay and was roaming the dockside taverns always in pursuit of the rough trade. I found him, and questioned him, and discovered you had been entered into the ship's company as Jack Nevis."

"Slough was murdered on one of those Portsmouth ambles," said James.

"Yes," said his father. "So I understand."

James did not ask him to elaborate.

"And the crew was dispersed, a wise precaution with a mutinous ship. I checked the Admiralty records and found you had ended up under Mungo McKenzie. It was then I checked his roster and found you had died. I visited your grave. There were flowers on it. I did not know who could have placed them there — and I knew McKenzie had perished of a fever in Calcutta that winter — but I hoped it meant that you had been loved by someone in those two years, when everyone and everything had been taken from you."

"James Sparhawk," said the man who bore his name, "was like a son to McKenzie, and a brother to me. We mourned him. And he knew of our plan. He asked me to make his a famous name. I suppose I have honored his request, though not in the manner he expected."

"Dear God," said his father. Sparhawk had never seen the man look afraid. "Have you evidence against Graves, enough to save you?"

"No," said Sparhawk. "I have a few incriminating papers taken off the *Diana* before she burned that implicate Thomas Graves in brokering a transaction with Micah Wild, but nothing to prove the admiral used the gold to buy her. The Rebels say they have the evidence to damn him, but they hold it hostage to a powder run."

His father shot up out of his chair. "You must leave, *now,* quickly. Graves and his marines will already be surrounding the building."

"So you meant to turn me over to them, whether I was guilty or not."

"No," said Sarah.

Trent turned to look at her. "I did it for Sarah. You in exchange for her safety, Tristan."

It was strange to be called by his real name.

"We must go," Sarah said. She placed her hand in Sparhawk's.

It was going to be all right, he realized. If she was going to come with him, they would have the *Sally* and her family and the

428

freedom of the sea.

The floor vibrated. Feet on the steps. The door rattling in the jamb. Too late, too late. He had left it too late.

"The window," said Sarah.

"They will be in the alley," said his father. "I left nothing to chance."

Sparhawk opened the casement. His father was right. Below in the alley was a thick line of red, blocking his escape. Marines. A dozen at least.

Sarah drew a little pistol out of her pocket.

"Put that away," Sparhawk said. There must not be any shooting, not with Sarah in the room. He turned to Trent. "You must let them take me."

His father nodded.

"I will get the evidence from Angela Ferrers," said Sarah. "Somehow."

"I will come with you," said Trent. "And once I know where they are holding you, I will see Tommy Gage."

The door burst open. Sparhawk was not surprised to see Lieutenant Graves leading the marines. "Arrest that man and take him to the *Preston.*"

Sparhawk held out his empty hands, but they knocked him to the floor anyway.

Sarah screamed.

"Her as well," said Graves.

"That was not part of our arrangement," said Anthony Trent. "The girl was to be left out of the matter of the gold."

"The girl is a pirate. We have a witness who will testify that she took a British officer captive and held him in her home in Salem."

"Micah," said Sarah, numbly.

Two marines took hold of her.

She wrenched free of them and reached for James.

As his mother had in the cottage.

He acted without thought, punching one marine in the throat, feeling the man's windpipe buckle beneath his knuckles, then sheathing his belt knife in another's belly and feeling the blood wash warm and sticky over his hand — anything to win her free of this, but they were too many. The marines closed in around him, overwhelming him with the press of their bodies and the butts of their muskets.

A blow to his jaw knocked him to the floor, and a kidney punch kept him down. Between their booted feet he could see Sarah being dragged out the door, hear her slippers scrabbling for purchase over the floorboards, her cries echoing off the plaster walls.

His father hesitated on the threshold, torn

between his son and the woman he so evidently loved.

"Go with Sarah," Sparhawk implored him. He knew what would happen to her, a woman without interest, accused of piracy, imprisoned in a British jail, if she was not plainly attached to a powerful man.

Reverend Edwards stepped forward. "I will stay with the boy, Anthony."

His face a mask of anguish, his father managed a responsive nod, then set off after Sarah and her escort. And shortly after he was gone, the remaining marines began beating Sparhawk in earnest, eager to get back a little of their own for the unlucky bastard who'd been stabbed, while Francis Graves looked on. The reverend begged that officer, with all his powers of persuasion and the best of precedents, to put a stop to things. But young Graves, it transpired, was not a God-fearing man.

TWENTY-ONE

They would have clapped her in irons, but Trent would not stand for it, and he stayed by her side as they marched her over the neck, through the streets of Boston, and down to the boats at the Long Wharf. He refused to allow them to put her in the cutter until someone rigged a sail to shield her from the late-afternoon sun, and he sat next to her on the bench, between her and the sailors, despite the protestations of the marine sergeant who had been assigned to lead the detail.

Castle William, sitting atop its rocky island in the harbor, was no Otranto. It had none of the gothic romance of Mr. Walpole's novel. The walls were squat and graceless, the scrubby slopes below the ramparts littered with refuse and slick with mud. The cell they led her to was dank and stank of mildew, with only a single barred window high on one wall.

The cell itself did not frighten her, but the sick expression on Trent's face told her that as he looked at the filth and squalor, he was cast back into scenes of horror that had played in his mind for fifteen guilt-ridden years, scenes in which he saw another prison, another woman.

"I will be fine," she said. Until they hang me. "I was born on a schooner. It was cleaner, of course. And drier."

"I will not let anything happen to you," he said. His hand returned again and again to the hilt of his sword, but his blade could not help her here.

He demanded a room for her above ground, with a guard on the door and a servant, preferably a woman, but the marine sergeant was only following the admiral's orders and did not have the authority to command anything better in the castle.

Something rustled in the far corner of the cell, and she did her best to ignore it.

"I will speak to the governor," said Trent.

The tight look on his face told her that he was still held captive by the horror of the past, but rustling corners were the least of their problems. She drew James Sparhawk's father deeper into the fetid chamber and out of the marine's hearing. "I am not James' mother. No one will pour lye down my throat."

He flinched.

"And this is not Nevis. I cannot be spirited off to some plantation. This is an English colony, ruled by English laws, and I will be fine passing a night in an English jail." Her brother had done so often enough, for drunkenness and fighting. And her mother had bailed Mr. Cheap and Abednego out on occasion, when rum and nostalgia had gotten the better of them.

The thought of those carefree days in Salem, of her loving, disreputable family, of the *Sally* and the home she had lost, threatened to overwhelm her.

"It may be an English jail, but you are an American, accused of piracy. The navy has always dealt harshly with pirates, but in the past you would have been protected by the due process of the law. Not now. The Port Act and the Administration of Justice Act have effectively suspended your rights as an Englishwoman. They permit Graves to hold you indefinitely, and transport you for trial."

And put an ocean between her and her family. Her mother would have told her not to picture it. To imagine herself safe, on the deck of the *Sally* . . . but that only made her ache to be there in reality, to be free.

"The admiral is commandeering fishing

boats to patrol the harbor," she said, trying to reassure herself. "He does not have a ship to transport me." She was not sure that was true, but she clung to this reasoning because it fended off despair. And there was still a slender hope that James at least might win free. "There is a woman, a rebel, who says she has the evidence to implicate Admiral Graves in the theft of the gold. You may be able to use it to save James." But it would not help Sarah.

Trent's hand closed around his hilt. "Tell me how to find her."

Sarah shook her head. "She will not just hand the papers over to you. Sentiment does not move this woman. Benji and I made a deal with her, but failed to honor it. We were to take the *Sally* to Lisbon on a powder run. In exchange, she was going to deliver the papers. But James learned that you were here and that I was to marry you, and he would not sail."

Trent made a bitter, desolate sound and said, "So again I have consigned my son to hell."

"It may still be possible to bargain with her," said Sarah. "Though I fear what she would ask from a naval man with money and interest."

"Sarah, I lost my son once. I will not lose

435

him again. You are here because you would not let the navy take your brother. I would do the same and more, trade places with you now if I could, to save you and Tristan."

He was not, she now understood, blameless in the death of his wife and the degradation of his son, and youth did not excuse his errors; but men changed and learned from their mistakes, and she believed Trent capable of sacrifice, so she told him. "There is a house in the North End. James bought it for me. The cook there can get Benji a message. He will know how to find this woman." She gave him the direction of the little green house with its side to the street and the three dormers in the roof, where she had lain with his son.

"I will go to this house in the North End, and send a message to your brother," he said, "but first, I will see you in more appropriate accommodation. If I allow them to keep you here, the guard will think you are fair game for abuse. No lady would be held in such conditions."

"Not even one who picks pockets?" she asked, trying to keep back the tears that threatened.

"Not even one who picks them badly," he said. "Don't worry, Sarah. All will still be well, and I will call you daughter as gladly as I would have called you wife."

It was kind and generous and meant to buoy her spirits, but she did not believe it. Angela Ferrers' evidence might save Sparhawk. He was innocent. Sarah was not.

Trent kissed her chastely on the forehead and promised to return within the hour. For good measure he told the guard his rank and title, and made it clear that Sarah was under his protection, and that any insult she suffered would be met with swift retribution.

The door closed. The corners rustled. The *Sally* had rats, of course. She and Benji had named the ones too clever for the cat to catch. There had been, over the years, a piratical roster of rodents aboard that schooner: a great beast called Teach, a weedy sly one called Rackham, and a plump mottled titch who had been named Quelch, but who was demoted to Squeaker when the cat finally caught him.

Trent was as good as his word, and returned, miraculously, within the hour.

"I have spoken to the military commander of the fort who reports to the governor. He is writing to Tommy for further instructions but agrees that you should stay with the fort major for now."

Most likely he had agreed because he did

not want to meet Trent at dawn over the matter.

"Fort major is an honorary post," Trent continued, "held by a veteran of Louisbourg who lives with his family in an apartment within the walls. And fortunately for us, his pension is miserly, so he is very amenable to bribes. Come."

He led her out of the dungeon and up into the yard, trailed by the marine sergeant, who did not like this change of plans but could not gainsay the commander of the castle.

The fort major's apartments were located on the second floor in the south wall, and the outside rooms offered a view of Roxbury, with the cupola of the old governor's mansion visible in the distance.

The fort major himself, one John Phillips, was avuncular and kind, and had been a chaplain in the army for many years. He no longer preached, but his extensive library of sermons was at Sarah's disposal. Their establishment was a modest one, as his position was honorary and the stipend accordingly small, but Sarah was invited to share their table and his spinster daughter's chamber.

"Once a day we have a boat. It is for the correspondence of the customs inspector and the tea agent, but the boatman's wife will make any purchases you might need in town. You will make a list straightaway, and I will give it to the boatman, and by tomorrow you will have all the little comforts necessary to life."

Trent left her a purse full of gold, and in private, a knife to keep in her pocket and use if anyone attempted to abuse her.

The fort major's daughter brought her ink and a pen and paper, and Sarah sat down to make a list for the boatman's wife, but she could think of nothing that was necessary to life except James Sparhawk.

James passed the night unmolested in a locked compartment on the *Preston.* The last time he had been confined aboard a man-of-war had been on Slough's *Scylla,* and child that he had been, he had still hoped that his father would appear to rescue him.

Rescue on that occasion had never come. Slough had summoned him, directed him to kneel and open his mouth, and when James had refused, had ordered him tied to the gratings and flogged. Sparhawk had realized then that his father was never coming, and accepted that it was Trent's actions that had put him there in the first place.

Now James knew his father was not the villain that he had thought, but that did not mean his father would come for him now. He had seen the devotion on Trent's face when he looked at Sarah in that shabby little room. In Trent's place, Sparhawk might be tempted to try to enforce the bargain he had made with Graves — to trade James' life for Sarah's. And thinking of her in the cells of the fort, at the mercy of the admiral's lackeys, Sparhawk wished he would.

The reverend had come with him all the way to the flagship, and finding the sailors of the *Preston* a more God-fearing lot than their marines, sent for and received water and bandages and a beaker of rum. He cleaned Sparhawk's cuts and bruises, examined and wrapped Sparhawk's ribs, one of which might be cracked and hurt like the devil, and asked him if he would like to pray.

Sparhawk attempted to explain his notion of the Divine, of stars and angles and cosigns and the map of the heavens, but after the rum and the beating, it came out sounding like a treatise on navigation crossed with the Admiralty Rules and Regulations, and James gave up. The Reverend Edwards proclaimed him a deist and produced a small book of sermons from his pocket that he claimed he kept close to hand for such occasions, which made Sparhawk wonder exactly what manner of "occasions" regularly came up in American colleges.

Edwards read to him for some time, the words less important than the reassuring sound of the divine's fluting voice, and it occurred to Sparhawk as he drifted off to sleep that the man had read to him before, though the text when he had been a child, if James recalled correctly, had been *Robinson Crusoe.*

Just after noon the next day, a midshipman brought James a meal from the mess, an indication that while the charge against him might be gross theft, someone on board thought it wise to treat him as an officer and a gentleman — of sorts. The rather sheepish young middy apologized for the quality of the meat and described the item on the plate — generously, to Sparhawk's mind — as a chop.

"Our servant is not allowed to go to the market," he explained, "until after the senior officers' servants, and he cannot get anything good now. It was different before the army made a hash of things at Lexington."

It certainly had been.

Sparhawk thanked him. He did not think Graves above poisoning him, but he was hardly likely to do so with anything so unappetizing as the "chop."

Sparhawk ate.

The afternoon passed.

The midshipman returned with a tankard of grog and waited until Sparhawk had finished, then lingered a moment more, screwing up his courage. Finally he said, "Ned Ward was a gentleman on the *Preston* for a week. Then he was transferred to the *Diana*. Captain Graves says that he deserted like a cowardly Yankee, but I thought he might have run away to join your pirate crew."

Sparhawk was unaware that he had a pirate crew. "And why would you think that?" he asked without rancor. He could recall those heady days, just after McKenzie had made him a midshipman, when life seemed like an adventure and the world was filled with wonders: monsters and pirates and corsairs. And the most terrifying creatures of all: girls, of course.

"Because Ned said that he knew you, and when you were arrested for stealing the admiral's gold, he said that if you had done it, then you had done it for a good reason, and probably because you were in love with his sister."

It was a twelve-year-old's understanding: wildly romantic, totally wrong, and, at the

442

same time, completely true.

Trent did not come back to the island the next day, or the day after that. A trunk from the mainland arrived, however, filled with her things, and in the same boat, her maid.

Trent had overseen the packing himself, the woman told her, though Sarah could have gleaned as much from the neat naval corners into which her garments had been folded and the efficient way they were wedged inside. A good sea chest was stuffed tight like an oyster, her father used to say.

At the bottom of the trunk was her sewing bag with her embroidery silks and a yard of fresh canvas with a letter rolled inside. It was from Trent, and it warned her that the admiral might bar him from visiting, but assured her that she was never out of his thoughts. It made no mention of Sparhawk. Sarah assumed that everything Trent sent to her would be opened and read, and that he could vouchsafe no confidences in his letters. He closed by reassuring her that he was working tirelessly for her release.

The fort major's wife lent her a frame and helped her stretch her canvas in their comfortable parlor, which she confided to Sarah had been much larger and better appointed when her husband had been the castle's actual commander, but such was the gratitude of princes, or governors, that Major Phillips had been turned out of his post with nothing just after his sixtieth birthday, a time of life when he could not possibly be expected to secure new employment. She hinted that these financial difficulties had contributed in some way to her daughter's disappointment. Major Phillips had only attained this poor sinecure through the strenuous efforts of her family's connections.

Sarah was not allowed to leave the apartment, and the marine posted at the head of the stairs refused her request to take a daily turn in the yard. From the windows Sarah could watch the soldiery drilling, which she did not much enjoy, and betweentimes, children playing, which she did. These, she was told, belonged to a pair of refugee families who had lost their homes to mob violence. But not their fortunes, or so Mrs. Phillips said: the tea agent's wife was always sending for fine things from the mainland, like lace and almonds and other luxuries.

"I invited them to dine when they first came to the island, but they did not reciprocate, and we could not bear the expense," she told Sarah on their third afternoon spent stitching in front of the window. "I am sure it is of little moment to them, the cost of a meal, and they did not even think upon it," she said. "But the governor might have considered these little social obligations, and made us some allowance for it. I fear it leaves my husband embarrassed that he cannot even ask the gentlemen into his study for a glass of brandy without making some sacrifice. And this leaves him in the unpleasant position of being forced to do errands and accept requests that plague his conscience terribly."

He procured *company* for the tea agent, she confided, and allowed him the use of some rooms set aside for the storage of the fort major's possessions, to enjoy such company, out of the sight of his wife. "I cannot look her in the face," said Mrs. Phillips, "knowing what he does with his trollop atop those crates."

A little past four, Sarah was summoned by the guard. She followed him across the yard and into a stairwell, then up to a set of second-floor rooms that looked out over the harbor toward the open sea.

The whitewashed chamber held only one chair, a table, and Francis Graves. His hair was shorter than she remembered, pulled into a stubby tail at the back of his neck, the ends singed. And his eyebrows were missing. Disfigurement was common among sailors, an accepted risk for those who followed the sea and enjoyed its freedoms. Sarah had never been frightened or repulsed by scars or missing limbs, but Francis Graves wore his injuries with neither dignity nor ease.

He followed the direction of her eyes, reached back to touch the frizzled ends of his hair, and gave her a grim smile. "Courtesy of Captain Sparhawk and his Rebel friends, when they took my brother's ship, the *Diana.*"

He did not offer her a seat, because there was only the one, and he occupied it.

"I thought the Rebels offered the *Diana*'s crew quarter."

"They did. And they looted her as well. But we would have gotten her afloat, when the tide came in, had they let her be. Not content, though, to humiliate my brother and my uncle and the king's navy, the rabble had to put her to the torch as well. She was not a year old, purchased and outfitted at great expense."

"With gold your uncle stole from the *Wasp,*" said Sarah, sick of this family and its lies.

"What gives you the right to question the decisions of an admiral?" demanded Graves.

"You are a provincial sailor's trull, for all that Trent dresses you in silk and lace. My brother will not get another ship on this station. Maybe not ever. He could not look on and watch her burn. It was the grossest criminal act, and we will see every man who was there that night hanged as pirates."

"Then you will have to hang every adult male in Chelsea," she said. And Salem, and Marblehead, when it happens there, she added in the privacy of her mind.

"The *Preston*'s yardarm will accommodate them. I have already sworn a statement that you did knowingly and willfully resist a lawful boarding and customs search by the king's navy, ordered the assault of myself and the marines under my command, and took prisoner and held hostage an officer of the king. There is further testimony from your countryman Micah Wild, whose loyalty to the government and material aid to the navy have earned the gratitude of the Admiralty, that you did hold James Sparhawk in your home in Salem against his will, and made statements admitting to this in Mr. Wild's hearing. There is also the matter of four bodies found in the wreckage of your house after the fire that consumed it."

"Is the Admiralty in the habit of hearing testimony from a woman's former lovers?"

she asked. "Because Micah Wild is not a disinterested party in my affairs."

"No indeed. Wild further asserts that you did deprive him of his rightful property, a schooner called the *Sally,* which had become his upon the failure of your father to fulfill his obligation on a debt."

"I see," said Sarah. "And the Admiralty will conveniently look the other way in the matter of Mr. Wild's investment in the *Sally,* which was carrying the French gold."

"The *Sally*'s log will hardly vindicate you, Miss Ward. It lists many investors, but only one owner — your father. You are no more than a pirate, from a family of pirates. Your father should have swung thirty years ago."

"Then why are we not already hanging from the *Preston*'s yardarm?" she asked, with more bravado than she felt.

"Because my uncle is a sentimental man. Your lover and your betrothed have deserted you. Sparhawk has been pardoned. He is the heir, I am given to understand, to a barony and a substantial fortune, and he and his long-lost father prepare even now to return home. It is a story worthy of Mr. Smollett, if only he were alive to tell it. Sparhawk is young, rich, handsome. He will be the talk of London. You, on the other hand, will hang, along with Red Abed, and when we find him, that little deserter, your brother Ned."

"I do not believe that James would abandon me," she said.

"Let us face facts. You are a buccaneer's daughter, Miss Ward. No man with such glittering prospects would ally himself with such as you."

"Trent planned to," she said.

"If you believe that, you are naive indeed. Every officer above the rank of lieutenant in this godforsaken town has a mistress he calls a fiancée because there is no other worthwhile entertainment to be had. And half these imbecilic women think they are truly betrothed. There was no formal engagement. No bans were read. *Lord* Polkerris has no obligation to you. Certainly, none he acknowledges now. He has not even troubled to visit."

Lieutenant Graves tried on a sympathetic look. It did not suit his face. "We are offering you the opportunity to save your father and your younger brother from the noose. Confess that you and James Sparhawk conspired to send a chest full of flint to Boston aboard the *Wasp,* and that you stole the French gold off the *Sally* for your own purposes and buried it on Cape Ann. Write it," he said, pushing a pen and ink across the table, "and sign it, and your father and Ned will go free."

Sparhawk was shackled and taken to the admiral's cabin under guard. He supposed after the mayhem at the Three Cranes it was to be expected, but with the beating the marines had given him, it was unlikely he could have attempted to escape again.

He had been belowdecks with only occasional lantern light for so many days that his eyes did not adjust at once to the brightness of the admiral's cabin. The admiral himself was not present in the stark white room with its long row of windows. At the table where the admiral had eaten his joint of beef and left untouched his bowl of fresh green peas sat his nephew Thomas Graves, lately the commander of the *Diana,* whom Sparhawk had watched madly attempt to climb back aboard the burning schooner after the Rebels had set it alight; and his younger brother, Francis, Sparhawk's one-time lieutenant, who had dragged Thomas from the flames.

Francis had escaped with singed hair and burnt hands. Thomas had not been so lucky. His right ear and cheek were bandaged, the flesh showing livid and oozing at the edges of the muslin. One arm was in a sling, the

450

hand completely swaddled.

They did not offer him a chair.

"Your slut has double-crossed you," said Francis Graves. "In exchange for a pardon, she has written a confession naming you as the instigator of the plot." He pushed paper and ink across the table. "I won't pretend to like you, Captain, but this is too much. I can't believe it of a brother officer, not even you. Describe how she tricked you into sending the flint to Boston aboard the *Wasp*, and bragged of it while her family held you prisoner in Salem, and she will hang, and we will see you free."

He had met Sarah under the most extreme duress, seen her face down the British Navy with nothing but a pistol in her hand, defy Micah Wild and the Rebel mob because her sense of honor demanded it, and risk hanging to reunite him with his father. And even if his father was not the saint Sarah had believed, Trent's failings, tragic as their results had been, were human and forgivable.

She put her faith in people, loving loyally and steadfastly.

He had not. Lashed to the gratings of the *Scylla*, with the blood running down his back, James had lost faith in his father, and never dared believe in anyone else like that again. If he had held on to hope a little longer, if his faith had survived until his meeting with Mungo McKenzie, if he had implored that good man to take him home, he might have known his father's love these past fifteen years.

"No."

Thomas Graves struck the table with his good hand. "Do you *want* to hang, man?"

"Not particularly," said James Sparhawk. "But I know Sarah Ward, and you manifestly do not. You're bluffing."

They returned him to his cabin. The next day he received a visit from Charles Ansbach, who brought with him a bottle of brandy and sent the middy for two glasses.

"They will not admit Trent," he said, pulling up a stool and sitting opposite Sparhawk, "but they dare not bar me, so I am here as his emissary. Though I am not sure what to call you," said the king's bastard nephew. "Is it Trent or is it Sparhawk?"

"I am not quite sure myself," said James honestly.

"Well, Sparhawk or Trent, you will be free by the end of the day."

"How?"

"Your father's efforts. Bribes and blackmail, I daresay."

"And Sarah?"

"She as well."

He had been right. "Where is she now?" asked Sparhawk.

"Miss Ward is at the castle, with the fort major, in his apartments. *Safe*. The admiral and the governor have been at odds over who has authority over her, but their disagreement has spared her imprisonment in the cells beneath the walls, and your father's money has ensured her every comfort."

Ansbach handed him a beaker of brandy. Sparhawk took it, his hands shaking with relief. He knew she would not have confessed of her own free will, but he had worried, in the dark watches of the night, that they might have coerced her — tortured her — and he had vowed that he would kill Thomas and Francis Graves if they had. He confessed to Ansbach the fear that had been eating him.

"They dared not touch her," said Ansbach, reaching into the dispatch case he had brought and pulling forth a printed broadside. "General Gage has arrested the printer's son, Peter Edes, and thrown him in Boston Jail, but not before the boy managed to print and distribute several thousand of these."

The image had been struck off an engraving, a political cartoon like those so beloved of the London broadsheets, and if the work showed a certain haste, this only added to its vigor. The central figure was a female form in heroic pose, young, pretty, slender but shapely, her hair streaming down her back. She stood on the deck of a trim schooner, holding off a party of lecherous marines with nothing but a pistol. One arm was thrown back to protect maybe her son — or conceivably, her younger brother — who peeked, eyes wide with fright, around her skirts; the other aimed the gun steadily at a drooling sergeant whose eyes were fixed on her ample bosom.

"The artist has taken some license," said Sparhawk.

"It is Tommy Gage's worst nightmare," replied Ansbach. "A British abuse tailor-made for the talents of Samuel Adams' pen and Paul Revere's burin. Another Boston Massacre, another Concord, another rally-ing cry for the Rebels if they hang her here. For all his other faults, Gage is too smart to allow it. The admiral must swallow his pride and free her, though he blusters even now that she committed piracy on the high seas."

"It was Marblehead," said Sparhawk. "The seas were not so high as all that. And resisting the press is a time-honored tradi-tion. If we began prosecuting women for it, we'd have to hang every fishwife in Bristol."

"No doubt that will be Parliament's next act," said Ansbach. "Or some similar folly. I have written to my uncle, the king, about the state of affairs in Boston Harbor. I tried to persuade your father to share some of the evidence against Admiral Graves in the matter of the gold with me, but he fears that any reprisals from that revenge-minded family would be directed against you. In any case, I have done my best to see the admiral recalled. The pamphlet is proof enough that his temperament is ill-suited to such a delicate post. Uncle George does not make war on women defending their children."

"And what of your own interest in this affair?" asked Sparhawk. They both knew he meant Benjamin Ward.

"Ah," replied Ansbach with a sigh. "You will not have heard. There is a Rebel privateer patrolling Boston Harbor this past week, and she has taken her first prize. Galling for the admiral, and a windfall for the American forces. The *Nancy* out of Portsmouth was carrying a hold full of the finest Swiss powder. She was three weeks overdue, her topsails gone in an Atlantic storm, two hands at the pumps at all hours. She had a sensible skipper, and that was her undoing.

He followed the navy's published remarks on navigation in Boston Harbor, and anchored at Boston Light to wait for a local pilot to guide her in."

Sparhawk thought he could guess what had happened next.

"Their pilot, alas, was waylaid, and the man who came aboard was an imposter. A notorious buccaneer named Cheap. He was Abednego Ward's sailing master at one time. Now he sails with his son."

"Cheap did not, I take it," said Sparhawk, "guide the *Nancy* to the Long Wharf."

"No. He took her up one of the little high-tide creeks, where a schooner named the *Sally* was waiting for her. To do these Rebel pirates credit, they did not molest or rob the British crew. They put them off in the ship's boat and allowed them to remove their personal possessions. But they took all of the powder, and they burned the leaky little brig to the waterline."

Benjamin Ward had told Sparhawk: he would always put kin and crew before king and country. And evidently, before his own passions as well. Angela Ferrers had demanded a powder run in exchange for the evidence against Admiral Graves, and as Benji had observed, there were nearer sources of powder than Lisbon. He could not count on Trent being able to bribe the Americans to save his sister, and so he had taken it upon himself to acquire a bargaining chip. And in so doing, he had perhaps driven a permanent wedge between himself and Charles Ansbach.

"What will you do now?" asked Sparhawk.

"The Graves family — the admiral and all four of his nephews — has vowed to hunt this Rebel pirate down and hang him, but I am determined to find him first."

To find him first. And no doubt keep him from harm if he could.

A few hours after Ansbach left, one of the *Preston*'s marines came for Sparhawk and led him to the gangplank without explanation or fanfare. From the top of that ramp James could survey the entire length of the Long Wharf, thrusting almost a mile into the harbor, lined with squat bulky warehouses. Once, ships had lined up along that mighty jetty end to end, an unbroken line of masts and rigging, promising to the sailors who came to Boston to make their fortunes the limitless freedom of the sea.

A few small shops struggled on: caulkers and carpenters employed by the fleet, merchants who were granted precious dispensations to sell the most basic sustenance, rice and flour and oats. There was a barrel maker open for business opposite the *Preston,* his awnings rolled out against the summer sun and his products on proud, if somewhat scanty, display.

His father stood beside a rack of barrels, waiting.

This time, he had come for him.

The day was hot, the air humid, and that was why Sparhawk could not draw breath. The caulkers were busy at their work, their pitch boiling noxious vapors into the air, and that was why his eyes were watering.

"You are free," said Anthony Trent.

"And Sarah?" James asked with what voice he could find.

Trent nodded reassuringly. "Expected from the castle hourly. Come, let us go home."

Sparhawk climbed into the carriage, glad of the shadows inside where he could hide the emotion that threatened to overcome him.

"How?"

"Nothing less than blackmail. I procured the receipts for the *Diana* and the admiral's other purchases from a certain widow of the Rebel persuasion. A formidable and intriguing woman. The documents are damning, as they specify the coin in which the sums were paid. Graves has been given copies of these documents. If you and Sarah were not released, I promised to send the originals to the Admiralty."

"And what did you give the Rebels in return?" Sparhawk asked.

"Information," replied his father, "the source of which, I fear, will become obvious within a very short time. Specifically, Billy Howe's plans for an attack on the Rebel positions at Roxbury. He is poised to make Gentleman Johnny's 'elbow room.'

"Billy shared his plans with Clinton, Gage, Burgoyne, the admiral, and me. When it is clear that their attack has been anticipated, I will become a man without a country or a livelihood, which is as much as I deserve. But it is my hope that both will be restored to you through my actions, and to Sarah as well."

Sparhawk had just gotten his father back. He was not prepared to lose him again. "You won't just stay here and let them arrest you," he said.

"No," said Trent. "After I have seen you and Sarah both free, I will leave with the Reverend Edwards for Cambridge. He has invited me to live with his family in their house near the college until such time as the troubles are settled or I make other arrangements."

"It is not so very difficult, I understand," Sparhawk said, thinking of Joseph Warren's midnight visits, "to slip across the lines. I could come to see you."

"I would like that. I cannot give you back your mother, or your childhood, or the years that we have lost, but I would give you a future with a woman who is worthy of the man you have become, and try to earn myself a place in it. That is, if you intend to marry Sarah."

"Of course I do."

"That is well," said Trent. "I almost feared, when I saw her house in the North End, that the resemblance you bear to my youthful self might not be *too* pronounced."

"I did not offer Sarah marriage because I did not know what would happen when I stepped forward and declared myself your son. If you had been the murderer I thought," he said, hearing the defensiveness in his voice and trying to curb it, "then you might have been a danger to her." Sparhawk was explaining himself as though an errant child, and this man his father.

Which he was.

"I'm not even sure it would have been legal to marry her under the name James Sparhawk," he added.

"I suggest you decide on that point

460

quickly, as I have asked the Reverend Edwards to meet us at the house. He is not terribly fastidious in the matter of licenses, fortunately. You will have to beg Abednego's permission, of course, and I must warn you in advance that you may find it a gruesome business."

Strange to think his father too had sought such permission.

"Did he offer you rum?" asked Sparhawk, remembering the sulfurous black liquor he had drunk in Abednego Ward's keeping room in Salem.

"No," said James' father.

"Then I think it will be just fine."

Sparhawk had never seen the spacious home Trent rented on the Common, but it equaled the size and luxury of the house Micah Wild had built for Sarah in Salem, and far exceeded it in opulence. It was a fit place for a wedding, but afterward, he wanted to take her to the snug little house in the North End, or better, to the *Sally,* where he would ask for her ration of grog, and convince her to walk across the deck for him in nothing but her chemise and stays.

Abednego Ward greeted Sparhawk in the hall and shook his hand, congratulating him on his escape from the gallows.

"He was not as near the rope as all that," chided Trent, who had cause to know how very near he had come, and the cost to set him free.

"It is a fine thing," said Abednego Ward, "a fine thing, to have a brush with the Almighty. It can change a man's direction entirely."

Sparhawk agreed that it could, although he thought he might always have been sailing in the direction of Sarah Ward.

The Reverend Edwards arrived and punch was served, but Sparhawk did not want to drink until Sarah was with them. He sat near the window in the parlor, waiting for the sound of her carriage, and discovered there an embroidery frame with Trent's coat of arms — no, *his* coat of arms — drawn in pencil and an outline begun in gold-wire thread. He traced its outline, the lines of the familiar griffin and brace of Cornish chough, and recalled the embellished curtains on the *Sally,* how she had confided to him in that antique bed in the North End her desire to sail with him to share the freedom — and discomforts — of the sea as Abigail had with Abednego.

"And there will be no dame schools for my daughters," she had vowed. But the delicate needlework, the ribbon tucked into the copy of *The Female American or the Adventures of Unca Eliza Whitfield* that sat snug between the sofa cushions, betrayed the pleasure she had discovered in these female accomplishments. The dame *had* broadened her mind, at least in some respects. Once he had a ship again, Sparhawk would broaden her horizons. And the children they created would have both the wonders of education and the freedom of the sea.

The sun dipped in the sky. The warmth of the day dissipated. And still, her carriage did not come.

Trent sent to the wharf for word of the boat he had hired. It had not yet returned from the island.

"Perhaps," suggested the reverend, "she was taken unawares by the good news and required time to pack."

Sparhawk did not believe it. He had never known Sarah Ward impractical, or vain of possessions.

"Send direct to the castle," said Sparhawk.

Trent agreed. An hour passed, and a dark certainty overtook Sparhawk. "Graves has double-crossed us. We should go to the castle ourselves."

"No," said Trent. "If the admiral is refusing to free her as agreed, we will not be able to effect her release on our own authority. I will go to Province House and speak to Tommy Gage, and if need be, row him to the castle myself to demand her return. But you should wait here, in the event that she or some news of her makes its way here."

Sparhawk knew that his father was right; he could not help Sarah by storming the castle like a knight of old. So he sat in the pretty parlor where she had begun to embroider his family's coat of arms in gold-wire thread and waited for Sarah Ward, her father sitting quiet and subdued, his earlier ebullience gone, on the settee opposite.

The shadows in the room lengthened, the sun set, the servants came to light the tapers, and finally Anthony Trent returned.

"I have been to the castle and back in the company of Thomas Gage. The admiral claims that he sent orders for her release, and the commander at the castle admits to receiving such orders and transmitting them to the guard at the gate. The guard says that she was taken ill and carried to a boat, and he was told that she was in the care of a family friend. The fort major is not to be found, but his wife tells the same story. Sarah's maid was out walking when all this transpired, and saw nothing. In the end we searched the fort, the outbuildings, and the beaches, and found no trace of her. Sarah Ward is gone."

TWENTY-TWO

The Phillips family was unfailing in its kindness. The guard would not permit Sarah to leave the apartments to see the natural beauty that Major Phillips swore was to be found on the island, so they brought that beauty to her. Mrs. Phillips picked wildflowers and refreshed the bowl in Sarah's room each day. Her wan, distracted daughter, Rebecca, dried and pressed the discarded blooms, and labeled them in a book in a neat flowing hand.

When Rebecca was searching for pencils one day, Sarah saw an abandoned project lying hidden at the bottom of a drawer: a compass rose made completely out of dried flowers, the points picked out in rich violet and the rings in bold, verdant green. There were three points yet to be completed, and it had clearly been made as a gift, with part of the recipient's name, Martin, visible in the corner, but when Sarah questioned her about it, Rebecca just smiled her sad, distracted smile and closed the drawer.

Looking out the windows seaward during the long afternoons when Mrs. Phillips and Rebecca walked the beach, Sarah was reminded of her first weeks at the dame school, when she felt imprisoned in the dame's rambling waterfront house, the sea sparkling within reach but forbidden. She had come to enjoy school, in the end, and cherish Elizabeth Pierce's friendship, now lost to her, but she had always felt the shackles of the dame's expectations, and when she became engaged, had thought that Micah Wild would set her free.

While Major Phillips' wife and daughter were out during the afternoons, he often invited her into his little study and encouraged her to borrow any books she might like — he had a prodigious library, as many as twoscore volumes — and discuss anything she might have read recently. He did not have any novels, but he had several histories, and these she enjoyed. He also had many trays of dried and pinned insects, which she did not.

He was not in the habit of offering her any refreshment during these interludes, and he always seemed vaguely embarrassed, like his wife, by the poorness of his hospitality, but today he surprised Sarah by placing a decanter of brandy on the table between them. She was even more surprised when he rummaged in his secretary and produced two cut glasses.

"My dear," said Major Phillips, pouring the brandy, "today your ordeal is at an end. You are to be released."

Her hand trembled. She was not going to hang. She brought her shaking glass to her lips and drank it off to steady herself. Phillips patted her hand.

Then panic overtook her. "And James Sparhawk? Is he to be freed as well?"

Major Phillips refilled her glass. "I believe so."

"When may I leave?" she asked, and then regretted it. They had been so good to her, and she did not want to appear ungrateful. "That is, your family's kindness has sustained me, but I long to see my own."

"Of course. Of course. That is my wish, to see you restored to your family. We will miss you, my wife and I and Rebecca. I believe that your stay with us has done her some good. You will have guessed, I think, that she was disappointed."

"Yes," said Sarah. "As was I, once," she said. But she had not been entombed on a rock. She had possessed the freedom of the sea. And now she would have James Sparhawk, who was necessary, for her, to life.

"That is what I was given to understand," said Major Phillips. "It is a fault of fathers, I think, to raise their daughters too protected from the world. Our Rebecca was not prepared to resist the lures of a rogue."

Sarah had not been protected. She had climbed rigging and picked pockets and cadged oranges, been raised by rogues and adventurers, and she had been taken in by Micah Wild as easily as Sparhawk's mother had been beguiled away from her country parsonage by Anthony Trent.

"I was commander of the castle in those days," said Major Phillips. "And Martin was a boat pilot and a frequent guest at our table. He thought Rebecca would have an income, but when I lost my post, there was no possibility of that. I told him as much, and when they ran away together, we knew to expect the worst. It lasted a few weeks, and he left her penniless and in debt in New York. She was preyed upon. By the time we found her, she was much changed."

"I am so very sorry," said Sarah, "but I do not believe there was anything you could have said to dissuade her." Abednego Ward had not been able to talk Sarah out of an alliance with Micah Wild. He had warned her not to go to him that night.

"No," Major Phillips agreed, recharging her glass once more. "That is why I am anxious to see you returned home safe."

"There is time, if I hurry, to make the mail boat," she said. There had been a clock beside the door, but in the shadows of the room she had to squint and could not make out the dial. She rose out of her chair, but too quickly. Relief made her light-headed, and she sat back down.

"My dear, you cannot go back to this Trent," Major Phillips said, reaching across the table and sliding the brimming glass into her hand. "He has worked to free you and that is well, but you do not owe him what he will expect when you return. And his reputation is such that I have reason to believe he has designs upon you."

Something was not quite right, but Sarah's thoughts were muddled. "Trent is a good man," she said. "He was going to marry me. But Trent is . . . now he will be . . . he will be my father," she said. "Father-in-law," she corrected. It was all suddenly very confusing.

The fort major looked concerned. "That is not what I was told," he said.

She tilted the glass in her hand, stared at the thick sludge on the bottom, tried to puzzle out what it might be. Sniffed it. Cinnamon, but not. A spicy scent that sometimes clung to her father's sea chest, and Mr. Cheap's. A captain's private cargo. As valuable as nutmeg or pepper, gram per gram. Opium.

"You've drugged me," she said, her tongue thick.

"You will take no harm from it," he promised, his voice a little anxious.

The door opened and Micah Wild stood framed in the light from the hall.

She stood up, grasping the table for support. "That man," she said, pointing at Wild, "burned my house down."

"That is the opium talking," said Micah Wild.

The room swirled around her, the red of the chairs, the black of the clock, the green of the fort major's coat blurring into streaks.

Then Micah was behind her, grasping her by the waist and keeping her from falling, pulling her back against his chest, and encouraging her to give in to the drug's pull and sleep.

"No," she said, but her vision was dimming, and the room was being taken from her by the opium one color at a time until all was gray and blurred.

"I don't like this," said Major Phillips.

Her head felt heavy; her limbs would not answer. "Please," she begged the fort major. "Send for Trent."

"Trent is a seducer," said Wild, his voice coming from far away. "He has tired of her and intends to hand her off to his son."

She clung for one last moment to consciousness, long enough to feel Wild lift her and carry her to the daybed, to feel him stroke her face and tuck a hair behind her ear and say in his honeyed voice, "Everything is going to be all right, Sarah. I've come to take you *home*."

General Gage sent a detachment of his own men to search Castle William for Sarah Ward. He also posted a guard at the Long Wharf to inspect the small boats putting in, but there were far too many little wharves and anchorages in Boston and Charlestown to search them all, and by that time Sparhawk and Trent had already come and gone from the island. They questioned the maid, Mrs. Phillips, her morose daughter, and the guard at the gate. And then they searched the island for Major Phillips.

They found him outside the walls on a secluded stretch of beach, staring out to sea. They did not need to resort to threats or bribes. The man poured forth his tale. He knew he had been deceived when he saw Micah Wild carry the girl to the daybed. His hands on her had been too possessive, too familiar, for a chastely devoted suitor and family friend. Major Phillips had taken money from Wild, as he had taken money from Trent, and he had received his thirty pieces of silver. The incident was a stain on his soul. The pieces could not be given back.

Wild had paid him to drug the girl. He had explained that it was a precaution, that she was highly excitable and liable to do herself an injury if he had to take her away against her will. His tale was one of innocence seduced, a simple seaman's daughter, promised to a doughty merchant, beguiled away from hearth and home and lawfully betrothed by a worldly rake named Trent.

There was enough of fact, when the fort major quizzed the girl on her family and origins, to burnish the story with the aura of truth. And enough similarity to his daughter's sad tale that he was predisposed to believe it. Sarah Ward was from Salem, her father had been a mariner, she had been engaged to marry, but had not. She lived under Trent's roof. Trent had a certain reputation with women, and he had paid for her upkeep at the castle. Her gowns were lavish and costly, the kind a kept woman wore.

Wild told him Trent was about to pass her on to another naval officer. It would be the beginning of a steep, fast slide into degradation. Unless Wild could spirit her away from her seducer before the man got his hooks into her once more.

Sparhawk saw his father's hand return again and again to the hilt of his sword, felt his own fingers twitch to do the same. But the fort major was a dupe, and his spiritual agony already exceeded any physical chastisement they might mete out. They needed two names from this man and nothing else: that of the ship on which Wild had taken her, and that of its intended port of call.

Sparhawk was not surprised when he learned the first, but taken aback at the second. The ship was the *Roger Conant*, with her four-pounders and her swivel guns and her twoscore hired men. And she was bound for Rebel Salem.

Sarah woke beneath a silk canopy in a soft feather bed. The posts of her bower were polished mahogany carved with swags and urns. The drapes were pale blue figured damask. A quiver of Cupid's arrows picked out in gold paint adorned the tester.

474

The dimensions of the room felt strangely familiar, but the mustard yellow walls, flowered carpets, and plump upholstered chairs did not. She could not place where she was, nor how she had come there.

Then she remembered the fort major's study, the drugged brandy, Micah Wild's hands upon her. Someone had removed her gown and loosened her stays, and she knew with certainty that Micah had touched her while she slept, could recall through the poppy's haze the way he had stroked her hair and her face on the daybed in the major's parlor, then as he held her across his lap in the boat.

Micah Wild had said he was bringing her home, but her home was gone, burned by his longshoreman.

She slid from the high bed and clung to the posts for a moment, her head still thick and fogged from the opium. Her gown lay across a chair, her shoes on the floor beside it. The dressing table and washstand were unfamiliar, but the size and placement of the windows, and when she looked out, the patchwork of rooflines and clapboard colors, told her where Micah had brought her, and whose house this was. She was in Salem, and the house was Micah Wild's.

The bedrooms had not been completed

by the time Micah broke their engagement; they had been only plaster and planks when she saw them, but if she remembered correctly, based on the views, this was the guest bedroom at the back of the house with the prospect of the North River. Another chamber across the hall, where Micah and Elizabeth must sleep, looked out on a similar view. She knew that room had been intended for the master and lady of the house, as it adjoined a small study where Micah had planned to conduct his more private business transactions, to keep ledgers and write receipts for French molasses and Dutch tea and all the other smuggled goods that flowed in and out of Salem.

She took a step forward, and then retreated to the bed. She did not feel well at all. She could still taste the brandy and the dusty dry spice of the opium in her mouth, and felt the tangle of dried saltwater spray in her hair. Micah could not have brought her all the way to Salem in a rowboat. He must have had the *Conant* hidden somewhere in the channels of Boston Harbor.

Even if Sparhawk or Trent discovered that much, they could not reach her here in Rebel Salem. General Gage had tried to send a column of regulars up under Colonel Leslie in February, and they had been driven back by the combined militia and townspeople.

Gage could not even break out of Boston now. The navy was unlikely to go haring off in pursuit of a woman it had only grudgingly released on a charge of piracy. And if Micah Wild was welcome in Salem once more, the *Sally* certainly wasn't.

Which meant that if she wanted to see Sparhawk and her family again — and stay out of Micah Wild's bed — she would have to get out of Salem herself.

Shoes and a dress would be material to a successful escape. And sweet cooling water. She drank half the pitcher on the washstand and bathed in the rest, combed and pinned the tangle of her hair, reserving the longest pins in the dressing table for a more important purpose than her coiffure.

It took her longer to pick the lock than it should have. Standing up, she became dizzy; kneeling on the floor, she began to sway. Finally she accomplished her task with her cheek pressed to the grain-painted door and her heart beating wildly from the exertion. She knew sailors who took opium because they enjoyed it, but she could not understand the attraction. Unconsciousness, strange dreams, and nausea held little appeal.

She kept the pin that had vanquished Micah Wild's brass door lock, and tucked it into the front of her gown. The hall, thankfully, was empty, because there was no way to slip discreetly down that broad curving stair.

The latch on the front door lifted just before she reached it. In a moment, she would surely be discovered. The parlors to the left and right offered no concealment. She darted instead for the opening beneath the stairs and found herself in the service ell, broader and taller than Sarah's whole house had been, and full, just now, of servants.

Their chatter stopped abruptly. There were three maids and two cooks and a burly footman in the mold of the late, loathsome Dan Ludd. He got up from his place at the table, where one of the maids had been feeding him slices of apple, and took a step toward Sarah.

The room spun. She felt hands reaching for her, then a chair being thrust under her, and she looked up to find an anxious sea of faces peering at her, including that of the cook, a smiling woman Sarah recognized, Mrs. Friary, the best baker in town. Micah had hired her for the new house because Sarah loved her ginger cakes.

"Get the captain," Mrs. Friary said to the wide-eyed maid beside her. "Miss Sarah," she said in the voice one reserved for children and invalids. "Miss Sarah, you've been very ill. Captain's only just brought you home, and you're not to be out of bed."

She was ill, certainly, but only because "the captain" had dosed her with opium. Even seated, she still felt dizzy, and when she attempted to stand, the yellow shutters on the windows, the copper pots over the fire, the iron hooks over the hearth, moved in a kaleidoscope of fragmented colors.

"Fetch some water," said Mrs. Friary.

"The poor thing," said the wide-eyed maid.

"Filthy British bastards," spat the youngest of the footmen.

Which was peculiar, because these were Micah's servants, and they seemed to be full of righteous indignation and sympathy *for her.*

Sarah heard booted feet running. The sea of faces parted. Micah Wild knelt in front of her, and the look of concern on his handsome face was unfeigned. "I'll take her from here, Mrs. Friary."

"What did you tell these people?" Sarah asked, trying — and failing — to stand.

He caught her as she slumped into the

479

chair and lifted her into his arms. She was too sick and dizzy to protest.

"I told them the truth," he said in his orator's voice, intended to ring through the house as he carried her out of the kitchen. "That you are a heroine. You were wrongfully imprisoned by the treacherous British in Boston for saving Ned from the press and took ill in their barbarous jail. And I brought you out of there, brought you home."

That explained their caring and concern, the kindness they had been too afraid to show her when she had defied Micah Wild and refused to become his mistress.

"Only the jailer, as it turned out, was treacherous," she said. "And only because he was deceived and bribed by you."

Wild sighed. "The doddering old fool gave you too much opium. I am sorry for that. But Mrs. Friary is making you ginger cakes. And you will recover quickly now that you are home."

Home and not home. The house he had built for her, with the furnishings she had picked out, and the cook hired to please her. The familiar voices outside her window, calling down the river, the sound of the water lapping at the reeded banks. The scent of molasses-sweet air from the rum distilleries wafting on the breeze, and beneath it, the salt tang of the sea. It was what she had longed for, shut up in Castle William — what she thought she might never see again.

Now if her head would only stop spinning, she might be able to take some comfort in these little things at least.

She had to close her eyes as he bore her up the winding stair to avoid being sick. If she had been capable of even crawling back to her room, she would have preferred that to enduring Micah's touch. She could not blame his servants for swallowing his lies. People would believe anything he said in that honeyed voice. In Sarah's experience, if there was a grain of truth in Micah's words, they were taken as gospel.

He deposited her gently on the bed in the blue and gold chamber and brought a wet cloth with which to dab her forehead. She swatted him away.

"Where is Elizabeth?" she asked, remembering that her former friend's family had called her home in light of Wild's newly precarious circumstances.

"Gone back to her family. This time for good. They are having our marriage dissolved."

"And how is it you are welcome in Salem once more?"

He refreshed the cloth and laid it across

her forehead, and this time she did not stop him. "I'm not, exactly. Or I wouldn't be without you. The pamphlet that Benji's friends printed has made you quite the heroine, defending Ned from the press and such. And now I am your rescuer. Salem's Committee of Safety allowed the *Conant* to enter the harbor because we carried you."

"Why Salem? And don't tell me because it is my home. You burned my home."

Another wave of nausea swept her, and she twisted on the bed. He replaced the cool cloth with a fresh one. "Your house would still be standing if you had been reasonable that night."

"And Ned would have been pressed aboard the *Wasp* if I had been reasonable that day." She sat up. "But I am not reasonable, and you are not a romantic. Why are we here?"

Wild laughed. "You may not be reasonable, but you are certainly made of tougher stuff than Elizabeth. You would not have run home to your father over a little double-dealing."

She was not so sure he was right about that, but she let it pass.

"We are here," he said, "to retrieve my property. It is my hope that the Committee of Safety and the Continental Congress will soon welcome me back into the fold, but I have made provision in case they do not."

For a moment she was puzzled; then she understood. "The French gold. The admiral paid you for the *Conant* and the *Cromwell* with the French gold. It is still here."

And it was the most damning evidence against both Micah Wild and Admiral Graves, if she could lay hands on it.

"Just so," he said. "If Salem will not welcome us, then Providence or Newport will. We have enough capital to provision the *Conant* for a profitable cruise. The *Sally*'s success in Boston Harbor has ignited a fever for privateering, and the admiral's latest threats of retaliation have sent the ports scrambling to arm vessels for their defense. Salem cannot fit out ships fast enough."

"What success?"

"You have not heard? Benji took a British supply ship, loaded with powder. Dr. Warren and his Provincial Congress may be willing to overlook my recent defection if I will fly their pine tree flag on the *Roger Conant* and do the same."

"And will you?" she asked.

"Yes."

"Why this change of heart? The admiral gave you letters of marque to hunt the *Sally*. The Congress may not." The Provincial

Congress, to judge by the machinations of Angela Ferrers, wanted James Sparhawk. Fast ships and bold seamen. Ones they could be sure of.

"I still mean to claim the *Sally*," said Micah Wild. "She is my lawful property, and the courts will return her to me. But the admiral betrayed me. He reneged on his promise to release the *Roger Conant* at the end of her lease, told me he had the right to press her into service, without payment, a necessity of war."

"How did you get her back?"

"I *took* her," he said.

From Admiral Graves, a man who brooked no insult, who would have hanged Sparhawk to conceal his own cupidity, who had ordered Sarah thrown into a dank cell, who threatened children like Ned, and who would have shelled Marblehead over a box of candles. There would be no changing sides again for Micah Wild. "Why?" she asked. "When you could not be sure the Rebels would have you back?"

"Because the admiral's 'necessity' was you. He intended to double-cross Trent and transport you for trial. I couldn't let him do it. It was always an abstract set of principles for me, liberty, the cause. I did not like anything that Parliament was doing, but that was because it hindered trade. I was always prepared to sail whichever way the favorable wind blew, for independence or reconciliation, but Graves . . . Graves was going to send you across the ocean and hang you," said Wild. "It was no longer about tea or pamphlets or taxes."

Sarah had dreamed of this, in her cold bedroom in her vanished house, after the curtains and carpets had been sold. And she had dreamed of it on the chilliest nights, when she slept down on the trundle with Ned and there was no other way to stay warm.

But Micah Wild was only saying it now that Elizabeth and her money were no longer available to him, and Sarah Ward was once more useful to him, a safe conduct to enter Salem Harbor.

"I should have married you, Sarah," he said. "I was going to. But then you came to me, and I knew I didn't have to."

When Sarah said nothing, he went on. "I thought I could have Elizabeth's money and you and no one would think the worse of me for it. On the contrary, they would envy me. But when I thought you were going to die, that the admiral would see you hanged, I realized that the only thing that mattered to me was you."

And a heavy chest of French gold.

"If my happiness matters to you," she said, "you will let me go."

"Your safety," said Micah Wild, in the voice that had long since ceased to sway her, "is more important than your momentary happiness. And there is no safety for you inside the British lines while Admiral Graves has control of the squadron. Whatever trick Trent used to free you will not work again. Nor would the admiral bother with the niceties of the law this time. If you go back to Boston and your lover, you will die."

The question was how to get into Salem Harbor.

"The guns on Winter Island and those at the point will blow you to bits," said Abednego Ward. He ought to know. He had helped place them there, before Micah Wild had jilted his daughter. "And you cannot run around them, or you will be holed by the chevaux-defrise." These were ten-foot-square pine boxes weighted with lead and sunk in the channel, bristling with iron spikes. "And then there is the chain across the harbor."

They returned to the question over and over again, late into the night, with the candles blazing in the parlor of Trent's mansion. The Reverend Edwards had stayed on, and though the cleric was not a military man, Sparhawk took some comfort from the presence of this fixture of his childhood.

Finally Sparhawk acknowledged the truth. "We cannot enter Salem Harbor without the permission of the Rebels there. It must be negotiated, and quickly."

Trent nodded. "I will go," he said.

"No, Father," said Sparhawk. "I will go." He knew what Angela Ferrers would demand, and he was prepared to give it.

He reached the Rebel camp at Cambridge before dawn, the pretty redbrick buildings of the college nestled in broad meadows within sight of the river. The smell was less appealing. The farmers and farriers and lawyers and innkeepers he had met on the road to Boston after Lexington were not soldiers. They did not know how to build a hygienic camp for ten thousand men, or how to set a picket line. Their officers had not been drawn from the ranks of military or aristocratic families and trained to leadership from a young age. They were elected by their men, or chosen by the Provincial Congress for their initiative, which was demonstrated by recruiting enough volunteers to form a command.

Sparhawk presented himself and asked to see Angela Ferrers. He was directed to a fine manor house of three stories with a hipped roof and carved balustrade, occupied at present by a company of mariners from Marblehead. He had a little sway with them, as their leader, a man named Glover, knew Abednego Ward and had overseen the refitting of the *Sally*.

Glover sent for the Merry Widow, and Angela Ferrers came down to meet Sparhawk in the parlor, wearing a blue silk night robe with her hair falling loose over her shoulders.

"Captain Sparhawk, or should I address you as the heir to Polkerris?"

"You knew, didn't you, that my father was no murderer?" he said.

"Your father is in point of fact a murderer, several times over. He has killed seven men in duels. The privilege of rank, private law. It is still murder, even if they all deserved it. And while I knew that the Milton family had engineered the death of Trent's first wife, your mother, I did not know how culpable Lord Polkerris himself might have been in the affair. That was not something I had the need, or the time, to investigate. Are you going after Sarah Ward for yourself or for your long-lost father?"

"Does it matter?" asked Sparhawk.

Angela Ferrers caressed the pearl-crusted mourning rings on her right hand. It was an unconscious gesture in a studied woman. "What matters is that this army is supplied with the matériel of war. We have veteran soldiers aplenty, but their cartridge boxes and powder horns are empty. And we lack guns. Benjamin Ward's victory in Boston Harbor was an easy one. The next British supply ship will not be so handily gulled. And blockade runners are bold when it is a cargo of rice or French molasses they carry, but few men have the nerve to sail with a hold full of powder into the jaws of the most powerful navy in the world.

"Smugglers have served our needs up to now, but with open war upon us, we need men who have been trained in piracy, who can fire a shot across a merchantman's bow and will blow her to flinders if she does not heave to. And for such as that — for genuine, old-fashioned piracy — there remains no better school in the world than the British Navy. If you wish to enter Salem Harbor with the *Sally* to find Sarah Ward, then I will require you to accept this."

She drew a sealed document from her robe and placed it on the tea table. He broke the seal and read its contents. "I was not aware that the Americans had a navy," he said.

"At present there are only provincial navies, mostly made up of flotillas of whale-boats and gun barges. You will notice that your commission is postdated. It will take effect on June fifteen, when I anticipate that a new commander will take charge of our forces, and it confirms you as captain in the army of the United Colonies, and charges you to seize and make a prize any British ships you encounter, though not to engage with men-of-war carrying superior guns. Fifty percent of civilian cargo will go to you and your crew, but all powder, muskets, cannon, uniforms, and ordnance must go directly to the army. I cannot sanction your actions in Salem, nor take any part in your quarrel with Micah Wild, but I *can* make certain that you are allowed to enter the harbor. I believe that Dr. Warren also offered other incentives, including real estate. You will find deeds for suitable properties enclosed."

He opened the document she indicated, and found deeds for a fine house he had seen in Salem, a warehouse and a cottage he had heard tell of, and the lease for a significant portion of Misery Island.

"It is a generous offer," said Sparhawk.

"But it is not an English barony. What say you? Will it be Captain Sparhawk, or my Lord Polkerris?"

"Sparhawk," he said without hesitation, because it was not an English baron's son but James Sparhawk who was worthy of Sarah Ward.

Micah sent for ice from his icehouse and fresh water, and once both arrived, he warned Sarah against making another escape attempt.

"I will tie you to the bed if I must," he said. Then he left to speak with Eli Derby.

Sarah rested for a little while and considered whether she might be able to climb down from the window.

The Ward house had been a humble antique structure in its bones, with ceilings barely seven feet tall — an easy drop from a second-story window.

Not so this monument to Micah Wild's ambition. The ceilings of the ground floor were a lofty twelve feet. There was a porch roof she might climb out to and use to lower herself to the iron railings, but it would take a clear head and a strong grip, neither of which she now possessed.

She resolved to use one of the Chinese vases lining the fireplace mantel to brain whoever next opened the door, and make her way out down the back stairs. She only hoped that it would prove to be Micah Wild.

It was not Micah Wild. When Mrs. Friary put her gray head through the door, her face a mask of worry, a tray of cakes in her hands, Sarah hid the vase behind her back and sat down on the bed.

The old woman praised her courage for saving Ned, asked politely after her father's health, and told her how happy everyone was to see her back where she ought to be. It wasn't for her to say, of course, but everyone knew Micah had made a mistake marrying Elizabeth Pierce. And no one was going to mind when Sarah moved into the bedroom down the hall, even if the divorce took time to arrange.

Sarah resolved to go out the window as soon as Mrs. Friary left.

She ate the cakes first. Then she knotted up her skirts the way she used to when sneaking out of the house with Benji to drink rum in the *Sally*'s cutter, and swung her legs out the window. The porch over the door below was two feet from her window, and she was forced to swing, jump, and scramble onto it, clutching the painted white balustrade and thanking the architect for fastening it to the slate tiles with iron spikes.

From there the way down to the ground was easier. She lowered herself from the balustrade, wrapped her legs around one of the supporting columns, and shimmied down until her feet met the iron rail. Then, with relief — and scraped knees and elbows smudged with roof soot — she found herself outside the back door, looking toward the river.

And unfortunately, standing on the granite steps below was Micah Wild. "Is that how you used to get out of your father's house to come see me?" he asked incredulously.

"It was easier with a smaller house," she said. "I am leaving, Micah."

He took her by the elbow. "We are both leaving. That damnable interfering Ferrers woman has poisoned the well with Eli Derby. There's nothing for it now. We must collect the gold and make for Providence."

She backed toward the door, but his men were waiting there for her, and when she tried to run, they caught her and forced her into the boat. Her screams, before they gagged her, brought Mrs. Friary and the servants to the door, but too late to help her, and then they were away down the river, heading for the harbor.

When they went aboard the *Conant,* Sarah recognized her skipper, Jerathmiel Finch, who had been her father's first choice to captain the *Sally* on the run to Saint Eustatius. Micah had vetoed the choice, judging Jerathmiel insufficiently dedicated to the Rebel cause, but Sarah had suspected he was just insufficiently dedicated to Micah Wild. He was a sensible man and a better sailor than Molineaux had been, and Sarah hoped she might be able to prevail upon him to release her.

Micah shocked her when he ordered Captain Finch to clear the deck for action and make for Misery Island.

"What is happening?" she asked her former betrothed as he scanned the harbor with a spyglass.

"Derby would not partner with me, but we have been friends since childhood, and he had the decency to warn me. Your lover has been given permission to enter Salem Harbor and retrieve you, with the *Sally.* "

"We should run for it," said Finch. "I do not have a man-of-war's crew. I have boys lured by the promise of prize money. Farmers' and shopkeepers' sons. They have never fired a cannon."

"We cannot run," said Wild, "until we have landed at Misery Island and taken my property off."

They made for Misery Island. Finch ordered netting rigged. It was meant to catch splinters during a battle, which meant he anticipated one. Next he called for powder. By the time the *Conant* came within sight of the windswept rock that Salem's early settlers had dubbed Misery Island, they had spotted a sail on the horizon.

It was the *Sally.* Finch turned to Micah Wild. "Take the girl with you in the cutter, and leave her on the island until this business is done."

Wild balked, but Finch, who, as Sarah recalled, had served in the navy in his youth, gave him no choice. "I won't fight Abednego Ward's schooner with his daughter aboard. It's not right. It would be dishonorable, and damnably unlucky."

Micah took his sword, two pistols, and a shovel and hurried Sarah into the boat. She watched the *Sally* draw near, her sails stiff in the breeze. Sarah's heart rose in her throat. She had not seen the schooner fly like that since her father had been well. She stood up and waved, hoping her brother or Sparhawk, whoever had command of the *Sally,* might see her and forgo engaging the *Conant,* and come for her.

Her heart sank when the *Sally* tacked and disappeared behind Misery Island. They had not seen her. They likely meant to engage the *Conant,* to come up into the wind and gain the weather gauge, the crucial advantage in any fight at sea.

Sarah lost sight of the schooner as she went around the other side of the island, and now she had no doubt that the *Sally* meant to fight the *Conant.*

Micah dragged the boat up the rocky strand, and Sarah followed him through the scrubby trees to a clearing within sight of the water. He checked one of the trees — Sarah saw notches in the trunk — then crossed to the other side of the glade, then paced, counting, to a point slightly north of the clearing's center.

Then he began to dig.

He did not look up when the guns of the *Conant* spoke, but Sarah did. Both ships were visible now from this vantage.

The *Conant* had fired high into the *Sally*'s rigging and struck a spar. One of her topsails tore loose and flapped in the wind. The *Sally*'s guns made no answer until she tacked and came up on the *Conant* again. Once more the *Conant* fired high, meaning, Sarah realized, to take her a prize. No doubt these had been Micah's instructions to Jerathmiel

Finch. He still wanted the *Sally,* after all.

The *Sally* exhibited no such delicacy. She fired on her downward roll, low into the hull of the *Conant,* and the *Conant*'s side exploded in a shower of splinters.

The *Conant* had been holed below the waterline — a crippling blow. She could not run now. And neither could Micah Wild.

Sarah turned to her former betrothed and saw that he had unearthed the familiar French chest. It was no longer filled as it had been in Molineaux's cabin, but a small fortune in Spanish gold remained, and Wild was filling his sack with the glimmering coins.

"The *Conant* is crippled," she said.

"But we have the gold," replied Wild, scooping coins out of the chest. "And there is a snow docked on the other side of the island. We can take her to Marblehead, buy another schooner, hire another crew."

"You may have the snow, sir," said James Sparhawk, who had approached silently through the trees, pistol in hand, "but Sarah, and the gold, belong to me."

Micah took the snow. As he crossed the island, his hangdog expression suggested he saw little scope now for his powers of persuasion and had no stomach to put his fencing lessons to the test.

"There is water aboard, and she is seaworthy," said Sparhawk as they watched Wild go. "Though where he will be welcome now is difficult to say."

"Providence, perhaps," she said. "The Browns have a reputation for boldness, and an idiosyncratic understanding of private property." When Wild's boat was out of sight and Sparhawk lowered his pistol, she threw herself into his arms.

"How is it that you are here? Who is commanding the *Sally*?" she asked.

"Benji captains her, and my father and yours shared command of her guns. They have cruelly mauled the *Conant,* by the looks of it. Mr. Cheap is with them as well, and Ned."

They returned, hand in hand, to the clearing, where Micah Wild's unburied gold lay glittering in the sun.

"It is evidence," she said, "against Admiral Graves. You can use it to prove your innocence, to regain your rank."

"Or I could use it to repair the *Conant.* Your brother, as Red Abed's eldest, lays a legitimate claim to the *Sally.* And means to rebuild your family's fortunes with her, as a privateer. And as it happens, I have already accepted a commission from the Americans, and been amply rewarded for it. I believe we hold the lease to a quarter of this island. There is a warehouse in town, no doubt intended for my ill-gotten goods, a cottage that I suspect we will sell immediately, unless my father wants it, and a house to which I understand you are attached."

"What of Polkerris? Your father has acknowledged you. If you went home to England, you would be a baron."

"England," he said, "has never been my home. I was born on Nevis. And raised aboard frigates. And my father cannot go home to England. He traded the Americans' intelligence to obtain the papers Angela Ferrers held, to obtain my freedom. He will settle, he tells me, wherever I do, at least until he has had time to correct my swordplay. The 'dropsical Spaniard,' apparently, has much to answer for."

She laughed. "Perhaps he can teach Ned as well," she said.

"Does that mean you will have us?" he asked. "I will not be a baron. Or a naval officer."

"I had always planned to wed a sea captain," she said. "That is, if you intend to marry me."

"I was waiting to do so in my father's house the day Wild took you off Castle

Island. I have been waiting ever since. I will marry you on the *Sally,* if you like. Or in Salem, if you would prefer." Then he added with a smile, "The Reverend Edwards is with us. And I do hope you can endure the man's Puritanical thunder, because my father has already paid him."

They were married on the *Sally,* in a mercifully short ceremony with less thunder than tenderness, because the reverend had known James Sparhawk from the day he was born, and had certainly not hoped to see an occasion as happy as this for the boy he had long thought dead.

Ned and Abednego and Benji and Trent stood by, and afterward Red Abed patted Sparhawk on the shoulder and kissed his daughter. Trent retired to the rail with the old pirate to share a jug of rum.

The *Sally* met no opposition entering Salem Harbor. Sarah had been unconscious when Micah had brought her in on the *Conant,* but now she saw that the wharves were alive with a bustle they had not known since her childhood, since the trouble had started with Parliament and the navy's predation had cast a pall over the port's trade. Now hammers and axes rang, and all up and down the waterfront vessels of every size and description, from tiny snows to substan-

500

tial schooners like the *Conant,* were fitting out.

There was a committee of Salem select-men, mariners all, and headed by Eli Derby, waiting for them when they dropped anchor at the Long Wharf.

Sparhawk and Abednego and Benji spent an hour closeted with these men, bargaining for water and cordage and spars for the *Sally* and repairs for the *Conant*'s hull. They paid for these in hard cash, Spanish gold to be exact, which was very warmly received.

Sarah took Ned and Trent to the house Micah Wild had built for her, and, after explaining the change in circumstances to the anxious servants and showing them the deeds and leases, she took up the responsibilities, so long delayed, of a new bride. She arranged for her father and Trent to have the principal chambers on the second floor, and chose a smaller, more modest room for herself and Sparhawk. Ned and Benji, she knew, would sleep on the *Sally.*

By the time her father and Benji and Sparhawk returned, there was a breakfast of sorts laid in the parlor, the best Mrs. Friary could do at the moment, with a ham and bread and a bowl of potent milk punch sprinkled with nutmeg; and because there was a tower of ginger cakes sparkling with

501

castor sugar, Sarah thought it was a very good breakfast indeed.

It was evening by the time she and Sparhawk were finally alone. Mrs. Friary had taken the ticking covers off the furniture for the occasion, and Sarah and her husband sat together on the sofa, looking out the windows at the river.

"I am very glad to have the house," she said, "but I do not intend to live in it. Not all the time. I want to sail with you, like my mother did with my father."

James Sparhawk turned to his new bride and drew her into his arms, then had a better idea and pulled her into his lap. "On runs to the sugar islands," he said. "And when we carry *safe* cargo. But never with a hold full of powder, and never when we are looking for a fight."

"Agreed," she said. *"Provisionally."* She unlaced the ribbon that bound his hair and kissed him, then kissed him again. She had the life she had hoped for, dreamed of, since girlhood, and she could not remember a time when her heart had been as full.

But for her joy to be complete, she had to know that it was the same for him. "Your father," she said, "has his son. Mine will see his schooner taking prizes once again. Benji has the *Sally*. Ned no doubt will serve aboard her. And I have a home, my family, and the man that I love, but what is there for *you,* James Sparhawk?"

"*Everything,* Sarah. Everything I need. The freedom of the sea. And you."

AUTHOR'S NOTE

While the battles of Lexington and Concord and Bunker Hill have been kept alive in popular memory, the skirmishes fought at sea during the spring of 1775 have largely been forgotten. So too has the role they played in winning the war for public opinion, in the colonies and abroad.

John Derby left Salem on the schooner *Quero* on April 29 and reached London with his printed broadside from the *Salem Gazette* on May 28. By the time the royal express packet *Sukey*, which had left Boston four days *before* the *Quero,* arrived in London on June 9 with General Gage's account of the conflict at Lexington and Concord, popular opinion had already accepted the American version of the events.

The battle of Chelsea Creek occurred on May 27 and 28, 1775, in the salt marshes and mudflats of what is now East Boston. It was the first naval battle of the American

Revolution, and a significant American victory. The burning of the *Diana* demonstrated, to Patriots and friends of government alike, that the British Navy in Boston Harbor was not invulnerable, and it set the stage for further small-scale actions and intensive privateering that advanced American interests throughout the war.

RECOMMENDED READING

Albion, Robert G., Baker, William A., Labaree, Benjamin W., *New England and the Sea,* Mystic Seaport Museum, Mystic, CT, 1994.

Archer, Richard, *As If an Enemy's Country, The British Occupation of Boston and the Revolution,* Oxford University Press, New York, 2010.

Bourne, Russell, *Cradle of Violence, How Boston's Waterfront Mobs Ignited the American Revolution,* John Wiley and Sons, Hoboken, NJ, 2006.

Coggins, Jack, *Ships and Seamen of the American Revolution,* Dover Publications, Mineola, New York, 1969.

Cordingly, David, *Under the Black Flag: The Romance and the Reality of Life Among the Pirates,* Harcourt Brace and Company, New York, 1995.

DeBerniere, Henry, *The Narrative of General*

Gage's Spies March 1775, reprinted by the Bostonian Society, Boston, 1912.

Druett, Joan, *She Captains, Heroines and Hellions of the Sea,* Simon and Schuster, New York, 2001.

Fischer, David Hackett, *Paul Revere's Ride,* Oxford University Press, New York, 1994.

Fowler, William A., *Rebels Under Sail, The American Navy During the Revolution,* Scribner, New York, 1976.

Johnson, Charles, *A General History of the Robberies and Murders of the Most Notorious Pirates,* Conway Maritime Press, London, 2002.

Jones, Marilyn and Tentindo, Vincent, *The Battle of Chelsea Creek,* Revere Historical Commission, Revere, MA, 1978.

Kaynor, Fay Campbell, *Province House and the Preservation Movement,* Old Time New England, Boston, Fall 1996.

Konstam, Angus, *The History of Pirates,* Lyons Press, n.p., 2002.

Morrissey, Brendan, *Boston 1775,* Osprey Campaign Series 37, Osprey, London, 1995.

Patton, Robert H., *Patriot Pirates, The Privateer War for Freedom and Fortune in the American Revolution,* Pantheon Books, New York, 2008.

Phillips, James Duncan, *Salem in the Eighteenth Century,* Essex Institute, Salem, MA, 1969.

Rantoul, Robert S., "The Cruise of the *Quero,*" *The Century Magazine,* n.p., September 1899, pp. 714–21.

Rodger, N. A. M., *The Wooden World, An Anatomy of the Georgian Navy,* W. W. Norton & Company, New York, 1996.

Taylor, James C., ed. *Founding Families: Digital Editions of the Papers of the Winthrops and the Adamses,* Massachusetts Historical Society, Boston, 2007.

Tilley, John A., *The British Navy and the American Revolution,* University of South Carolina Press, Columbia, SC, 1987.

Tuchman, Barbara, *The First Salute, A View of the American Revolution,* Ballantine, New York, 1988.

Various, *Naval Documents of the American Revolution, Volume 1, AMERICAN THEATRE: Dec. 1, 1774–Sept. 2, 1775, EUROPEAN THEATRE: Dec. 6, 1774–Aug. 9, 1775, Part 2 of 8,* United States Government Printing Office, Washington, DC, 1964.

Wilbur, C. Keith, *Pirates and Patriots of the Revolution,* Globe Pequot Press, Guilford, CT, 1973.

■ ■ ■ ■

READERS GUIDE:
THE REBEL PIRATE:
RENEGADES OF THE
REVOLUTION

DONNA THORLAND

■ ■ ■ ■

A CONVERSATION WITH
DONNA THORLAND

Q. This novel tells a side of the American Revolution that was completely unknown to me. Can you fill in some of the background? What new understanding do you hope that readers will take away?

A. During the French and Indian War, America had three working powder mills. By the eve of the American Revolution, she had none. All the matériel of war — the powder for muskets and cannon, the lead for bullets — had to be stolen from British arsenals, a risky business, or imported, which was a riskier business still. For up to a year before the fighting broke out at Concord and Lexington in April 1775, the colonists had been smuggling powder and weapons into North America, running their fast little schooners past the British Navy's blockade of Boston Harbor. Gunrunning was rife with international intrigue, and the

French and Spanish were only too happy to help, to spit in the eye of their old enemy. But most of the risk was borne by the scrappy American mariners who made powder runs to Europe and to the tax-free Dutch ports of the Caribbean like Saint Eustatius.

Q. *When the book opens, Sarah Ward's fiancé, Micah Wild, has called off their union because her family has suffered a change of fortune. Was it common for men (or women) to break engagements when their finances took a turn for the worse?*

A. Property was an important part of betrothal agreements for the middle and upper classes, and a material change in either family's status was grounds for nullifying the contract. Both before and after the Revolution, vast New England fortunes were made — and lost — at sea. American ships were vulnerable to pirates, search and seizure by the British Navy, and bad weather. The mansions lining Salem's common and Chestnut Street are testaments to the rewards of bold seamanship. But many of those houses were built and furnished, only to be occupied for a short time — a matter of months in some cases — before their owners were ruined by a single failed venture.

Q. Micah Wild burns Sarah Ward's house down under the cover of a night of mob violence. How common was such rioting during the period?

A. The story of British Loyalists during the American Revolution hasn't received the attention it deserves. Their plight reminds us that the War for Independence was as much a civil war as it was a revolution, with families, including those of some of the founding fathers such as Franklin, torn apart by conflicting loyalties. Riots, common throughout the 1770s, particularly in port cities like Boston and Salem, often focused the ire of the rebel mob on prominent Tories. Governor Hutchinson had his house torn down. In Salem, Judge Ropes, the inspiration for Judge Rideout, was dragged from his bed while he lay dying of smallpox. Several British officials and their families were forced to take refuge on naval vessels or in forts like Castle William. Many Loyalists were tarred and feathered. Those whose assets were primarily real property, farms, businesses, homes, lost everything. And the Continental Congress, on more than one occasion, seized property from

Loyalists and awarded it to Patriots.

Q. How typical for the time is Sarah's sexual knowledge and experience?

A. We tend to view eighteenth-century American sexuality through a Victorian lens, but cohabitation was common in the colonies. Between one-third and one-half of colonial American brides were pregnant at the time of their marriage. In port towns, sailors often cohabited with women who acted as temporary wives while their ship was in. Prostitution, particularly in the port towns, was common. Marriage was also less "permanent" than we often imagine: legal divorce was available to the wealthy, and many husbands and wives effectively divorced their partners simply by moving away or publishing the dissolution of their union in a newspaper.

Q. Was it common for pirates who plied the Caribbean to hail from New England, and to retire there after their adventures?

A. Many of the pirates who terrorized America were born in England. Only a few famous buccaneers are known to have hailed from the New World, most notably Ned Low and Thomas Tew. Most of the pirates who frequented New England ports met violent ends, like Blackbeard, William Kidd, and Thomas Veal, but legends of their buried treasure persist, especially on Cape Ann.

Q. Margaret Gage, wife of General Thomas Gage — who I assume is based on a historical figure — seems to have strong Rebel sympathies, which I find shocking in the wife of a British commander. Can you explain?

A. Margaret Kemble Gage was a noted beauty from a prominent New Jersey family. Her husband, Thomas Gage, like several of the British commanders who followed him (including General Howe, featured in my previous book *The Turncoat*), had strong American sympathies. Gage himself was seen as a timid commander, but he had been given an impossible task. Parliament refused to send him the men necessary to pacify America, and at the same time urged him to bring the brewing conflict to a head. The disastrous retreat from Concord and Lexington was the result. In *Paul Revere's Ride,* historian David Hackett Fischer raised the possibility that Margaret Gage tipped the Rebels off on the eve of Concord and Lexington, allowing Hancock and Adams to escape arrest.

Q. What role did Boston play during the later years of the war? Did it remain under British control?

A. The siege of Boston ended, and the Americans regained control of the city in March 1776 when Washington placed cannons captured from Fort Ticonderoga on Dorchester Heights. Powder captured by American privateers in Boston Harbor enabled Washington to keep his army supplied through that tenuous winter. Boston was to remain in the hands of the Rebels for the rest of the war.

Q. Much is made in the novel of the British Navy's policy of "pressing" men into service to man its ships. Was life as a lowly sailor so bad that the navy had to resort to physical force in order to ensure it had enough men?

A. Life at sea in the eighteenth century was hard, but civilian sailors were free to negotiate their terms, to change ships at the next port, to go home. Many American sailors were young men who signed on for a single voyage to get a start in life, to earn enough money to open a business or marry. When the British Navy pressed these sailors, sometimes off incoming ships or even from the docks of port towns like Salem and

518

Marblehead, it abducted them into the service, and a New England man might find himself on the other side of the world with no way to communicate with or support his family. Understandably, many Americans were less than enthusiastic about being conscripted in this fashion!

Q. *While writing this novel you moved to Salem, Massachusetts, which plays a significant role in the book. What drew you to Salem, and how do you like living there?*

A. Salem played a crucial role in privateering during the Revolution. Of the 2,200 British ships captured by American cruisers, 458 were taken by Salem vessels. Naumkeag privateers accounted for more captured tonnage than privateers in any other American port.

Salem launched 158 privateers over the course of the war, and 85 of those were outfitted by Elias Hasket Derby, America's first millionaire, who loosely inspired the character of Micah Wild. It was Derby's *Quero,* under the command of his younger brother, John, that reached London first with the news of Lexington and Concord and ensured that the American version of events would be heard and would shape both the debate in Parliament and the public perception of that battle.

My first career was in public history, and I started out as an intern in the departments of Early American Architecture and Asian Export Art at the Peabody Essex Museum in Salem. I rose over the years to manage the institution's interpretation department, and fell in love with early America in the process. After many years splitting my time between Boston and Los Angeles, where I wrote for film and television, I'm excited to be back in Salem as a resident, where history really does come alive, from the Puritan settlement at Naumkeag to the adventure of the Revolution and the China Trade.

Q. What have you most enjoyed about readers' responses to The Turncoat?

A. I'm excited that readers are rediscovering the drama and danger of the American Revolution, and that they identify with the remarkable women of the period. The response to Kate and Angela Ferrers (who also appears in this book) in particular has been very gratifying.

Q. I, for one, can't wait for the third book in the trilogy. Can you tell us a little about it?

A. Playwright and historian Mercy Otis

Warren penned seditious dramas under a pseudonym. Her work placed her on a British hanging list. The heroine of my next book is loosely based on Mercy, and follows her adventures as she flees the British. The story will take us to Saratoga and pit Mercy's alter ego against British author, general, and man-about-town "Gentleman" Johnny Burgoyne.

QUESTIONS FOR DISCUSSION

1. What is your overall response to the novel? What do you like best? Do you mind that the story takes place before events of *The Turncoat,* the first book in the Renegades of the Revolution trilogy?

2. Were you surprised to learn of the naval skirmishes between the British and Rebels that took place in Boston Harbor and all up and down the New England coast, even as the more familiar events in Lexington and Concord were unfolding? How has your understanding of the American Revolution changed after reading this book?

3. Which secondary characters did you like best, and why?

4. Angela Ferrers also appears in *The Turncoat.* Discuss her role in both books.

5. Many of the characters in *The Rebel*

Pirate lack strong political conviction, but by the end many of them have joined the Rebel side. Discuss the events that lead each character to this conclusion, and the various ways in which each is "radicalized" to take up arms against the prevailing government. Does this have implications for our own age?

6. James Sparhawk and Sarah Ward are drawn to each other right from the start. Does Donna Thorland convince you that their attraction goes deeper than mere lust? How does she accomplish that? Do you find their romance satisfying? What future do you envision for them?

7. Without realizing that Anthony Trent and James Sparhawk are related in any way, Sarah becomes engaged to the father of the man she loves. It's a risky plot twist. Does Donna Thorland pull it off?

8. Anthony Trent is not quite the murderer that his son believes, but he's not entirely innocent either. Discuss the choices he has made and his efforts to make amends. Do you believe he is thoroughly reformed?

9. Discuss the relationship between Benjamin Ward and Charles Ansbach. What role

does honor play? How does their unequal social status affect their relationship and the Ward family's fortunes?

10. Discuss the role of money in the book, and during this time period. What happens to the characters when they get it, and when they lose it? Who plays false to acquire money, and what happens to them when they're found out? What do you think of the way captured ships, and their cargo, were taken as "prizes" to enrich the captors? Can you think of a modern-day equivalent?

11. Betrayal is a pervasive theme. Discuss the various perceived or confirmed betrayals that the characters commit, what motivates them, and what consequences follow. Who, on the other hand, chooses loyalty over betrayal, and how do they fare?

12. Sarah had a happy childhood growing up in Salem. Drawing upon the few details that we're told, discuss what her childhood might have been like. How does it compare to Sparhawk's upbringing? How do their experiences compare to the ways children are raised in this country today?

13. What do you think you will remember about this book six months from now?

ABOUT THE AUTHOR

Graduating from Yale with degrees in classics and art history, **Donna Thorland** managed architecture and interpretation at the Peabody Essex Museum in Salem for several years. She then earned an MFA in film production from the University of Southern California School of Cinematic Arts. She has been a Disney/ABC Television Writing Fellow and a WGA Writer's Access Project Honoree, and has written for the TV shows *Cupid* and *Tron: Uprising.* She is the director of several award-winning short films, her most recent project having aired on WNET Channel 13. Her fiction has appeared in *Alfred Hitchcock's Mystery Magazine.* Donna is married with one cat and splits her time between Los Angeles and Salem, Massachusetts.